VAMPIRESLAYER

KURT REACHED UP and grabbed his shoulder. 'Oh no, you don't. You can't simply walk away from this one, my friend.'

Adolphus glared down at him, allowing his anger to show in his eyes. Kurt quailed away and for a moment Adolphus thought he might actually let him walk, but the pig-faced lout was too drunk and stupid to listen to his instincts. He tried to restrain Adolphus who shrugged off his grip easily. 'On your own heads be it,' he said, watching the young fools follow him out into the night.

He glanced around. They were in an alley. There was no sign of the watch. There were no witnesses about. As they slouched out behind him, they made fists, fitted knuckledusters over their hands, drew small weighted truncheons. Experienced tavern brawlers these, Adolphus thought. Not that it would do them any good.

'Now you're going to get what you deserve,' said Kurt.

'One of us is,' said Adolphus and smiled, for the first time showing all his teeth. In the dim light it took a few moments for the youths to register what they were seeing. Then their faces blanched. Kurt began to scream.

Adolphus kept smiling, knowing that he was going to kill them all, and that he had always intended to.

Gotrek and Felix

VAMPIRESLAYER

By William King

A BLACK LIBRARY PUBLICATION

First published in Great Britain in 2001.

This edition published in 2004 by
BL Publishing,
Games Workshop Ltd.,
Willow Road, Nottingham,
NG7 2WS, UK

10 9 8 7 6 5 4 3 2 1

Cover illustration by Geoff Taylor,
Map by Nuala Kennedy.

A CIP record for this book is available from the British Library.

ISBN 1 84416 053 X

Distributed in the US by Simon & Schuster
1230 Avenue of the Americas, New York, NY 10020, US.

Printed and bound in Great Britain by
Cox & Wyman Ltd, Reading, Berkshire, UK.

See the Black Library on the Internet at
www.blacklibrary.com

Find out more about Games Workshop
and the world of Warhammer at
www.games-workshop.com

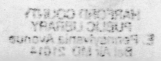

THIS IS A DARK age, a bloody age, an age of daemons and of sorcery. It is an age of battle and death, and of the world's ending. Amidst all of the fire, flame and fury it is a time, too, of mighty heroes, of bold deeds and great courage.

AT THE HEART of the Old World sprawls the Empire, the largest and most powerful of the human realms. Known for its engineers, sorcerers, traders and soldiers, it is a land of great mountains, mighty rivers, dark forests and vast cities. And from his throne in Altdorf reigns the Emperor Karl-Franz, sacred descendent of the founder of these lands, Sigmar, and wielder of his magical warhammer.

BUT THESE ARE far from civilised times. Across the length and breadth of the Old World, from the knightly palaces of Bretonnia to ice-bound Kislev in the far north, come rumblings of war. In the towering World's Edge Mountains, the orc tribes are gathering for another assault. Bandits and renegades harry the wild southern lands of the Border Princes. There are rumours of rat-things, the skaven, emerging from the sewers and swamps across the land. And from the northern wildernesses there is the ever-present threat of Chaos, of daemons and beastmen corrupted by the foul powers of the Dark Gods. As the time of battle draws ever near, the Empire needs heroes like never before.

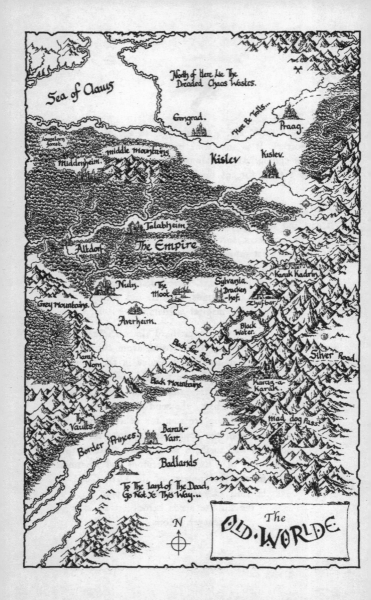

BOOK ONE

Praag

'At that time, in the depths of that dreadful winter, I thought myself well acquainted with horror and pain. During the siege of Praag I had endured the loss of many trusty companions to the fiends of Chaos. But all the travails I had previously undergone shrank to insignificance compared to what was to come. For, through some strange quirk of fate or jest of the Dark Gods, the Slayer and I were destined to encounter an ancient, terrible evil and to lose several more of those who had been closest to us in the most peculiar and terrible of ways. The darkest of our days were yet to come.'

— From *My Travels With Gotrek*, Vol IV, by Herr Felix Jaeger (Altdorf Press, 2505)

ONE

FELIX JAEGER STRODE through the ruins of Praag – burnt out buildings, ruins, and rubble, as far as the eye could see. The remains of a few collapsed tenements poked their scorched heads from the all-enveloping snow. Here and there men piled bodies on carts to be taken away and burned. It was a thankless and probably fruitless task. Many corpses would not now be found until the spring thaws, when the snow covering them melted. That's if they were not excavated and eaten first, Felix thought. The effects of starvation were written on the faces of people all around him.

Felix pulled his faded red Sudenland wool cloak more tightly around him and strode on towards the White Boar – or where it had been, before the battle. He had grown bored with the triumphal banquets in the Citadel and the company of the Kislevite nobles. A man could only stand to listen to so many speeches praising the valour of the city's defenders and the courage of the relieving army before his ears felt as if they would fall off. His tolerance for listening to nobility congratulating themselves on their heroism was not as great as it once had been. It was time to see what the

Slayers were up to. They had left the banquet early the previous evening and not been seen since. Felix had a shrewd
idea that he knew where he could find them.

He walked through the remains of what had been the
Street of the Silk Merchants, surveying the burned out
remains of the great warehouses. Pale, lean and hungry people, wrapped in ragged coats, were everywhere, trudging
heads down through the snow, taking shelter in the ruins of
the old storehouses. Many eyed him as if wondering
whether he carried enough money to make him worth the
risk of robbing. Some looked at him as if he might be their
next meal, quite literally. Felix kept his hand near the hilt of
his sword, and wore the fiercest expression he could muster
on his face.

In the distance, the temple bells rang out in celebration.
Felix wondered if he was the only one who found anything
ironic in their joyous clamour. Considering their dire straits
it was surprising how many of the people looked cheerful.
He supposed most of them had expected to be dead by now.
Nigh unbelievably the great Chaos horde of Arek Daemonclaw had been thrown back, and the mighty Chaos warlord
had been defeated. The Gospodar muster and a ferocious
bombing attack mounted by the airship, the *Spirit of
Grungni*, had delivered the city from that vast army. Against
all odds the heroic city of Praag had been saved from the
mightiest army to attack it in two centuries.

It had been a victory bought at high cost. More than half
of the Novygrad, the New City, that vast, densely populated
warren of narrow streets between the outer wall and the old
inner wall surrounding the Citadel, was gone, burned to the
ground when the rampaging Chaos warriors had broken
through into the city. Nearly a quarter of the city's population was dead according to the quick and informal survey
conducted by the duke's censors. The same number again
were expected to die of hunger, disease and exposure to the
bitter chill of the northern winter. And that was assuming no
more marauding armies emerged from the Northern Wastes.
The outer wall was still breached in three places, and would
not withstand any more assaults.

In the distance Felix could smell the sickly sweet scent of burning flesh. Somewhere out there people were warming their hands around funeral pyres for the slain. It was the only way to get rid of so many corpses quickly. There were too many now to be buried, the earth too hard to be broken by spades. There were still worries about plague. The dreadful diseases unleashed by the worshippers of Nurgle, the Lord of Disease, during the siege had made a resurgence in the aftermath of the battle. Some claimed it was the Plague Daemon's revenge for the slaughter of his followers. The wizard Max Schreiber thought it more likely that the cold, the hunger and the depressing effects of the Kislevite winter were making the population more prone to the spore daemons that carried disease. Felix smiled sourly; a man with a theory for everything was Max Schreiber, and depressingly correct most of them had proven too.

A wailing woman tried frantically to stop two of the carters bearing off the body of a dead man, her lover, her husband or her brother perhaps. Most of the people in the city had lost at least one kinsman. Entire families had been wiped out. Felix thought about the people he had known who had died in the battle. Two of the dwarf Slayers, young Ulli and the hideously ugly Bjorni, had been burned on those huge funeral bonfires.

Why had this happened, Felix wondered? What had driven the Chaos worshippers from their remote realms in the uttermost north, and compelled them to attack the city? Why had they chosen the weeks before the onset of winter for their assault? It was an act of insanity. Even if they had taken Praag, they would have suffered quite as much from the effects of the cold and snow as the people of the city now were. More so, for such was the grim determination of the Kislevites that they would have burned their entire city to the ground rather than see it fall into the hands of their bitterest enemies. Felix supposed that the daemon forces would have had fewer qualms about devouring corpses or even each other, but even so their attack had been madness.

He shook his head. What was the point of trying to understand them anyway? You would have to be mad to willingly follow the daemon gods of Chaos, and that was all he needed to know. It was pointless for any sane man to try and understand the motives of such lost souls. Of course, Felix had heard many theories. Max Schreiber claimed that a huge tide of dark magical energy was flowing south out of the Chaos Wastes, and that it was goading the daemon worshippers to new heights of insane fury.

'Repent! Repent!' shouted a lean man with burning eyes. He stood on the pedestal once occupied by a statue of Tsar Alexander and ranted at the crowd. Foam gathered at the corners of his mouth. His long hair was lank. He looked like he had lost touch with sanity a long time ago. 'The gods are punishing you for your sins.'

It seemed the zealots who preached in the burned out squares of the city had their own theories. They claimed that the end of the world had arrived, and that the Chaos horde had merely been a harbinger of worse things to come. That theory only lost plausibility slightly when you considered that these were the same people who claimed that the end of the world had arrived with the Chaos horde. They had been forced to change their story a little when the horde had been defeated. Felix fought down the urge to shout at the man. People had enough troubles without being harangued by a furious lunatic. A quick glance told him it was pointless. Nobody was paying the zealot any heed despite the way he had bared his breast and pummelled his own chest in fury. Most folk walked swiftly by, trying to finish whatever business they had and get back to whatever meagre shelter they might possess. The man might as well have been shouting his anger at the wind.

A few stalls had been set up at the corners of the Square of the Simoners. Men in the winged lion tabard of the duke's household doled out a ration of grain to a queue of hungry folk. The measure was now down to half a cup. Of course, the duke was now also feeding the assembled force of the Gospodar muster, nearly five thousand warriors and their mounts. They were camped out in the remains of the city and the burned out farms that surrounded it. Felix pushed his way quickly round the edge of the square, doing his best to avoid being caught up in the teeming mass of hacking, coughing, scratching flesh. He kept one hand on his sword hilt and one on his purse. Where crowds gathered you could never be too careful.

Felix had heard people say that the Ice Queen, the Tsarina of Kislev, had power over the winter weather. If that was so, he thought, why did she not loosen winter's grip on the throat of her people? Perhaps such magic was beyond her power. It looked as if not even the Lords of Chaos had the power to do so, and surely they, most of all, had reason to do that, unless this whole invasion was just some sort of grim divine jest for their own amusement. From what he had seen when he had flown over the Chaos Wastes, Felix would not put it past them.

As he exited the square huge, thick flakes of snow began to fall, brushing coldly against his cheek. It frosted the hair of the folk about him. Felix was sick of the sight of it. He thought he was used to snow. Winters in the Empire were long and harsh but they were a summer picnic compared to what winter brought here. He had never seen so much snow fall, so quickly, and never known it to be quite this cold. He had heard rumours of huge, white dire wolves stalking the city's outskirts and making off with children and the weak. He had heard tales of other worse things too. It seemed the Kislevites had horror stories for everything concerned with winter. Hardly surprising, he supposed, and he had seen enough of the world to know that there was most likely a grain of truth behind all of them.

Felix told himself not to be so dour. After all, he was alive when he had fully expected to meet his death during the Chaos horde's attack. He could even leave the city on the mighty airship, the *Spirit of Grungni*, when Malakai Makaisson departed. True, that would mean returning to Karak Kadrin, the squat savage home of the Slayer cult, but surely even that would be preferable to spending the winter in Praag. Only a fool or a madman would want to do that.

Felix knew that really he had no choice in the matter. He was sworn to follow Gotrek and record his doom. Wherever the Slayer chose to go, he was bound to follow. Surely not even Gotrek would choose to remain in Kislev? Felix shook his head. The Slayer would most likely do it out of sheer pig-headedness. He seemed happiest when things were most uncomfortable, and Felix could imagine few places more guaranteed to provide a healthy measure of discomfort than this snowbound, burned out shell of a city.

Now that he and Ulrika Magdova had finally separated, there was no real reason for him to stay. Briefly he wondered where the Kislevite noblewoman was. Most likely she was still with Max Schreiber, back at the banquet; the two of them were thick as thieves these days.

Ulrika claimed it was because of the honour debt she owed the wizard for saving her life during the plague. Felix was not quite so sure. It was hard for him not to feel jealous of the mage, even though, theoretically, he and Ulrika were not a couple any more.

Yes, he told himself, moving on was for the best.

The snow crunched under his boots. He walked towards a charcoal brazier where a vendor was selling skewered rats. He did so more because he wanted heat than any of the four-legged chicken the man was selling.

The vendor seemed to read his thoughts and gave him a glare. Felix met the man's look evenly until he glanced down and away. Despite his scholarly appearance he felt there were few men in the city who would give him trouble at times like this. Over the long period of his association with the Slayer, he had learned how to intimidate all but the most confident when he wanted to.

From over by the entrance to the Alleyway of Loose Women, above which a red lantern still burned even in this gloomy daylight, he heard the sound of weeping. The more cautious part of his mind told him to move on, to avoid any trouble. The curious part egged him on to investigate. The battle was over in heartbeats, and he marched over to the mouth of the alley. He saw an old woman weeping. She was bent over something and then leaned back and let out a terrible wail of anguish. No one else seemed to be paying much heed. Misery was abundant in Praag this season, and no one had much reason to go looking to share someone else's.

'What is it, mother?' Felix asked.

'Who you calling "mother", priest boy?' the old woman responded. There was anger in her voice now, as well as grief. She was looking for someone to focus it on, to distract herself. Felix guessed he had just made himself the target.

'Did I offend you?' he asked, still polite, studying the woman more closely. He could see that she was not really all that old. She just looked that way. Her face was covered in rouge to hide the pockmarks. Her tears had smudged her makeup horribly. Black rivulets ran down her powdered cheeks. A streetgirl, he decided, one of those who sold herself for a penny a tumble. Then he looked at her feet and a faint thrill of shock passed through him as he saw why she was crying. 'Was she a friend of yours?'

It was the pale corpse of another girl. At first he thought she had died of the cold, then he noticed how utterly unnatural her pallor was. He bent down and saw that her throat was bruised. Some instinct told him to run his fingers over it. The flesh was torn, as if a beast had gnawed at it.

'You a watchman?' the woman asked aggressively. She reached out and grabbed his cloak, thrusting her face close to his. 'You secret police?'

Felix shook his head and gently removed her hand. It would be a very bad thing to be marked out as one of the duke's spies and agent provocateurs in this rough quarter. A crowd might gather and lynch him. Felix had seen such things happen before.

'Then you're just a ghoul and I don't have to tell you nuthin'. The woman coughed and he heard the phlegm rasping through her lungs. Whatever she had, he hoped it was not contagious. She did not look like a well woman. Felix looked at her coldly. He was chilled to the bone, he was tired and he was not really in the mood to be the focus of this sick madwoman's anger. He stood up straight and said, 'You're right. Deal with this yourself!'

He turned to go, and noticed that a small crowd had gathered. To his surprise he felt a tug at his wrist, and turned to see the streetgirl looking up at him and crying once more. 'I told her not to go with him,' she said after another hacking cough. 'I told her, I told Maria, but she wouldn't listen. I told her he was a bad 'un, and there have been all these killin's recent, but she wouldn't listen. Needed the money for medicine for the little 'un she said. Now who'll look after him?'

Felix wondered what the woman was babbling about. He felt the urge to walk away as quickly as possible. He had seen many corpses in his life but there was something about this one that sickened him. He was not sure why, but he just knew that he wanted nothing further to do with this. And yet...

And yet he could not just walk away. The meaning of the woman's words passed into his numbed brain, just as he heard a commotion at the back of the crowd and the sound of marching feet crunching snow underfoot. He turned to see a squad of halberdiers in winged lion tabards had forced their way through the gathering crowd, hard-faced veterans of the city watch, led by a grey-haired sergeant. He looked at Felix and said, 'You find her?'

Felix shook his head. 'Just passing by,' he said.

'Then keep on passing,' said the sergeant. Felix stepped to one side. He wanted no arguments with the duke's guards. The sergeant bent down over the corpse and muttered a low curse. 'Damn,' he said. 'Another one.'

'That's Red Maria, sarge,' said one of the troopers. 'From Flint Street.'

'Have you seen something like this before?' Felix asked.

The sergeant looked up at him. Something about his expression made it clear that he was not in the mood to give answers to any passing civilians. Felix wasn't sure why he had asked. This was surely no business of his. But something about the man's tone rankled him, and something about this killing niggled at the back of his mind. He knew it would most likely go unsolved anyway. He had been a watchman himself in his time, back in Nuln, what seemed a lifetime ago, and he knew the watchmen were not likely to expend any more effort on a murdered streetgirl than to carry her to the funeral pyres. Looking down at the corpse he began to see her as a person finally.

Who were you, he wondered? What was your life like? Why did you die? Who killed you? Your friend said you had a child. Did you love him? Must have or you would not have gone out with a deadly stranger on a winter night and walked off to your death.

He felt a faint familiar surge of anger at the sheer injustice of it. Somewhere out there a monster was free and a child was most likely going to die for want of food, and there was not much he could do about it. He reached down to his waist and fingered his purse. It was a bit flat, but there was gold in it. He turned so his body covered the action, and pushed it into the woman's palm.

'Take that, find the child and look after it. Should see you for a while. Take it to the orphanage at the Temple of Shallya. They'll care for it, if you give them a donation.'

Stupid, stupid, stupid, he told himself. The woman will most likely keep the money herself. Or will be robbed, or the child is already dead. But what else could he do? He was a fool, he knew, but at least he had done something, made some small gesture in the face of the vast uncaring universe.

'Same as the one down on Temple Street two nights ago,' he heard one of the troopers murmur. He turned in time to see the man make the sign of the wolf's head against evil. First finger and little finger extended, middle two fingers pressed into the palm by the thumb. The guard was a follower of Ulric then, like most of these Kislevites.

'Another lunatic most likely,' said the sergeant.

'Or a daemon,' said the soldier superstitiously. Rumour had it that some of the daemons summoned when the Chaos horde attacked the city were still at large. Felix knew this was unlikely. He had sat through enough of Max's lectures on the subject to know why. There was simply not enough magical energy in the area to support one now.

'It would not be a daemon,' he said.

'You'd be an expert on that, I suppose,' the sergeant said. Felix thought back over his long career as the Slayer's henchman, and all the vile creatures he had fought, including the great Bloodthirster of Karag Dum.

'More than you would ever guess,' he murmured.

'What was that?' the sergeant asked abruptly. Felix snapped his mouth shut. Claiming knowledge of daemons in this city was a sure way to get yourself invited to a witch hunter's confession cell. He was not ready for the rack and the iron boot just yet.

'Nothing,' he said. The sergeant looked at him as if he really wanted to pick a fight just now. Felix could understand why. The sight of the body was very disturbing, a cause of both fear and anger, and the man was looking for a target to focus his on. Suddenly the streetgirl came to his rescue.

'He's right. It wasn't a daemon. It was a man,' she said. 'I saw him.'

'Daemons can take human shape,' said the gloomy soldier. He obviously wasn't going to give up on his theory without a struggle.

'It was a man,' she said. 'A rich man. A nob. With a foreign accent like the stranger here.'

The sergeant was giving Felix an even harder, appraising stare now. Felix could see what he was thinking.

'Wasn't him,' said the girl quickly.

'You sure, Nella? I saw him slip you some money there. Pretty suspicious if you ask me.'

'Wasn't him,' she said even more emphatically. She too could see the deep waters they were sailing into now. 'Was taller, thinner, darker. And there was something about him that just made my flesh creep.'

'There's something about this one that makes my flesh creep,' said the sergeant. His witticism drew guffaws from the troops, all except the gloomy soldier who repeated, 'Daemons make your flesh creep. It was a daemon for sure.'

'Don't look like a man's work. Look at her throat. More like a dog did that. Never saw a man kill anyone like that before.'

'I have,' said the sergeant. 'Remember Mad Olaf? Chewed his way through quite a few bar girls in his time.'

'Olaf is in the madhouse,' said the soldier with the daemon theories.

'Who knows?' said the sergeant. 'Madhouse burned down in the siege. Who knows if all the loonies burned with it?'

'Does the girl's description fit Mad Olaf?' Felix asked, keen now, to divert any hint of suspicion from himself.

'Not at all. Mad Olaf was short, bald and worked in the Street of Tanners. Smell could knock you down at six paces. I'm sure Nella would have noticed it, wouldn't you, Nella? Unless you're just making this up to put us off pretty boy here's tracks.'

'Wasn't anythin' like Mad Olaf,' she said, shaking her head. 'Though he did smell kind of odd…'

'Odd? How?' asked Felix and the sergeant simultaneously.

'There was a perfume about him, like something the nobs wear but stronger. Like those spices you used to be able to buy down at the Pepper Market. Like cinna… cinnabor… cinna…'

'Like cinnamon?' Felix finished for her.

'That's the word.'

'So we're looking for a tall, dark man, dressed like a noble, smells of cinnamon,' said the sergeant sarcastically. It was obvious he thought Felix really was wasting his time now. He glared at Felix as if considering hauling him off anyway.

'Where were you last night, stranger?' he asked. Felix was glad he had a good answer for that.

'The palace,' he said. 'Maybe you would like to ask the duke a few questions while you're about it.'

The sergeant looked suddenly a bit more respectful, but only a bit. Felix could tell he was wondering whether he was being mocked. After all, how likely was it that someone as scruffily dressed as Felix would be eating with the ruler of Kislev's second most powerful city-state?

'Perhaps you'd care to come along to the palace and make sure of what I am saying?' Felix said. He was confident that things would go his way there. He and Gotrek had been given a heroes' welcome, along with Snorri Nosebiter, after their heroic stand on the outer wall and their despatch of Arek Demonclaw. To tell the truth, Felix knew he was probably only welcome because he was associated with the dwarfs. They had, after all, proven to be the Kislevites' best and only allies in this struggle so far. Their airship had done as much to lift the siege as the entire Gospodar muster.

'That won't be necessary,' said the sergeant after a long moment. 'Come on, let's get this body to the pyres.'

Felix exchanged looks with Nella, and they went their separate ways.

MAX SCHREIBER LOOKED around the massive feasting chamber wondering if the celebrations would ever end. It seemed the Kislevites liked to commemorate their victories with enormous meals and endless toasts. It seemed like he had barely gone to sleep when he was woken for the next instalment of the grand debauch. His stomach was so distended it felt as if it would burst. Fortunately, he had decided to drink nothing but water since his embarrassment with Ulrika at Karag Kadrin, and he had stuck to the resolution. It had given him an opportunity to study the Kislevites around him. It had been a long time since he had moved in quite such exalted company.

At the head of the table, at the place of honour normally reserved for the Duke of Praag himself, sat the Ice Queen Katarina, the Tsarina of Kislev, a cold and perfectly beautiful woman with eyes like chips of blue ice. Today her hair was the colour of winter frost. Max knew it changed at her whim. She had the ageless sculpted beauty of a statue, a perfection of face and form that had something inhuman about it and she appeared none the worse for two days of eating and drinking. Looking at her, Max could easily believe the tales of inhuman blood that was said to flow in the veins of the royal line of Kislev.

Whatever it was that gave her beauty, it also gave her a fearsome aura of magical power. A wizard of great strength himself, Max could recognise a potent mage when he met one, and the Tsarina was certainly that. No, he thought, that was not quite right. There was something strange and not quite human about her powers as well. She did not feel like any human wizard he had ever encountered, and when he studied her with his magesight he could see the swirls of power surrounding her were quite unlike those of any human mage too. She had a frosty, chill blue aura that seemed to extend outwards beyond his field of vision. Patterns of magical energy swirled around her like snowflakes in a blizzard. She seemed to be connected directly to the cold energy of her land. He doubted that there was anything subtle about the magic she could wield, but he knew it would be effective as a battering ram. She was in receipt of great energies from somewhere.

She seemed aware of Max's study and turned her cold gaze speculatively on him. Max had heard rumours of her, and her legion of lovers too, and had no great desire to find out if they were true. He swiftly looked away. A faint mocking smile played across the Tsarina's lips as if she could read his thoughts. Max stroked his beard with his hand, to hide the flush that came to his cheeks. He was not quite used to the forwardness of Kislevite women. They were very unlike the ladies of his homeland, the Empire.

Automatically his eyes sought out Ulrika. She sat across the table from him, side by side with her father, the huge old March Boyar, Ivan Petrovich Straghov. Looking at the two of them, Max wondered how it was possible that the massive bear-like man could be the father of such a slender and lovely woman. Ivan Straghov was a giant, huge of shoulder, and just as huge of belly. A long beard, almost dwarf-like, descended to his waist. Sweat shone on his bald forehead. He held a stein of beer in one massive fist. It looked little larger than a delicate wine goblet in that massive ham-like hand.

His daughter by contrast was slim as a blade, with high cheekbones and wide-set eyes. Her ash-blonde hair was cut short as a man's and she held herself with a dancer's poise. She was garbed in tunic and riding britches, the true daughter of one of the horse lords of Kislev. She laughed and joked with her father just like any common trooper and her quips were rewarded with huge bellows of laughter that set the old man's belly shaking like a jelly.

Seated beside Max, the duke, a tall, dark saturnine man with long drooping moustaches and sunken cheeks, leaned forward to pour more wine for the Tsarina. A peculiar gleam was in the duke's eye and Max recalled the rumours that Enrik was not quite sane. Hardly surprising – ruling the haunted city of Praag was likely to drive even the most normal man over the edge. Since the death of his brother at the hands of Chaos worshipping assassins he seemed even sadder and more sardonic than usual. Max wondered if the duke knew of Felix Jaeger's theory that his brother had been a member of the Chaos cults himself, but knew he would probably never find out. Who was going to risk asking such a loaded personal question of such a high-ranking noble? Not Max, for a certainty.

Max glanced around and looked at the others. This was the high table where the Tsarina, the duke and the favoured few sat to be waited on by court favourites. At the other tables were the leaders of the great muster of Kislev. Leaders of tens, fifties and hundreds of horse-soldiers, formidable warriors all. They looked more like barbarians than nobles to Max, but he kept the thought to himself. These men were allies of his homeland, the Empire, and great nobles in their own land.

It never paid to antagonise such people under any circumstances. Max had spent enough time around the courts of the rich and the powerful to know this only too well. At the bottom of the main table, looking as uncomfortable as a man waiting his own execution, sat the dwarf Malakai Makaisson, the only Slayer who had bothered to accept the duke's invitation to dine today.

Makaisson was short and like all dwarfs very, very broad. Without the great crest of dyed hair rising above his shaven skull, his head would only have come to the top of Max's stomach, but he outweighed Max by far, and all of that extra weight was muscle. Crystalline goggles, pushed back from his eyes, sat in the middle of his forehead, looking for all the world like the eyes of some giant insect. A leather flying helmet dangled from his neck. A fur-collared leather flying jerkin covered his massive torso. Tattoos depicting entwined dragons covered the back of his hands.

The dwarf caught Max looking at him and gave him a gap-toothed smile before raising his pitcher of ale. Max answered the smile for he liked Makaisson, who was just about as friendly and outgoing as it was possible for a dwarf Slayer to be, as well as a genius in his own field.

Max was a sorcerer not an engineer, but he had seen enough of Malakai Makaisson's work to recognise that the dwarf was master of a power that was, in its own way, quite as great as wizardry. He had seen the massive airship, *Spirit of Grungni*, break the siege of Praag with the use of alchemical fire. He had seen it resist the attack of a dragon and rout an army of orcs. He had seen the Slayer's modified firearms slaughter dozens of goblins in seconds. He had heard tales of mighty ships and siege engines created by this dwarf, and he recognised an intellect as great in its own warped way, as anything ever produced by the Universities or Colleges of Magic of the Empire. Quite possibly greater, he admitted.

'It is a pity none of your comrades could be here tonight,' said the duke sardonically, addressing Malakai Makaisson. 'They seem insensible to the honour of dining with the Tsarina.'

If the Slayer was embarrassed he gave no sign of it. 'That wud be their bizness, yer dukeship,' he said. 'Ah cannae answer fur them. Gotrek Gurnisson and Snorri Nosebiter are as thrawn a pair o' dwarfs as ever lived.'

'And that's saying something,' said the Ice Queen lightly. The favourites around the table laughed.

'Among dwarfs it wud be considered a great compliment,' said Malakai Makaisson judiciously, as if no mockery were intended. Perhaps the dwarf was too blunt to notice it, Max thought, or perhaps he chose to ignore it in the interests of diplomacy. Max considered the latter an unlikely eventuality, but you never knew. No one had ever called Malakai Makaisson stupid, just mad.

'Present or not,' said Ivan Straghov, 'they did well in the last battle.'

'They did a great service to Kislev, and shall be rewarded for it,' said the Tsarina. Malakai Makaisson spluttered into his ale. Max wondered if he should explain the situation to the Ice Queen. Gotrek and Snorri did not seek rewards or honours; they sought death to atone for their sins. He decided that it probably wasn't his place to share the information. Besides, the Tsarina seemed to be an extraordinarily well-informed woman. She probably already knew.

'We shall have great need of such fighters before this war is over,' continued the Ice Queen. Max shivered. It was war all right, quite possibly the largest in history. Before the siege he had not really had time to take it in, he had only been concerned with the seemingly unwinnable battle to come. Now, he knew that the whole of the Old World had a huge fight on its hands. The massive drift of Chaos worshippers out of the north ensured it. The Ice Queen turned her gaze on Malakai Makaisson once more and it swiftly became obvious why he had been invited to this feast. 'Have you thought more of our proposal, Herr Makaisson?'

Malakai took another swig of his beer and met her gaze levelly. 'If there's ocht ah can dae, lassie, ah wull dae it. But ma airship and ma services are already spoken fur. Ah must gan back to Karak Kadrin and help the Slayer King muster his forces.'

'Surely you can spare us a few days, Herr Makaisson, a week at the most,' said the Tsarina. Her tone was silky but Max could hear the danger in it. He wondered what she would do if Malakai Makaisson had the gall to refuse her outright. She did not have the look of a woman who was used to taking rejection well. 'Your airship is worth an army of scouts. In days you could cover more terrain than ten thousand of my bold riders could in a month.'

'Aye, ye're right,' said Malakai. 'Ah could. An' ah can see the value such kenning would have. Who kens where those Chaos-lovin' basturds will strike next, excuse ma language.'

'So you'll do it then?' said the Ice Queen decisively. Malakai Makaisson sucked his teeth loudly. 'Ah'll dae ma best, but there are ither factors tae be considered. What if ma lovely airship gets shot doon, or blasted fae the sky by sorcery, or attacked by them bat-winged gets that are always hoverin' above the daemon worshippers? It wouldnae dae onybody ony guid if that happened. An ah don't own the *Spirit of Grungni*, ah'm only the builder. It's no really mine tae risk.'

Max almost intervened. He had put the Chaos-repelling spells on the *Spirit of Grungni* himself and he knew how strong they were. Few mages would overcome them quickly. And he was just as certain that the heavily armed airship would be able to repel anything that attacked it. As for taking risks with the airship, the Slayer engineer had taken a number of crazy ones with it, to Max's certain knowledge. He forced himself to keep his mouth shut, knowing that Malakai must be as aware of all these things as he was, and if he wanted to refuse the Ice Queen he must have his own good reasons.

The Ice Queen gave the dwarf another one of her dangerous looks. Most men would have quailed before it, but Malakai just took another slug of his beer. 'We could of course compensate you for any risk you might run...' she said softly.

Max half expected Malakai Makaisson to protest that he was a Slayer and that risk did not enter the equation. Makaisson surprised him. 'Ah might be able tae dae somethin' wi' that. Depends on yer terms.'

With that, Malakai Makaisson and the Ice Queen began to dicker. Max did not know why he was surprised by this turn of events. Malakai Makaisson was a dwarf after all, a race of beings famous for their love of gold.

Still, thought Max, such constant advancement of self-interest among supposed allies did not bode well for the conduct of the war.

FELIX JAEGER WAS surprised. The White Boar was still standing. Well, almost. Part of the roof had been burned away and hastily patched with timbers salvaged from the ruins of nearby tenements. A blanket covered the doorway and two heavily armed mercenaries stood on guard beside it, keeping a wary eye on everyone who came along the street. He squared his shoulders and strode up, doing his best to behave as if he could not feel their suspicious glares on him.

Once inside he was surprised by how packed it was. It looked like half the sellswords of the city had tried to squeeze inside out of the cold. Felix half suspected that even without the huge fire blazing in the hearth, the press of bodies would have kept the place warm. He heard two familiar voices bellowing and strode towards the table where the two dwarf Slayers were arm-wrestling.

Gotrek Gurnisson looked none the worse for the terrible wounds he had taken during the siege. The healers of the

temple of Shallya had done a good job of patching his
wounds. Right now a look of insane concentration glittered
in his one good eye. Veins bulged in his forehead and his
enormous crest of orange dyed hair stood on end. Sweat
beaded his tattooed skull, running down his forehead into
the ruined socket covered by a huge eye patch. Massive
cable-like sinews bulged in his huge arms as he strove
against another dwarf even more massive than he.

Snorri Nosebiter looked even dumber than usual, Felix
thought. The dwarf licked his lips moronically as he concentrated. He looked as if arm wrestling were about the
most intellectually stimulating pursuit he had ever engaged
in. The three painted nails driven into his shaven skull were
a testimony to his sheer brute stupidity. He was almost as
ugly as Bjorni Bjornisson had been. One ear had been
ripped clean away; the other resembled a massive cauliflower. His nose had been broken so many times it seemed
to have spread across his face like wax from a melted candle.
His arms were thicker than a strong man's thighs. They
bulged and flexed as he strained to overcome Gotrek's grip.
Slowly, inexorably, the one-eyed Slayer's enormous strength
began to tell. Snorri cursed as his hand was slammed into
the tabletop almost upsetting his beer.

'That's another one of these piss-weak manling brews you
owe me, Snorri Nosebiter,' said Gotrek. His gravelly voice
sounded even more contemptuous than usual.

'Snorri thinks we should make it best of twenty-seven,'
said Snorri.

'You would still lose,' said Gotrek with certainty.

'Maybe Snorri would surprise you, Gotrek Gurnisson,' said
Snorri.

'You haven't so far.'

'There's a first time for everything,' said Snorri Nosebiter, a
little petulantly, Felix thought.

'What have you been up to, manling?' asked Gotrek. 'Your
face is tripping you.'

Swiftly Felix told the tale of the dead girl and his escape
from the clutches of the guards. Gotrek listened with the sort
of unreasonable interest that Felix knew boded no good.

Even Snorri was hanging on his every word. After he finished his story, Felix said, 'You don't seem at all surprised by what I have been saying.'

'I've heard several versions of this story over the past few days. Seems like there's a mad dog killer on the loose out there. One that needs to be put down.'

'You think you're the one to do it?' Felix asked worriedly. When the Slayer got such ideas fixed in his head, he usually ended up in some dark and nasty place along with him. Gotrek shrugged.

'If I run into the bastard, manling, I will do it happily, but I'm not planning on going out looking for him just yet.'

'Just yet? That's good.'

'Snorri wonders whether it really might be a daemon,' said Snorri. 'That soldier sounded quite clever to Snorri.'

Gotrek shook his head. 'If it was a daemon every wizard in the city would be shouting spells and every priest casting exorcisms from the temple roofs.'

'Then what could it be?' Felix asked.

'Your guess is as good as mine, manling,' said Gotrek and took a long swig of his ale. 'One thing's for sure though. Nothing good.'

THE BOW AND Bard might be the finest inn in Praag, Adolphus Krieger thought as he glanced around, but this was not saying much. He had seen finer inns in any small town in the Empire. He should have remained in Osrik's mansion, he knew, but the strange restlessness that had filled him recently had driven him out into the night once more. When this mood was on him, he could not even stand the sight of his loyal manservant, Roche.

He drew his cloak around him and studied the tavern crowd. He could smell each individual scent, hear every heartbeat, was aware of the thrum of crimson through every vein. So many people, he thought, so much blood. He felt like an epicure studying a Tilean banquet.

Where to begin, he thought? Perhaps with that young noblewoman sitting over there with her lover? She was almost beautiful but there was something about her he found vaguely repulsive. As a rule, Adolphus did not care for Kislevite women with their flat peasant features and short muscular bodies. No, not her.

The tavern wench gave him a broad smile, and offered to bring him more wine. It was possible she was responding to his good looks, he thought, but more likely to the cut of his clothes. She sensed money, either in tips or afterwork activities. Adolphus shook his head and smiled at her affably. He had only just surreptitiously poured half his current goblet on the floor. It had been a long time since Adolphus drank wine. The barmaid moved off with a saucy flick of her hips. Once, a long time ago, she might have interested him, but now he was not even interested in her as prey.

Adolphus shook his head and began to draw patterns on the tabletop with his fingertip using some of his spilled wine. He was in a strange mood, and he had not lived as long as he had without learning to recognise the dangers of such things. He was becoming prey to all manner of odd impulses and he wondered what that foreboded.

Last night for instance, he had drained that girl dry when he had only meant to sip. There had been no need for it. Her blood had been flat and thin and not even remotely interesting. She herself was mere cattle, barely worth his interest. Why had he done it? Why had he drank so deep that she had died, and why had he torn out her throat with his teeth in that pathetic attempt to cover his trail?

It was difficult to understand. A delirium had come over him such as he had not experienced in centuries. He had sucked the girl's blood like a whelp on his first night after rising. He had done the same the night before, and the night before that. Looking back on his feverish actions, it seemed almost unreal. It was as if some madness were overtaking him, and the madness was becoming stronger.

Adolphus had always despised the Arisen who slew indiscriminately. It was unsophisticated, boorish and deeply, deeply counter-productive. That way lay witch-hunts and mortal sorcerers and priests with their deadly spells at least until Adolphus fulfilled Nospheratus's ancient prophesy. One for one, or even one for ten, the Arisen might be more than a match for any mortal, but the cattle had the numbers, and they had potent allies and magic.

It was not like the old days that the Forebears spoke of with such fondness. Mankind had grown much stronger since the time when they were skin-clad barbarians to be hunted through the woods.

Of course, things would change. Human civilisation had collapsed into anarchy before. Adolphus could remember the Time of Three Emperors and von Carstein's efforts to re-establish the superiority of the Arisen. It had been a brave effort but a doomed one. Von Carstein had not been potent enough and clever enough to win his war. Adolphus knew that when his time came, things would go differently. He was the chosen one. He was the Prince of the Night. The Eye and the Throne would be his!

If only that old fool would give him the talisman there need be no unpleasantness. Adolphus fought down the urge to simply go round to the old man's mansion and take it, but that would be too loud, too unsubtle, such an action might well be noticed in certain quarters before Adolphus wanted it to be. It would not do for the countess or others of her faint-hearted ilk to discover what he was up to ahead of time. No, he told himself, it would be best to wait.

He turned his attention to the noblewoman. She really wasn't so bad, he thought. The best of the bunch present tonight certainly. He saw that she sensed him looking at her, and she glanced at him out of the corner of her eye. Without thinking, Adolphus exerted his will. The woman froze and stared at him, as if seeing him for the very first time. Adolphus smiled at her, and she smiled back. He looked down at the table again and let her go. That was enough for now. The connection was made. He would pluck her later, when the moment was ripe, perhaps not tonight, but some other night, when the thirst came upon him. He saw that her companion, perhaps a young aristocrat of some sort from his dress, was looking at him, and then at her. He had obviously noticed the exchange between them, and was most likely jealous. He leaned forward and whispered something furiously in the woman's ear. She shook her head as if denying something. If he had wanted to, he could have listened in on their conversation simply by focusing his mind on it. Like all of the Arisen, his senses were fantastically keen. The cattle were always so predictable, thought Adolphus.

He dismissed the mortals from his thoughts. They were irrelevant. What was worrying him was his own lack of control. He could not afford it now. Not with the consummation of all his plans so close, not with everything he had worked so hard on almost within his reach. He needed all his wits about him now. He needed all his guile and cunning. He needed to keep his plans a secret until it was too late for the rest of the Arisen or anyone else, for that matter, to stop him. Instead he had gone on a blood binge, killing and drinking indiscriminately, leaving a trail that the right sort of hunter could follow with the ease of a forester tracking a mastodon. He simply could not understand it. Such a thing had not happened to him since his first mistress had given him the red kiss all those long centuries ago. Why was this happening to him? And why now?

He had heard of such things happening before. The Arisen were sometimes subject to a strange madness that got into their blood and drove them to crazed sprees. When that happened they were just as often hunted down by their own kind as by the cattle. None of the Arisen particularly cared to have the cattle stirred into a frenzy. Adolphus knew that if he kept up this sort of behaviour it would only be a matter of time before one of the Council came looking for him, and he could not afford that, at least not until the talisman was in his hands. Once that was accomplished and the thing was attuned to him they could send whoever they liked. But until then, he very badly needed to get himself under control unless he wanted to end up with a stake through his heart and his brainpan stuffed with witchroot as a warning to others not to behave as he had done.

He was aware, as he was aware of everything in the room, that the young lover had risen and walked over to a pack of his richly garbed friends, who were standing by the bar. He was gesturing in Adolphus's direction, pointing aggressively. Not now, you young idiot, Adolphus thought. I do not need this. The group of youths began stalking over towards his table, hands on their sword hilts. Adolphus had seen lynch mobs in small towns walk towards their victims' homes with exactly that stride. He watched them come towards his table, hoping vaguely that they would pass him by, knowing that it really was not all that likely. Now he wished he had brought Roche. His hulking henchman was always a good distraction in situations like this.

'So you are the one who's been seeing Analise,' said a voice from close by. The accents belonged to the wealthy merchant class of Praag, the tone of voice was at once arrogant and self-righteous and petulant. A young jealous man, thought Adolphus, and one about to make the biggest mistake of his short life. Adolphus did not answer but studied the contents of his goblet closely. A hand lashed out and knocked his goblet over.

'You, sir, I am talking to you. Don't ignore me.' Adolphus looked up and studied him closely. A foppish young fool clad in the latest fashion, long coat, bright pantaloons, a wide-brimmed hat with a feather in it. He had a narrow face, white sharp teeth and a savage, feral look in his eye. Makeup covered some of the pockmarks on his not unhandsome face.

'You are making that very difficult, sir,' said Adolphus, looking up. He could smell the drink on the young man's breath. He gazed into his eyes and tried to make contact but the youth was too far gone in drunken jealous anger to be reached. Too bad for him, thought Adolphus, feeling the devil of rage begin to stir in his own unbeating heart. He glanced over at the youth's friends. All cut from the same cloth, he thought, all young, all drunk, all viciously certain that they could do anything they wanted to a stranger here, and get away with it. Under normal circumstances, Adolphus thought, they would most likely be right. These were not normal circumstances, however.

'I want you to get up and leave now, and I want you never to show your ugly face in here again.'

Adolphus shrugged. Under normal circumstances he would probably have done what these boors asked. He wanted no trouble that he could avoid, not now. But somewhere in the back of his mind, the lurking daemon, the thing that had caused him to drain those women dry, was stirring. He felt irritation build up within him, a small nagging thing that swiftly ballooned into a compulsion to be contrary. Who were these oafs to be ordering him around? Mere cattle, insects barely worthy of his notice. He looked at them with loathing, letting his contempt show upon his face. He saw the answering anger written on theirs.

'And how are you going to make me do that, boy?' Adolphus asked. 'Why should I listen to a child who needs half a dozen of his playmates to deliver a simple warning? Is this the usual behaviour of Praag's so-called men?' The internal daemon made him add, 'Is it any wonder Analise prefers a real man to a beardless boy like you?'

Fury contorted the youth's face. He had trapped himself and he knew it. Adolphus's accent marked him as a noble, albeit one from some distant corner of the Empire. It would be dishonourable to simply gang up on him. The only course open to him was to call Adolphus out, to fight a duel. He saw the youth begin to look at him as if for the first time, taking in the height, the breadth of shoulder, the superb self-confidence with which Adolphus was facing down a whole gang of armed men. Obviously, even his drunken brain retained enough sense not to like the implications of what he was seeing. Adolphus wondered how he would deal with it. The response was predictable.

'Take this piece of scum outside and beat him within an inch of his life,' the youth said.

'A coward as well as a cuckold,' Adolphus sneered. He looked at the others. The part of him that was still relatively sane suggested that he should at least attempt to give them a way out from what was about to happen. Slaughtering six sons of the local wealthy was sure to bring him a lot of unwelcome attention. 'Are you really going to fight this coward's battles for him?' he asked.

He could see that the justice of his words struck at least one or two of them. They did not really want to fight at these odds, any more than he did. They realised the dishonour of their act. One or two of them were wavering. Adolphus caught one's eye and began exerting his will. The youth wavered and said, 'I think Kurt should call this man out if he feels so strongly.'

Kurt obviously did not like this idea at all. 'Are you all cowards? Do you all fear one scurvy outlander so much?'

This obvious appeal to their Kislevite patriotism was having as strong an effect as his questioning of their manhood. He could sense the gang wavering once more. 'Take him outside and show him what happens to arrogant outlanders who shoot their mouths off in Praag.'

Adolphus looked around once more. He could see a lot of sympathetic looks but no offers of help. Obviously this gang of youths was well known and greatly feared around here. There was going to be no other way out than fighting, he could tell. How unfortunate. He only hoped he could restrain his bloodlust.

The real problem now was a tactical one. How was he going to deal with this bunch of young thugs without arousing suspicion of his real nature? Perhaps he should simply leave after all. He rose from his chair and loomed over Kurt. 'Do not bother yourselves, I am leaving. The smell of yellow-bellied swine is too strong in here for my stomach.'

He cursed. What had made him say that? If he had simply strolled confidently for the door, the chances were that they would have let him go. Now there was no chance of that. He knew the answer to his own question. Deep in his heart, he did not want to let these arrogant cattle live. He was as bad as they were. It was not a thought designed to enhance his self-esteem, and he knew he was going to make these youths pay for making him think it.

Kurt reached up and grabbed Adolphus's shoulder. 'Oh no, you don't. You can't simply walk away from this one, my friend.'

Adolphus glared down at him, allowing his anger to show in his eyes. Kurt quailed away and for a moment Adolphus thought he might actually let him walk, but the pig-faced lout was too drunk and stupid to listen to his instincts. He tried to restrain Adolphus who shrugged off his grip easily.

'On your own heads be it,' Adolphus said, as he stepped through the doorway, watching the young fools follow him out into the night.

He glanced around. They were in an alley. There was no sign of the watch. There were no witnesses about. The idiots had done his work for him. As they slouched out behind him, they made fists, fitted knuckledusters over their hands, drew small weighted truncheons. Experienced tavern brawlers these, he thought. Not that it would do them any good.

'Now you're going to get what you deserve,' said Kurt.

'One of us is,' said Adolphus and smiled, for the first time showing all his teeth. In the dim light it took a few moments for the youths to register what they were seeing. Then their faces blanched. Kurt began to scream.

Adolphus kept smiling, knowing that he was going to kill them all, and that he had always intended to.

TWO

FELIX LOOKED DOWN from the cockpit of the *Spirit of Grungni*. Below him he could see a seemingly endless waste of snow and ice. Far off at the horizon was the grey zone where the wastelands met the leaden waters of the Sea of Claws. Cold winds tore at the steel walls of the cupola and made the great gasbag above creak. The noise of the mighty engines was barely audible above the howling of the wind. He glanced across at Malakai Makaisson who stood at the huge control wheel, pulling levers and studying gauges with all the assurance of the experienced pilot.

'Are you really going to get 5,000 gold crowns for this, Malakai?' Felix asked. He had been surprised when Max had told him. He had never figured on the Slayer engineer being particularly gold-crazed. On the other hand, he was a dwarf, and a little of that lurked in every dwarfish soul.

'Aye, young Felix, ah am! Tae tell the truth ah would have done it fur nithin' but the bloody icy bezum kept gaun on and on at me, so ah figured ah might as well make it her pay fir it.'

Felix nodded: it sounded quite possible. Malakai Makaisson was as stubborn as any other dwarf and did not

like being pushed into things. Felix was surprised he had
not refused outright. He was quite capable of it, despite the
Tsarina's exalted position. Dwarfs cared little for human
titles or nobles. And Slayers didn't show the least respect for
their own rulers, so why should they show it for other
races?

'So why did you agree to do it?' Felix asked curiously.

'Coz she was bloody well right. We dae need tae ken what
the Chaos basturds are up tae, and the *Spirit of Grungni* is the
best thing fur the job.'

Felix was also a little surprised that Malakai was capable of
seeing things so clearly; he normally seemed obsessed with
only one thing, his machines. Unlike most Slayers he did
not seem to spend much time brooding on his own death or
sins. He was not stupid, Felix had to admit, and he supposed
that anyone capable of designing this airship had to be only
too aware of its military possibilities.

A tide of movement out of the corner of his eye caught
Felix's attention. He focused the spyglass on it and the scene
jumped into view. He shivered. It was another huge force of
beastmen, heading southwards, following the coast of the
Sea of Claws. They trudged along with implacable determination, their massive banners fluttering in the breeze.

Seeing the symbols of the Chaos gods so nakedly visible
filled Felix with horror. They were signs which from his
childhood he had been taught to fear and loathe. This one
took the shape of an eye from which radiated eight arrows.
It was stained in blood on a white sheet, and fluttered on a
crossbar made of human bones and topped with the horned
skull of some huge monster.

'That's the tenth warband in this area,' said Felix.

'How many?'

'At a guess over a thousand.' Felix did not need to count
them any more. Over the past few days, flying these recon-
naissance missions, he had become quite adept at judging
the size of the Chaos forces. 'Where are they all coming
from?'

Suddenly he caught sight of something else, and swiftly
focused on it. At first he could not believe his eyes, then

slowly the reality of what he was seeing forced itself on his brain. It was a huge ship, driving through the icy sea. It was made all of black metal and no sails were visible. The whole prow was carved in the shape of an enormous daemon's head. Red runes glowed along its side.

'What in hell is making that thing move?' he asked. Malakai Makaisson snatched the spyglass from his hand.

'Tak the controls, young Felix, an' tak us closer tae yonder ship. Ah want tae hae a guid lang look at this.'

Felix took the controls with practiced ease and aimed the prow out towards the sea. Malakai had taught him how to fly the ship long ago, and he had had a lot of practice on their trip back from the Chaos Wastes. It was one of the reasons why, along with his keen eyesight, he was the observer on this flight. Such was the airship's speed that they were soon passing over the turbulent water.

'Whit in hell wus right,' said Malakai Makaisson. 'Ah cannae see ony paddlewheels, and there's nae wake that wud indicate some sort of drive screw under the thing. All ah can think o' is dark magic, an' that isnae ma field. Cannae think o' onythin' else that wud shift somethin' that big. Bloody hell. I niver guessed they Chaos basturds were capable of ocht like this. It's movin' as fast as a steamer under full pressure and it's as big as onythin' ah hae ever seen on water.'

'That's all very well, Malakai,' said Felix. 'But what does it mean?'

'It means ye'd better pray to all your manling gods that they don't hae a fleet o' those things, young Felix. Coz if they dae they'll be able tae land an army onywhere they like alang the coast of the Old World. By Grungni, they could head right up the bloody Reik as far as Altdorf and Nuln.'

Felix shivered as Malakai took the controls and returned the spyglass.

'I don't think Sigmar is in the mood to answer any of my prayers,' said Felix.

'Why?'

'Look over there,' he said, pointing to the fleet of black ships driving headlong through the storm-tossed sea.

'Let's head fir hame,' said Malakai. 'Ah think we've collected enough bad news fir yin day.'

Felix was forced to agree.

FELIX WAS GLAD to be back in Praag, even gladder than he had been to see the lights of the city winking below them and the huge citadel blazing with light ahead. Sitting in the White Boar he was looking forward to getting a hot meal inside him, and then some sleep. These days the airship always seemed cold inside, and no matter how many extra layers of clothing he wore, he could never quite get warm. His mouth felt a bit dry, and there was an odd tingle in his fingers and toes. He hoped he was not coming down with something.

All around him he could hear the buzz of conversation, the gossip of all the mercenaries and merchants cooped up in the city by the snows of winter. The guild wanted permission to raise the price of corn once more, but the duke would not approve it. He wanted all of his citizens as well fed as possible, and no starvation. Felix felt that though he could never like the duke, he could respect the man and like his policies. He appeared to be about as fair as it was possible for an aristocrat to be, though Felix had never really lost the suspicion of the ruling class that had been burned into him by his merchant father.

It seemed six young nobles had died in a brawl down in the merchant quarter last night. According to rumour they had taken some wealthy foreigner outside to teach him a lesson and never come back. Their corpses had been found in the snow. The guess was that the foreigner must have had bodyguards or friends of his own waiting outside for it was deemed unlikely that one man could best six at blade work or brawling. Felix wasn't so sure. He had seen Gotrek overcome many times that number in combat and occasionally had done it himself when desperation drove him.

Felix pushed the thought to one side. It was no business of his, even if the youths' families were offering a huge reward to help them find the killer. What did he care? He could just picture the young men, spoiled dandies of the

sort he had once been forced to deal with every night in the
Blind Pig tavern in Nuln. He could not find it in himself to
feel much sympathy with anyone who thought it fun to go
outside six against one. Most likely they just got what they
deserved.

This was not the only tale of slaughter in the night.
Another two streetgirls had been found dead and drained of
blood. Now there was fearful talk of some daemon stalking
the night, and someone had even mentioned the dreaded
word 'vampire'. Felix shivered. His old nurse had told him
chilling tales of the blood drinkers. As a child, he had spent
many a sleepless night fearing that one might find its way
into his room. He tried to push aside his fears and found
that he could not. He had seen far too many other childhood terrors prove to be real in this terrible world. It would
not surprise him in the least if one of the soulless ones were
abroad in the city. He only prayed he would never encounter
it. They were said to be terrible foes.

He noticed that one man was paying a lot of attention to
this conversation. A tall nobleman, dressed in fashionably
foppish clothes, a pomander clutched in one hand. His features were a little pale, perhaps from the powder applied to
his face. His eyes were cold and his face wore a look of
intense concentration.

The man caught Felix looking at him, their eyes met and
Felix felt a flicker as of some sort of contact. He was suddenly filled with a desire to look away, but his own native
stubbornness would not let him. He matched the stranger's
glare and studied him closely. The man wore his hair in an
odd archaic style, cut square to cover his forehead, and long
down the sides. There was something about him that made
the hair on the back of Felix's neck prickle. He had the same
sort of aura as Max. Most likely a magician then, Felix
decided, and someone best not to start trouble with. This
time he looked away, just in time to see Ulrika and Max
Schreiber enter the White Boar. They strode over to his table
with a determined step.

What's got into them, Felix wondered?

* * *

ADOLPHUS LOOKED UP and watched the wizard and the woman enter the crowded tavern room. By all the gods of darkness, she was a beauty. Neither her mannish garb nor the sword she carried could detract from her loveliness. In a strange way they enhanced it. He felt the surge of an attraction the like of which he had not felt in a long time. It was a pity the man she was with wore power like a mantle.

In his long existence, Adolphus had encountered few more potent sorcerers. He was skilled enough in the art of magery to recognise a master when he saw one. He only hoped his own cloaking spells were sufficient to keep the man from noticing him.

He cursed himself for a fool. He should have stayed at the mansion and studied Nospheratus's damn book. These nightly peregrinations might prove the end of him. After killing those louts last night, he had come to this squalid place to avoid any more attention. And what was the first thing he had done when he came down to the common room? Seeing the blond man staring at him, he had decided to use his gaze to make the man look away, but the mortal had proven unexpectedly strong-willed and could not be commanded. That in itself was unusual. Now the man had proven himself to be the associate of a master wizard. Perhaps this explained his strong will, perhaps not. Whatever it was, it was a bad thing. He only hoped the mortal would not draw the wizard's attention to him, that was the last thing Adolphus wanted. He cursed; as so often in his long unlife, it seemed the gods were playing tricks on him. Now, with all his dreams almost within his grasp, nothing was going right.

He had given in to his bloodlust last night and slaughtered those young fools like the cattle they were. At least he had had the sense not to drink from them. He had managed to restrain the thirst until later when he had drained those two streetwalkers dry. Despite all his best efforts, he had not been able to resist the compulsion; he had not even wanted to. The thirst had not been so strong in him since he first arose. What was happening to him? What madness was overtaking him? Why did this constant lust for blood burn in his veins like a fever? He did not understand.

Perhaps it was this place. Praag was said to be a haunted city. Perhaps the strange forces of the town were working on him. Or perhaps it was the huge Chaos moon burning in the sky and haunting his dreams. He did not know, could not tell. He just knew that it was happening at the worst possible time for him and his plans. If only the old fool would prove more tractable. Adolphus resolved that if he did not give way in the negotiations soon, he would kill the man and have done with it.

Even as he thought this, he knew it was another symptom of the madness overtaking him. He knew he must hang on. It was all almost within his grasp. He could not afford any more mistakes now. He rose to return to Osrik's mansion, taking the back exit. Best to get no closer to that wizard than absolutely necessary.

On his way out he paused to take a last long look at the lovely woman. Some night, he promised himself, I will come looking for you.

'WHAT IS IT?' Felix asked. Max and Ulrika seemed both grim and excited at once.

'Where is Gotrek?' Max asked.

'Out drinking with Snorri Nosebiter. Doubtless if you follow the trail of broken bodies along the street you will find them.'

'That's not funny, Felix,' said Ulrika. Since the split she had taken to using a very cold tone towards him.

'I wasn't joking,' said Felix. 'You know what they are like when the mood is on them. What do you want with them anyway?'

'We have been offered a job.'

'We?'

'All of us. You too.' Privately Felix wondered who would be crazed enough to offer a job to a couple of Slayers. Someone pretty desperate, he guessed. Or badly in need of having a lot of violence done.

'Does it involve killing big monsters, or fighting against insuperable odds?' Felix asked sardonically.

'I don't think so,' said Max. 'At least I don't know for certain.'

'Then they probably won't be interested.'

'There's a lot of gold involved,' said Ulrika.

'That would most likely change things.'

'Then let's go find the dwarfs and introduce ourselves to our potential employer.'

'Who is he?' Felix asked, rising and adjusting his sword belt. He noticed the rather sinister-looking nobleman had vanished.

'A distant relative of mine,' said Ulrika.

'Half the nobles in this city are distant relatives of yours,' said Felix.

'That's the way it is with Kislevite nobility,' she said, a little huffily Felix thought.

THE MANSION WAS big and rather impressive in a scruffy down-at-heel sort of way. Felix paused to glance out of the window, taking in the huge pleasure garden, surrounded by spike-tipped walls. The place must be worth a small fortune, he thought, before turning to follow the others. So much space came at a high premium inside the high walls of Praag.

Inside the house, bric-a-brac filled every nook and niche. Odd exotic weapons, and masks from the distant Southland lined the corridors through which the elderly servants led them. A porcelain statue of some four-armed monkey god, which Felix guessed was from far Cathay, guarded the entrance to a vast sitting room in which the owner lolled on a huge antique couch.

Count Andriev, Ulrika's distant cousin, rather reminded Felix of a mole. He was a short man, very broad and bulky. He had a huge nose and vast whiskers that drooped below his chin. Little round glasses perched on his mountainous nose and obscured his small weak eyes. The count wore a long silk robe in the Cathayan style. He did not look like much of a warrior, although Ulrika had assured them he had been a famous swordsman in his youth. Now he leaned on a long black walking stick, clutching the silver ball at its tip with clawed arthritic fingers. He gazed around the room, taking them all in. A pull of a bell-cord summoned a tall, lean butler almost as ancient as himself.

'Would you – ahem – like anything to drink? Some tea perhaps?'

Snorri Nosebiter and Gotrek looked at each other unbelievingly. They seemed to be wondering what they were doing here. They had been lured from the tavern by talk of lavish sums of gold. When Felix had found them they had been busy brawling with some Kislevite horse-soldiers. Felix and the others had stood aside while the two Slayers trounced four times their number before they could get their full attention.

'Beer,' grunted Gotrek.

'Vodka,' said Snorri. 'In a bucket.'

'I will have some tea,' said Max. Ulrika nodded. Felix shook his head. He was interested now almost against his will. It was fairly obvious that this old nobleman was wealthy enough to have his own bodyguards, and without a doubt the treasures in this house were worth a lot of money. Why did he need them? More to the point, how had he found out about them anyhow?

'What do you want with us, old man?' said Gotrek. Ever the diplomat, Felix thought sourly.

Andriev leaned forward. He seemed slightly hard of hearing. There was a faintly crazed glimmer in those weak eyes. 'A member of the Slayer cult,' he muttered to himself. 'Fascinating.'

'I know what I am, dotard. I asked what you wanted with us.'

The count cleared his throat and began to speak in a thin, quavering voice. 'Forgive me,' he said. 'This might take a little time.'

'Snorri thinks it would take less time if you got on with it,' said Snorri Nosebiter. Patience was not a strong suit with him, Felix noted.

'Ahem – well – yes. I shall begin.' The old man paused and gazed around as if to make sure he had all their attention. Felix was starting to feel a little impatient with Andriev's querulous manner himself. 'I am, as you have probably noticed, a collector of curios, antiques, all manner of ancient and interesting objects. It has been a hobby of mine ever since I was a boy when my grandfather gave me a particularly fine carved war mask from the Southland, a truly exquisite piece, marked with the three sigils of the black gods of Tharoum. It was–'

'Perhaps it would be better if you stuck to what you wanted our help with,' suggested Felix as gently as he could. The old man leaned back, looking faintly startled, and put his hand across his mouth as if in surprise.

'Of course – ahem – sorry, sorry. I am old and my mind tends to wander. It's been a while since I had company and well–'

'The point,' Felix added, a little more harshly.

'Sorry. Yes. As I said, I am a collector of antiquities. Over the years I have acquired many pieces of considerable interest. Some of these pieces are said to be… well, mystical. I am not a sorcerer myself so I can't really say, but Brother Benedict, my appraiser, assured me this is so.'

'So?' said Gotrek. It was obvious that he was fast losing patience. Doubtless he was feeling the lure of the tavern particularly strongly right now.

'I have been assured that some of my pieces would be very valuable to mages of a certain sort. After a few incidents among the collecting fraternity many years ago, I paid not inconsiderable sums to mages of the Golden Brotherhood to protect my mansion and my collection with all manner of spells. I believe these spells might have helped preserve my house during the late inconvenience with those Chaos chappies.'

Felix wondered how sane the old man was. The siege had been something more than an 'inconvenience' to most of the city. On the other hand, he supposed that if he were an old man locked away deep within the city in his own fortified manor house, surrounded by servants and bodyguards, he might have been able to ignore the worst of it too.

'So you have some valuable stuff here,' said Gotrek. 'So what?'

'A few days ago, my appraiser, Brother Benedict, a former priest of Verena who left the temple after an incident which was, he assured me, none of his doing but rather–'

'I am sure Brother Benedict is a fine man,' said Max hastily. 'But could you perhaps stick to the point.'

'Yes, yes, ahem, sorry. A few days ago, a stranger, a nobleman from the Empire who claimed to be interested in purchasing one of my pieces, approached Brother Benedict. Benedict told him that my collection was not for sale, but the offer price was so high that he thought I should know about it. Of course, I love my collection and I would not part with any of it, not even that small chipped piece of Nipponese porcelain with the painting of the two herons–'

'Please,' said Felix. 'Have mercy.' Ulrika glared at him. She appeared to be the only one capable of tolerating this old bore. All very well for her, he thought. She was his relative, and her head was probably not starting to ache. He rubbed his nose with the edge of his cloak and was unsurprised to discover that it was running. He really hoped he was not coming down with something.

'Yes, sorry. Well, I thought it would be interesting to meet a fellow collector. One rarely encounters any kindred souls. My hobby is rather a specialist field and not many people are that interested in it...'

Probably it's you they are not interested in, Felix thought, but kept the thought to himself. Instead he coughed loudly. His cough sounded a bit phlegmy.

'Yes, yes. Anyway, I agreed to meet the man. And I don't mind telling you there was something about him I did not like. Not to put too fine a point on it, he scared me.'

'That must have been difficult,' said Gotrek sarcastically.

'Ahem, believe me, sir,' said the old man testily. 'I am not all that easily daunted. As a youth I rode to battle along side Tsar Radhi Bokha and single handedly slew the great Ogre of Tronso. It was a feat of considerable renown and–'

'No one doubts your courage,' said Max. 'Please tell us what so frightened you about this man that you felt you needed to make an offer for our services.'

'There was something very sinister about him. Something daunting. Something about his eyes... When he looked at me, I wanted to do what he told me, and it took all my willpower to refuse. I think the man was a magician of some sort, and a powerful one. For a moment, after I refused his offer, I thought he was going to attack me, in the presence of my own guards and my own house magician. Brother Benedict thought so too. He said he suspected that only the protective spells in place around the mansion stopped the man from turning nasty. I ordered my guards to escort him from the house, and he went. But he said he would be back, and told me I had seven days to reconsider his offer. This was several days ago.'

'Where is Brother Benedict?'

'I do not know. Normally he visits me every morning. He has not shown up for two days. This is another reason I am worried. He is a man of regular habits. Only serious illness would have prevented him from coming, but this cannot be the problem. I have sent servants to his house and his office, and he seems to have disappeared.'

Felix glanced over at Gotrek and Snorri Nosebiter. They were quieter now and seemed more interested. The mention of evil magicians seemed to have got their attention. The mysterious disappearance of Brother Benedict had gotten his.

'Are you sure he has not simply left town.'

'Maybe Benny went on a bender,' suggested Snorri Nosebiter.

'Impossible on both counts. Brother Benedict would have informed me of his departure. He has been in my employ for twenty years. And as for your suggestion, Herr Slayer, he was an abstinent man. Never touched anything stronger than water. Claimed anything else interfered with his ability to concentrate.'

This seemed reasonable to Felix. He had often heard Max claim the same thing.

'So your magician has disappeared. Anything else?' asked Gotrek.

'Ahem, I think so. The guards report the house is being watched.'

'By this mysterious stranger?' Felix asked.

'No, by others, well-dressed men and women, trying not to be noticed but obviously – ahem – not good enough at it to escape detection.'

'Not a gang of professional thieves then,' said Max. Seeing all eyes on him, the magician shrugged and said, 'I used to make my living casting all manner of protective enchantments for people. It has given me some familiarity with the way such people operate.'

'That is one reason I wanted to hire you, sir. Your reputation precedes you. The duke himself is said to think highly of you, and my dear kinswoman here says you are the most competent mage she has ever met.'

'Why do you need us then?' asked Felix. 'Surely you have hired swords enough.'

'That is another strange thing about this whole affair. Even before Brother Benedict vanished some of my guards failed to report for duty. Mostly the day guards, the ones who do not live here in the mansion, but even a few of the residents went out and never returned.'

'These are strange times,' said Felix. 'The city has been under siege. Many folk are starving. Perhaps they left the city. Perhaps they felt they could get more gold or food elsewhere.'

'Herr Jaeger, I am, without wishing to appear to be boasting, a very, very wealthy man, and I pride myself on seeing that my people are well taken care of. I doubt they could be better paid or fed anywhere else in this city under current distressing circumstances. My cellars are very well stocked. I keep the house prepared for the harshest of winters. As an old man, in Kislev, you know how to do these things.'

'Why not take this matter to the duke?' Ulrika asked.

'And tell him what? That one stranger has threatened me in my own house? That my guards are disloyal and my mage has disappeared? The duke has more important things to worry about right now! Why should he trouble himself with one old man's problems when there is a war on.'

'Have you made inquiries why your guards did not report for duty?' asked Felix.

'Again, I sent servants. Some were not at their lodgings. In some cases, the servants thought there was somebody at home, but no one was answering.'

'That's very strange,' said Felix.

'The whole business is very strange, Herr Jaeger. Which is why I need your help and am prepared to pay handsomely for it.'

'How handsomely?'

'If you resolve this matter for me, I will pay each of you one hundred gold crowns, plus a bonus depending on how matters turn out.'

'That sounds fair to me,' said Felix. A glance at the dwarfs told him that they agreed.

It was Max who began to dicker.

'Normally I am paid for the spells and wards I cast, separately from any other fees.'

'I will pay your normal fees – in addition to the amount mentioned previously.'

'Fine.'

'Then you will do it?'

A glance at the others told him they were all willing to get involved. It seemed it was left to Felix to ask the obvious question: 'What was it the stranger wanted to buy from you?'

'Come, I will show you.'

COUNT ANDRIEV'S FAVOURED treasures were certainly well protected. The old man had led them into the centre of his mansion, and then down into a cellar guarded by thick walls worthy of an emperor's tomb.

The entrance to the vault was through a series of huge counter-weighted doors. 'Dwarf-built,' the old man said proudly.

'And protected by several very strong wards, unless I am much mistaken,' said Max. He sounded impressed.

'You are not mistaken. The great Elthazar himself cast these for me. I brought him especially from Altdorf two decades ago. You know of him, of course?'

'He was one of my tutors at the College of Magicians,' said Max in a neutral tone of voice. 'A great wizard but very… conservative.'

'You… ahem, sound as if you don't like him.'

'We had a few disputes before I left the College.'

'Do you not think his work is good?'

'No. I am sure it is very fine. He was very capable and strong in the power.'

'I am glad to hear you say this. But if there is anything you feel can be improved do not hesitate to mention it.'

'I will not, believe me.'

The vault reminded Felix of a cave from some tale of the riches of Araby. In it were many precious and beautiful objects: golden statuettes from the deserts of the Land of the Dead; complex patterned amulets from Araby; beautiful carpets from Estalia; detailed dwarf metalwork carved with all manner of intricate patterns, and vials of precious liquids engraved with the flowing scripts of the elves. Felix understood why the old man had spent so much money to protect it. He also understood just how desperate he must be to hire five near strangers to help him guard it.

Of course, Ulrika was his cousin, and Max was so renowned in this field of wizardry that the dwarfs had hired him to protect their airship so maybe it was not all that strange. And he supposed Ulrika's recommendation would be good enough to get the Slayers and himself the job. He considered the fee. One hundred crowns was a small fortune. Enough to allow a man to live like a noble for months.

The old man showed them a massive sealed chest. He produced the key from under his robes. The chest and the lock looked like dwarf workmanship too. One thing was certain, Felix thought: he knew how to look after his treasures.

'Ah – here it is. The Eye of Khemri,' he said, retrieving a small dark object from out of the strongbox. He held it up to the light. After the long tale, Felix was expecting something more impressive-looking. Max held out his hand: 'May I see it?'

Count Andriev seemed almost reluctant to hand it over, but Max kept his hand outstretched and eventually the old man gave the object to him. Felix moved closer, standing next to Ulrika so he could look over Max's shoulder. He saw a small oval carved from what looked like black marble. A central eye gazed out from strange pictograms depicting animal-headed men and women, perhaps representations of some elder gods. The stonework was encased in a silver

hand that gripped the disc with pointed talons. The whole
amulet depended from an age-blackened silver chain.

Felix looked at Max's face; he saw the wizard was frown-
ing.

'What is it?' Ulrika asked. Max pursed his lips and a look
of concentration passed across his face. Felix could see dim
pinpoints of fire blazing within his eyes and knew that the
wizard was summoning his power.

'I don't know,' said Max. 'There is something very odd
here. The talisman is magical, but seems to contain little
power...'

'And?' Felix asked.

'Why would anyone go to the trouble of obtaining it, if
such were the case?'

'You are saying this trinket could indeed be a magical artefact?' said Andriev.

'Certainly. At this moment I cannot say more. Would you
mind letting me study this, count?'

'If you do not take it out of the vault, I would be fascinated to learn more. I always assumed it was some relic of
the Tomb Kings. The man who sold it to me claimed it had
been found in the rubble of Khemri. I always assumed he
was exaggerating. Now I am not so sure.'

'It is certainly ancient. I have never seen its like before.'

'The question is, what are we going to do about the man
who wants it? Do we go looking for him or do we wait for
him to return?' Felix was not sure he liked the idea of
going looking for a magician, even in the company of Max
and Gotrek. They were too powerful, and too unpredictable, and too many things could go wrong. Felix had
witnessed what Max could do with a wave of his hand and
a word, and did not like the idea of standing in the way of
a lightning bolt.

'No reason why we cannot do both, manling,' said Gotrek,
of course exactly what Felix had feared he would say.

'Where would we start? Did the stranger give you his
name, Count Andriev?'

'He said his name was Adolphus Krieger.'

'That's an Imperial-sounding name,' said Max.

'Easy enough to give a false name,' said Felix. 'Particularly if you are going to go around threatening people, it would seem like a good idea.'

'True enough,' said Ulrika. 'He must be a very confident man, to threaten a Kislevite noble, in the middle of Praag, in his own palace.'

Felix thought about the disappearing magician and the desertion of the guards.

'Perhaps he has cause to be. He could be a very powerful magician.'

'I've killed wizards before,' said Gotrek. Felix wondered why such a feeling of foreboding had come over him. For once, all the odds appeared to be in their favour. They were in a fortified mansion. Max was a sorcerer of great skill, and Gotrek, Snorri Nosebiter and Ulrika were as formidable a trio of warriors as any man could hope to fight beside. Why then was he worried? There was something wrong here. Something troubled him. He wished the feverish feeling would go away. He was having a little difficulty concentrating.

'We could start by looking up those guards hiding in their houses,' said Gotrek. 'Find out what put the wind up them.'

'That seems like a logical starting point,' said Felix, turning the problem over and over in his mind. A few more thoughts occurred to him.

'Did Brother Benedict keep records?' Felix asked Andriev. 'How did this Adolphus Krieger know you had the Eye? How did he get in touch with Benedict?'

'Of course Benedict keeps records,' said Andriev. 'He was a meticulous and methodical man, and as a former priest of Verena he was a great believer in written records. You could try his chambers on the Street of Clerks. Tell his scribes I sent you and they should help. As for your other questions I do not know how this Krieger found out I had the artefact, but I can guess.'

'If you could share your speculations with us, I would be most grateful,' said Felix.

'The market for exotic collectibles is a small one. Few people have the interest, and – ahem – to be frank, the gold to indulge in a hobby like mine. There are a few dealers who make a living in this way and they tend to know all the potential customers in their area. I deal with certain reputable houses in Middenheim and Altdorf. Brother Benedict used to make purchasing trips for me once a year. I used to go myself until I became too infirm. Those were the days, let me tell you, to stand in the great hall at Zuchi & Petrillo's and gaze upon their collections with my own eyes. It makes me want to weep when I think of all those treasures. I recall–'

'You seem to have trusted this Benedict a good deal,' said Felix, interrupting the old man before he could begin another of his rambling reminiscences.

'He was a good man, worthy of trust. He accounted for every pfennig he spent, and I was always satisfied with his accounts.'

Felix returned to his original line of questioning. 'You think this Adolphus might have traced the Eye through the dealers you bought it from, Zuchi & Petrillo?'

'They are models of discretion, Herr Jaeger. It's part of what their clients pay for.'

'Men can be bribed or… daunted with sorcery.'

'That is true. Yes.' The old man seemed genuinely shocked by the thought that his favourite dealers might have betrayed a confidence. On the other hand, he was not denying the possibility either.

'It seems to me that there is another point to be considered here,' said Max.

'Go on…'

'Why is this Adolphus fellow prepared to go to all this trouble to acquire the Eye? What does he hope to gain from it?'

'You're the magician. You tell me.'

'I think it's imperative I begin studying this artefact,' said Max. 'Perhaps if I can divine its purpose I can work out what our friend wants with it.'

Felix nodded. That seemed reasonable. 'One of us should stay here with you and help watch this place.'

'I will,' said Ulrika, rather too quickly for Felix's liking.

'Snorri will too,' said Snorri Nosebiter. 'If there's going to be a fight here, Snorri wants to be around for it. Better than talking to clerks.'

Felix looked at Gotrek. 'It looks as if we will be asking all the questions.'

The Slayer shrugged. 'Let's get on with it then, manling.'

THE SKY WAS overcast and more snow was falling. Felix could feel the chill right through the extra layers of clothing he wore, and he resolved to use some of the money Andriev was paying them to buy a new pair of boots. As ever there were people watching them. It was not unusual. Gotrek was a colourful figure, although one no one would think of bothering. He showed no sign that the chill bothered him in any way.

'What do you think?' Felix asked the Slayer. Around them crowds packed the narrow streets of the merchant quarter. Old buildings leaned over them. It was dark and mazy and he was glad they had paused to get the directions to Benedict's office from Andriev's steward before leaving.

'I think Count Andriev is a rich old man who can afford to indulge whatever whims he has, manling. I think his gold is as good as anybody else's.'

'You think he's imagining things?' said Felix. He stepped out of the street to let a patrol of lancers pass. After a moment's consideration Gotrek did the same. He eyed the horses with hostility. He had never had much love for cavalry or their mounts.

'No. I think there is most likely something going on here. Wizard's business by the sound of it.'

'Do you think the others will be all right?' Felix asked.

'You have seen Max Schreiber use magic, manling, and you have seen Snorri Nosebiter and Ulrika fight. They are in a fortified mansion surrounded by guards. What do you think?'

'That they are most likely safer than we are.'

Gotrek grunted as if considerations of personal safety were the last thing on his mind. Felix fought back a cough. There was an odd tickling at the back of his throat, and he seemed to be sweating a little more than normal. He hoped he was not coming down with anything nastier than a cold.

'You think it might be Chaos cultists?' he asked. They had encountered followers of the dark gods in the cities of man before. During the siege they had interrupted an attempt by the Chaos worshippers to poison the granaries. Felix did not think they had killed all of them, by a long chalk.

'Who knows, manling? Doubtless we will find out soon enough.' Felix wished he could emulate the Slayer's unconcerned attitude, but knew he would never be able to. His imagination was too active, he thought too much. It probably helped that Gotrek did not care whether he lived or died either. Felix did. He knew that he wanted to live; there was much he wanted to see and do yet.

'Doubtless you are right,' he muttered and they trudged on down the street.

THE STREET OF Clerks had been mostly untouched by the siege. It was in the old town, within the inner wall, in the shadow of the citadel. The buildings were mostly red-roofed tenements and shop-houses. Even in the winter chill people were coming and going. From his long experience of such things in Altdorf, Felix judged them to be merchants and lawyers and the people who ran errands for such men. Winter or no winter, war or no war, business went on as usual. It was just like his father had always said.

Brother Benedict had an office in one of the more prosperous-looking buildings, a tall tenement that leaned right out over the alley, joined by a high bridge to the building across the way. With its white-washed walls and timbered frame, it reminded Felix of the buildings in Altdorf, although it was not so high or so beautiful and the gargoyles perched on the ledges over doors and windows were far too grotesque for his home city.

They entered the building and made their way up the narrow winding stairs. On the third landing was the office where Andriev's agent had maintained his business. Felix knocked on the door and then entered. A clerk looked up in surprise as they came in.

'What... What do you want here?' Felix handed him a scroll emblazoned with the count's seal. 'We're here on Count Andriev's business. I want to check your records.'

The man inspected the seal closely and then broke it and read the message on the scroll. 'It says I am to give you my fullest co-operation.'

The man's voice sounded querulous. Gotrek showed him a ham-sized fist. 'I think that would be a good idea, don't you.'

The man looked at the dwarf and then nodded silently. 'Where does your master keep his records?' Felix asked. The clerk indicated a large cabinet. 'Keys?' Felix demanded. The man reached into a purse and produced them. Felix tried them and found that they worked.

'When did you last see your master?' he asked.

'Two days ago.'

'Was there anything unusual about his behaviour?'

'No. It was just before he locked up for the night. I was about to leave. He lived here in the small flat at the back of the office.' Felix jingled the keys.

'Did he meet a stranger here, a noble from the Empire? Adolphus Krieger by name.'

'The name sounds familiar. I think he met Krieger here one evening.'

'One evening? Isn't that a little unusual? Normally merchants do their business during the day.'

'In our line of work we often meet people at unusual hours – couriers from the Empire, shady characters with something interesting to sell.'

'Shady characters?'

'Not all collectables are legitimately acquired, Herr Jaeger. And many are quite valuable. Thieves often try and pass them on to new owners. Not all collectors are as scrupulous about such things as the count; not all brokers as scrupulous as my master either.'

'Your master worked exclusively for the count?'

'Yes. Since before I was apprenticed. Over a decade ago.'

'Do you remember anything about an artefact that might have come from Araby? The Eye of Khemri.'

'I do. We purchased it for the count about two years ago. It was part of a collection belonging to an elderly merchant in Nuln, a very good one with many exquisite pieces. To me the Eye seemed nothing special, but my master thought it might be magical. He should know – he was a wizard after all.'

'Magical?'

'Nothing special. Some sort of protective talisman. Old; most likely the power in it had drained away over the years. He thought it came from Khemri in the Land of the Dead.'

You wouldn't have to be an expert to make that deduction, Felix thought. He could have made it himself. Still he was a little disturbed. The Land of the Dead had an evil reputation. It had once been the oldest of human kingdoms but had fallen into desolation millennia ago. Felix had never read anything good about the place, and a lot that was terrifying. All of the inhabitants were rumoured to have died of some terrible plague, and the cities were said to be vast haunted tombs. Worse than that, it was said to be the original home of the Great Necromancer, Nagash, a name which had been used to frighten children for hundreds of years. Felix said as much to the clerk.

'Nehekharan relics are particularly prized by certain collectors. It was the oldest human civilisation in the world. Its people were civilised two millennia before the time of Sigmar.'

'Civilised was not a word I would have used to describe them,' said Gotrek. It no longer surprised Felix when the Slayer displayed unexpected depths of knowledge. The dwarf kingdoms were far older than the kingdoms of man, and the dwarfs kept extensive records in their great books.

'Go on,' said Felix.

'They were half savages who built huge cities for their dead. They practised all manner of dark magic. Their nobles drank the blood of innocents in depraved ceremonies intended to prolong their own lives. They studied dark magic and daemon summoning.'

Felix could remember reading about such things in the great library of Altdorf University. He also remembered other things.

'They were not all bad. There were many city-states. The rulers of some fought against the blood drinkers. And

Alcadizaar fought against Nagash himself and destroyed him for a time.'

'Be that as it may, manling, they all fell into darkness in the end. Their cities are terrible places, haunted by the restless dead. Believe me. I have seen them.'

'You've seen them?'

'Aye, and it's not a sight I would care to look upon again.'

'What were you doing there?'

Gotrek looked at him and shrugged. He said nothing. Felix knew that unless the dwarf wanted to tell him, he would learn nothing. He was surprised. He knew the Slayer had gone through many adventures before they met, but Felix had never suspected he had travelled to the distant lands east of Araby.

'We don't have all day,' said Gotrek. 'If you're going to check the records here, you'd best get on with it.'

'What are you looking for?' asked the clerk.

'I'll know when I find it,' said Felix. 'You can go now. Have lunch,' he said. The man looked at him for a moment.

'You can read?' he asked. Felix wasn't surprised. Reading was not a common skill. 'Yes,' said Felix. He jerked a thumb at Gotrek. 'So can he.'

'I will leave you to it then, unless you want some help.'

'I don't think that will be necessary.' Felix went over to the record cases and opened them. He picked the ledger that had been worked on most recently and began to skim through it. As he told the clerk, he was not sure what he was looking for; he only hoped that they would find some clue, and that Max was having better luck than they were.

MAX SCHREIBER STARED at the Eye of Khemri. The more he looked, the more convinced he became that there was something odd about it.

He inspected the stone closely. He had seen its like before during his early studies at the College. He was certain that it was obsidian, a stone often used by the ancient Nehekharans. He was less certain about the pictograms. He had never undertaken any particular studies of that obscure and near forgotten language. It was a field only necromancers studied closely, and Max had never felt any great interest in that dark and dangerous art.

There was something about this talisman that niggled at him though, a subtle wrongness that Max could not quite put his finger on. The thing seemed to have a faint residue of dark magic, as if it had once been used to store dark magical energy. Such unholy objects were common enough, and Max had encountered many of them in his travels. The Eye had obviously once been used to contain such energies, and they had long since been discharged. At least they appeared to have been. Max was not entirely sure that they had been totally used up. He knew he would need to employ some complex divinatory spells to ascertain whether that was the case. Before he did that though, there were a few elementary precautions he wanted to take, just in case of mishaps.

He closed his eyes and focused his magesight, then reached out to bind the winds of magic to him. It was difficult here. The mansion was woven around with protective spells and this vault was the most densely defended area within it. It would be near impossible for anybody save a master wizard to draw any power at all here. Fortunately Max was a master, and he did not require much energy for what he had in mind.

He felt the power slowly trickle into him. He had not felt the flows of energy this weakly since he was an apprentice. Much as Max disliked Elthazar, he had to admit the old wizard knew his business. The spell walls were tight and strong. It took all of Max's efforts to maintain his concentration and tie the simple weave around the talisman. It took much longer than it normally would have, and by the time he was finished Max was sweating profusely. He felt drained and ill but he knew that his spell was in place. He studied the matrix of energies around the talisman closely, nipped off a loose flow here, tightened a skein there, until he was completely satisfied that the spell would hold for as long as he wanted it to. Good, he thought, the first stage of the work was complete.

Now it was time to begin his examination. He opened his magesight to the fullest and disregarded his own weave. He let his vision roam over the Eye, seeking out any slight hint that the thing was not what it appeared to be. At first nothing would come. He could tell just from the aura of the thing that it was old, and that it had indeed once held a fair amount of dark magic. It appeared to be the sort of talisman that any reasonably powerful necromancer would create to help him with his casting, one that had long ago served its purpose and discharged all its energies. It appeared to be a worthless burnt-out relic. Had he not had reason to think otherwise Max would have ended his examination there and then. But he did have reason and his curiosity was piqued and he was not a man to give up easily once his need to know was aroused.

He continued his search, focusing his magesight ever more closely on the talisman, seeking any hint of abnormality, the slightest trace that it was not quite what it seemed. He had heard of such things before. Mages sometimes camouflaged powerful artefacts with cloaking spells to prevent their enemies knowing their worth and purpose until it was too late.

Max suspected that something like this might be the case with the Eye but so far he had failed to find any evidence of it. If the thing was cloaked, then someone had done a truly masterful job. Max doubted that the mighty high elf mage Teclis himself could have hidden anything from the kind of minute examination he was giving the Eye, and still he found nothing.

The thought crossed his mind that perhaps he was wrong. Perhaps this talisman was simply just what it appeared to be, and there was nothing to be gained from any further examination. Max considered this and then considered the possibility that the thought might have originated outside his own mind, that it was in fact some sort of subtle suggestion spell placed on the Eye itself.

Part of him wondered that this might be taking suspicion too far; another part of him sincerely believed that no master magician could ever take suspicion far enough. There were far too many subtle snares that could be placed by jealous rivals. He inspected his mental defences and found them unbreached. He felt like laughing. Any suggestion subtle and potent enough to worm through his hard-held mental shields would certainly be able to hide any such tampering after the fact. This was getting him nowhere.

Once again, he returned to his painstaking search, fixing his fullest attention on finding any discrepancies in the aura of the stone. There! What was that? Perhaps nothing. Just the faintest hint of an echo of magical current, a strange resonance of an old spell. Max almost ignored it, and then realised that it was the only thing he had spotted so far. He focused his mind on it, drew on whatever magical power he could and followed the resonance trace.

It was like touching gossamer, a trace so faint that for several heartbeats Max was not sure that he had encountered anything at all. Perhaps he was imagining it. At first it truly seemed as if there was nothing there, then he noticed just the faintest hint of a weave so thin and so complex it seemed well nigh impossible that any human sorcerer could have woven it. He moved his awareness to a new level, shutting out all external visual stimuli and the pattern expanded to fill his field of vision.

As certainty bloomed within him Max was suddenly overcome with awe. He knew he was looking on spellwork of the highest order, far beyond anything he himself could perform, possibly far beyond anything anyone now living could perform. Someone had bound the most slender filaments of dark magical energy into the talisman in a way that was almost beyond Max's ability to perceive, let alone unravel. And they had done this beneath a cloaking spell so subtle that Max had almost missed it entirely.

Max knew that he was dealing with the work of one of the true masters. Perhaps the mysterious Adolphus Krieger did have a good reason for wanting this thing after all, although, as yet, Max could discern no hint of the thing's purpose. He was guided only by the suspicion that it was no good one. Few indeed were those who worked with dark magical energies for the benefit of mankind. He checked and rechecked his mental defences and wove the swiftest, most powerful wards around himself before continuing.

By concentrating all his powers he could just about manage to make out the pattern. He selected one thin strand of energy and began to follow it. It was an exercise he had performed many times during his apprenticeship, studying the weaves of spells cast by his tutors: now the stakes were much higher. He knew he truly had to be careful now. Anyone capable of going to so much trouble to shield the true power of the talisman was more than capable of leaving booby traps for those who might seek to uncover its secrets.

He traced the weave slowly, gingerly, like a man advancing along a rotten wooden bridge over a chasm that he knows might give way at any moment. Slowly he began to discern the order and logic of the pattern. There was some sort of zone of compulsion locked on the talisman, designed to affect minds other than human, although what sort was not entirely clear. That spell was layered over and interwoven with several other spells. Max could see that the user could somehow draw on the energies of dark magic through a lattice so subtle and powerful that it filled his mind with the sort of awe that an architect might feel in the inner sanctum of the great Temple of Sigmar in Altdorf. Max knew, without doubt, that he was looking on a work of genius.

As he continued he saw that these spells were interwoven with dozens of others, the purposes of which he could not divine. It was breathtaking. He no longer doubted that Adolphus Krieger, or whatever his real name was, really did want the Eye. If he had even an inkling of the thing's true power, any dark magician would kill for this artefact.

Overcome with fascination, Max continued to trace the weave, overwhelmed by the subtle labyrinth of power that someone had created. He let his awareness slide along the intricate sweeps and curves of magical power, following them ever faster, certain as he reached towards the core of the design that he would be able to unravel its purpose fully and completely.

Faster and faster his mind raced along, his magesight sweeping to the very centre of the pattern. He felt excitement build within him, as if soon all the innermost secrets of the magical universe might be revealed to him. Too late part of him realised the unnatural nature of the feeling. Too late part of him realised that the Eye was indeed trapped.

Frantically he tried to shore up his mental walls, knowing that soon an assault would come. Even as he did so, his awareness finally reached the centre of the elaborate magical structure. At that moment, just before the wave of blackness swept over him, Max saw that the creator of the Eye, in a fit of megalomania or vanity, had left his signature upon the thing. Doubtless he wanted anyone who had unravelled his secrets to know their author before they were destroyed.

Looking upon that mystical seal, as certain and as recognisable to any fellow mage as handwriting, Max felt himself overcome with wonder and terror. Before the darkness took him, he knew without doubt the identity of the Eye of Khemri's creator, and he was very, very afraid.

THREE

'WHAT HAVE YOU found out, manling?' asked Gotrek. He sounded bored and annoyed and Felix did not blame him. Several hours of searching Brother Benedict's records had revealed next to nothing. The Eye of Khemri had been purchased from Zuchi & Petrillo's in Altdorf, part of a lot sold to the auction house by the widow of one Baron Keinster of Warghafen. Felix had never heard of him, but it was hardly surprising. There were many old noble families in the Empire, far too many for anyone to ever keep track of. All he knew was that Warghafen was a small town near Talabheim, which was not a great deal of help. He coughed again, feeling a little shivery.

There were references to a meeting with Adolphus Krieger. There were even two letters from the man, written in bold flowing Imperial script, requesting a meeting with Benedict and his patron, and referring to Krieger as a fellow enthusiast of antiquities. The address given was in Middenheim and they referred to an upcoming visit to Praag. There was no way to check the address now, unless Malakai Makaisson could be persuaded to take the *Spirit of Grungni* all the way to the mountain city state, and given the present circumstances that seemed like a frivolous use of his time. Anyway, Malakai was preparing to leave the city and head back to Karak Kadrin to ferry more dwarf troops into Praag for when the war renewed in spring, if not before. He had better things to do than go on a wild goose chase after someone who had most likely not been using his own name and address. Felix took the letters anyway. At least they were evidence that the mysterious Krieger existed and was not some figment of Andriev's imagination.

'Not much,' he told the Slayer. 'Benedict was a meticulous man, and he recorded all of his appointments, but there is not the slightest clue as to where he is and why he disappeared.'

'Time to visit the mysteriously deserting guards then.'

Felix nodded. He could not think of anything else to do. They had wasted the whole afternoon and a good part of the early evening here.

ADOLPHUS STALKED THROUGH the snowbound streets. His cloak was drawn tight about him; its hood obscured his features. In the present weather conditions no one would find this in the least surprising. The streets were near empty, and those who were abroad this evening were often even more muffled than he. Adolphus still felt a little weary. Like all his kind, daylight slowed him and hurt his eyes. Too much exposure to the light of the sun would leave him badly burned and in considerable pain, and it would take a good deal of warm, fresh blood to heal him.

He was feeling a little torpid. He knew that he had been feeding too much recently and too much blood could be as bad for him as too little. His head ached. His thoughts were restless and hard to focus. He wondered if some of the blood he had drunk was tainted, or whether he was succumbing to one of the insidious madnesses that the centuries sometimes brought to his kind. Once, when young and desperate, he had drunk the blood of a mutant whose veins had been tainted with warpstone. That had given him a similar feeling to this, only not nearly so bad.

It was hard to concentrate. Anger burned deep within him. He felt an urge to rend and tear, to find prey and simply kill for the sake of killing. He fought hard for control. He did not need this, not now, not with so much at stake, not with the talisman he had sought for so long and so hard this near at hand. He needed all his wits about him, in case the others got wind of what he was up to. If the countess or some other representative of the Council of Ancients should learn of his presence here and divine his purpose, all might yet be lost. After all, they were as familiar with Nospheratus's prophesies as he, even if they were too gutless to try to fulfil them. No, he could not afford any mistakes.

Could it be that he wanted to fail? He had seen stranger things happen in his long existence. He had known some of his kind who used long quests to keep themselves motivated and interested, but who had allowed themselves to falter and fade once they had fulfilled their purpose. Maybe part of him wanted to avoid such a fate.

He sensed that he was being watched, and allowed his awareness to balloon outwards. Footsteps padded after him. He could tell there were only two of them, and that they were not too close. Footpads most likely and desperate ones, to be abroad on a night like this. He speeded his step. He had business to be about this evening, and did not want to be distracted. He had wasted too much time in negotiations with the stubborn old man. It was time to take more direct measures. He had sent out his manservant Roche to summon the coven. It was a risk he would have to take; if the council's agents found out about it, then too bad. The hour was getting late. He had other things to worry about. He wanted to find the Eye before the madness fully overwhelmed him. Perhaps with the talisman he could overcome its effects. Or perhaps the madness was a product of this accursed city, in which case the sooner he left the better.

He realised that as he had increased his speed, so had his pursuers. He shook his head, trying to fight off the urge to turn on them and rend them asunder like a beast of prey. Quietly, he told himself. Be calm. There is no need for this.

The beast that had taken up residence in the back of his head told him differently. The men were fools and they needed to die. It was an insult that such cattle dared to pursue him. Their rightful role was prey, not predator, and he should teach them the error of their ways.

He slowed his pace. His pursuers were committed now. They came on as swiftly as before. How well he knew that feeling. The decision had been made. It was time to close for the kill. He waited until the last minute before turning to meet them. Two men, as he had known there would be. Medium height. Wrapped in thick tunics. His keen eyes picked out every stitch of the patches. Their faces were intent. Long knives glittered in their hands. They intended to show no mercy. They were going to kill him and take whatever he had – or so they thought.

Adolphus did not even bother reaching for his sword. He knew he did not need it. The humans moved with appalling slowness compared to him. As the first reached him, Adolphus stretched out his arm, easily sliding round his attacker's clumsy strike and grabbing his throat. One quick jerk and the man's neck broke. Adolphus felt the vertebrae grind beneath his fingers, saw the light go out of the man's eyes. The robber's partner had not even realised what had happened yet; Adolphus did not intend to give him time to.

He decided he would teach this foolish mortal the meaning of horror. He punched out with his hand. Such was the force of the blow that his fist penetrated flesh and dug deep into the man's abdomen. Adolphus felt wet slimy things surround his hand. With the expertise that only centuries could bring he reached out and closed his fingers. Something squished; there was a curious gurgling sound as he ripped it free.

The man only started to scream when Adolphus held a slab of meat up before his eyes. It took the robber a moment to realise that it was his own liver.

THE GUARD LIVED in no salubrious area, Felix thought. No matter what Andriev claimed about paying his watchmen well, it was obvious that the money did not go on rent. The tenement was old. Rats watched them with glittering eyes as they made their way up the alley. Felix was uncomfortably reminded of the skaven he had encountered in Nuln.

The door swung open on partially broken hinges. There was a grinding sound as the wood dragged across stone. The place smelled of cheap cooking oil and chamber pots, and too many people cramped too close together. Perhaps, Felix told himself, things had been better before the siege, before so many people had been made homeless, but somehow he doubted it. This building had the look of a place that had been allowed to go to seed a long time ago.

As they entered, he became aware that other eyes than those of rodents were watching. An old woman glared at them.

'Wot you want?' she demanded, in a harsh, cracked voice that reminded him of a parrot's screech.

'We're looking for Henrik Glasser, grandmother. Have you any idea where we might find him?'

'He owe you money too does he? And I'm not your grandmother!'

'No. We just wish to talk to him.'

'You don't look like the sort that just come around for a quiet conversation, and Henrik ain't much of a one for small talk either.'

'Just tell us where to find him, hag, and less of the backchat,' said Gotrek. His voice sounded even more flinty than usual. The old woman looked as if she was going to say something cutting, but a glance at the Slayer's brutal features and one mad eye convinced her otherwise.

'Up the stairs, first landing. Door on the left,' she said, and disappeared into her cubbyhole beneath the stairs rather more quickly than she had emerged. Felix heard a key turn in the lock.

'We don't want no trouble here,' she shrieked once the door was securely in place behind her. 'This is a respectable house.'

'And my mother was a troll,' muttered Gotrek. 'Come on, manling, we don't have all evening.'

Felix strode up the stairs. Ten heartbeats later, he was banging on Henrik Glasser's door. There was no answer. He glanced down at the Slayer.

'There's someone in there,' said Gotrek. 'I can hear breathing.'

Felix could hear nothing but he had learned long ago that the Slayer's ears were far keener than his own. 'Open up, Henrik!' he shouted. 'We know you are in there.'

Still no answer.

'If you don't open up by the time I count to three, I'll break the door down,' said Gotrek. Felix could hear no sound of movement. He looked at the dwarf.

'Three,' said the Slayer, and his axe smashed the door to kindling.

'That wasn't very nice,' said Felix, leaping through the doorway.

'He wasn't going to answer, manling.'

The stench of the place slapped Felix in the face, then rammed two fingers up his nostrils just to get his attention. The place reeked of unwashed clothing, unwashed flesh and uneaten food, as well as a lot of rotgut booze. A solitary candle guttered on a plate sitting on a broken table in the middle of the room. Felix heard rather than saw something slithering away out of the corner of his eye. Gotrek was already past him and in a moment, had dragged a pale-faced, fearful man into the light.

'What do you want with me? Keep away! I won't tell you nothing,' said the man.

'We'll see about that,' said Gotrek. His tone conveyed as much menace as a wolf's warning growl.

'All we want are the answers to a few questions.'

'I don't have any money,' said the man. 'I told Ari that, and I'm telling you the same. Maybe next week. Maybe once I find some more work. Breaking my arms won't help. Ari will never get repaid that way.'

'We're not from Ari,' said Felix.

'It's no use threatening me. I don't have the cash. Tell Ari gold doesn't grow on trees, you know.'

'We're not from Ari. We just want to ask you a few questions.'

'You're not from Ari?'

'No.'

'Then you have no right to come bursting through my door like that.'

'Says who?' said Gotrek in his most menacing voice.

The man looked as if he wanted to say something smart but then thought the better of it. Felix did not blame him. When he wanted to, the Slayer projected more menace than a school of sharks.

'We're from your former employer, Count Andriev. Remember him?' Felix asked.

The man nodded. He looked a bit saddened. A little grieved even. 'I never worked for the count, that was my brother, Henrik.'

'You're not Henrik Glasser?'

'No. Pauli. Henrik's gone. He vanished. Not that I blame him, mind you. Winter's been hard, there was the siege and all. I figured he just got fed up working for that old madman and shipped out with a caravan.'

'There's no caravans leaving Praag at this time of year,' said Felix. 'None coming in either.'

'Is too, if you know where to look.'

'What do you mean?' asked Felix. He had the feeling he already knew.

'Smuggling's always profitable, particularly at times like now, what with the duke's tax collectors clamping down and all. You get my meaning?'

'Only too clearly.' He remembered his father's constant grumbling about tax collectors in Altdorf and the fact that his old man had many connections with smugglers. It was one of the things that had built the Jaeger company to the size it was. Felix could see only too clearly how such things came about. There were always men willing to make a dishonest penny or two, even in times of catastrophe.

'You think your brother left with smugglers?'

'Where else would he be? He might have left me some word though, instead of running off without a by your leave and us owing on the rent and all. I don't suppose you could see your way clear to lending me a couple of silver pieces, just until I get some work and…'

Felix looked at the man, not quite believing his cheek. 'How long has your brother been gone?'

'A couple of days. About that silver – one would be enough.'

'Anything else unusual about his disappearance? Aside from the fact he left no word of his going.'

'I will have to replace that door after all. Old Gerti is most particular about things like that, and you two did smash it–'

'It's not the only thing I'll smash, if you don't start answering the questions,' said Gotrek. Felix fumbled for his purse, as if he was considering looking in it for money. He knew the value of the carrot and the stick when it came to getting answers.

'No. Except he never told Nell, his girl, either, and they were close as two thieves in a thicket. Closer. She's been round a few times asking for him and doesn't believe I don't know where he is.'

'I don't believe you either,' said Gotrek. He raised his axe menacingly.

'There's no need for that. I've told you all I know. Honest. As Ulric is my witness, why would I lie about it? To tell the truth, I wish you luck finding my brother. Remind him about his share of the rent when you see him.'

Felix looked at the Slayer. He could tell they were thinking the same thing. There was nothing more to be learned here.

'THIS IS A bit of a wild goose chase,' Felix said, drawing his cloak closer against the cold. The Slayer glared off into the darkness.

'Tell me about it, manling.'

'Well, at least we know that Krieger or someone calling himself that exists, and that Andriev wasn't lying about his guards or his tame wizard disappearing. I don't think we need check on any of the others. I have a pretty good idea of what we will find. I don't think Pauli will be seeing his brother again.'

The Slayer nodded once again.

'Back to the mansion then.' They trudged into the night and the deepening snow.

* * *

ADOLPHUS GLANCED AROUND the room. It was warm. It was luxurious. Osrik always liked to do well by himself, and his guests. He could smell wine and fresh cooked food and blood – lots of human blood. Thick hangings of brocade covered the windows, keeping out the night chill. Portraits of noble ancestors covered the walls. The carpets were thick, the furniture old and polished and heavy. The place suited the wealth of its other occupants. They looked on him with adoring eyes.

He was used to it now. He had selected them himself, just after he reached the city. Some of them he had known in other places, and other times. He had first met Baroness Olga nearly a decade ago. He had drunk from her veins in a scented garden in the warm south of Bretonnia, and she had been his willing slave ever since, finding new chattels for him, introducing him to other nobles, ensuring that his coven grew in size and influence.

She had proven most useful, although her thinness and the sickly light in her eyes told him that soon she would be fading. Standing too close to the sun was not good for mortals. Being on intimate terms with the Arisen had a tendency to drain them of youth and strength before their time, if they were allowed to survive at all.

Not that it mattered. There were always others willing to step up and take their place. Their owners always fascinated the cattle. None knew better than Adolphus the way the aura of immortality and power and beauty affected them. He had been overwhelmed by it himself when he had first met the countess all those centuries ago, and she had chosen him.

And that was what this was all about, he knew. Being chosen. All of these rich and powerful people present this evening hoped that eventually he would grant them the embrace. All of them knew it was unlikely he would choose to, but the hope of it kept them going, motivated them to do what Adolphus wanted willingly. Not that they had much choice anyway. He had tapped all of them for blood and that created a bond that was hard for all but the strongest to break.

He looked at them again. Everyone present had surrendered their will to him gladly. They were all in his thrall, would gladly do whatever he required of them. He felt nothing but contempt for them all. They were slow, stupid, greedy, ugly, grasping, foolish. They had all turned their backs on conventional morality, on all their old gods, and they had raised him up in their place. It was written all over their faces. He wondered whether this was what it felt like to be a god. Perhaps they were the only creatures left, aside from the Arisen, with whom he had anything in common. Perhaps the world was not divided between predators and prey, as he had always thought; perhaps it was divided between worshipped and worshippers.

Where were these thoughts coming from? Why was he thinking them now? It did not matter what these people were or who they thought they were. All he really needed them for was tools. Like all the followers of the Arisen, they provided money, blades, adulation and blood. That was all they were really good for.

He looked around once more. There were nobles here, men and women who craved immortality the way a drunkard craves drink. They were all rich and powerful, that was why they had been chosen, but right at this moment they looked like a group of desperate children keen to be the one chosen for the favour of a distant parent. Good. That was the way he liked to keep them.

The only one who stood out was Roche. His hulking servant stood to one side, a cynical smile on his brutal pockmarked face, the fingers of his massive strangler's hands intertwined in a parody of prayer. Roche knew what was going on. Roche had seen the likes of the coven before, and he shared his master's contempt for them. He was secure of his place in Adolphus's favour, just as his father had been, and his grandfather before him. Roche's family had served Adolphus for generations. In them he had placed as much trust as he placed in any mortal. They looked after his interests among the mortals, guarded his crypt while he slept, drove his coach in the daylight when he travelled, spoke with his voice to the cattle when he did not need to be present. Roche was a servant, but he knew he possessed more power than many lords and that arrogance was written on his face.

Adolphus did not mind, just so long as he remembered who was truly the master here. Perhaps this evening he would allow Roche to pick out one of the noble women and begin breeding his successor. After all, Roche was not getting any younger; his close-cropped hair was iron grey now, and the lines around his eyes were deep. So soon, Adolphus thought. Mortal lives passed like those of mayflies.

Adolphus studied his slaves, wondering if he really needed them. He had disposed of most of old Andriev's guards, and the corpse of the greedy magician would not be found until the spring thaw. Either the old man would give him the talisman at the price he offered, or he would take it from his cold, dead hands. At the moment the latter option seemed preferable. Subtlety was no longer going to get him anywhere. He had made himself too visible now. If the countess or any of her agents were in the city, then it would be only too obvious to them that another of the Arisen was also present.

He could see that one of his followers, the fat merchant Osrik, was desperate to speak. The man obviously felt he had something important to say. He rubbed his double chin and his oiled hair, his eyes fixed on Adolphus with blazing intensity. He wondered if he should let the man suffer a bit longer but dismissed the idea. A god should be above such petty games.

'What is it, Osrik? You seem keen to speak.'

'Yes, master, I have important news to impart to you.' He ignored the glares of the rest of the coven, all of whom were equally desperate for Adolphus's attention. The image of a sultan in his harem sprang into Adolphus's mind. It was not an idea he liked.

'Then go on, share this revelation with us all,' said Adolphus mockingly. The coven smiled at his tone. One thing they could always be relied on to do was toady well.

'As you know master, I have had my agents watching old Count Andriev's house day and night.'

'I commanded nothing less.'

'The old man has had visitors.' If Adolphus's heart had still beaten it would have skipped a beat now. Immediately, he assumed the countess or some other agent of the council had found out what he was doing.

'Who?' he asked calmly. He had centuries of practice at concealing his emotions, and it never did to show any dismay in front of the cattle.

'He has summoned aid. A magician and two dwarf Slayers, as well as a pair of human warriors.' Adolphus allowed himself a small, satisfied smile. These did not sound like any agents the countess would have used. Dwarfs were almost never part of any coven. There was something about their blood that disagreed with most of the Arisen.

'This hardly sounds like a major problem, Osrik.'

'The magician is very powerful, master. He is an advisor to the duke. I have made enquiries and found out a few more things about him. His name is Maximilian Schreiber. He is famous for casting protective enchantments. He was an advisor on such things to the Elector Count of Middenheim and has been employed by the Duke of Praag in a similar role. By all accounts, he is a very formidable magician.'

This was sounding less promising. Adolphus feared few mortals, but mages of the first rank were a cause for caution. Given time to cast their spells they could prove a threat to even one of the Arisen. It seemed that the old man was not going to give in without a fight.

The madness that lurked in the back of Adolphus's mind welcomed this; more deaths, more blood, more killing. He had to fight back the urge to show his fangs.

'I believe we can overcome any single mage.'

'The Slayers too are formidable.' Adolphus allowed a smile to crease his features. He feared no mortal warriors.

'I do not think we need trouble ourselves with them,' he said confidently. To his surprise, he saw that Osrik looked troubled, almost as if he wanted to contradict Adolphus. That was unusual for a coven member. He was about to dismiss the fat merchant's qualms but some instinct told him not to. 'I can see you are troubled, Osrik. Why don't you tell us why?'

The fat man sighed. His blubbery cheeks shook. 'One of the Slayers is Gotrek Gurnisson. I met him once on the walls of the city before the siege. He is terrifying.'

It was interesting, Adolphus thought, that Osrik could describe this Gotrek Gurnisson as terrifying. After all, Osrik was a coven member and had encountered one of the Arisen. After that, few mortals were impressed by anything less. This Slayer might indeed prove to be a problem. His fame had reached even Adolphus's ears. The dwarf had become quite famous during the siege. He was said to be the possessor of a magical axe and had slain the Chaos warlord Arek Daemonclaw. He had rallied the defenders on the walls at the height of the siege and was even said to have destroyed the great daemonic siege engines. Adolphus had been deep in slumber at the height of the battle so he had not witnessed this for himself.

Adolphus rubbed his forehead. He had bad experiences with dwarf rune weapons in the past, at the battle of Hel Fenn. He knew that they could hurt him and from all he had heard the Slayer was very skilled with his axe. Even so, Adolphus doubted that he would prove much of a threat, but it never paid to take chances.

'You have done well, Osrik. And you appear to be thorough. Who are the other mercenaries the old man has hired?'

'With all respect, master, they are not mercenaries. One of them is a noblewoman, Ulrika Magdova, daughter of the March Boyar Ivan Petrovich Straghov, and a distant relation of Count Andriev. The other Slayer is a certain Snorri Nosebiter, a dwarf of great strength. The last one is Felix Jaeger, a swordsman and associate of Gotrek Gurnisson's. He too played a major part in the siege of the city and enjoys the favour of the duke.'

This was getting worse and worse, thought Adolphus. It was as if the Old Powers were intervening to thwart him. If the count appealed to Ulrika's father then he could have a small army of troops at his disposal. Adolphus was familiar enough with Kislevite politics to know that the march boyar had the ear of the Tsarina and, if the others had the ear of the duke, a formidable coalition of foes could be raised against him. In numbers, even the cattle could prove dangerous. Worse, if this Max Schreiber was a competent wizard, and by all accounts he appeared to be, then he might unravel the true nature of the talisman and seize it for himself.

Adolphus snarled and all of the coven shivered and looked pale. He realised that unconsciously he had allowed his fangs to extrude from his gums. It was not a sight that most mortals looked upon without qualms. Events were running out of his control. All of this time, he had been worried about the countess or the council finding out his plans, and now it appeared he had been blindsided by a stupid, old madman. He knew that he would have to act quickly now. The time for waiting was past. Even if it meant revealing his presence to any Arisen in the city, he would have to act, and act quickly before the mortals could assemble their forces to stop him.

He had spent far too long tracking down the talisman to allow himself to be thwarted now. He was the Prince of Night. He would fulfil the Prophesies of Nospheratus. If anyone got in his way at this late stage then they would have to die.

He began giving instructions to the coven. He knew with their aid, he could assemble a small army of henchmen quickly. Which was good, he thought, for it looked as though he was going to need one.

ULRIKA LOOKED DOWN at Max. She was worried. A few hours ago the wizard had screamed and fallen from the chair in which he sat. The odd talisman lay near his hand. Ulrika had checked and found out that Max was still breathing and his heart still beat albeit slowly, but nothing she could do would wake him. She had sent out for a physician but there had been nothing the man could do either. Now Max lay unconscious on the floor of the vault. It did not look as if he would be awakening any time soon.

Ulrika felt helpless, and it was not a feeling she liked. She owed Max Schreiber for saving her from the plague, and she had not had a chance to repay the debt. Now there seemed to be nothing she could do. It would take another wizard or perhaps a priest to revive Max. She wondered if she should send word to the Temple of Shallya, or to the duke. She was beginning to wish she had never become involved in any of this strange business. She could just have ignored Andriev's message. After all, he was only a distant cousin on her mother's side. She could barely remember her father ever mentioning him when she was growing up, and when he had it was with a mixture of pity and contempt. Her father was a warrior and he had no interests outside horses, battle and the managing of his estates. To him, Andriev's hobby seemed to be something childish and unmanly. Ulrika shook her head. That summed up the relationship between the border nobles of Kislev and those who dwelled in the cities. Most of the country folk thought their city-bred kin were decadent and effete. Most of the city dwellers looked down on the border nobles as little more than barbarians. There was some truth in both points of view, Ulrika thought, and then brought her attention back to the matter at hand. She knew she was just trying to distract herself from it anyway.

Snorri Nosebiter looked up at her. His brutish eyes held a look of dismay. 'Snorri thinks Max is not getting any better,' said Snorri. 'Of course, Snorri isn't a doctor.'

Ulrika tried to smile at the Slayer. Snorri was stupid but he had a good heart and had been a good companion in many desperate adventures. He did not deserve to feel the cutting edge of her tongue now, no matter how much she felt like giving him it. She wondered when Felix would get back. Perhaps he would have some ideas about what to do. He was a clever man. Too clever, she often thought. Too clever, and too superior by far, when really he was only the son of a merchant. She wondered what she had ever seen in him now. Still, he had the power to make her angry even when she just thought about him. Just at that moment she heard the sound of the doorbell ringing.

Within moments, Felix and Gotrek were in the room.

'What happened to him?' asked Gotrek jerking his thumb in Max's direction. Ulrika told him. Felix looked at him closely then at her. 'Where is the talisman?' he asked.

'Is that all you're concerned about?'

'No – but if we summon another magician to look at him, he might want to study it too.'

'It was studying the thing that did this to Max,' she said.

'Are you sure?'

'It's possible that he might have had a fit at the exact moment he was examining the thing but I prefer to believe the two things were connected,' she said.

'There's no need to be sarcastic.'

She glared at him. He was such an infuriating man when he wanted to be. 'Do you think summoning another magician is a good idea right now?'

'I can't think of anything better to do, unless it's to summon a healer, or send him to the Temple.'

'Best send for the healer then.'

'The healer will want a donation to the Temple. They nearly always do.'

Andriev looked at them. 'I will pay. After all this happened when the man was in my service.'

At that moment there came a crashing sound from above.

'What was that?' Ulrika asked.

'Sounded like somebody breaking the door to me,' said Gotrek. Felix did not doubt the Slayer was right. He usually was about such things.

'Snorri thinks we should go and break some heads,' said Snorri Nosebiter. Gotrek growled his agreement and the two Slayers rushed for the stairs. Felix glanced after them, and then looked around the open vault, and at the recumbent figure of Max.

'Snorri is not exactly a master strategist,' said Felix. 'We're supposed to be guarding this place.'

'Sometimes the best form of defence is offence,' said Ulrika. 'Go and help them! I will stay here with Max and make sure no one gets into the vault.'

Felix could see she was determined and what she said made a certain amount of sense. If any intruders could be stopped before they got in here, it would go much better. Felix looked at Andriev. Somehow he did not doubt that Snorri Nosebiter and Gotrek would be capable of handling anything short of a small army.

'Can the vault be opened from the inside?'

'Ahem – yes. It can. There is a hidden lever in here.' Good, Felix thought. 'I will close the door behind me. If we have not returned within an hour, make your own decisions as to what to do.'

As he raced up the stairs, Felix wondered how long the air would last in the sealed vault. Long enough, he hoped.

From up ahead came the sound of fighting. Felix recognised the bellowed war cries of the two Slayers and the butcher-block sounds of weapons impacting on flesh swiftly followed by screams of agony.

It sounded as if the dwarfs were doing the work they were paid for. It was time for him to do the same.

His sword felt light in his hand. His heart raced. He was not exactly scared. He just felt a little weak. Everything seemed to be happening a little slower than normal. Felix recognised the signs. He was always like this before going into action.

He emerged into the atrium and took in the whole scene at a glance. Snow and cold night air blew in through the door that swung wide on its hinges. A mass of cloaked men, armed with swords and daggers, engaged the two Slayers. Servants and men-at-arms lay sprawled in their own blood everywhere. It looked as if the intruders had not been too choosy about who they slaughtered.

The shoe was on the other foot now though. Gotrek thundered through them like a raging bull. His axe left bloody corpses every time it struck, and it struck often, moving almost too fast for the human eye to follow. As Felix watched, the Slayer cut down two more assailants and dived headlong into the pack of men trying to force their way in through the door.

Snorri was no less dangerous. In one hand he held his broad-bladed axe, in the other a heavy warhammer. He wielded the two weapons as dextrously as most warriors would use one, lashing out almost simultaneously with both, whirling like a dervish maddened on locoweed to face his foes. As soon as one cowled man went down beneath a thunderous hail of blows, Snorri sprang over his corpse to get to grips with another. All the while an idiot grin of enjoyment played across his lips, and occasionally mad bellows of mirth erupted from deep within his enormous chest.

Even as Felix watched, more men emerged from other entrances to the halls. Either they had been there earlier slaughtering the servants or they were coming through the windows. Felix did not want to think about the implications of that. Whoever wanted the talisman had brought a small army with him. It was not a reassuring thought. Felix shouted a challenge and raced to join the melee.

He wondered if the mysterious Adolphus was somewhere in the milling throng. To be honest, Felix was not all that keen to meet him.

ADOLPHUS KRIEGER MOVED silently through the house. It was a place he could have learned to like given time. Every corner was stuffed with curios and artefacts of an earlier time. Adolphus recognised vases that must have emerged from the potter's kiln before he arose. Some of the tapestries on the wall had been woven when he was still a child. It almost made him nostalgic. Almost.

Behind him he could hear the sounds of battle. It appeared that the coven's retainers were providing the distraction he required. Perhaps they might actually overwhelm the guardians of the manor. Somehow though Adolphus doubted it. Maybe with his aid they might have stood a chance, but they were on their own. The beast that lurked at the back of his mind wanted to go back there, to tear and rend and drink blood, but he was not going to give in to it. Why should he risk his centuries-long life if he did not have to? The chances were that he could defeat the dwarfs, but why chance it if there was even a one in a thousand possibility they might win?

If you took enough thousand-to-one risks, then eventually one of them would kill you. Consequently, he avoided them when he could, which was doubtless why he had lived so long when others of his kind had been snuffed out like flickering candles. No, if he absolutely had to, he would face the dwarf and kill him, but there was no sense in tempting fate when it was not utterly necessary. Despite this though, it took a great effort of will not to run towards the fray, not to rush to where he knew all that warm hot blood was flowing.

Moving so silently he doubted that even a cat could have heard him, Adolphus stalked deeper into the mansion. The magician Benedict had provided him with detailed descriptions and a rough map of the layout before his unfortunate demise. Adolphus had the near perfect memory of the Arisen, which, combined with his darkness-piercing vision, enabled him to navigate the shadowy corridors without difficulty.

A sense of relief filled him as he put more distance between himself and the battle, and the urge to kill decreased slightly. He had entered the part of the mansion where magical protections were in force. He opened his mage senses to the flow of energy moving around him. There were no magical traps that he could see, simply spells of warding and protection, weaves designed to keep prying eyes from gazing into the place with scrying spells, and wards designed to negate a head-on magical assault. Whoever had cast these spells had known his business, but had drawn the line at using harmful magical energies, just as the builders of the vault had not used any physical traps such as deadfalls.

Adolphus could understand it. Certainly, there were those who were paranoid enough to use such things but they were a minority. After all, who wanted to dwell in a building where a slight misstep could put you in a pit, or blast you with a firebolt? Despite what mages might tell you about how careful they were, such things did occur. And when they did you were usually not around afterward to complain about the consequences.

Adolphus fought to keep a smile from his lips. He was making assumptions that might prove fatal. He did not absolutely know this was the case here. It might simply be that the magician who had cast these wards was a better sorcerer than he, and he just could not perceive the traps. It would be best to proceed with the utmost caution until he had established whether this was the case or not.

He was at the top of the flight of stairs now. He knew they led down through the cellars and into the vaults. He paused for a moment, and allowed himself to savour the anticipation. He was close now, so close he could almost taste it. The thing he had sought so long and so hard for was almost within his grasp, and with it the power to do what none of the Arisen had dreamed of since the time of the Vampire Counts. He would be the one to fulfil the prophesies in the *Book of Shadows* and the *Grimoire Necronium*. Surely the time had now come to pass? The armies of Chaos were on the march, the old order was ending, and a new world would be born in fire and blood. Most of all, in blood. He would be the King of the Night, and his reign would be eternal, dark and filled with poisonous beauty.

He shook his head. Such musing brought him no closer to his goal. It was time to take the last few steps that would lead him to ultimate glory.

FELIX GLANCED AROUND at the scene of carnage. Dead bodies were piled up all around them. Blood splattered Gotrek and Snorri making them look as if they had been working in an abattoir. Felix guessed that he did not look much better. Not all of the blood belonged to his opponents. He was nicked and cut in half a dozen places though he guessed that none of the wounds were major.

'Hardly a fight at all,' grumbled Gotrek. 'Even for humans these were poor warriors.'

'Snorri has killed tougher cockroaches,' agreed Snorri Nosebiter sourly. 'Snorri squashed an ant once that put up a better fight. Nasty acid sting it had.'

Felix could not entirely agree with the Slayers about the toughness of their foes. By virtue of sheer numbers, he had been almost overwhelmed on several occasions, and his body's aches reminded him that this fight had been dangerous enough. Still, they had a point. These men had not fought as well as many he had faced. It was not just that they were indifferent warriors; it was something more. They had fought like sleepwalkers. Their timing was off, and they had been indifferent as to whether they had lived or died. Their parries and thrusts had possessed a purely mechanical quality. A thought struck him.

'They fought like men who were under a spell,' he said.

'A spell of being very bad fighters, maybe,' said Snorri Nosebiter.

'I think you are right, manling,' said Gotrek. 'Not even humans are usually so bad. They fought as if they did not have all their wits about them.'

'That's never stopped Snorri from putting up a good fight,' said Snorri. From the peevish tone, anyone would have thought the men had tried to cheat him out of a copper pfennig. He was obviously still disappointed by the quality of the opposition they had faced.

Felix ignored him. His mind was already racing ahead, searching out reasons for why this might have happened. This Adolphus Krieger was a magician of some sort, and obviously these men had been in his thrall. The question was why he had sent them to attack now. The answer was obvious.

'This was a diversion,' Felix said. 'The magician is already in the building.'

He and Gotrek exchanged glances. 'The vault,' they said simultaneously.

ADOLPHUS STOOD BEFORE the entrance to the vault. The door was large and very strong and could probably resist a team of men with a battering ram. Not that there would have been room to swing it in these corridors. There were several potent wards on the doors designed to neutralise spells of opening and unlocking. Adolphus doubted that he could overcome them with magic. He was a very knowledgeable mage but not a particularly potent one. The countess, for one, had been much stronger. That would change when he had the talisman.

He did not need to be a great mage, under the circumstances. The concealment of the dwarf-built pressure pads would have fooled most eyes, but not his. They were far, far keener in the darkness than any human eye could ever be. Even the hairline edges cunningly concealed in the

stonework were as clear to him as the edges of a paving
stone would be to a mortal.

He took out his dagger and slid its edge through the narrow gap of the nearest one. He heard a click and the stone
slid out, revealing the pressure pad within. He pushed it,
and was rewarded with another click that told him the way
was partially open. He repeated the process on the other
side of the door. There remained only the main lock on the
door itself. Fortunately he had an easy solution for that too.
He had made his preparations with care.

Reaching inside his jerkin he carefully pulled out the two
containers he had made earlier. He smiled. He might not be
the greatest of sorcerers but his knowledge of alchemy was
considerable and had been perfected over long centuries.
When the contents of the two containers were mixed they
would create a powerful corrosive capable of eating through
solid metal in a short time.

Carefully he dribbled some fluid onto the area around the
lock. When the green fluid encountered the red fluid, an
acrid chemical smoke rose. There was a hissing, spluttering
sound and the metal of the lock began to melt away like
snow under a soldier's piss.

Very soon now, the talisman would be in his grasp.

'WHAT WAS THAT?' asked Andriev nervously. Ulrika looked up.
She too had heard the odd bubbling sound. A few moments
before they had both heard faint clicks as if someone had been
working with the locks. She could only hope it was Felix and
the others coming back. Somehow she did not think it was.

'I don't know,' she said. A faint reek as of noxious chemi-
cals reached her nostrils. She was reminded of the scent of
alchemical fire but it was not that. She sniffed again. The
scent was coming from the direction of the doorway. She
thought she heard a faint hissing sound now as well.

'There's someone outside. I think they are trying to get in,'
she said, raising her sword to the guard position. Andriev
clutched his own weapon tighter. Even as they watched, the
door began to bend inwards, as if being subjected to a force
as slow and irresistible as the action of a glacier.

'Whatever is out there, it isn't human,' Andriev said. Ulrika shuddered. She could remember Felix's tales of his encounters with daemons all too clearly. What was it Adolphus Krieger had sent to collect the talisman?

CAREFULLY AVOIDING THE spot where the corrosive still bubbled, Adolphus exerted his strength. He was much stronger than any human, and knew in a few heartbeats the weakened door would give way. He could simply have waited for the acid to do its work, but he felt he was running out of time. The sounds of fighting had ceased behind him. That might mean his cats' paws had succeeded in killing the defenders but somehow he doubted it. It was more likely that the Slayers were coming for him. He was not going to risk a fight now if he could help it, not when he was so close to his goal.

Inside he could hear the sounds of voices. One of them belonged to Andriev, the other to a young woman. They would not stand against him for long.

FELIX RACED THROUGH the house, wondering if what he was doing was wise. His legs were longer than the dwarfs' and he was a much faster runner, so he was outdistancing them by quite a way. What if more of the enthralled warriors were in the house? What if he came upon the mage all by himself? Unless he could take the man by surprise, it would most likely prove to be a fatal encounter. He had no illusions about the outcome of any struggle between himself and a competent sorcerer.

On the other hand, Ulrika was in danger and, despite their feelings for each other, he did not want to see any harm come to her. She might be an arrogant, overbearing, inconstant, misguided snob but he did not want to see her dead. To tell the truth, he wondered at the intensity of his own feelings now that he knew she was in danger. Not quite over her yet, he thought, sourly.

He reached the top of the stairs and halted. From below, he could hear the shriek of tortured metal. It sounded as if the entrance to the vault was being shattered by the application of enormous force. Impossible, he told himself – it would take a siege engine. But the man down there was a magician. Who knew what he was capable of? Perhaps the wards woven on the vault were not quite as strong as Max had claimed, or maybe the magician was a lot more powerful than they had expected. It was not a reassuring thought.

He listened to see if he could distinguish anything else. He hoped to hear Gotrek and Snorri Nosebiter approaching but there was nothing. He could not hear their booted feet ringing on the stonework. He could hear Ulrika's indistinct voice shouting some sort of challenge, and the murmur of a response too low for him to hear. Then from down below too came an ominous silence.

Better go and learn the worst, he thought. Reluctantly he padded down the stairs, thinking, perhaps Gotrek will be the one to write the tale of my heroic doom.

ULRIKA WATCHED AS the door exploded inwards. Stone screeched against stone. She expected to see a gang of warriors armed with a portable ram or a mage surrounded by the incandescent glow of power. Instead, she saw a tall, stately-looking man, garbed in fashionable clothing. A longsword hung scabbarded at his side. There was an eerie grace about him that she would have associated more with acrobats than a mage. He glanced at her but made no threatening move.

'If you can use that blade, magician, I suggest you draw it. I hate to cut down an unarmed man.'

To her surprise he smiled, showing gleaming white teeth. His eyes when they met hers were dark and piercing.

He was a very handsome man, Ulrika thought, almost beautiful. He bore himself with an air of command that a Tsar might have envied.

'And I would hate to kill a young woman so lovely,' he said pleasantly. He sounded as if he came from the Empire but there was just the faintest trace of a foreign accent in his voice. If she had been forced to guess, she would have said Bretonnian.

'I am not afraid of your magic, wizard,' she said, and was proud of how steady her voice was. Something about the man's manner told her she could easily die here. He laughed – an eerie, velvety sound.

'Is that what you think I am?'

'What else could you be?'

'Something beyond your ability to imagine,' he said.

ADOLPHUS RECOGNISED THE woman from that night at the White Boar, just as he recognised the unconscious man lying nearby. What a small world, he thought. Then again, Praag was a small city and not many taverns remained open after the destruction of the siege. Once again he felt the surge of attraction.

She was certainly beautiful, and she held herself well. There was something about her courage in the face of her obvious fear that he found quite touching. He wished he had had time to talk to her, but he had already wasted enough time. He could see what he had come for. It lay on the table beside the recumbent form of the man in wizard's robes.

Adolphus could see the man still lived, but life pulsed so faintly in him that he would not recover any time soon, if at all. No threat there then.

The only ones who stood between him and the talisman were the young woman and the old man. He would not even need his sword to take them.

Behind him on the stairs came the footsteps of a man trying to move quietly. A mortal might not have detected him at all, but Adolphus could tell where he was from the sound of his breathing, let alone the soft scuff of boot leather on stone. He smiled. One lone man was no threat to him either.

'Step away from the talisman and I will let you live,' he told the girl quietly. 'Interfere with me and you will most assuredly die, and that would give me no pleasure.'

The woman lunged at him with surprising speed. She was obviously not unskilled with that long blade of hers. Adolphus stepped easily aside. She was quick for a mortal, but compared to him she moved like an arthritic cripple. While she went for him the old man reached for the talisman. Adolphus was not going to allow that.

He extended his stride and reached the amulet at the same time as the old man. A quick buffet from his open hand sent Andriev flying across the room to smash into the wall. There was a sickening crack and he slid down to the floor. Blood pooled from his broken head. Triumph filled Adolphus as he picked up the amulet.

He was disappointed to feel no surge of power, no enormous burst of magical energy. Thunder did not roar. Lightning did not flash. The world did not change in an instant. He had been foolish to expect any such thing. The talisman would need to be studied and attuned before he could use it. There was no doubt he had found what he had come for in his mind though. It was exactly as described in the grimoire and the *Lost Book of Nagash*. There could not be more than one artefact fitting this description in the world now. He had what he came for. It was time to leave.

He turned just in time to see the woman racing towards him, and a tall blond man filling the doorway. Surely these fools did not intend to try and stop him?

FELIX DID NOT think he had ever seen a man move so fast. His swiftness was eye-blurring. Some sort of spell must be enhancing his speed. At least there was only the sorcerer. It was a small mercy. Watching the man, he knew that there was no way he could stand against him if he drew his sword. Best not to give him the chance to then, he thought, and advanced into the room.

Ulrika raced forward too, aiming a slash at the man's neck that would have severed his head from his shoulders if it had connected. It didn't. Krieger ducked and the blade passed above his head. With a motion like a tiger pouncing on a deer, he sprang forward. In an instant he had Ulrika immobilised, his arm around her neck; her struggles were as weak as those of a mouse in the grip of a cat.

'Ulrika,' Felix shouted.

The man looked up at him, and Felix was in no way surprised to see the red glow in his eyes. Mage, he thought, and then realised that there was something naggingly familiar about the man. Felix suddenly put his finger on it. He was the wizard in the tavern, the one who vanished just as Max and Ulrika came in.

Felix could hear Gotrek and Snorri Nosebiter on the stairs. Help was on its way.

'If you care about this girl, stand back,' said Krieger. 'Or I will snap her neck like a twig.'

'If you harm her in any way I will kill you,' said Felix, and was surprised to find that he meant it. Whatever it took, however long, he would hound this man to his grave.

'Somehow I doubt that,' said Krieger in his suave tone.

'If the manling doesn't then I will,' said Gotrek, from beside Felix. There could be no doubt at all that he meant it.

The tall man laughed but hell was in his eyes. 'It's been tried before, by your kin, and they did not succeed either. Now stand aside or the girl dies.'

The Slayer glared at the dark magician. Felix wondered if Gotrek was going to attack and let Ulrika die anyway. He knew he could not allow it.

FOUR

'SNORRI THINKS WE should take him,' said Snorri Nosebiter.

'I don't,' said Felix. 'If we do, he will kill Ulrika.'

'And then Snorri will kill him,' said Snorri, his battle lust unsated by his encounter with the magician's minions. He was ready to attack no matter what Felix said. Felix looked at Gotrek pleadingly. No sign of any understanding entered the Slayer's one mad eye. The silence lengthened. Gotrek and Krieger glared at each other. An odd glow appeared in the mage's eyes once more. There seemed to be some sort of contest of wills going on. Neither looked away.

Felix's mouth felt dry. The room stank of dust and death and the faintest hint of something else, cinnamon perhaps. Andriev lay near, his broken head testimony to how fragile life could be. Max did not look much better.

'Kill him,' gasped Ulrika. 'Don't worry about me. I would rather die than be dishonoured.'

Her words were cut off abruptly as Krieger tightened his grip on her throat. For a magician, he was strong. Felix was not at all sure he would like to face him with a sword in his hand. Ulrika's face was very pale now. Felix could see she was having trouble breathing. The Slayer continued to glare. Felix could feel that things had come to a very delicate pass, it might go either way now. There was a tension in the room that begged for violent action. Unfortunately, Felix knew that when the explosion came it would end up with Ulrika dead.

'Let her go and you have my word you can leave here,' he said, hoping to sway the Slayers with talk of honour and oaths. This approach usually worked on dwarfs. Gotrek tensed. The Slayer did not like what he was doing. The magician merely laughed.

'Much as I would like to take you up on such an offer, I fear it would be unwise under the circumstances. This girl is my shield and before a battle it's a foolish warrior who throws aside his shield.'

'You are no warrior,' grated Gotrek. 'You have no idea of what the word means.'

Krieger's smile was sour, and oddly sad. 'Once I did, probably more than you. Alas, things change.'

Gotrek was about to throw himself forward. Foam frothed from Snorri's mouth as he champed at the bit for battle. Still he waited to take his cue from Gotrek. Ulrika tried to bring her heel down on Krieger's booted foot, but he eluded the move easily. A further tightening of his arm brought a squeal of pain from the Kislevite noblewoman. Her neck could not be far from breaking.

Felix put a hand on the Slayer's shoulder. He knew he had no more chance of restraining the dwarf if he decided to attack than he would have of holding back a dire wolf, but he felt he had better try. 'Don't,' he said. 'There has to be a way out of this.'

'There is,' said Krieger. 'Let me go and, after I am free, I will let her go whenever she wishes.'

'You would not accept my word,' said Felix looking at the sorcerer. His faint complex smile had widened. 'Why should I accept yours?'

'You don't have any choice,' said Krieger with assurance. He raised the pomander dangling from his neck to his lips, and took a long satisfied sniff. He looked utterly calm and collected. He had the poise of an aristocrat. Felix had always disliked them.

'Let him go,' said Felix. 'We can always hunt him down later.'

'You can try,' said Krieger.

Gotrek seemed to emerge from his killing trance. 'However long it takes, however far you travel, I will find you and I will kill you,' he said.

'That goes twice as much for Snorri Nosebiter,' said Snorri.

'Step aside,' said Krieger. Slowly and reluctantly, the dwarfs did so. Lifting Ulrika as if she weighed nothing, clutching the talisman in his fist still, Krieger strode between them and up the stairs.

Silence filled the vault.

'What do we do now?' Felix asked.

'Follow him,' Gotrek replied. 'He won't get too far.'

They moved up the stairs in Krieger's wake but when they emerged into the night he was gone, and so was Ulrika. Felix thought he heard a sledge hissing off into the distance but it was night, and there were many sledges going to and fro between the mansions of the nobles.

Icy, freezing fog filled the streets. It had gathered almost too quickly to be natural. Felix wondered if the mage had cast some sort of spell to obscure his tracks. It seemed all too likely. Despair filled him. Ulrika was in the hands of an evil mage and so was the talisman they had agreed to protect. Andriev was dead. Max was in a coma. Failure tasted bitter in his mouth.

'He must have used magic to remove himself once he was clear of the vaults,' said Felix. 'The wards would no longer have held him there.'

'I don't know,' said Gotrek. Rage filled his voice. He liked their situation no more than Felix. 'I am not a magician.'

'Neither is Snorri, but we'd better work out how to find him soon. Snorri Nosebiter swore an oath, and if Snorri has to search this city house by house Snorri will.'

'Chances are we will be joining you,' muttered Felix. 'Come on, let's go inside and see to Max.' None of them suggested ringing the alarm bell and summoning the watch.

* * *

KRIEGER LOUNGED BACK in the padded seat of the sleigh. Roche's broad back obscured his view as he handled the horses. He put an arm around the unconscious Ulrika. It was good cover. They were just two lovers returning from a sleigh ride in the night, a scene Krieger had enacted many times in the past, with the cattle, before he drank of their blood. No one would notice them.

The warm glow of triumph filled him. He had thought things might all go terribly wrong there for a while. Close up, the power of that dwarf's terrible axe had been evident to him. There was no doubt in his mind that the weapon was capable of ending his immortal life with one blow. He had never seen anything so filled with terrible killing power. To one with mage senses as keen as Krieger's, it was practically incandescent with deadly energy, and its wielder had been almost as worrying, a grim, fell-handed creature indeed.

The man's weapon had not been as powerful, but to Adolphus's surprise had been magical also, and thus capable of hurting him. Amazing really that Andriev had found two such guardians at short notice. If he had known, he would not have been quite so confident. He did not doubt he could have won any fight with the pair, but there would have been a risk, and right then, with the talisman in his grasp, it would have been foolish to take it.

Still, the part of him that craved violence and death wished that he had initiated combat, wished that he had fought, and torn his opponents limb from limb. The raging beast was still within him. He tried to tell himself that there was more to it than this. It galled him to leave enemies alive and unharmed behind him. He was annoyed by the arrogance of the dwarf. That any mortal should dare threaten one of the Arisen seemed near sacrilegious. He was also certain that the dwarf would attempt to make good on his promise, would spend years if need be hunting him down.

Not that it mattered now. Soon he would have enough power to master the world, and take his revenge on them. It would not be the dwarf who sought him out. Once he fulfilled Nospheratus's prophesy he would take his revenge. He tried telling himself that powerful though that axe was, he was not frightened by it, but he was wise enough to know that he was lying to himself. That was why the beast was snarling within him so strongly. It felt threatened. He shivered a little. For the first time in many, many years, he had encountered something that caused him to fear.

Perhaps he should try to enjoy the novelty of it. After all, amid the ennui of the long centuries, any new emotional experience was to be welcomed. Somehow he could not quite make himself believe it. Best to get away as quickly and as quietly as possible and leave the Slayers to their futile efforts at pursuit. He could travel so quickly and so secretly that they would have no chance of finding him until he wanted it.

The main thing now was that he needed time to work out how to unleash the power of the talisman, to attune it to him, and learn to draw upon its energies. Once that was accomplished, there was little he could not do, at least according to Nospheratus, and that vampiric seer had been well placed to know.

The girl beside him whimpered but did not come to consciousness. He looked down at her. Ancient malice woke in his brain. It was obvious that the man back there had cared for her, and that the dwarfs had enough regard for her to restrain themselves from attacking. She might prove a valuable hostage and, by all the Dark Gods, she was beautiful. On his long journey a companion to while away the time might prove interesting, and he could always get rid of her if she proved dull. He doubted that she would, at least for a while. She knew the dwarfs and the man with the magical weapon, and thus she could tell him something of his enemies. He would need to know at least their names when the time came to hunt them down.

Of course, he had given his word to the man that he would let her go, and he had never broken his word in all his long centuries of unlife. It was just as well he had carefully worded the promise to suit himself. He had said he would let her go whenever she wished. He had ways of ensuring that she would not wish to leave him.

Gently he pushed back the collar of her tunic, and stroked her neck, looking for the lovely vein he knew he would find there.

FELIX LOOKED AROUND the wreckage of the mansion. There were corpses everywhere: the remains of Andriev's ancient servants, the mangled bodies of the men he, Gotrek and Snorri had slain. The air smelled of blood and opened innards and corruption. It did nothing to improve his mood. He wished now that he carried a pomander, as the mage did. Its perfume might cover the stench of death.

That thought tickled something at the back of his mind. It reminded him of something, just as the faint elusive scent he had smelled in the vault had done. What was it? Why did the image of a dead woman spring into his mind now?

Obviously because you are surrounded by corpses, idiot, he told himself, but knew that was not the answer. He remembered seeing the body of the dead woman found in the snow, remembered what her companion had said. She had gone out with a nobleman. She had remembered a very distinctive scent like cinnamon. That was what he had smelled in the vaults. Was it possible that the man who had killed the streetwalker and mangled her corpse was the same as the one who had taken Ulrika?

He prayed not. Many Imperial nobles carried pomanders to cover the smell of the streets, surely this was just one more. Cinnamon-based perfumes were common. No, it could not be the same man – could it? Why not? He was a dark magician and who knew what atrocities they might commit. Felix had heard tales of evil mages devouring the brains of their victims to absorb their souls, maybe those tales were true and maybe this was such a man. Suddenly, he wished Max were awake. He would know much more about such things than Felix ever would. He mentioned his suspicions to the Slayers.

'Snorri thinks you should have let us kill him,' said Snorri Nosebiter almost petulantly.

I should have let you, Felix thought. As if there were anything he could have done to restrain the Slayers if they had taken it into their heads to fight.

He looked over at the two sullen dwarfs. It was obvious that they were not in the best of moods. They glared at him as if he personally were responsible for costing them their chance of a heroic death. In a way, he supposed he was. Not that he was going to let it bother him all that much. Ulrika's life was far more important than their deaths. They would have another chance when they caught up with the mage. Somehow, Felix did not doubt that they would. Now he only had to work out how.

The first thing they needed to do was get Max to a healer. He was the expert in this field, and if anyone knew how to go about finding a dark mage, it would be him. Felix thought he had better notify the authorities what had happened here. Not the city guards: they would most likely throw all four of them in the cells just on suspicion and, once there, who knew when they would get out? That's if Gotrek and Snorri didn't start a battle with them for their temerity in trying to make the arrest in the first place. Best take the matter straight to the top, to the duke. He would listen to them, perhaps even help.

And then there was Ulrika's father. Felix was not looking forward to breaking the news of his daughter's abduction and possible death to the old nobleman. Not that he was prepared to admit that Ulrika might not be alive. Such a thought did not bear thinking about. No – they would tell Ivan Petrovich Straghov and doubtless he would lend them aid, even if the duke would not.

He considered his plan from every angle. There was no sense in heading off on a fruitless search for the magician in this fog, no matter what the Slayers might want. He could perhaps convince the duke to seal the gates, and have his men scour the city. That way the guards might prove to be of use, and several thousand men would be more effective in a search than three.

Swiftly, he outlined his plans to the others. They headed out into the night.

FELIX LOOKED IN on the sickroom where Max lay. The priestesses had finished their rituals. Healing magic had been invoked. Felix could only pray that it worked better for the wizard than it had for his mother all those long years ago. The duke looked up from his place beside the bed. Even in this place of healing two guard captains flanked him. These were dangerous times.

Enrik's expression was melancholy. From his large eyes with bags beneath them, to his long drooping moustaches, he seemed to radiate sadness and depression. Felix had heard he was given to moods of black depression, and even madness, but had seen no sign of it himself. The Duke of Praag was one of the most competent and energetic nobles he had met. He had guided the defence of the city against the Chaos horde with vigour and courage. It was evident that the loss of his brother, under somewhat mysterious circumstances, had hit him hard. He moved like an old man, and not just because of his wounds.

'Yours is very grave news, Felix Jaeger,' he said. His voice was clear and commanding and completely at odds with his appearance. It held all the arrogant command that one might expect from the ruler of Kislev's second greatest city. 'Ulrika was kin to me, and so was Andriev very distantly, although there was no love lost between us. He had more in common with my brother. They were both keen on ancient things, and magic.'

Felix suspected that the duke's brother had been involved with the cults of Chaos. Was it possible that Count Andriev had been as well? That would explain his interest in magical things, and his wish to avoid attracting attention to himself. But if he had been, then perhaps he would have had allies both magical and human of his own, and he would not have needed to call on himself, Ulrika and Gotrek. Not unless there was something he wanted to hide from his fellow daemon worshippers. Felix was familiar enough with the treachery and backstabbing that all the followers of the Dark Gods wallowed in. It was enough to make his head spin just thinking about it.

Perhaps the old man had been involved in such things, perhaps not. It would be best not to think about it until he had clear proof either way. Right now there were plenty of other things to think about.

The duke turned and barked commands to his guard captains and they departed. Felix knew that soon there would be a watch kept on every gate and the city guard would be alerted to look for anyone like Ulrika or her captor. The duke's instructions sent soldiers hurrying to obey.

'I am sorry I cannot do more,' said Duke Enrik, 'but a house-to-house search is all but impossible at the moment. And there are other things to worry about right now.'

Felix knew what he meant. With the Ice Queen in his palace and the army bivouacked on the city, there was the problem of seeing to her security and maintaining public order, not to mention planning what to do about the oncoming Chaos horde. It was a reminder to Felix that the whole world had not stopped because of his personal problems. The greatest invasion of the Old World in two centuries was still under way. The duke seemed to consider the matter settled but Felix decided to risk persisting for the moment.

'Have you informed her father, your grace?' Felix asked.

'I have summoned him. It was wise of you to bring this to me first. I think such news would be best coming from a kinsman. He is very fond of Ulrika. She is his only 'surviving' child.'

Felix heard the hesitation on the word surviving. The duke too was trying to put his best face on things.

'And you have no idea what this talisman was or what it was capable of?'

Felix could recognise a deliberate change of subject when he heard one.

'I have no idea, but it must be important considering all the effort this Adolphus Krieger put into getting it. We had best hope that Max recovers soon. Perhaps he can tell us something.'

'It was investigating the talisman that did this to him?'

'So Ulrika said.'

'I will have you informed when he recovers,' said the duke. His tone made it clear that this was a dismissal. He looked like a man with the weight of the world on his shoulders.

'Thank you, your grace,' said Felix and withdrew.

* * *

ADOLPHUS LOOKED AROUND the chamber in the mansion. Osrik had given up his best suite of rooms so that his master might occupy them. The tapestries were thick and heavy, the best wine sat unopened on the heavy mahogany table, the fire blazed brightly. Although Adolphus no longer felt the cold and took no pleasure from wine, he always found it best to keep up appearances. Tongues always flapped otherwise, and you could not browbeat or mindbind every servant. They all looked alike to Adolphus anyway. And he admitted to having a taste for luxury that persisted from his former life, before the countess chose him. It was a taste that his status as one of the Arisen allowed him to indulge.

The only thing that was really necessary about the rooms was the thick curtains that kept the sunlight out. He had never got used to daylight. It still hurt his eyes, and burned his skin painfully. No matter how much blood he drank, he had but a fraction of his true strength when exposed to it. It made him almost as weak and feeble as a mortal. The sluggishness he felt now told him it was still light outside.

Few of the servants thought it odd that he was not to be disturbed through the day. As far as they were concerned he was a distant kinsman with a taste for lowlife and debauchery, who spent his nights in the taverns and bordellos of the city, and his days recovering from his nightly indulgences.

He was not sorry to be leaving Kislev. It was a barbaric place, and likely to become more so as the Chaos horde advanced. Bloodletting on a massive scale always seemed to bring out the wild rider in the Kislevites.

Still, he thought, the situation was not without its advantages. One could easily exploit the anarchy of the coming months and years, and he would be powerful enough to do so. The prophesies of the *Grimoire Necronium* would be fulfilled. This was the Time of Blood of which the ancient tome spoke, of that he was certain. And he was the Pale King who would arise to rule the night. The talisman would make that come true. With it, none of the others would be able to stand against him, all of them – even the countess and the Council – would have to swear fealty.

The woman in his bed stirred. She was almost too beautiful, he thought. She had none of the bovine stupidity that was usually written on the faces of Kislevite noblewomen. She looked hard, and sharp and fierce as a hawk. There was something predatory in her beauty. She would perhaps be worthy to be chosen, worthy of the dark kiss. Perhaps she was the one.

For long centuries, ever since the countess had explained to him how the bloodlines had thinned since the time of the Lahmians, he had resisted creating his own get. Most of the Arisen of his generation could create only one, and even that might turn out to be only an insipid counterfeit of what it should be – moronic, weak, mad, the cause of all those bizarre stereotypes of monsters mortals seemed to have about the Arisen. He himself had never risked trying to create one, for he had never found any worthy of his embrace. Over the centuries he had occasionally thought he had found someone but always there had been a flaw in them.

Let's see. There was the Bretonnian noblewoman, Katherine, who had turned out to be nothing more than an empty, posturing fool. Her beauty had dazzled him for a while into thinking she might have the intelligence and the grace to be worthy of eternity at his side.

How wrong he had been. The woman had cared more for her mirror than she had for anyone else. It had been a distinct pleasure to watch her squeamishness as the lines appeared on her face, grey appeared in her hair, and age had eaten away her beauty.

Then there was the peasant girl turned courtesan from Nuln, what was her name? Oh yes, Marianne. She had been all that he had desired. Beautiful, intelligent, witty, charming, cultured even, with the erudition of those who have painfully acquired it by their own efforts. She had possessed a playfulness and a curiosity that had promised she would not have succumbed easily to ennui, and he had been drawn to her for many reasons. But she had been treacherous, and selfish, and deceitful. Remembering how he himself had turned against the countess, he had foreseen that she too would eventually turn on him, and that would have been too painful to endure. So he had watched over her, aided her and protected her until eventually she had died wealthy, respected and one of the great noblewomen of the Empire. Her rise had provided them both with amusement.

There was Alana, that strange bitter woman, half witch, half-seeress who had taught him all those dark secrets and opened his eyes to the power of mortals' magic. To her as much as to the countess did he owe his knowledge of sorcery, and the knowledge that mortals tried to hide even from themselves. She had died before he had ever had a chance to make his mind up about her, torn apart by some appalling creature she had summoned in a blasphemous ritual on Geheimnisnacht, a victim of her own overwhelming ambition and desire for control. He was not certain, but he guessed that he would not have embraced her. Their relationship had always been about power, who would have it, who would wield it. She would have wanted to bind him to her with magic, as much as any one of the cattle had ever been bound by the dark kiss.

There had been others, so many others, down the long centuries. Their faces sometimes drifted before him when he entered the trance state that in the Arisen replaced sleep. Sometimes they all blended together, sometimes they changed into faces he had never seen, but would eventually. One thing you learned over the centuries was that sooner or later most things would occur.

It was strange, he mused, how much of the flesh was left behind and how much stayed when you were embraced. He no longer craved meat or drink or sex or drugs. But still he craved companionship. Perhaps it was the only thing he had in common with the cattle any more. He still was on the lookout for that one special woman now, as much as he had been when he first met the countess back in Parravon three centuries ago, as much as when he had been little more than a boy attending his first ball at the king's court.

He pushed the thoughts aside. Here he stood on the brink of the greatest triumph any of the Arisen had ever managed, on the brink of madness goaded by something he could not explain, and he was thinking of women. He smiled wryly. It was one of the few habits of mortality he had not been able to rid himself of.

Perhaps, he thought, he should kill this woman now, drain her dry in the ecstasy of the kiss, just to prove to himself that he could still do such a thing. Pointless, he told himself, you know you can. It has been something you have done all too easily over the past few weeks. If you really want to prove you are still in control you should let her live. The reaction of the beast in his brain as it resisted the idea showed him that he was correct. For the moment then, he would let her live. She could travel with him for a while. It never hurt to have an extra vessel lying around in case of need. He could not afford to weaken Roche by tapping him on this journey, and he utterly loathed drinking the blood of animals. Only the direst of necessities could drive him to it now. Anyway, it would not be seemly for the soon-to-be lord of all vampires to drink from a deer.

He identified the footsteps approaching down the corridor long before he heard the knock on the door. Roche had a very distinctive gait. He walked very softly for such a heavy man. Adolphus's keen senses told him that there was no one else close by. He walked to the door and turned the key in the lock. It was an elementary precaution that he never forgot to take in rooms like this ever since a chambermaid had entered his room and found him with the drained corpse of a streetwalker in the days after the countess had first embraced him.

Roche looked down on him unsmilingly. Adolphus gazed back, measuring him. He was a huge man, strong as a blacksmith, quick as cat, with the manners of a chamberlain and the morals of an assassin. Like his father and his grandfather before him, Roche served as Adolphus's most trusted personal retainer, and was privy to all but his darkest secrets. It was a position he had been groomed for since he was a small child.

'The sledge is ready, master,' said Roche. His voice was melodic and not a little sad, it should have belonged to the priest that he so often impersonated. 'We can leave as soon as you are ready.'

'Very good, Roche.'

'The young lady, master?' Roche's voice was mild. He just wanted to know what to do. He could be told to wrap her in a sheet and take her to the coach or to chop her into little pieces and feed her to the dogs. He would do either with the same quiet, calm efficiency, had done so often in the past.

'She will be accompanying us.'

'Very good, master. I considered the possibility that you might wish to do this and have taken the liberty of loading extra supplies. I hope this meets with your approval.'

'As always, Roche, you think of everything.'

'It is my pleasure to serve, master.' They exchanged knowing smiles.

'Let us be away, Roche. We have a long road ahead of us, and the sooner we are out of this backwater kingdom, the happier I will be.'

IVAN PETROVICH STRAGHOV was calm now. Felix was glad. He had been shouting threats and curses strong enough to make a dockworker blanch just minutes before. Now he was restricting himself to just a few choice anatomical epithets. He turned and glared at Felix. The younger man suddenly felt that the tent had become far too small.

'We will find her,' he said, in a challenging tone, as if Felix had just contradicted him. 'And when we find the man who has taken her, I will string him up by the balls and...'

He went on to describe exactly what he would do. With most people, Felix would have assumed they were speaking metaphorically, but Ivan Petrovich was a march boyar. He fully intended to carry out those threats no matter how physically impossible they sounded. Felix did not envy Adolphus Krieger if the old nobleman ever got his hands on him.

'First, we have to find him,' Gotrek said. His harsh gravelly voice sounded almost calm compared to the Kislevite's but for all his bluster Ivan Petrovich would never in a hundred lifetimes be able to match the menace in it. The effect was like a dash of cold water in the Kislevite's face.

'How will we do that?' The Slayer shook his head. He looked baffled and frustrated. Felix knew this would just make him even more short-tempered. Felix moved over to the charcoal brazier and warmed his hands. Ivan Petrovich could have had chambers in the Citadel if he wanted, but he chose to stay with his men, who were bivouacked in tents on the edge of the city in the old Kislevite horse-warrior style. Felix would have complained about the cold, but he'd already heard enough comments about soft southerners to last him a lifetime.

The march boyar's question was a good one though. Felix had not held out much hope that Krieger would keep his promise and release Ulrika, and over the past few days even that tiny flicker had died. How did you find one man and his prisoner in a city as large and chaotic as Praag? How did you prevent them leaving if that is what they sought to do? Ivan Petrovich had his riders, but in the cold and the snow a sweep around the city would be difficult. On the plus side, anyone setting out would be more noticeable than usual. Not too many people were leaving the city at the moment. Trickles of refugees were still streaming in.

Felix was baffled. He needed to know more. He needed to know what the purpose of the talisman was, and what the dark magician intended to use it for. He desperately needed to know whether Ulrika was still alive.

If I were an evil sorcerer and I wanted to keep myself hidden in Praag, how would I do it? In the books and plays he had read as a youth it was always easy. Evil mages lived in ruined towers, crypts in cemeteries and huge mansions built with their ill gotten gains. A search of all such locations in the city should turn him up. Unfortunately, Felix had long ago learned that things were rarely that simple. If Krieger had any sense, he would be keeping a very low profile indeed, disguising himself somehow. How would he do that? Felix wished he knew.

'You are looking thoughtful, manling,' said Gotrek. 'Have you got any useful suggestions?'

Despite the apparent irony in his tone, Felix could tell that the Slayer was serious. During their long association, the thinking in situations like this usually fell to him. Sadly, at the hour of their greatest need, his mind was a blank. He shook his head and sat down on the thick rug covering the tent floor, and began to trace the convoluted weave with his fingers. His head hurt, his eyes ached and his nose was running. He was definitely coming down with something.

'We need a magician,' he said.

'We had one,' said Gotrek. 'Unfortunately, he seems to be no longer with us.'

'That might change,' said Felix.

'You're saying we should be patient,' said Ivan Petrovich. His tone implied that Felix had suggested they take up molesting goats.

'Sometimes, it's the only thing you can do,' said Felix wearily.

'Spare us the pearls of wisdom, manling.'

'If you have any better ideas,' said Felix. 'I am open to them.'

The silence was deafening.

ROCHE DROVE THE sledge towards the gates. On the back was a cheap wooden coffin, bags of feed for the ponies, a ragged tent and a few other things. He cracked the reins to keep the animals moving. The runners hissed on the snow as they moved towards the gate.

The guardsmen on duty looked at him with more suspicion than they normally might. Roche met their gazes easily. The sergeant looked at a scroll, and then eyed him once more, as if checking to see whether he matched a description. Roche kept an expression of bovine stupidity on his face. It matched the peasant garb he wore. If these fools were looking for the master, they would be looking for a nobleman, and maybe a blonde-haired girl. They would hardly be looking for him.

He was confident. If they searched the sledge he had his story ready and all the evidence would confirm it. Even so, he felt a slight tension rising within him. Things could go wrong. They had in the past; they might do so again now.

'What's your business, peasant?' asked a short man who had emerged from behind the guards. His fine uniform and his swaggering arrogant manner marked him as an officer of some sort, most likely one of these so-called Kislevite nobles. Roche did not like his manner. He memorised the man's face, in case an opportunity for vengeance should arise in the future. It wasn't likely under the circumstances, but you could always hope. A few minutes alone with Roche and his flaying tools would soon rid him of that cocky manner, along with a lot of skin.

'Going back to the farm, bury my brother,' said Roche. He could do a convincing impression of the thick guttural Kislevite commoner accent when he had to. 'I promised him I would. Said before he died that he wanted to lie alongside ma and I said I would see to it.'

'Take him back and burn him, that's my advice. There's beastmen in those woods now, despite the patrols.' It was the sergeant who spoke now. His tone was not unfriendly. There was a certain amount of sympathy in it. The hard-faced officer glared at the man. The sergeant's face became a blank mask, his mouth snapped shut. The Praag city guard still used the lash to enforce discipline. Roche had found there was nothing like it for instilling obedience.

'People try and smuggle things in coffins,' said the officer. 'People try all sorts of things.'

Roche looked at the arrogant idiot but kept his face blank. Most smugglers would be trying to get things into the city, not out. Still, it was not a peasant's place to point these things out to a nobleman. Peasants in Kislev were obedient, just like they were back home in Sylvania.

'I promised him,' said Roche, as if he were so stupid he was still answering the sergeant. 'He made me swear by Shallya and Ulric that I would do it. He loved ma. He loved the old place. He said we should never have come to the city. Said he wanted to be buried under the pines.'

'Open the box,' said the officer. It was obvious that for some reason he had taken a dislike to Roche. People often did. Roche was used to it. It was his appearance he supposed. Still, there was nothing he could do about it now.

'But he's dead,' said Roche.

'If you won't open it, I'll have my men do it.' Roche saw the soldiers flinch. They might not have any objections to cutting a man down in hot blood, but none of them wanted to open a coffin that might contain a week-old corpse.

'What did he die of?' one of the guards, a whey-faced boy, whose tunic barely fitted, asked nervously.

'The coughing sickness. A month ago he was healthy as you. One day he starts coughing and wheezing, says it's difficult to breathe. Two days ago he was gone, after a month of sweating and fevers and wracking his lungs. It wasn't pretty.'

The soldiers looked even more nervous now. There had been many strange plagues in the city since the siege. Maybe they were remnants of the evil spells cast by the followers of Nurgle, the Plague Lord. Maybe they were just a product of overcrowding, rotten food, the cold and bad sanitation. It was said more folk had died of sickness since the siege ended than had ever died in the battle. Roche could believe it. It was often the way.

'I said open the box. Let's take a look at what you got in there.'

'A corpse,' said Roche sullenly.

'You'll be one soon if you don't open it,' said the officer. He was obviously one of those small men who liked using every speck of power he had been granted. And he obviously liked venting his authority on such hulking giants as Roche. Roche would definitely remember this man. He might even make a special trip back to Praag for him, if the master allowed. He did not like being bullied.

Roche clambered down off the sledge and walked back to the coffin. The soldiers all drew back slightly save the officer who strode officiously along beside him. Just one minute with the flaying tools, that's all I ask, thought Roche. He levered open the coffin, and did his best to stand so that his shadow fell on the master. He knew how the sun affected his tender skin.

The officer looked down on the recumbent form. The master was garbed as a peasant too, and his hair was messed up. His pallor did not require make-up; the smudges of dirt on his face served to highlight the paleness of his skin. They had done this several times in the past when they needed to leave a city in a hurry. Roche could remember his father and grandfather telling him tales of similar departures, some in considerably more dangerous circumstances than this one.

The officer removed his glove and laid a hand on the body's chest, as if not wanting to quite believe his eyes.

'Definitely dead,' he said disappointedly.

'That's why I am going to bury him.'

'And I'll have less of your sauce,' said the captain. 'Another word and I'll have my men peel your hide off.'

Roche looked at his boots to hide the fury in his eyes. He loathed these petty jumped-up officials with a passion and he had been forced to deal with more than his fair share down the years. Now is not the time, he told himself. He did his best to look like the absolute embodiment of brow-beaten peasantry.

The officer looked like he was seriously considering having his men tear the coffin apart. That would not be such a good thing, Roche thought, for then they might find the hidden compartment beneath the master that held the talisman. Who knew what the master might do under those circumstances. Roche knew all about his obsession with that ancient trinket, had been forced to listen to tales of it on countless evenings, till even he was sick of it, and his master's plans. If I hear the name of Nospheratus one more time, thought Roche, I will…

The officer took another closer look at the master. Roche held his breath. He had a dagger hidden in his boot. If anything happened, the first thing he would do was stick it in the cocky officer's gut and twist. Men took a long time to die when you did that right. Roche knew this from practical experience. Eventually though, even this man seemed to tire of his petty bullying.

'Get out of here,' he said. 'Go bury your dead.'

Roche nodded dumbly, clambered onto the sledge and cracked the reins. He could see looks of something like sympathy in the soldiers' eyes.

'IT LOOKS LIKE your friend is starting to heal,' said the priestess of Shallya. There was grey in her hair but her calm face was very pretty. She smiled as she spoke. 'He's still very, very weak but I think he has come back from the brink. I believe he will live.'

Felix glanced around the small spartan chamber. Max had been moved to the hospice on the temple grounds at the duke's insistence; that way the most powerful of the healers would always be on call. Felix smiled back at the woman. 'I am glad to hear it.'

'Herr Schreiber is a very strong-willed man, and there is a power in him that aids the healing.'

'Do you know what happened to him?'

'No – the Mistress of Healers claims that some malign energy entered his brain somehow. It cost her an enormous effort to drive it out. She has been confined to her own room for a day now. Your friend must be a very important man for the duke to insist she did this.'

'I am sure he will make a very large donation to the goddess,' said Felix sourly. It seemed that even the supposedly independent and altruistic sisters of Shallya, helpmates to the poor and weak, were subject to political interference. He did not know why this should leave him feeling surprised and disappointed but it did. The woman caught his hard tone and her face became less friendly.

'Can I look in on him now?' he asked, forcing a smile. It was best not to antagonise the priestesses. You never knew when your own life might depend on their help. Their prayers and herbs seemed to have helped his own illness. He felt better now, even if he was not entirely healed.

'If you wish, but be quiet. He is asleep, and he must rest to heal. And cover your mouth with a handkerchief. It would be terrible to have him recover from his own ailment only to be taken away by your flux.'

Felix nodded and walking as softly as he could, entered the sickroom. It smelled of mint and camphor and other herbs he remembered from his childhood when he had visited his mother during her last long illness.

Felix was shocked. Max had always been a powerful, energetic man. Now he looked pale and feeble indeed, as drawn as a consumption sufferer. It was such a dreadful change in so short a time. At least his breathing was deep and regular.

Felix looked up at the dove icon on the walls, and offered a prayer to Shallya for mercy and healing for the wizard. If the goddess heard she gave no sign.

Felix turned to leave and heard a change in the wizard's breathing. He turned to see that Max's eyes were open wide, and there was a wildness and fear in them. His hand stretched out feebly and he whispered one word that sent a chill running down Felix's spine.

'Nagash,' he said, and slumped back into unconsciousness.

'NAGASH,' SAID GOTREK grimly. Even in the warmth of the tavern, surrounded by a hundred drunken warriors, the smell of beer and the sound of singing and dancing, the word was enough to chill Felix like the ague. He tried to tell himself it was his lingering fever but knew that this time it was not. The name conjured up an image of a remote time when dark gods wandered the world and slew entire kingdoms. Not even the cruellest of mothers would use it to frighten the most disobedient children.

'A name of ill omen indeed,' said Ivan Petrovich, sending another glass of vodka tumbling down his throat. His hand shook as he did so.

'Snorri doesn't like this one little bit,' said Snorri, and for once Felix had to agree with him whole-heartedly.

'So, our pet wizard thinks this talisman is somehow connected with the Great Necromancer, manling?'

'We didn't exactly discuss the matter. It was the only word he said before he fell back into a coma. It would explain why this Krieger was so keen to get his hands on the thing though.'

Felix considered this as he took another slug of vodka. The fiery liquid warmed his belly, but did nothing to remove the chill from his heart. The Great Necromancer, he thought. A being who had fought with the man-god Sigmar before the Empire was even founded and who, if dark legend were to be believed, was responsible for the slaying of an entire nation in the dawn ages of the world. Nagash was by all accounts the mightiest wizard the world had ever known, a necromancer who had mastered the darkest secrets of life and death. Who knew what instrument of ultimate evil he had been capable of creating? Whatever it was, it was now in the hands of Adolphus Krieger, or whatever his true name was. Along with Ulrika.

Felix did not want to consider that. He was having a hard enough time keeping the idea that Krieger was the blood drinker who had killed those women out of his aching head.

Felix shuddered. This was all they needed. Ulrika abducted, Max in a coma, the Chaos hordes on the march, and now an ancient artefact in the hands of a mad sorcerer. How could it get worse?

ADOLPHUS FELT BETTER. It was night, and his skin was starting to heal. The moon's eerie light gave the snow-covered landscape a spectral beauty and filled him with the urge to hunt. From the window of the hunting lodge he could see fat Osrik and his men approaching. There were a number of sleds and bodyguards. His keen eyes could make out the men and women wrapped in heavy furs. Doubtless they had not had trouble getting out of the gates. They were after all a pack of well-known local nobles, and if they were so foolish as to want to go on a hunting trip, no gate guards were going to contradict them.

He could see that the girl Ulrika was with them, her head leaning against Osrik's fat shoulder. She was still stunned by the kiss he had given her last night. Adolphus was looking forward to another sip of her blood. It looked as if the plan had worked. They were all outside the city now, and preparations were being made for the trip to Sylvania. His coven had seen to it that he was well provided with everything he, Roche and the girl could need for the trip. They would all soon be ready to go.

He clutched at the talisman. It hung around his neck now. He could feel something in it, something that was responding to his presence. He put his hand on it just to feel the cool stone under his fingers. It was certainly a fascinating thing, at least to his kind, and that was what made it so dangerous.

Once he was back in his adopted homeland it would grant him power undreamed of over the aristocracy of the night. He would become the Lord of Vampires in truth, and his reign would be eternal.

Now it was time to go and greet the girl. Perhaps she might prove to be the one.

BOOK TWO
Sylvania

'Winter was no time to travel in Kislev. The snow, the wolves, the unending tedium of sleigh travel made this journey even more miserable than my usual experiences when travelling with the Slayer. This was in no way helped by the recurring illness that plagued me, or by the general gloominess of my companions. Nonetheless, after what I experienced on arriving at our destination, I would rather make a hundred trips across the ice wastes of Kislev, than a single journey through the bleak pine forests of Sylvania.'

— From *My Travels With Gotrek*, Vol IV, by Herr Felix Jaeger (Altdorf Press, 2505)

FIVE

'HOW LONG HAVE I been... ill?' asked Max Schreiber. He felt weak, and there was a horror in his mind that had not been there before. He raised his hand. It looked more like a claw, all muscle and bone. His nails were long and untrimmed. The skin appeared near translucent. Moving it took so much effort.

'Three days,' said Felix Jaeger.

Max raised himself up in the bed and focused his eyes on the renegade poet. Felix did not look so good either. His eyes were red and he was unkempt and unshaven. Max could smell him from where he lay, a mixture of booze and unwashed clothing. He coughed hackingly into his bunched-up fist. Max attempted a smile. It felt as if the skin of his face would crack from the effort.

'And you have been on a drinking binge all of this time, by the look of it.'

'Near enough,' said Felix. He sounded grim, and he looked even grimmer. There was a wildness in his eyes that had not been there before. He looked more like the Slayer than his usual amiable self.

The effort of sitting up had drained Max. He allowed himself to slump back onto the bed and stare at the ceiling. It was whitewashed. The room smelled of mint and healing herbs. The walls were white as well. From the corner of his eye he caught sight of a dove icon.

'It pains me to be so clichéd, but where am I?' he asked. He could guess the answer but he wanted to know for certain.

'The hospice of the Temple of Shallya.'

'I have been that ill?'

'Yes.'

Max let out a long breath and tried to gather his thoughts. The last thing he could remember was the house of the nobleman Andriev. No. He had examined something, a talisman. After that, his memories were... confused. He could remember nightmares, a skeletal giant with a face of death and horror, teeth that grinned like those of a skull, flesh peeling away from the face, eyes that were pits of greenish putrefying slime. He remembered strange visions of a desert land and a huge black pyramid; of wars in which the dead fought the living and pale aristocrats drank blood from bronze chalices and practised dark sorcery to prolong their unnaturally extended lives. From his studies he thought he could put a name to that figure and to that distant dusty land of death. He did not want to. He found his thoughts shying away from those memories. There were things there he was not ready to deal with yet. Perhaps not ever.

He reached up with his hand and felt his face. His beard was long and unkempt. His cheeks felt gaunt. He touched his heart. It still beat. Somehow he had been afraid that it would not.

'You look like a man who has seen a ghost,' said Felix.

'In a way, I think I have.'

'When you were ill you were raving. You kept mentioning a name.'

Max could guess what that name was. He did not want Felix to say it, to remind him of the things he had seen. The man would not stop though.

'Nagash.'

Max stiffened. He knew he would have to face the thing sooner or later. He had not become a master sorcerer through lack of a strong will. He forced himself to breathe normally, to control his racing heart, to ignore the cold sweat on his brow.

'Yes,' he said eventually. 'Nagash.'

Memories flooded back. There had been so much power concealed in that amulet, woven with such cunning and skill that Max could still not quite believe it. The thing had been trapped against just such an investigation as Max had attempted, and he had triggered the trap. It was a wonder that he had survived at all. He guessed he almost hadn't. Nagash had certainly gone to a lot of trouble to protect his secrets but that was understandable. The Great Necromancer was hardly the only magician who had ever tried to keep his secrets from other mages. His protections has simply been more effective than most.

With just an instant's warning Max had managed to shield himself against the brunt of the attack, yet still it had overwhelmed his defences. He knew he needed time now, to check for damage, to see if his mind had been tainted, if his memories were whole, if his skill…

Instinctively he reached out to grasp the winds of magic. Power flowed. He grasped at its flows and wove them into a probe; then, realising how weak he still was, he released the power. At least he could still work magic, he thought. His skills were still intact.

He realised that Felix was gawking at him and his hand was on his sword. 'What is it?'

'Your eyes started to glow and you sat directly up. From the look on your face I thought you might attack me.'

'No. I was just testing to see if… if I was still capable of working magic.'

Felix nodded, although it was plain from his expression that he still did not understand. 'What has Nagash got to do with the Eye of Khemri?'

'He made it. He made it a long time ago, and with a specific purpose. I managed to divine at least that much before the trap was sprung.'

'What does it do?'

Max thought about it. He was sure that he had known the purpose of the Eye, but it was buried in his mind now underneath the cascade of horrific dreams and visions. Given time, he would be able to put it all back together. Given time he would remember. At least he hoped he would.

'I don't know yet.'

'Yet?'

Max did not feel like explaining the whole situation to Felix at that moment. 'Things are still a little confused in my mind. It will come back.'

Another thought struck him. 'Where's Ulrika?'

Felix's reaction surprised him. If he had blasted the young man with magic he could not have looked more pained. Suddenly it occurred to him that there might have been a reason for Felix's drinking, and his slow, hesitant tone of voice. 'She's not dead, is she? What happened? What happened in Andriev's mansion?'

Felix told him. Max listened. What he heard did not make him happy. When Felix finished, he glanced around. 'Where are my robes? I must be up and about. We must find her.'

Felix gave him an ironic grin. 'How? Gotrek and I have walked our feet off looking for her. We've wandered all over the city, checked every graveyard, and followed every rumour of a magician's presence. Nothing. Ivan Petrovich has had his men sweep the area around the city. Nothing. The duke has given Krieger and Ulrika's description to every gate guard. Guess what? Nothing.'

Max did not like Felix's tone or his appearance. 'So after that you took to investigating every tavern and the bottom of every beer glass to see if you could find her there?' he asked nastily.

Felix's fingers whitened on the hilt of his sword then a guilty expression played over his face. 'I could think of nothing more to do. I tried everything I could think of and nothing worked. I was hoping that you would be able to do something, when you recovered. That is why I was waiting here.'

He sounded so obviously distressed that Max took pity on him. 'You did the right thing then. I can find her. At least I hope I can.'

'How? Magic?'

'Yes.'

'Then you are better at this than half the diviners in the city.'

'I have an advantage over them.'

'What is that?'

'I cast a spell of location on the talisman before I began investigating it. With any luck it still holds and I can track it down.'

'So you can find the amulet. That doesn't mean you can find her.'

'Don't be obtuse, Felix. Krieger went to a lot of trouble to get the thing. I doubt he would just fling it away. Particularly not if it's as powerful as I believe it is. No dark magician would do anything other than keep it and try and use it. If I can find the talisman, I can find him, and if I can find him, we can find Ulrika.'

'If she's still alive. If he hasn't offered her up as a sacrifice to some dark god. If…'

Max cut Felix off with a gesture of his hands although his words had almost stopped his heart with fear. Ulrika must be alive. She could not be dead. Max loved her and he would not allow it to be so. Realistically, there was every chance that Felix's suspicions were correct but he would not allow himself to consider the possibility.

'Pull yourself together, man. If we find him and she's alive, we will free her. If she's dead…' His mouth went dry just saying the words, and he felt like his tongue would not move. He forced himself to go on. 'If she's dead, I will have vengeance on Krieger and all who might follow him.'

Felix straightened, and the wild glint in his eye died down slightly. He let go of his sword and ran his hand across his chin as if realising for the first time how unkempt his stubble had become.

'How soon can you start?' he asked.

'As soon as I am out of this bed. And Felix…'

'What?'

'Get some rest. You look like hell.'

'ARE YOU SURE this will work?' asked Ivan Petrovich Straghov for the hundredth time.

Max sighed with exasperation and glanced back at the walls of the city. Felix could tell he was still exhausted. He was keeping himself going by sheer force of will, and the march boyar's constant badgering was wearing him out.

'If you do not trust in my magic you are welcome to take your men and ride off in any direction you please,' said the wizard. His tone made it clear he was at the end of his patience. For a moment, the old man looked as if he might just do that. Worry about his daughter was making him even less restrained than usual, and he had not been a patient man to begin with.

'I am sure Max is more than capable of finding your daughter,' said Felix diplomatically. Felix wanted the old man and the twenty riders he had brought with him. Riding through Kislev in the depths of winter was bad at the best of times. Now, with the Chaos horde on the move, and maybe skaven in the area, it could be downright suicidal. This might well suit Gotrek and Snorri but Felix had every intention of living to set Ulrika free, and twenty hardened veterans of the northern marches along with their stout leader greatly increased the odds of this.

Ivan stood for a moment, then slapped Max so heartily on the back that he started a coughing fit. 'I did not mean to insult you, Max, my friend, it's just...'

Max looked wretched but he gave the boyar a wan smile, and said, 'I understand. We are all worried about her too.'

Felix looked at their small caravan. Each of the riders had brought two extra ponies. There were three sleds, for the supplies, for Max and for the dwarfs. All of the sleds were piled high with food and grain. Felix hoped that it would be enough. Not for the first time he wished he had known when or if Malakai Makaisson would return with the *Spirit of Grungni*. There had been no word of the great airship for days and they could wait no longer. The Slayer engineer had muttered something about refitting at the Iron Tower when last he had seen him. If only he were here now, their mission would have been so much simpler.

Gotrek and Snorri eyed the ponies warily. Both dwarfs were of the opinion that horses were only good for eating but even they could see the point of taking sledges in this weather. Felix only hoped the beasts could endure the cold better than he was doing. Even through two layers of clothing and the thickest cloak and gloves he could find he was freezing. He wished he were back inside the White Boar warming his hands by the fire and glugging down hot spiced wine. The illness that had plagued him for weeks had returned during his drinking spree, and neither the priestesses' herbs nor Max's spells seemed to be of much help. He just hoped things did not get any worse.

'Time to go,' said Gotrek, clambering onto the sled behind Felix and giving the ponies a threatening look. If the animals were capable of reading murderous glares they would have known that they had better behave themselves. Snorri clambered up beside Max. Ivan himself took the reins of the third sledge. The riders spread out in formation. A pair of scouts moved ahead, another two pairs watched the flanks, and a rearguard dropped back to watch their tail. The rest rode along in a double line ahead of them.

Snow crunched beneath hooves and hissed beneath runners. The sledge jerked forward as Felix tugged the reins. They were off. Behind him the golden-domed towers of Praag receded into the distance.

MAX CLOSED HIS eyes and invoked the finding spell once more. Flows of magic swept into him and reinforced the long, thin cords that tied him to the Eye of Khemri. It was as if a long incredibly fine cable bound him to the talisman. He could not tell exactly how long, but he knew the distance was great, and that the direction they had to go in was south-west.

Hopefully, as they got closer, he would be able to divine more, but at the moment this would have to be enough. He was lucky the tenuous link held at all over so great a distance.

Hell, he was lucky to still be alive, after his encounter with the traps left by the Great Necromancer.

Max had spent a great deal of time over the past few days wondering about that. He was still capable of invoking the power. His skills and memories seemed to be more or less intact. He could discover no taint on his soul left by that overwhelming tide of dark magic. In itself that meant nothing. Any spell capable of corrupting his thoughts would also be able to prevent him from seeing it. Max knew that it would take a mage of incredible power and skill to be able to do that. Until a few days ago he would not have believed it was possible. Now he knew it was. Just from the weaving left on the Eye of Khemri, Max knew Nagash would have been capable of such a thing. The man, or whatever he had become, had been a being of almost god-like power.

How was that possible, Max wondered? How could any mage have been so powerful? Perhaps magical energy had been more abundant when the world was young. Perhaps he had lived in a time when the tides of dark magical energy had risen to peaks undreamed of in modern times. Perhaps that was what was happening now, as the Chaos Wastes expanded and the armies of the Dark Powers marched south.

Or perhaps the Great Necromancer had simply been born with powers far beyond those of any modern magician. It was possible. All sorcerers varied in power and potential. Max had known men twice his age and experience that did not have a tenth of his current strength. He had seen apprentices who he had thought with practice could become stronger than he. At least, he had believed that at the time.

His encounter with the defences Nagash had laid on the Eye of Khemri had left him filled with doubt. In all his life he had never encountered the work of a magician so much superior to him. The mages who had cast the spells for the Chaos horde during the siege had been stronger than he, but at least he had understood what they were doing. And he had known that their power came in part from the huge torrent of dark magic they were tapping into. That skaven grey seer had been more powerful because he had used warpstone to enhance his strength, and Max doubted that he had truly been that much stronger or better when it came to working magic.

But Nagash was something else entirely. Max had never encountered spellcraft as sophisticated as that laid on the amulet before, nor natural strength so great it could leave a resonance down through three millennia. When he had discovered the defensive spell on the Eye he had encountered the work of a being as far beyond him as he was beyond most ordinary people when it came to magic. He knew that no matter how hard he struggled to learn or how much power he acquired he would never be a match for that being.

What had happened to him had been more than the hideous visions and nightmares. It was corrosive to his self-esteem, damaging to his confidence, and Max knew that for a mage that could be fatal. So much of spellcasting was dependent on sheer willpower, and anything that weakened your will diminished your ability. If you suffered a lapse when weaving a dangerous spell, it might have deadly results. Max had heard of it happening. The outcome had not been pleasant either for the mage or for the people around him. He knew that he could afford no such lapses at the moment. Not with Ulrika's life at stake.

He wondered if his feelings of inferiority were in some way a product of the defences on the talisman. It would be a very subtle way of destroying an enemy magician, to undermine his confidence in this way. He doubted that Nagash would have need of such subtlety, although doubtless he would have been capable of it. Why had he concealed the power within the talisman? Why had he protected it with such defences?

Max could at least answer the latter. He had brooded on it long enough. A magician as powerful as Nagash would have had many adversaries, and it would have been only common sense to shield his work against falling into the hands of his enemies. The thought of enemies brought another image out of the whirling chaos of nightmares and visions into his mind. He saw those pale blood-drinking nobles again, and knew that the talisman was something to do with them – but what? All he could hope for was that soon the turmoil in his mind would settle and he would be able to make sense out of the mad whirl of strange thoughts the talisman had left there. He told himself that Ulrika's life depended on it. And just as importantly, his own life depended on it too, in more ways than one. He needed to know what they would face when they finally overtook Adolphus Krieger. And he needed to start rebuilding his own self-confidence.

Think, he told himself. Look on the bright side. Learn what you can from this experience and use it to make yourself a better man, and a better magician. You have always known that there were more powerful mages than you. It in no way diminishes your accomplishments. You have done the best you can with the gifts you have been given.

You survived what happened, and you have not been broken by it. You've learned things. Granted you could have lived without learning some of those things but it happened. How many people can say they have had direct insight into the mind of the Great Necromancer? How many people have survived being crushed by one of his spells?

Slowly, a little at a time, Max wrestled with his self-doubt. He knew that finding himself again would be a long slow process but at least he had made a start. He only hoped he would be ready to face this dark magician when the time came. As his thoughts raced another, more frightening possibility, entered his mind.

He had triggered the trap himself, had taken the full brunt of its energies. Would the spell reset itself? Or would Krieger find the way open to easily attune the amulet? Another thought struck Max. The defences on the amulet had not been triggered until after he had tried to analyse its structure. Perhaps the amulet was intended to be used: perhaps it had some sinister, secret purpose the Great Necromancer wanted hidden. For a moment, Max could almost feel that vast skeletal hand reaching out across the ages to tug at the destinies of mortals.

He shivered, and wondered whether or not they would be doing Adolphus Krieger a favour by killing him.

* * *

IVAN PETROVICH STRAGHOV clutched the reins of the sled through hands made clumsy by the thick fur-lined gloves he wore. Snowflakes fell, muffling the stamp of ponies' hooves and the jingle of harnesses. The wind bit at his skin. All around thick pine forests loomed over the road. Behind him he could hear the other sledges moving over the snow.

He cursed the weather. He cursed the man who had kidnapped his daughter but most of all he cursed himself. He had not been there when his daughter needed him. He had been indulging himself at the duke's banquet when she was being borne off by some crazed magician. He had spoiled her shamelessly since the early death of her beloved mother, let her do most anything she wanted, even run after that young outlander Felix Jaeger, when she should have been safe at home.

Only there was no home, not now. His mansion had been all but destroyed by a skaven assault months ago, and doubtless anything left had been reduced to rubble by the oncoming hordes of Chaos. All of his vague hopes for a quiet old age, surrounded by grandchildren, had gone now. He felt strangely restless and rootless. The previous month of guerrilla warfare and riding with the muster had made him realise that he was not a young man any more. He was a fat old man, used to his creature comforts and grown soft with good living. It had taken an enormous effort of will to keep up with the younger men in his troop and not to show his fatigue and despair. It was taking an even more enormous effort not to give in to it now.

He tried telling himself that she was a brave and resourceful young woman, as well schooled with weapons as any warrior in his band. It made no difference. He could only hope and pray that Ulrika was still alive, and not sacrificed to some dark god. He could only hope that Max Schreiber knew what he was doing. He drove on, guilt and worry eating at his heart, his thoughts as bleak as the weather and the desolate surroundings.

ADOLPHUS KRIEGER LOOKED around the inside of the coach. It was comfortable. The seats were plush leather; there was plenty of room for himself and the girl. It had been built for Osrik by the best coachwright in Kislev and the quality showed. It was a rich man's toy. A luxury coach built on runners. Perhaps in a country where the winters could last six months, and where snow covered the ground for most of that time, owning it made as much sense as owning a coach. In any case, whatever the reason, he was glad Osrik had indulged himself.

The girl gave him a sullen look. She looked pale, drawn and defiant. She did not understand what was happening to her. Few mortals did understand the effects of the dark kiss. She was fighting against it. That was all right, Adolphus thought. He would enjoy breaking her will. He smiled at her, not showing his teeth.

'Admit it,' he said silkily. 'You enjoyed it. Last night you bared your neck before I even asked.'

That was not quite true but it was close enough. She had not fought very hard when he had embraced her. He knew the pleasure that most mortals took from being tapped. It was an ecstasy unlike any other. Once addicted to it, they would do anything to experience it again, even if it killed them. As it often did.

The girl glared at him, unwilling to admit that there was even the slightest grain of truth in what he had said, unable to acknowledge even to herself that there might be. And yet, he knew there was. Slowly that knowledge would become undeniable. Slowly it would overcome her fears, revulsions, and denials. Just the element of doubt it created would undermine her resistance as she learned she could no longer trust her own judgement, her old sense of morality. He had seen it happen many times before over the centuries. Once begun, the process was inevitable unless he chose to stop it.

He flipped open his book, an old tattered vellum copy of the *Prophesies of Nospheratus*, bound in manskin leather. It fell open at the section concerning the portents of the Age of Blood. Sure enough, the signs were all there. The armies of beasts were on the march. The hungry moon was devouring the sky. The cities of men burned. And now the Pale Prince had recovered the Eye of the Great Undying. It was here, burning on his throat. He could feel the subtle power of the thing. Out of the corner of his eye, he caught sight of sudden movement.

Swift as a snake the girl went for her dagger. He smiled. He had expected her to. It was one of the reasons he had let her keep the weapon. She was very fast. The dagger would have been in a mortal's heart before he could even have reacted. Adolphus was no mortal though. He caught her wrist and almost gently forced her hand back. The pressure was no less irresistible because of the gentleness. Within moments, he had forced the weapon back into its sheath. He let the book fall onto his knees.

'Temper, temper, my sweet,' he said mockingly, and caught her wrist again as she attempted to slap him. She would have to learn that she was helpless here; that there was nothing she could do to stop him. First, she would learn that physically, and then inevitably she would learn it in her heart and soul too.

'Bloodsucker,' she said spitefully and turned and glared out the window. Adolphus could see the two small punctures in her neck. He found the sight strangely arousing and felt the urge to sample her blood once more. He forced the urge down although it was difficult – there was something in the girl's blood that gave him great pleasure. Perhaps that was why he spent so many waking hours working on her, subtly questioning her about her companions. He was pleased that he had managed to resist temptation. The more leagues they put between them and Praag the less the beast within troubled him. Or perhaps it was the distance they put between themselves and the north. In any case, it did not matter; what was important was that his self-control was returning.

'I am,' he said, allowing some of his pride to show in his voice, 'and it's no bad thing to be. I have lived for centuries, and I have seen wonders beyond your ability to imagine.'

'You bought those centuries with the blood of innocents.'

He laughed. 'Most gave themselves to me willingly enough, as you will soon.'

'Never,' she said, and sounded like she meant it. 'I would rather die first.'

'Oh, don't be so melodramatic. You have no idea of what you speak. You are a long time in the grave, after all. Why rush to get there? Why hurry to let the worms eat those beautiful eyes, or maggots crawl through those full and lovely lips?'

For a moment there was no answer, then she spoke: 'What do you know of death? Of true death? Of eternal rest? You are a walking corpse kept alive by the blood of the living.'

So she was going to be difficult after all. Good. The struggle always made things more interesting. Breaking her would give him something to do, until he got to the keep and could attune the talisman to his will. 'I know enough to realise that I would prefer not to experience it.'

'That is not an answer.'

'What would you have me say? I am not a priest to speak knowledgeably of things I have never seen, nor talk of realms I have never been. I tell no lies.'

Adolphus suspected he had gotten her attention now. He sounded sincere, and while he was perfectly capable of counterfeiting sincerity when he wanted to, he was not doing so in this instance. There was no need to. He merely addressed himself to the doubts and fears that all mortals felt, that he himself had felt when he still breathed, and which he still felt even occasionally now.

'You are saying the priests lie? That the *Book of Morr* is not true? That the words of the gods are lies?'

He reached out and grabbed her by the chin, gently but inexorably turning her head so that he could look into her eyes. 'Have you ever spoken to a god, pretty one?'

'I have prayed.'

'And has the god ever spoken back to you?'

'My prayers have been answered.'

'I do not mean did you get what you asked for, or something you thought you had asked for. I meant: has a god ever spoken to you directly?' He saw she was breathing harder now. Her gaze met his challengingly.

'No. Of course not.'

'Yet you are willing to take the priest's words for what they claim to be true. You are willing to believe in entities you have never seen.'

'I have never seen Altdorf but I know it's there.'

'You could go to Altdorf if you wished, but could you speak with your priest's gods?'

'There have been miracles, worked by priests in the name of their gods.'

'We both believe in magic. I believe you know a wizard. I am sure he could duplicate the effects of most of those miracles. Who is to say that the priests are not simply magicians themselves?'

Silence. He let it draw out and smiled at her mockingly. She did not flinch but glared at him. He decided to surprise her. 'I do believe that gods exist. I have seen enough evidence to know it. I just do not believe they are what the priests tell you.'

'You have seen evidence?'

'So have you if you think about it. Only a fool could have looked on the Chaos horde and deny the Lords of Chaos exist.'

'What about our gods?'

'*Your* gods, you mean?'

'If you would have it so.'

'I believe that something exists but I do not think they are what mortals believe they are.'

She refused to be drawn so he continued. 'I think the gods are beings as much beyond ordinary mortals as mortals are beyond dogs. When a dog looks at you, do you think he understands what goes on in your mind?'

'My old dog did.'

'Could he understand poetry?'

'I don't see what that has to do with it.'

'I mean there are things that you can understand and think about that no dog ever could, no matter how well he understood your emotions or moods. I think your gods are creatures like that. I think they look down on you mortals and are amused. After all, they have the perspective of aeons and knowledge that far surpasses yours.'

'I think you are projecting how you see yourself onto the gods. I think you no more understand them than you claim I do.'

Adolphus looked at her, surprised at how perceptive the point was. Obviously the girl was intelligent. Excellent, she would provide stimulating company on this rather dull trip. He had become rather bored with the company of Osrik and the rest of the coven. Fawning respect and devotion grew as wearisome as anything else when overindulged in. Anything else except blood.

Now that the immediate threat was past he found he rather missed the prospect of the Slayer and his companions showing up. It had added a touch of excitement to the proceedings. Still, these lands were said to be dangerous. He was fairly sure that something interesting would turn up before the trip was over.

'AT LEAST WE are heading back towards the Empire,' said Felix, squinting into the snowfall. The cold wind made his eyes water, and the liquid was freezing on his cheeks. He was glad he had invested in an extra pair of gloves before they left Praag. Even through the thickness of both pairs he thought his hands might freeze to the reins. All of it increased the misery brought on by his illness. Perhaps going out drinking all of those nights back in Praag had not been such a good idea. He had never recovered properly.

Gotrek said nothing, merely glared out into the snow as if it were a personal enemy. His face was set in the grim expression that dwarfs always wore when forced to endure hardship. Underneath it he suspected the Slayer was quite enjoying himself. Dwarfs seemed to delight in undergoing physical travails. It was one of their least appealing characteristics as far as Felix was concerned. Hardship was something he could cheerfully live without.

Ahead of them, Max and Snorri were barely visible, and the riders were but dim shadows in the snowfall. Felix wondered how the scouts would ever find their way back through this grim weather but somehow they did. He supposed they were used to weather like this coming from the wilds of Northern Kislev. They had sneered at Felix's claims concerning how cold it was, saying that this was like spring compared to the weather back home. Felix was unsure whether they were kidding him or not. He suspected they were not.

Certainly, they had shown an uncanny aptitude for finding and building shelter. Last night Ivan Petrovich had even showed them how to build a little circular house from snow and ice. It had proven surprisingly warm once they were inside, certainly more comfortable and less drafty than the tents had been.

Their progress was slow though. Moving across this part of Kislev as winter's grip tightened was a nightmare. Had it not been for his concern over Ulrika, Felix would have begged them to turn back. He was fed up with the unending chill, the biting wind and the distant howling of wolves. They reminded him only too well of his encounter with the Arisen of Ulric under similar circumstances back in the Empire. Three days of this was more than enough for one lifetime. He knew though that he would have to endure much more. According to Max there was at least a hundred leagues between them and the talisman, and it had not stopped moving.

There were times moving through these white wastes when Felix felt the sheer futility of what they were doing. It was a kind of madness to chase after a magician with such a long head start through this dismal chilling landscape, in the faint hope that they might find Ulrika alive.

At least that was what he and Max were doing. He was certain that Gotrek and Snorri and Ivan would follow this Krieger to the ends of the earth now, for vengeance if she was killed or, in the case of the Slayers, simply to fulfil the oaths they had sworn.

There were a few small mercies to thank Sigmar for. So far they had not encountered any beastmen or Chaos warriors. From the airship the landscape seemed to have been teeming with them, but on the ground things were different. The speed of the *Spirit of Grungni* had been deceptive. On the ground, you came to realise just how vast and empty a land Kislev was, and quite how much distance really separated the various forces.

He wondered what was going to happen afterwards, if they did overhaul Krieger and reclaim Ulrika. The danger was not past. The winter had merely slowed down the great Chaos invasion and prevented almost any movement at all on the human side. Once the spring came, it would be total war on a scale the world had not seen for two centuries. Maybe trying to save a single woman in the midst of all this was futile. Perhaps they would all be dead soon anyway. At Praag they had succeeded only in slowing down and defeating one small part of an immense army. The forces of Chaos seemed limitless, and their daemonic masters did not care how many lives they expended in the pursuit of their goals. In the face of such opposition, it sometimes seemed inevitable to Felix that they would be defeated, and the world would end in fire and ruin.

But what could he do? Only what he saw best. And to tell the truth he would not mind a little fire right now, even if he could live without the ruin. Poor as the joke was, it cheered him up a little, for a few minutes until the cold started to sink into his bones again and his hacking cough returned.

It had been a village until quite recently. Now, the few stone buildings were soot-blackened rubble. The wooden palisade had left a few charred stumps rising above the snow. The evidence of human habitation had been buried beneath the drifts, along with most of the corpses. Felix felt guilty, as if somehow his thoughts of a few minutes ago had brought this into being. Don't be ridiculous, he told himself, this place was destroyed days ago. Still, the feeling stayed with him and added to his gloom.

'Look at this,' said Marek, the tracker. He brandished something long and white and mottled with brown. Felix joined Gotrek as he stamped over. Ivan Petrovich was already there. Flakes of snow drifted down from the sky. All around the rolling plain was silent save for the eerie sweep of the wind.

'What is it?' Felix asked.

'Human bone,' said Gotrek, glancing at the thing in Marek's hand.

'A thigh bone,' said Marek. He had a long thin thoughtful face, and he rarely spoke more than he had to. 'Part of one, at least. Broken for marrow.'

'Wolves?' asked Felix hopefully. As soon as the words had left Marek's lips other, more horrible possibilities had entered his mind, but he did not want to be the one to voice them. Wolves did not attack fortified villages and burn them to the ground.

'Nah, this was split lengthways, and the break's not made by wolf teeth. Men or things like men did this.'

'Beastman work,' boomed Ivan Petrovich. 'I've seen enough like it up along the marches to recognise it.'

'They must have got hungry and stopped for a snack on their long march,' said Gotrek. His scowl was ferocious. He loathed beastmen.

Max came over and joined them. He moved slowly as if still husbanding his strength. A huge bearskin robe covered his thick woollen robes. His gloved hands clutched his staff.

'Do you think Ulrika and Krieger might have been here when the attack came?' Felix asked, voicing a question that was in all their minds.

Max shook his head. 'The talisman is still on the move.'

'The beastmen might have it,' said Felix sourly.

Max glanced at him coldly. 'There is no residue of magic about this place. If it were attacked, Krieger would surely have summoned the dark to defend himself. If he had I would know. I do not think he was here when this happened.' He sounded so certain that Felix let the matter drop. Perhaps he just did not want to acknowledge any other possibility.

'Do you think the beastmen are still about?' Felix asked, casting a nervous glance about them.

'No. This is two days old. They're long gone,' said Marek.

'Pity,' muttered Gotrek running his thumb along the blade of his axe till a drop of bright blood was drawn.

'Do not fear, Gotrek Gurnisson. There will be plenty of work for your axe before we're done. All the hordes of hell are on the move this winter.'

'Bring them on,' said Gotrek, gazing bleakly out into the woods. 'Some exercise will help ward off the chill.'

FROM OUT OF night and distance, Adolphus heard the howls: wolves, baying in pursuit of prey. His little caravan was the prey. Normally, the beasts would not have given them the slightest trouble, but there were other voices mingled with those of the wolves: goblins, wolf riders. The greenskins must be desperate, he thought, to come so far into the lands of men this winter. No doubt they had been displaced from their homelands by the southward drift of the Chaos horde. Not just men were running before it like deer before the beaters. Well, let them come on; they would soon learn the folly of attacking him.

Ulrika's blood filled him with its sweetness. It left a warm glow in him like fine wine once had. He had heard that some of the Arisen drank down the memories and emotions of those they tapped but he had never experienced anything like that himself until now. It seemed some of the girl's fire had found its way from her veins into his. It was an odd feeling but not unpleasant. The girl herself lay asleep and drained on the leather seat, a satiated smile on her face. Adolphus knew that look from other times and other feedings; she would be asleep for hours. He could sense some of her emotions now. The blood bond between them was growing.

The sledge shuddered to a halt. There was a tap on the window and Roche's ugly face appeared, as pockmarked as the face of the greater moon. 'It seems we are pursued, master,' he said as calmly as if there had not been half a hundred hungry greenskins on their trail. 'Do you wish me to drive or tell the others to make ready to fight?'

'I do not believe there will be any need for a fight, Roche,' said Adolphus. 'I doubt the wolves will attack us. I have an understanding with their kind.'

He opened the door and stepped down into the chill night air. He did not feel the cold the way he had once done, and he found the wind's chill bite refreshing. All around them snow blanketed the trees. He had always liked snow. It was the colour of bone, of blank paper. It spoke to him of innocence and fresh starts. Osrik and the other nobles gazed worriedly at him from the windows of their own sleds. The surviving bodyguards looked as if they could not decide quite whether to make ready to fight or to run. Adolphus favoured them with a smile that he guessed they would find in no way reassuring. 'Don't worry, my brave friends,' he said. 'I will protect you.'

He strode back along their trail, until he stood between the small circle of sleds and their oncoming pursuers. He inspected his nails while he waited. There was just the faintest of pink flushes beneath them from the blood he had just drank.

The baying was coming closer. The sound was lonely, even coming from the throats of a pack, and it spoke to him. Despite what he had said to Ulrika about dogs and poetry, he felt that there was a bond between him and the creatures. They both understood the loneliness of the predator. He shook his head. Such thoughts had no place in his mind at a time like this. It must be the girl's blood, or the presence of the talisman.

Suddenly the pack erupted from the woods, snow fountaining behind them as they ran. Huge creatures, larger than normal wolves by far, white furred for the winter, red eyes burning with fierce hunger. They were beautiful creatures, but their riders were not.

They were smaller than men, perhaps the size of a big ten year-old boy, green-skinned, and wrapped in the thickest of furs and clothes that looked like old chequered coloured rags. Their mouths were filled with huge, sharp snaggly teeth. Their eyes were yellow and the size of saucers, and Adolphus knew they could see in the dark almost as well as he. Their arms were long in proportion to their bodies, perhaps half as long again as human arms. In their huge gnarled hands they clutched spears and bows and scimitars. Adolphus strode confidently towards them.

This took them aback. It was not what they were expecting. One of the goblins, larger and more ugly than the rest, raised his paw and the line of riders came to a ragged halt. A rider took aim with his short bow and loosed an arrow. Adolphus stepped to one side and let it pass by so that it thunked into the side of the coach behind him. He doubted that the stone-tipped arrows could harm him, but they would smart, and Adolphus was no more fond of pain than anyone else. The leader turned and glared at the smaller goblin who had shot. Sensing Adolphus's approach and catching his scent on the wind, the wolves began to snarl and slink alternately. The leader of the pack, a massive beast, glared at him with eyes that matched the goblin chieftain's for fury.

Adolphus stopped twenty paces away from the goblins. By now, he knew Roche would have unlimbered his crossbow behind him and have taken a bead on the leader. It would not be necessary but he supposed it gave his servant something to do. He doubted that the bodyguards would be much use if it came to a fight but he did not care. He put his hand on the hilt of his sword and surveyed the wolf riders contemptuously. They shifted uneasily in their saddles, not sure of what they were dealing with now, but knowing it was well outside the ambit of their usual experience.

'Go now and I will let you live. Stay and you will surely die,' Adolphus told them confidently, eyeing the leader directly. He felt the connection as their eyes met and the battle of wills began. The goblin was fierce, stupid, ambitious, and did not like being balked. The contest was far from being one-sided.

The rest of the riders brandished their weapons and howled challenges and jeers in their crude guttural tongue. He doubted very much whether they understood a fraction of what he had said. It was just their nature to behave this way. The leader looked at him, clearly uncertain what was going on. He sensed the presence of magic, and it unnerved him. And his anger was turning to fear.

'Kill magic man,' he shouted then bellowed orders in his own speech. The wolves snarled, and crouched to spring. The goblins couched their lances, and raised their scimitars. Adolphus shrugged. It had been a slim hope but it had been worth trying. Now he would have to use his alternative plan.

His gaze flashed over the wolves, and he let them see the beast that dwelled within him, let them know they were in the presence of a predator far more dangerous than they. The change was immediate. The wolves' hackles rose and they cringed like beaten curs – their tails drooped between their legs, their mouths hung open and their tongues lolled out. Their riders' battle cries dropped to feeble protests of dismay.

Adolphus reached for the dark magical energy that filled the night and projected his will onto the animals. Perhaps it was his imagination but it seemed easier now that he had the Eye. He sensed momentary resistance from the animals but his will was too strong. In moments, the beasts were his to command and he drove his orders directly into their minds.

Almost as one they reared and bucked, throwing their riders from the saddle and pouncing on them to rip their throats. It took long moments for the goblins to get over their surprise and realise what was happening. By that time, over half of them were dead.

They were not going to go down without a fight. Some of them managed to stay in the saddle. Adolphus saw the chieftain reach forward and slash his mount's throat with a dagger. Wolf blood crimsoned the snow. The chieftain rolled clear of the saddle and came racing at Adolphus, dagger dripping red. Adolphus almost smiled at his foolish bravery.

He strode forward to meet the creature, not even drawing his sword. As he met the goblin he sidestepped and got his arm round his throat. With a single twist, he snapped the chieftain's neck. Vertebrae ground. Something wet and sticky flopped down the goblin's leg into the snow. He raised the corpse above his head and tossed at another struggling rider.

A crossbow bolt flashed past him and took another goblin through the throat. He could hear the bodyguards begin to advance towards the melee now that it appeared won. It was all too much for the greenskins. Within heartbeats the survivors had turned and fled, only to be run down by their own mounts. Within a minute the snow was awash with yellowy-green blood, and all the goblins were dead.

Adolphus gave the wolves permission to feed. They fell to with a will. Obviously the winter had been hard and their former masters had not fed them well. He turned and strolled back to the coach. Roche watched him expressionlessly. His coven gazed on him with expressions somewhere between worship and terror. Fear blazed in the eyes of the bodyguards as they parted to let him through.

'When we move on,' said Adolphus, 'I believe we will have an escort.'

'Very good, master,' said Roche. 'I shall wait for your new followers to finish their repast.'

'I DON'T LIKE the look of this at all,' said Max Schreiber. 'These tracks are unnatural.'

Felix felt a deep-seated unease. The woods were thick and dark all around them, the trees frosted with white flakes. Ahead of them the snow had been churned as if a large number of men or other things had passed this way quite recently. Felix seriously doubted that any sane or honest man would be abroad in this weather without some overwhelmingly important reason. As the cold intensified and the weather became grimmer and grimmer, he himself found the thought of giving up becoming ever more appealing.

It was not that he did not want to save Ulrika. It was just that the more time passed, the less chance there seemed to be that she was still alive. Swearing to avenge her was all very well, but men frozen to death in the snow, or losing their limbs to frostbite were not very likely to avenge anyone.

For the moment, Felix was keeping these thoughts to himself. They were not likely to find much favour with the Slayers, Max or Ulrika's father. There were times when they did not find much favour with him. They sometimes left him disgusted with himself, but more and more often recently they had been creeping into his mind. He knew he was ill; the flux had returned with a vengeance. He hoped he was not going to go down with pneumonia.

He tried telling himself that no hero in the stories he had read as a boy ever gave up just because he was cold, hungry, had a splitting headache or the thought of eating another mouthful of beef jerky left him feeling nauseous. But as the days had drawn out, he had found it was just these things that left him feeling the most discouraged.

The threat of violence Felix could deal with. While he was not completely enamoured with the idea of facing physical danger, he knew he had done it in the past and acquitted himself well. It was the little things that were slowly but surely wearing him down and out: the way his lips were cracked, the way his belly rumbled, the constant pain in his temples from the flu that never quite went away no matter how often Max healed it or gave him herbal infusions. He was just feeling strung out, as if his vitality were being leeched away by the spirits of the winter woods. Sometimes he thought that if they did overtake Krieger he would be too weary to fight him.

He found that it took an effort of will to conjure the image of Ulrika to his mind now, to imagine her in peril. It was alarming. You thought you loved her. No, you did love her, and yet now you are seriously considering abandoning her. This was another area he had discovered where things were not quite like the storybooks. There all the heroes dared everything to rescue their loved ones. They blazed with unquenchable passion and utter certainty. They never suffered from doubts or wondered whether they really were in love at all.

Such feelings were all too common for him. Sometimes when he was hungry or tired or hungover or scared, he could easily forget that he loved her. He could easily remember all the times she had hurt him, or snubbed him or told him he was foolish. All the little resentments he harboured crowded into his brain and clamoured for his attention. Detlef Sierck had never bothered to mention any of this in his plays. He wondered if he were the only man on the face of the earth who felt like this. Somehow he doubted it.

Then, just when he thought all feelings were extinguished, they would return in the oddest ways. He would find himself remembering the strange Kislevite way in which she stressed certain syllables, or the way she shook her head but smiled when he said something particularly stupid. He was not sure why he found these things endearing, he just knew that he did. They were some of the links in the chain that still somehow bound him, even when he thought time, distance and hunger had corroded it. He might never be really certain of how he felt about her, but he knew that as long as she lived he would have the chance to find out. If she died…

Just keep moving, he told himself. Just keep following this trail. Just keep eating the disgusting Kislevite iron rations. Just put up with the cold and the aches and the grumbling of the dwarfs and the boasting of the Kislevites and Max's constant worried expression. Just endure them. One way or another, you will get through this. One day, if you are lucky, you will look back on this and remember it fondly, in the way you can look back on hardships you have endured once they are safely long in the past.

He knew the strange tricks his memory could play would, if he lived, somehow edit this trial down into its highlights. He would remember the camaraderie, and the shared dangers survived. He would remember the sudden, surprising way beauty would spring on you even in the depths of this winter wilderness. He would remember enchanted vistas of frozen forest groves glimpsed from the corner of his eye as they bumped along the trail. He would remember a startled deer bounding off into the distance as it caught sight of them, its hindquarters flickering as it covered the ground in mighty leaps. He would remember the clear, clean frozen air, the sound of the runners cleaving the snow, and the ponies whickering to one another as if to keep their spirits up. He would remember the odd feeling of tranquillity as the horse-soldiers sang their winter hymns around the fires in the ice huts they carved for themselves each afternoon.

Without the immediate feelings of pain and nausea and worry and fear his memory would translate this into a wonderful adventure.

It would all be a lie of course, but it would be a glamorous lie far, far better than the real thing, and perhaps like all the other tale-tellers he would pass on that lie and make them think there was something wonderful about it too. And strangest of all, he knew that he would be sincere when he did it. He would genuinely believe what he was saying.

Marek had dropped back to look at the tracks. He was studying them carefully. 'Not too far ahead of us, I would guess,' he said. 'Not friendly either.'

'How can you tell?' Felix asked.

'Easy. Some of the footprints are mixed with hoof prints. Cloven ones. Beastmen are the only things that leave tracks like that. If we're lucky we'll overtake them soon.'

There will be nothing lucky about it, Felix thought, nursing his aching head.

MAX WAS WORRIED. Not by the prospect of facing an indeterminate number of beastmen but by the length of time the pursuit was taking. They had been on the move for almost a week now and were still no closer to the talisman. If anything, the distance was increasing. Whoever Krieger was, he certainly knew how to move through this winter landscape.

In a way it was good. He was reassured that the dark magician could keep going, and not be slowed by any of the perils of the way. It implied that if he wanted to keep Ulrika alive he was capable of it, and that was Max's one remaining source of hope. It was not a good one, though. Knowing that Krieger was powerful boded ill for their chances of recovering the girl, particularly if he had learned to tap the powers of the talisman.

Max shivered, and not with the cold. Since Ulrika's capture he had driven himself far beyond anything he would have believed possible. He sometimes felt he was keeping himself going by sheer willpower alone. He had turned into a man of stone. He did not feel the cold, he did not feel weary and he did not feel any hunger. He just wanted to get the woman back.

In a way he was almost grateful for the situation. It had helped him recover from the terrible mental ordeal of putting himself back together after his encounter with the wards on the talisman. It had given him a reason to overcome his feelings of weakness and self-pity and to confront the abyss of doubt that loomed within his mind. He knew that he must pull himself back from the brink as much for Ulrika's sake as for his own.

He had thought he had loved her before but what he had felt then was but a pale shadow of what he felt now. The prospect of losing her was almost more than he could bear. He had never felt anything so deeply before in his life. The urge to find her was an overwhelming drive; it dwarfed any of his bodily needs or any of his own weaknesses.

He begrudged every minute lost on the trail. He resented the possibility of encountering the beastmen as much because it would slow them down as because there was a possibility of injury or death. He hated every moment lost that enabled Krieger to put distance between them. He resented the time it took to make camp at night, to build the icehouses, make fires. If he could, he would have gone without them, without food or drink or sleep if need be.

Part of him knew this was madness. If he did not get those things he would die, and be of no help to anyone, least of all Ulrika. But it was one thing knowing these things rationally and another to feel them in the depths of his soul.

His life had simplified down to one true and real thing: he must save Ulrika. He thought he might go mad if he did not.

So FAR, THEY had found nothing, overtaken no monsters, and seen no sight of any beastmen. The only ones who were sorry were the Slayers. Everyone else was relieved. Felix wondered how the beastmen could survive in the depths of winter. Ivan had the answer.

'They eat each other when they can't get manflesh. The big ones eat the little ones. The strong devour the weak. I suppose they think it's their gods' way of testing them, so that only the hardiest survive. I don't know. I only know that I have seen enough corpses and fought enough battles against them in the winter to know the truth of it.'

Gotrek nodded as if he agreed with every word. Felix shuddered. This was the sort of knowledge he could cheerfully have spent his entire life without ever acquiring. Unfortunately it appeared that fate had other plans for him.

'Best keep moving,' said the Slayer. 'Every foul Chaos beast in the world appears to be moving this winter. Sooner or later we're going to run into some of them.' His evil smile left Felix in no doubt as to what would happen then.

SIX

THE MOONS BLAZED brightly overhead. The snow lay thick upon the forest. Gnarled ancient trees surrounded them, growing out over the road. Adolphus breathed deeply. Finally they were here. The air tasted different: it was sharper, with a tang of blood and dark magic and ancient secrets. He knew he was home. There was no place in the world that smelled quite like Sylvania.

He had not been born here, of course, but he had spent many centuries of his undeath here. It was a haven for his kind. A land which had been ruled by undying counts for centuries, where the peasants and the lesser so-called aristocrats had long ago realised their true place in the great scheme of things and bowed their heads and given their service to the Arisen. He would see that those days returned once more. The Time of Blood was here. The Council and those who followed them would change their ways or go to hell. He would send them there personally.

With the wolves trailing along behind him like a pack of obedient dogs, he strode in the wake of the coaches. It was easy enough for him to keep pace with it even in the deep snow. It was no obstacle to one such as he. The cold did not slow him, and he had long ago left such human weaknesses as suffering from frostbite behind him. On this night, the night of his return, he wanted to be outside, to stalk the night like the hunter he was, to sniff the wind for prey, to seek blood in the old way. Here of all places it was possible to do so without fear of reprisal. And he wanted to be alone to savour the moment, away from the pettiness of the coven and the cold amusement of Roche.

In this ancient stronghold of vampiric power, the cattle knew better than to rise up against their masters. Even in the dark times, when the forces of the so-called Emperor had driven the Arisen underground, they had been feared and respected in Sylvania. The mortals knew that no matter who claimed sovereignty over this land, there would only ever be one true set of rulers. Human power was transitory here. The sway of the Arisen would always return. An accommodation had been reached between the mortals and their masters that Adolphus knew satisfied a deep-seated need in both. For the brutish short-lived peasants what could be better than one who combined all the characteristics of feudal liege and undying god? Such people always needed to know their place in the world, and the Arisen had made sure that they did. In a way, the cattle were even grateful to feel the smack of firm government. They were happiest when they knew their place, when their thinking was done for them.

Adolphus knew that one day the whole world would be like this. Sylvania was a model for what was to come. Now that the talisman was in his hands, he would soon have the power to make it so. He had never been the most accomplished of magicians – his talents had always lain in other directions – but once he reached Drakenhof and tapped the ancient node of power there, he would claim the Eye for his own.

He smiled. It had taken decades of research and years of studying cryptic books and prophecies but the key to ultimate power was now in his grasp. In his hand, he held an artefact of the Great Necromancer, created at the peak of his power, an item that the mighty liche had once held in his own claw, and imbued with a fraction of his own limitless strength. Nagash had been subtle and relentless in his hatred of all the powers that might challenge his. He had forged the talisman when it became obvious that the ancient Vampire Queens of Lahmia and their followers might eventually rise to challenge him. He was not going to risk having such potent undying sorcerers dwelling in the same land without taking precautions against them, so he had created the Eye of Khemri to work their undoing.

It contained runes which when properly activated would bend the Arisen to its wearer's will. With it he had created the Hounds of Nagash, kin who served him loyally while under its spell. The rest of the Arisen had fled and hidden themselves in the distant corners of the world. Of course, Nagash had never intended for the Eye to leave his presence. For all his power he had not foreseen his own defeat first by the hero-king Alcadizaar then by the man-god Sigmar. Upon his destruction the Eye had vanished into history, passing through the hands of a succession of unknown bearers until it had re-appeared on the throat of Vlad von Carstein. Not even his closest associates had known what it was even as they fell under its sway. Sometimes, Adolphus wondered whether the first and mightiest of the Vampire Counts had truly realised what it was he owned. Vlad was gone forever now and Adolphus regretted he would never have the chance to ask him. It had passed through the hands of his successors, none of whom had guessed its true power until its eventual loss at the Battle of Hel Fenn. It had been years later, perusing the section of one of the three extant copies of the dread *Liber Occultus* dealing with the history of ancient Nehekhara, that Krieger had realised what the Eye was. So had begun his long search.

Now the talisman was in his hands, and he almost had it attuned to his will. With it, he could make himself undisputed ruler of the Arisen. He could unite all of Sylvania behind him and create an invincible army. It would take time and patience, of course. In many ways the Arisen fancied themselves the secret rulers of the world, but the main thing that prevented this, in truth, was their disunity. They spent more time plotting against each other than they did seeking to extend the dominion of their kind.

Adolphus would put an end to this. He would organise the Arisen and replace the vacillations of the Council with his own ironhanded rule. He would be their king, but he would see to it that they had a hierarchy as strict as any Empire with every one knowing their place, and having their own clearly defined fiefdoms. He had travelled. There was enough room for all of them, and big enough herds of human cattle to keep them all through eternity. He was excited now. Visions of what was to come burned in his brain, and he found he wanted to share them.

Leaving the wolves, he strode back past his followers and vaulted up into the coach. The girl looked up at him. He could see the resistance was slowly draining out of her along with the blood. Her anger was mixed with desire now and yes, even need. The ecstasy of the dark kiss did that to them, no matter how much they denied it. Still she reached for her dagger; still she intended to make a show of fighting him off. Casually he reached out and took it from her, the way a man might take a toy from a child. He was in no mood for games this evening. He wanted to talk, and it was either to her or Roche or the wolves. He felt somehow that telling her was the right thing.

'I am going to rule this land soon,' he said.

'You are mad,' she said. Her weakness made her voice soft and breathy. Adolphus felt the urge to sip from her blood rise in him once more. He pushed it back. He wanted to explain his plan to her, to force her to see what he saw, to make her acknowledge him for what he was and what he would be.

'No,' he said. 'I am not. I am in a position to do everything I claim.'

She shook her head disbelievingly, but he could tell he had her interest. 'The Arisen are many and their covens have a great deal of influence in the world. You would be surprised how many of the rich and powerful are secret members.'

'So?' He liked the way she raised her chin challengingly as she spoke, despite her weakness, despite the way the kiss must have made her head spin. It made things interesting.

'I am going to rule the Arisen.'

'How?'

'Don't be sullen, Ulrika. It doesn't become you. I am going to use this talisman, which you and your friends so valiantly defended. It has a great deal of power within it. It was created by the Great Necromancer Nagash to allow him to command my kind many centuries ago. The power is still within it. I will rule the Arisen, and through them I shall rule this land.'

'The Emperor might have something to say about that. You may have money and influence but that won't defeat an army.'

'Ulrika, Ulrika, sometimes I think you deliberately pretend to be stupid in order to make me underestimate you. We both know that money and influence can recruit soldiers, and we both know that many of the people who have them also already employ soldiers. More to the point, Nagash was the Great Necromancer. I can use the power of this talisman to raise an army from every cemetery and every burial ground if necessary. And many of the Arisen are also potent necromancers. United we will create an army so vast that no mortal force could stand against it.'

'An army of walking corpses.'

'I am sure they will not object. After all, they are already dead. Only the gods and the Arisen live forever.' He let those words and that thought hang in the air for a moment. Most mortals were eventually seduced by its power. Even if he never offered to make them one of the Arisen, they would begin to think about it. They would begin to see the possibilities of what pleasing him could bring. No fear of ageing; no fear of the grave. No fear of having to leave this world behind. It was this promise more than anything else that made them give themselves up so willingly. It was a coin that only his kind could demonstrably offer. He thought he saw the temptation occur to her, and he could tell by her expression that she dismissed it. He was not worried. Many mortals did the first time, before they truly had time to think about it. Once they did...

'The forces of Chaos may object as well. They seem hell-bent on having the world themselves.' She gestured at the window, to the bloated face of Morrsleib glaring down garishly from the sky.

'They will be thrown back, as they have before. United, the Arisen will have the power to do that. They are possibly the only ones who could. Do you think the decaying kingdoms of mankind have the strength?'

'They will have strength enough to stop you. Just as von Carstein was stopped at Hel Fenn.'

He smiled, showing her his teeth, all of them. She shivered. Partly from fear he was sure, but also partially from desire. 'Hel Fenn? I remember it well. Von Carstein should never have fought there. It was a bad site for a battle. No place to retreat except the swamp. He was confident we would not need to. Foolish...'

'You were at Hel Fenn?' He could see the dawn of knowledge in her eyes. She was beginning to realise what he was, what he was capable of offering. She now knew he had been present at a battle fought over two centuries ago.

'I am still here,' he said. 'How many of the so-called victors can say that?'

She had no answer. There was none.

'WE'RE GETTING CLOSER to the beastmen at last,' said Marek. Felix looked at the tracker through the gathering twilight. His weather-beaten face was tense with suppressed excitement. All of the Kislevite lancers looked ready for combat. Max stretched his limbs and Felix thought for a moment he saw a faint nimbus of light play around the wizard's flexing fingers.

'I hear the sound of fighting up ahead,' said Gotrek. Felix heard nothing but that did not surprise him. The Slayer's ears were keener than his, just as his eyes were better than a dwarf's in daylight.

'Who is fighting?' Felix asked.

'Men and beasts and Chaos warriors. The name of Khorne is being chanted, but we will soon put an end to that.' Felix wished that he felt so certain. Ivan Petrovich nodded. His lancers broke into a trot. Felix cracked the reins and urged the ponies forward.

Soon he could hear the sounds of battle himself.

BLOOD STAINED THE snow. A group of men armoured like Imperial knights made a last stand in the centre of the clearing. They were attempting to protect a coach. Men-at-arms lay dead in snowdrifts, their pikes fallen from their nerveless fingers. All around them were beastmen, horned horrors, part man, part goat, clutching weapons in their misshapen fingers, stamping on the fallen with their cloven hooves. Their eyes gleamed red with bloodlust. Froth dripped from their mouths.

As Felix watched a horse whinnied with terror. The rider, gaudily caparisoned in red and gold, was tipped from the saddle. A massive beastman clutching a standard depicting a bloated hungry moon face, tipped with a human skull, strode forward and drove the iron-shod base of the banner into the man's chest with a sickening, squelching sound. The man gurgled as he died.

The beastmen turned, alerted by the sound of hooves crashing through snow. Ivan bellowed orders to his men and twenty lances dropped into the ready position. The Kislevite horse thundered forward and crashed into the unprepared ranks of the beastmen. They went down screaming, impaled on lances, trampled by iron-shod hoofs. Gotrek and Snorri were right behind, weapons ready, irresistible as thunderbolts. Max chanted a spell and the clearing became bright as day.

A glowing solar disk appeared over the wizard's head and then, at a word from its creator, bolts of searing light erupted forth, burning the fur from the beastmen and filling the air with the smell of charred flesh.

Felix barely had time to rip his sword from the scabbard and climb down from the sledge before it was over. The savage beastmen, unprepared for such an onslaught, broke and ran for the woods. Most of them did not make it. They were overrun by the horsemen or slain by Max's mystical bolts.

Gotrek and Snorri finished off the wounded, looking utterly disgruntled.

'Hardly a proper fight,' said Gotrek.

'Beastmen are not what they used to be when Snorri was a lad,' said Snorri. 'They would have put up a bit of a fight then.'

Felix was glad they had not. Slowed by his illness, and worn out by the chill, he wondered if he would have survived a battle with a beastman. Best to push such thoughts aside. He strode over to the carriage the knights had fought so hard to defend. Even as he did so, one of them, a huge man with a mane of golden hair, strode between him and the vehicle. He raised his blade, obviously intending that Felix come no closer. Felix shrugged and stopped.

'We mean you no harm,' he said. Gotrek and Snorri clumped over to stand beside Felix. They did not look quite as unthreatening as Felix would have wished. They were obviously still keen for a fight, and perhaps this knight would give them one. He certainly looked as if he were considering it. Felix thought he'd better say something before things got out of hand. 'In Sigmar's name, put your weapon down. We just saved your lives.'

The four surviving knights had gathered around the gold-haired man. From the way they looked to him for their cue, Felix gathered that he was their leader.

'We were doing fine by ourselves,' he said eventually. His voice was rich and commanding and filled with utter self-assurance. He seemed to believe every word he said.

Just what I need, thought Felix, another aristocratic idiot. There was something odd about the man's accent, a thickness that was not quite Imperial and not quite Kislevite. A stress that reminded him of the way characters spoke in old books.

'The way your men threw themselves on the beastmen's spears was all part of your strategy then, was it?' Gotrek asked sarcastically. 'A great plan.'

Felix thought the knight was going to raise his sword to Gotrek. He was tempted to let him. If this idiot wanted to throw away his life fighting the Slayer why should he interfere, he thought uncharitably? He wiped his nose on a fold of his cloak and waited.

'What is going on here, Rodrik?' asked a woman's voice from within the coach. 'Why aren't you thanking these kind strangers for their aid against those fiends?'

'My lady, their manner is insolent and lacking in true courtliness. You should not sully your chaste ears listening to their words.'

Gotrek and Felix exchanged glances. If Felix had not known better he would have guessed the Slayer was amused. 'I think it is you who are lacking in knightly graces, Rodrik. A truly chivalrous man would express gratitude under these circumstances, not look for excuses.'

The knight looked crestfallen and when his gaze returned to the Slayers, he executed a perfect courtly bow.

'I apologise for my manners,' he said. 'My only excuse is that I let my concern for the safety of a fair lady overcome me. I beg your pardon.'

Gotrek spat on the ground at his feet. He was not one to accept an apology graciously. To his credit, Rodrik did not even blink. Max limped over. He looked even more tired and drained than usual. Working his magic on the beastmen must have cost him dearly.

'It is unusual for people to be abroad in weather like this, with the land so dangerous,' he said. The knight looked at him suspiciously. Felix had been around the wizard for so long he had forgotten how much many ordinary people disliked sorcerers.

'I could say the same about you,' Rodrik said. There was more intelligence behind the answer than Felix would have given him credit for. Perhaps he was not as stupid as he looked.

'We have a mission,' Max said suavely, although a pained look passed across his face. 'A quest, you might almost say.'

It was a well-considered response. Felix could see that Rodrik was intrigued. Quests were the sort of things knights understood, particularly ones like Rodrik who appeared to think he was living in some courtly romance. Felix had heard that there were still some like him, but he would never have believed it until now. He had thought only Bretonnians went in for that sort of thing.

'And what might that be?'

'A fair young lady of our acquaintance has been kidnapped by an evil sorcerer. We intend to rescue her or avenge her.' The words should have sounded ludicrous but the way Max said them invested every word with weight and seriousness. Felix could tell Rodrik was impressed.

The curtains of the coach window were drawn back and a pale, beautiful face cowled in black and partially obscured by a thin mesh of veil looked out at them. 'If it would not delay you too long in your quest, perhaps we could offer you shelter for the night. There is a keep not too far from here where we are expected. The least we can offer you after your efforts on our behalf is a hot fire and warm spiced wine.'

Not even the Slayers seemed ready to object to that.

Rodrik and his men rode ahead of the coach. Ivan Petrovich's scouts rode ahead of them. The sledges brought up the rear.

'I notice they did not tell us what they were about,' said Felix.

'Doubtless we will find out soon enough, manling,' said the Slayer.

'IT's LIKE A haunted castle in a Detlef Sierck melodrama,' murmured Felix. The Slayer looked at him. Felix wondered if he knew who the playwright was. 'I don't like it.'

The keep clutched the top of the hill on which it stood, like a hawk on a perch. There was something predatory about it. It made Felix think of robber barons, bandits and other things less pleasant from old stories. The scene was somehow ominously familiar. He told himself not to let his imagination run wild. He was sick, it was cold, and any place in this icy land would look sinister. The place looked strong; the walls thick. The turrets of the inner bailey looked built to resist a siege, and yet there was something about it that suggested other things. Felix thought of torture chambers, ghosts with clanking chains and wicked old barons threatening heroines with a fate worse than death.

'It's a castle, manling, and a strong one. Some good stonework there, for human work that is.' He might have guessed the dwarf would see things in the most prosaic terms possible. Not a terribly imaginative people, Felix thought, though at this moment it was a trait he wished he shared. There was something about this place that set his nerves on edge.

'It makes me nervous,' Felix said. 'There's something about the style of the building that...'

Even as he said the words, it came to him. He remembered where he had seen the likeness of this keep before. It had been in a book of horror tales he had read as a boy, tales set in the land of Sylvania. This place was an almost exact replica of one of the keeps in the book. It might have been the original model for the picture. He hoped that it was only the memory that made it seem so sinister.

THE TOWN BENEATH the castle was mostly ruined. The destruction was not recent, Felix could see. Most of the buildings had tumbled down decades ago. The city looked as if it had been built for a population of five thousand and now held only a tenth of that number. Even in the city centre, on the main thoroughfare leading to the castle only about one in every three houses appeared occupied and those seemed to be half rubble. The people were surlier and more brutish than any Felix had ever encountered. They wandered through the near-deserted streets listlessly, with no sense of purpose. The air stank of rot and human excrement.

And this was Waldenhof, a large and prosperous town, by local standards. Felix decided he would not like to live here.

The road led up the steep hillside towards the grinning gatehouse. Even as they approached the entrance, the gateway reminded Felix of the mouth of a great beast, and the portcullis of its fangs. A shiver ran down his spine.

Fever, Felix told himself, but did not quite believe it.

'WELCOME TO WALDENSCHLOSSE,' said the man who waited for them in the courtyard. He was a tall florid aristocrat, garbed in a slightly antiquated style. The padding of his tunic's shoulders and codpiece had not been fashionable in the Empire for half a century. Felix had only seen its like in old portraits. The others around him were garbed in a similar fashion. Somehow it suited their slightly antiquated manner of speaking. 'We thank you for the service you have rendered my sister-in-law, the Countess Gabriella, and my son Rodrik. It seems that without your intercession we would not have the pleasure of greeting her now. Nothing we could do can express our gratitude for your kindness, but we will do our poor best.'

'I am Rudgar, Count of Waldenhof, and you are my most honoured guests. I hope before you leave that you will discover the true meaning of Sylvanian hospitality.'

Felix's mind reeled a little with shock. They had come further than he had thought, or, indeed, would have wished, if they had crossed the borders of the ill-famed province of Sylvania. It was not a place he had ever harboured a strong desire to visit, not even in high summer, and without the beastmen filling the woods. It was a place of very evil reputation.

More introductions followed, but Felix's head still spun with the fever and he remembered none of them. He did recall noticing that the Countess Gabriella was looking at him, and, despite her widow's veil he could see that she was a very beautiful woman.

'YOUR HEALTH,' SAID Count Rudgar, raising his glass. Sweat glistened on his bald pate. The tips of his long moustaches drooped into his wine. He tipped his glass back and downed it all in one long swallow. A silent servant glided forward to refill it almost automatically.

Felix had to admit that he felt better now after a few hours sitting at the dining table in the great hall, near a warm fire, his stomach filled with beef and roast potatoes and capon and gravy. Half a bottle of the count's fine wine had done wonders too, and left him feeling a little better disposed to his surroundings as well. He could see that most of the others did not quite feel the same way.

Only Gotrek glared around suspiciously with his one good eye, as if expecting armed enemies to attack him at any second. Nothing unusual about that. He normally looked that way, but it was an unwelcome reminder to Felix that perhaps he should keep his guard up as well. Max was not drinking, and although the sorcerer chatted amiably enough with the Sylvanian nobles Felix could tell he was not entirely at his ease either. He saw Felix looking at him and nodded as if to say that he, too, shared his companion's suspicions of the place.

The Kislevite horse-soldiers and Snorri Nosebiter dug in with a will however, throwing back food and wine as if this was their last chance at it. Come to think of it, it might be. Ivan Petrovich shared the table with them. His men had another table down the great hall with the off-duty castle soldiers and the other troops.

Felix was surprised to find that they and the countess's party were not the only guests. It seemed many Sylvanian nobles were visiting Waldenschlosse, though why they should choose to do this in the middle of winter eluded him. He had read too many stories and seen too many plays in which terrible things happened at feasts in Sylvanian castles for his own comfort. Even through the pleasant warmth of the wine in his belly, part of him half expected to hear an order given that would have hidden warriors fall on the guests in an orgy of bloodshed. Such things were all too common in the tales.

He looked around trying to put faces to names once more. This time he was sure he had got things right. The frail old man on his right, skeletally lean and with a full head of pure white hair was Petr, Count of Swartzhafen. He seemed pleasant enough, mild-mannered and polite, but there was something about his eyes, a haunted quality that made Felix think that here was a man who had seen things that few mortals had. Facing him across the table was a tall man in his prime. Kristof, Baron of Leicheburg, had pure black hair and an arrogant hawk-like face dominated by blazing black eyes. To his right sat Johan Richter, a good-looking young man who shared something of the Count of Swartzhafen's haunted air. From what Felix had gathered, all of them were important noblemen in this part of the world, and reading between the lines, all of them were scared. All of the assembled company except Gotrek raised their glasses to the toast. Felix felt as if eyes were on him, and looking to his left saw the Countess Gabriella was looking at him appraisingly, her blue eyes startlingly clear above the veil.

'And to the health of our most unexpected and most welcome guests,' said Rudgar. 'They have my gratitude for saving the life of my son and my esteemed sister-in-law.'

Rodrik looked a little embarrassed by this, but kept his mouth shut. Doubtless he did not want any more lectures about gratitude from his father or the countess. Murmurs from around the table agreed with the count's words. Whatever else you said about the Sylvanian nobility, Felix thought, they were certainly polite, in an old-fashioned courtly sort of way.

'Now that we have eaten I suggest we get down to business,' said Baron Leicheburg. His voice was deep and resonant, the sort of voice that could fill a theatre or a room, or rise effortlessly over a battlefield. Felix envied him it. 'I have not come all this way through the worst winter in two hundred years merely to sip your wine, old friend, no matter how fine a cellar you keep.'

The count inclined his head graciously at the compliment and spoke at once.

'Aye, there is the rub. It is the worst winter in two centuries and not just from the snow. Wolves multiply in the forests, beastmen clog the Emperor's highway, and other things, worse things are stirring once more.'

Felix was not sure he liked the tone of the count's voice. It made the hackles on the back of his neck rise. Count Swartzhafen raised his fist to his mouth and gave a dry, desiccated cough. 'You are saying the ancient curse has returned to trouble us once more?'

Felix glanced over at Gotrek. The Slayer had sat up like a hound that scents prey straining at a leash. Doubtless he thought there was work here for him. Great, thought Felix, as if getting Ulrika from the clutches of a dark sorcerer was not bad enough, now they were going to get themselves mixed up with some ancient evil. Just what he needed.

'Can you doubt it?' said Richter. He leaned forward and placed his goblet carefully on the table but his eyes blazed with a near insane intensity. Felix was not sure he wanted to know what could put a look like that in a man's eyes. 'The signs are all there. A merchant saw witch lights burning on the Dark Moor two weeks ago. Black coaches have been sighted on the Old Road to the Red Abbey. Something had been disturbing the graves at the cemetery in Essen. On my way here I entered the crypt at Mikalsdorf, and found it empty. Grave robbers had been at work there.'

'That does not sound good,' said Count Swartzhafen mildly. Mirthless laughter from the rest of the nobles greeted this pronouncement, which also caused the men-at-arms to fall silent at the other table for a moment and glance at their masters. Only for a moment though, and then conversation was resumed.

Baron Leicheburg glanced at them all and continued. 'Maidens have started to vanish again in the Grim Wood, and the peasants have started hanging bundles of witchbane and bloodroot over their doors. Normally I would have thought nothing of it. The winter has been so bad, and the Chaos tainted so numerous, this would be reason enough for their precautions, but black-garbed men with pale faces have been seen too.'

'I don't think there can be any doubts,' said Rudgar. 'The undying ones have returned.'

Something in the man's tone made Felix shiver. 'The undying ones?' he asked. He guessed that he already knew, but he wanted to be sure.

'The followers of von Carstein, the drinkers of blood,' said Johan turning his blazing gaze upon them.

'Vampires,' said Max Schreiber. 'You are talking about vampires.'

Rudgar gave him a bitter smile, a mere flashing of teeth with no mirth in it. 'This is Sylvania,' he said. 'The land of the Vampire Counts.'

Silence fell once again. Not even the servants moved. It was as if someone had laughed at a funeral or voiced an awful truth that everybody thought but no one had dared put into words until that moment.

Wonderful, thought Felix: evil sorcerers, the coming of Chaos and now the return of the Vampire Counts. How do I get myself into these things?

'More wine anybody?' asked Count Rudgar to break the silence. His moustaches seemed to droop even more. He looked like a man who had just been told that his family had contracted the plague and there was a good chance he had caught it himself. Felix knew exactly how he felt.

Max glanced down into his still full wine cup as if he could see the secrets of the future there. Gotrek rubbed his massive hands together almost gleefully. Ivan Petrovich looked even more grimly determined to find his daughter. Felix stifled the urge to moan.

'There will be time enough for these discussions later,' said the Countess Gabriella, her musical voice sounding cool and amused. 'Perhaps our guests would care to tell us what brings them here in this time of troubles.'

Max looked at Felix as if asking which of them should explain. Felix gestured for Max to speak. Doubtless the mage could tell the tale better than he. Max spoke of the kidnapping of Ulrika and their pursuit across the frozen lands. In the telling he was forced to speak of the siege of Praag and the Chaos invasion.

The Sylvanian nobles remained silent for a time after he had finished, then looked at each other. Their faces were calm for the most part, but Felix was certain he could see fear in their eyes, and by now he was certain that these were people who did not frighten easily.

'It sounds like the end of the world,' said the Count of Swartzhafen eventually.

'We live in evil times indeed,' agreed Baron Leicheburg. 'More evil even than I had imagined.'

'The Emperor will be summoning his armies,' said Max. 'I am sure that come spring he will move to meet the foes.'

'Be that as it may,' said Rudgar. 'None of us will be moving with him.'

Felix felt a vague sense of outrage. Nobles were always ones to talk about their rights and privileges. As he recalled they had some duties too, and one of them was to defend the Empire when called upon to do so. Of all those present it seemed Rodrik was the only one who noticed his looks, and he had the good grace to look embarrassed.

'It is not that we don't want to,' he said quickly. 'I could ask for nothing more than to ride by the Emperor's side into battle but our duty is here with our people. If the undying ones have crept once more from hiding it is our duty to see that they are cast back into the pit from which they crawled.'

The last part of his speech was said with a great deal less confidence than the first part. Felix was not surprised. If his history was correct, the last time the Vampire Counts had risen it had taken all the military might of the Empire and its allies to cast them down, and that had taken many years and the loss of countless lives.

'I agree with young Rodrik,' said the white-haired old Count of Swartzhafen. He coughed dryly once more. 'It will do the Empire no good if the Emperor marches to meet the spawn of Chaos only to find an army of undying ones on his flank. Actually, I fear it would spell disaster.'

Felix was no expert on military matters but it sounded plausible. With such a powerful foe before it, any threat to the Imperial lines of supply or to flanks would be catastrophic. And now he recalled other things about the armies of the Vampire Counts. Their followers tended to be walking corpses animated by the darkest of sorcery. The snows of winter would slow them not at all. Indeed it would be a time when they were at their strongest. Even as they spoke the forces of darkness were gaining a mighty ally.

'The best we can do for the Empire is to smash the undying ones before they grow to their full strength, and then march to the Emperor's aid.'

'Let us pray that is possible,' said the Countess Gabriella. All of them made the sign of the hammer over the table save for Gotrek. He just grunted and took a swig of his wine. She leaned forward over the table and a feral gleam entered her cold blue eyes. 'It seems to me that the gods smile on us. It is not by chance that our friends came here today.'

Felix saw Gotrek and Max turn to look at her. Ivan was deep in his wine but something about his manner told Felix that he too was listening intently. 'What do you mean?' Max asked.

'The name Adolphus Krieger is not unknown to us,' she said.

Max sucked in his breath. 'He is a necromancer?'

'Worse. He is one of the undying ones. A very dangerous progeny of the Carstein bloodline.'

'And what is that exactly?' Felix asked. He felt he had to say something to conceal the fear that swept through him.

Krieger was a vampire! It explained a lot about him: his uncanny quickness, his incredible strength. And maybe there was a connection too between him and the killer who had stalked the streets of Praag, draining bodies of blood. He remembered how Nella, the street girl, had mentioned the smell of cinnamon, and the pomander Krieger had carried in the vault.

The countess's laugh was silvery. 'Forgive me, Herr Jaeger: sitting at this table it is sometimes easy to forget that not everyone shares our obsessive interest in, and knowledge of, the undying ones. If you are a Sylvanian noble, it is something you grow up with.'

'I thought most Sylvanian nobles were vampires,' said Gotrek nastily. It was not the most tactful thing to say but it was what Felix had always heard anyway, although most of his knowledge on the subject had come from a nurse who liked to terrify the children under her care with tales of horror.

In response to the Slayer's words, the temperature at the table seemed to drop. Rodrik's hand stole towards his sword and Felix felt sure that only a cool glare from his father prevented the youth from challenging Gotrek on the spot.

'Your knowledge is a little out of date,' said Baron Leicheburg. He studied the Slayer as if he were a nasty insect that had just crawled onto the table. If Gotrek cared, he gave no sign. He took another swig of the wine and belched loudly. This time it took his father's hand on his shoulder to prevent Rodrik from surging to his feet and issuing a challenge. There was a look of concern on the older man's face. He most likely could guess the outcome of that challenge as well as Felix could.

'I can see you are keen to correct me,' Gotrek said.

'Two centuries ago, you would have been absolutely correct,' said the Count of Swartzhafen. 'Two centuries ago this land lay under the heel of the Vampire Counts and their allies. After Hel Fenn they were… exterminated, and the Emperor gave these lands in fief to trustworthy vassals.'

Felix remembered reading something about the subject in the University Library in Altdorf. The book had said nothing about trustworthy vassals though. It had said that the lands of Sylvania were given to impoverished noble houses, and second sons keen to own land who could not get it any other way. The book implied that you would have to be very desperate indeed to want to rule over any part of the province.

'I have heard tales of vampires in Sylvania far more recently than Hel Fenn,' said Max. 'Reliable sources have informed me they have ruled large tracts of this land until even quite recently. I believe the Templars of the White Wolf besieged Castle Regrak ten years ago when it was discovered that the occupant was a blood drinker.'

'Regrak was a blood drinker,' said the Count of Swartzhafen, 'but he was as mortal as you or me. He merely thought that consuming the blood of virgin youths would keep him young and give him mystical powers. As far as I know it did not. Believe me, if he had been a vampire, the Templars would have had considerably more trouble burning down his manor.'

'Nonetheless, our learned friend is quite correct,' said the countess. 'There have been other instances of the undying ones ruling in Sylvania since Hel Fenn, as we all know only too well. If the number of these instances is less than popular rumour would have the ignorant believe it does not change the essential truth.'

'You haven't answered my original question, countess,' said Felix. He realised from his tone of voice and the slurring of his words that he was actually getting quite drunk. Not surprising really. He had been ill for days, and not taken any wine for the length of their journey. He was out of practice at drinking. 'What did you mean by the Carstein bloodline?'

Again Felix was surprised when Max replied. He could never quite resist showing off his knowledge when given half a chance. 'Scholars of these things believe the undying ones can be… classified is perhaps the best word, into several bloodlines. These are believed to be descendants of the original vampires of the city of Lahmia in the kingdom of Nehekhara created by Nagash over three thousand years ago. Each bloodline is supposed to share some of the traits of its progenitor and to have different strengths and weaknesses depending on its ancestry.'

Felix saw the countess staring at Max with a mixture of amusement, respect and interest. He felt a little jealous. She certainly was a very good-looking woman. Suddenly he felt disgusted with himself. What was he thinking? Ulrika was in the hands of something far worse than a madman and a dark magician, and here he was lusting after another woman. The more cynical part of his mind told him that feeling ashamed would not in any way change the facts of the situation.

'You are a very learned man, Herr Schreiber. I am surprised. These are not matters of common knowledge. We must discuss how you came to acquire such scholarship some time.'

Max nodded his head condescendingly. 'Thank you,' he said. 'I have studied much dark and forbidden lore and–'

'Nonetheless, you are wrong in one or two particulars.'

'Wrong?'

'The vampires were not created by Nagash. They were mighty mages in their own right who acquired some of his knowledge in the long wars of the Dawn Ages.'

Max looked dubious but remained silent.

'That was an age at least as fractious as our own.'

'The Carstein bloodline?' Felix prodded, hoping still to get an answer to his original question.

'It is one of the major vampiric bloodlines,' said the Countess. 'In the Empire it is perhaps *the* major bloodline.'

'The name is certainly the most familiar,' said Felix dryly. 'What with the wars of the Vampire Counts and all.'

'That is why the bloodline is known as the Carstein line. The original Vlad von Carstein was the most famous of all the counts, and popular legend gives his name to all of his progeny.'

'You sound as if you disagree with this?' said Max, ever the scholar, quibbling over a minor point of terminology not discussing a mass murderer whose insane plans of conquest had resulted in the deaths of tens of thousands of people.

The countess gave a small shrug, a gesture Felix associated with the wealthy Bretonnian merchants who often visited his father's premises. 'I do not see that it matters. We know little of von Carstein's antecedents. He was the first of his line who achieved notoriety. Since then, his descendants have been quite active, particularly here in Sylvania.'

'It looks like they have become a lot more active just recently,' said Felix. 'I wonder why.'

'I think that is something we need to find out,' said Count Rudgar. 'Many lives might depend on it.'

Not least our own, thought Felix. He forced himself to concentrate once more in spite of the wine and the heat and the feeling of wellbeing brought on by consuming rich food for the first time after many days of hardship. 'You seem to know a bit about Adolphus Krieger,' he said, trying not to slur his words too much. 'Would you care to share your knowledge with us?'

'Later,' said the countess. 'It's been a long day and I am sure we are all weary. The matter will wait for tomorrow. There are some things best discussed when the sun is high.'

Under the circumstances, Felix could not fault her reasoning.

THE CHAMBER WAS large, chilly and dominated by a huge portrait of a cold-eyed Sylvanian nobleman who seemed to study Felix with murderous intent. Briefly, he considered checking the rooms for secret passages. In the old tales Sylvanian castles were riddled with such things but the room was too cold and he was too drunk to bother. He did take the precaution of latching his door and leaving his sword propped against the wall within easy grasping distance of his bed.

As he drifted off into a cold and fitful sleep, he could have sworn he heard the distant howling of wolves.

SEVEN

IT WAS DARK. The coach slid through the night silently and swiftly. Behind them, the wolves padded along in the snow like wraiths. Their eyes burned. Their breath billowed forth in clouds. They looked at once beaten and fierce. There was something deeply unnatural about them now, as they slid further and further under the domination of the vampire.

Ulrika knew how they felt. She was confused. Her emotions were awhirl and it sometimes seemed to her that the darkness of the night had invaded her mind and her soul. She hated Krieger. She loathed him. He was arrogant, supercilious, sure of himself, domineering, contemptuous of those he deemed beneath him, which consisted of most of the world. She was sure that what he planned was evil, and yet sometimes she wanted to be part of it.

When she stopped to think, she knew that she must get away, that somehow she should escape from the coach and flee or find some way to kill him.

And yet it was impossible. He was too strong, too powerful. Often she had tried to strike him with her knife, and he had taken it from her as an adult might snatch a toy from a child. Twice she had tried to flee over the snows, into the depths of the winter woods. She had raced off, uncaring of whether she died of cold or starvation.

Once he had simply followed her trail, overtaken her in the darkness and carried her back to the coach. She could no more resist being snatched up than a mouse could have resisted a cat. The second time, she thought she had got away clean, but the cold had bitten through the thin clothing she wore, and she had passed out in the snow. She had woken to find herself back in the coach, warmed by some unnatural means, and quite certain that he could have overhauled her at any time, that he was toying with her, that he had let her think she had escaped just to be able to dash her hopes further. The most astonishing thing was that none of the vampire's servants tried to stop her. It was as if they had been commanded not to interfere.

She had kept her eyes peeled for a village where she might break free and find shelter, but they never stopped in one for long, and Roche or the others purchased all of the supplies while she was held immobile in thrall to his master's burning gaze and unnaturally strong grip. She could not even begin to make herself scream or shout for help, and that too made her wonder.

There was a darker side to her captivity, she acknowledged. In the vampire's burning embrace there was an ecstasy the like of which she had never known, a pleasure fiercer than anything she had ever experienced. She had heard that some devotees of the daemon god Slaanesh became addicted to certain drugs and became completely dependent on them. She was starting to suspect that she knew how they felt. There were times when she found herself looking forward to the coming of night with longing, and times when she was disappointed when Krieger did not wish to sip her blood. There were times when she felt jealous when she saw him descend from the coaches of one of his followers, with that sleepy sated look on his face.

And worse yet, she suspected that he knew this. Certainly the amused glances he gave her implied as much as his talk. He seemed very certain of this; very sure, as if he had done this hundreds of times before, and watched hundreds of women become his mindless slaves.

That thought brought a spark of resistance to her mind. She was not going to be anybody's mindless servant. She was not going to become his willing victim. If he thought she would, he was in for a surprise. Some way, somehow, she would find her way out of this trap and then…

And then what? There were other things to be considered as well. She was a long way from home, with no money or equipment or friends. She was sure they were in the wicked land of Sylvania now, a place of dark legends – not a place to be stranded alone in the depths of winter. There were the wolves loping along steadily behind them. Without Krieger's protection they might well tear her limb from limb. She glanced out into the gloom and saw Krieger there, striding along among them, a predator among predators.

With the sight of him, the darkness in her thoughts returned, and with the darkness, temptation. Of late he had taken to talking to her more softly, of offering her things. Not bribes, not gold or jewels, but power and immortality. He did it in a mocking, teasing way, so she could never be sure whether he meant it, or merely intended to torment her before killing her.

She was not interested in such offers, she told herself. She did not want to become immortal at the price of her soul. She did not want to unnaturally prolong her life at the cost of others' blood. She had no desire to learn the darkest secrets of sorcery. No. She wanted none of these things. There was no temptation there.

But at times she had found herself considering things. If she became immortal, she could some day become his equal, she could learn his secrets, and make her escape or extract her revenge. Unlife would eventually grant her that power, she was sure. That was the only real temptation there, or so she tried to convince herself. Unfortunately, she was not sure it was exactly true.

Sometimes when he talked, he seemed to be giving her glimpses into a greater, darker world, one possessed of an ancient and terrible beauty, ruled over by an aristocracy of the night, who held court in shadowed palaces, served by legions of more than willing servants. He talked of the far places he had been, and the things he had seen there, more places than any mortal could visit in a lifetime she was sure.

He had seen the Land of the Dead, and the great Black Pyramid of Nagash at midnight. He had heard the whisperings of the dead men as they stirred within the tomb cities. He had visited the edges of the Realms of Chaos and they seemed to hold no terrors for him. He had visited Bretonnia, Estalia, Tilea and every one of the known lands of men. He had talked with famous painters, and poets, as well as kings and queens and lesser rulers. He had discussed philosophy with Neumann, and playwriting and poetry with von Diehl and Sierck and Tarradasch.

He possessed a knowledge and a sophistication that made every man she had ever met seem shallow and venal. Even Max did not possess his depth of knowledge. Of course, she thought, Max had not stolen centuries of lives from innocents to acquire his scholarship either.

Krieger strode up to the side of the coach and wrenched the door open. The night's chill entered with him. He reached out and touched her cheek with one icy hand. She flinched away but not as quickly as she would have liked.

'Have you thought about the question I asked?'

'You are not a teacher and I am not your pupil,' she said. 'I do not need to answer any of your questions.'

He smiled, showing teeth like any normal mortal's. The killing fangs were still retracted. 'I did not ask you to answer. I asked you to think about it,' he said quietly. 'Actually, I know you have thought about it. How could you not?'

Again that smug self-assurance, again that certainty that she could not but do what he wanted. The annoying thing was that he was right. He had a way of putting things that, combined with the situation itself, made it impossible not to think about what he wanted her to. Once again she felt like a fly snared in a particularly strong and subtly woven web. She ignored him, knowing that to say anything would be to grant him another victory. He shrugged and glanced out of the window into the moonlight.

Despite her efforts to keep them out, the questions he had asked her blazed through her brain. It was as if his presence transmitted them into her mind by some mystical power. He had asked her what the difference was between him and her. He preserved his life by taking the life of mortals. She preserved hers by taking the lives of cattle, birds and other living things.

The answer had seemed so simple at first. He killed people, sentient things with loves and hates and thoughts and passions. He had asked her how she could not be certain that animals did not feel the same things. After all, once she had said her old dog had understood her.

'Are you prepared to kill to defend yourself or your family? You don't need to answer. I already know what you will say.' She spoke just to be contradictory. 'Of course I would.'

'What is the difference between doing that and killing to prolong your life?'

'The difference is that I would not be the aggressor. I would be defending myself.'

'What about to protect your land?'

'I would fight to protect it.'

'So you are saying you value your land more highly than another person's life.'

'If they tried to take my land, yes.' He shook his head and gave her a mocking smile.

'And if your allies call on you to fight, you would kill to protect their lands?'

'I would be honour bound to.'

'So now your honour is worth more than another person's life. I think I am more honest than you. I can truthfully say I value my existence more highly than I value theirs.'

'That is your privilege,' she said. 'What happens when you run into someone who feels the same way about you?'

'You already know the answer.'

Ulrika fell silent. She knew his questions were just another one of his games, designed to make her feel inferior and weak, to break down her resistance. She could not understand why he bothered, other than perhaps because he got some sick sadistic pleasure from it.

She did not regard herself as having a particularly philo-sophical turn of mind. Such a thing was hardly a necessity for the daughter of a frontier nobleman of Kislev. All she needed to be able to do was manage an estate and wield a weapon, not be able to answer complex ethical riddles. She felt out of her depth here, confronted with a puzzle that was way beyond all her previous experience.

She was willing to admit that eternal life and eternal youth were not without their attractions. But the price being asked here was too high.

Beside her, Adolphus Krieger smiled as if he knew exactly what she was thinking.

She really wished to put a dagger through his heart at that moment, but she suspected that if she could, it would make no difference. He seemed so invulnerable.

MAX WATCHED THE sun rise from the walls of Walden-schlosse. It did not cheer him. The meat he had eaten last night sat in his stomach as if made of lead. The weakness he had felt since recovering from his investigation of the Eye of Khemri stayed with him. He summoned a splinter of power, and wrapped himself in it, to keep out the chill, to warm himself. His old masters would have shuddered to see him use power in such a way but, right at this moment, he did not care.

The warmth spread over his skin and brought a flush to his cheeks but it did not touch his heart. It was no wonder; the view from the castle was enough to chill the blood of any man. The keep stood atop a great rocky crag. As the shadows of night retreated he saw the corpse of the town. That was the best way he could describe the ruined and half-deserted township. Waldenhof seemed less like a living city than a prison or a camp in which the refugees of some terri-ble disaster huddled, waiting for the next dreadful doom to descend on them.

In the distance, beyond the tumbled-down town walls, lay a seemingly endless dark forest. There was a brooding sense of presence about it, as if ancient evil things still lurked there, waiting to strike. It was said the woods of Sylvania had been a haven for creatures of darkness since the time of Sigmar. Max found it easy to believe. Not even the plumes of smoke rising from the snow-covered hovels below reassured him much. The town looked even less prepossessing by daylight than it had the night before.

Max had thought he would have slept well last night. After all, he had had a real bed and a real room heated by a real fireplace. He had not done so. His sleep had been full of nightmares. His body had become so accustomed to hard ground that he had constantly shifted on his mattress in a futile search for rest. The room had seemed stuffy and it had been hard to breathe. Perhaps he was becoming ill, but his routine monitoring of his physical health had shown no signs of it. His protective spells seemed to be working. He doubted if he was coming down with a flux or plague. It must simply be worry and exhaustion.

He invoked the location spell on the Eye of Khemri. It had stopped moving, as it often did at this time of day. Well, at least he had answered one mystery. If Krieger were a blood drinker, that would explain why he travelled mostly at night. Max prayed that finally the vampire had reached his goal and they would soon overtake him. It seemed logical that they would: Sylvania was most likely his destination. The question was, what horror did he plan when he reached his eventual goal? He surely intended to use the Eye for some unspeakable purpose.

Max saw Felix emerge onto the battlements. He looked considerably the worse for wear. He was pale and sweating, despite the cold. His hair was lank and his beard unkempt. The tattered red cloak was drawn tight about his shoulders. He gave a great hacking cough that made his whole body shudder. He shuffled along the battlements towards Max like an old man, moving very cautiously. The wizard was not surprised. The stone was slippery, and it was a long drop to the hard flagstones of the courtyard below.

'Morning, Max, you're up early,' he said. His voice was hoarse, and Max was sure he could hear a wheezing noise coming from his chest.

'I did not sleep well.'

Felix smiled. 'You look how I feel.'

'I could say the same about you,' said Max.

'This is a depressing place.'

'You can say that again.'

'And it's a depressing time. The winter is deep. The hordes of Chaos are on the march. The forces of the undead muster, and we're right in the middle of it. It's funny – when I was a child I always wanted to have adventures like the ones I read about in books. Now I find myself having adventures and I wish I was a child back in my father's house again.'

'These are dark times,' said Max. To his surprise, Felix burst out laughing, and kept laughing till his mirth ended in a spasm of coughing. 'What was that about?' Max asked.

'You really do sound just like a wizard should sometimes, Max. Would you care to make some ominous prophesies now?'

'I don't think you are in the right frame of mind for them. Maybe I will wait till it's dark and the wolves are howling outside. Maybe then you'll shiver appropriately at my oracular pronouncements.'

'I think I'm shivering quite enough at the moment.'

Max turned and looked away towards the horizon. In the distance, he could see a huge plume of dark smoke rising. 'What is that?' he asked. He answered his own question. 'Most likely just the fire from some townsman's hut.'

Felix shook his head. 'No. The billows are too big and too dark. It's no normal fire. Not unless he has set fire to his whole street in an effort to keep warm. Not that I would blame him if he had.'

A horn sounded from one of the nearby watchtowers. The call echoed through the courtyard and was answered from other towers.

'It would seem we are not the only ones who have noticed,' said Felix.

Within minutes, a company of men-at-arms had assembled in the courtyard. 'I suppose we had better go and help them investigate,' said Felix without much enthusiasm. He coughed long and hard before shuffling towards the stairs.

Even as Max watched a mass of people appeared before the castle, emerging from the tumbled down streets of the decaying city. They looked as if they had been running for their lives. There were raggedly clad men, women clutching babies to their breasts, and small children. A few of the men clutched pitchforks and other weapons. Some had pitifully small sacks over their shoulders that Max guessed held a few possessions. All of them seemed to be scared. The villagers in the huts below emerged from their homes to meet them. After a few seconds of chatter they began to shout for their masters to open the gates.

'IT SEEMS THERE has been another raid in the night,' said the countess. She strode over and glanced at Max and Felix. Max looked at her. She was pale and very beautiful, very much the languid aristocrat, and there was something about her that he disliked. 'Rudgar and his men will ride out and investigate, although I doubt that they will find anything. The creatures will have melted away into the woods by now. They always do. They are very good at it.'

Even as she spoke, Rudgar, Rodrik and a group of knights thundered past, going hell for leather through the snow into the woods, looking for all the world as if they were out hunting. A few even let out wild whoops of excitement, and blew upon their horns exactly as if going to hounds. Max was not too impressed by their grasp of tactics. Why warn your foes that you are coming? He had never suspected the count and his son as being the brightest of men and here was proof of it. Gotrek and Snorri Nosebiter were stomping down the stairs now, hefting their weapons and looking as cheerful as men on their way to an Elector countess's ball.

'Better hurry,' he said ironically. 'Otherwise you'll miss the battle.'

The two grinned as if he was not being sarcastic and began trotting in the direction of the smoke. Felix coughed behind his hand, and began to move off too. Max supposed he had to fill the conditions of his oath.

'Wait,' said the countess. 'Get horses from the stable. We'll all get there quicker.' Max noticed that he seemed to have been included in that. He found himself moving towards the stables almost automatically. There was something very subtly commanding about the countess.

IT WAS A twenty minute ride through the snow-covered streets to where the outskirts of the city touched the woods. All around rotting buildings loomed, frightened people glancing out from shadowy doorways. Max's breath steamed in the air. The horse raced along smoothly underneath him, great muscles bunching and uncoiling. Riding was exhilarating, and he thought he might be able to understand the behaviour of the young nobles earlier.

'Your face is very grim, Herr Schreiber,' said Countess Gabriella. 'Any particular reason, or are you always this way?'

Max forced himself to smile, and to relax a little. He might not like the countess much, but there was no need to be rude. It served little purpose. And really, who was he to judge her? He hardly knew the woman, after all.

'I am worried. About Ulrika and about Adolphus Krieger.'

'You have every reason to be. He is a very wicked man.'

Max glanced over at her. In the cold clear morning light, he could see that she was not as young as he had first thought. Over the veil, small lines were visible at the corner of her eyes. Expertly applied make-up almost concealed them but they were there. And there was a sheen to her black hair that suggested to Max that it was dyed. She was older than he was by ten years at least, he guessed.

'Are you talking from personal experience?' Max was not sure why he said that, the words just slipped out. He could see Felix give him a warning look. Perhaps his tone had been a bit insensitive, he thought, but he could not help it. The woman brought out the worst in him for some reason.

'You could say that,' she said. 'He is an old enemy of my husband's family. Or rather, they are old enemies of his.'

'Why?'

'The Emperor granted us the castle that he had occupied before the Wars of the Vampire Counts, before everyone knew what he was. He resented that a great deal, and he swore to take it back and have revenge on my husband's entire line.'

'He certainly knows how to hold a grudge,' said Felix. There was a note of mild irony in his voice.

'You don't understand, Herr Jaeger. You have no comprehension of the way the undying ones think. They look like mortals, but they are not like mortals. They are not sane, as you would judge sanity. What they are twists their minds. They are no more comprehensible to most people than a spider would be, if we could read its thoughts.'

'That's an uncomfortable idea,' said Felix, and the tone of irony was gone.

'The undying ones are disturbing things. They are predators and mortals are their prey. They are driven by needs and drives that are incomprehensible to the living.'

Max fought down a shiver. Somewhere out there Ulrika was in the hands of a creature like this, and that was the best he could hope for, if the thing had not simply slain her out of hand and drunk her blood to sustain its unnatural existence. Somewhere deep in his heart red-hot anger began to blaze. If that had happened Adolphus Krieger would pay; it would not matter how long it took, Max would hunt him down and make an end of him. It did not matter how powerful the creature thought he was, he would discover there were other powers in this world.

Max reached out and touched the weave of his location spell again. It was still there. He could still feel it. Suddenly, he just wanted to be away from here, for the chase to be on once more. They were wasting time here. Every heartbeat might prove vital. He pushed the thoughts back. This woman could tell him things that might help. It was always best to know your enemy, particularly if they were as powerful and dangerous as he feared Adolphus Krieger might be. Surely remaining here for a few more hours would not make that much difference. Just the extra rest would let them move faster over the next few days. Surely that alone would make this delay worthwhile.

He tried to convince himself, but he still felt guilty. 'Tell me more of Adolphus Krieger,' he said.

'Little enough is known of him. He was one of von Carstein's most trusted minions. He led armies in the field for him during the Winter War. It is said even von Carstein feared him. He vanished after Hel Fenn. Many thought he had perished with the other undying ones. My husband's family did not.'

'Why?'

'Things happened. My kinfolk died under mysterious circumstances, and always after reports of someone who looked like Krieger had been spotted in the area. Some thought his ghost had returned to haunt the family. Others knew he still existed and was taunting them. The undying ones can afford to take a long time over their revenges, and they like to spin these things out. Compared to them a cat toying with a mouse is merciful.'

She spoke on, telling bloodcurdling tales of Krieger's misdeeds, and anecdotes from her family history. As Max listened he began to build a picture of Krieger that chilled the blood. And this was the man who had Nagash's amulet! Putting aside rescuing Ulrika it occurred to Max that it would be a very bad thing to allow the Eye of Khemri to stay within his clutches.

Felix listened to Max and Gabriella talk as he rode. His cough was worse. His lungs felt clogged but he managed to stay upright on the horse. He kept his eyes peeled studying the surroundings. If there were beastmen about, he wanted to see them before they saw him. These half-abandoned streets were perfect for an ambush. Idly he wondered where the Slayers were. They had not overtaken them on the road, but he would not have put it past Gotrek and Snorri to have taken a shortcut.

His nostrils twitched. From up ahead he could smell burning. It seemed that they were closer than he had thought. A pity. He had a few questions he wanted to ask of the Countess Gabriella. She seemed the best informed of all the Sylvanian nobles, although he supposed it was quite likely that any of them could answer his questions. There was a lot he wanted to know about the undying ones, and the Carstein bloodline, particularly since he felt a cold certainty that one of these nights he was going to find himself in some out of the way place hunting Krieger or others of his ilk. Such episodes had all too frequently punctuated his career as the Slayer's henchman.

He wanted to know how many of the tales concerning vampires were true and how many were old wives' tales, and it seemed to him that the Sylvanians were best placed to be able to answer them. No time like the present, he told himself.

'Countess, is it true that the undying ones are much stronger than ordinary men, strong enough to rip a man's heart out with their bare hands?'

If Max was displeased with this interruption he did not let it show. He looked at the countess expectantly. She considered for a moment.

'Some of them certainly are. Krieger is… if the old tales are to be believed.'

Wonderful, thought Felix. I stood in a room with a man capable of rending my flesh with his bare hands, and I was quite prepared to fight him. I may have to do so again.

'Why do you say "some of them"?' Max asked. It was a good question, and Felix wished he had thought of it.

'The undying ones vary in their characteristics far more than humans. You hear many stories of them, and it's a certainty that all of them have some basis in fact. It's just that not every tale holds true of every blood drinker.'

'Can you give me an example?'

'They are said to be unable to abide the sign of the hammer, or to pass any window barred with daemonroot. In some cases this is true. There are documented reports of the undying fleeing from priests of Sigmar when presented with holy symbols. But equally there are believable accounts of them tearing apart priests who confronted them, and trampling on the holy signs and laughing.'

'I would be surprised if these tales involved the same vampire though,' said Max. The countess looked at him with some respect. Felix wondered what the wizard's point was. He wished his head did not hurt quite so much. He wished the motion of the horse did not make him quite so nauseous.

'You would mostly be correct, Herr Schreiber. And where the stories do overlap there is always the possibility of confusion.'

'There are some simple possible explanations,' said Max. 'Such things might be completely dependent on what the individual creature itself believes. It happens all the time with wizards. Some can only cast spells when they have their favourite staff. Some believe implicitly that their spells will have no effect on certain things like priests or people bearing the sign of the hammer and, strangely, this is the case. Even though other wizards have no difficulty doing this whatsoever. Magic is in many ways as much about confidence and willpower as it is about tapping the currents of magic, and certainly the undying ones must be even more steeped in magic than even wizards.'

'You are referring to Karel Lazlo's theory of belief systems,' said the countess. Max smiled.

'I would have thought I was the only person in a hundred leagues to know about that book, much less to have read it.'

'In Sylvania we know the utility of much strange lore, and we set ourselves to acquiring it.'

Felix's head reeled but he still had questions he wanted answered and he wasn't about to let these two get sidetracked into some long-winded discussion of what some centuries' dead philosopher thought, no matter how much it might have interested him under normal circumstances.

'Is it true they die if exposed to sunlight?' he asked, once again forcing his way into the conversation.

'Again it varies,' said the countess. 'Some become very badly burned by daylight, some die, some seem able to bear it without major damage. All accounts agree, though, that unless they have just consumed a great deal of blood, or enhanced their powers with magic, that they are considerably less formidable during daylight. No one knows why.'

'I have read that some of them are capable of going abroad by daylight even, provided they protect their skins from exposure,' said Max. The countess adjusted her veil and looked at him.

'That is most likely true too.'

Felix wondered how much of what he thought he knew about the creatures was true and how much of it was conditional, or applied only to some and not to others, or was merely an old wives' tale? He pushed on.

'Can they fly or transform themselves into bats or wolves or other animals? I have read that they can.'

Both Max and the countess stared at him for long moments in silence. He could not make up his mind whether they were giving his question serious consideration or looking at him as if he were an idiot, but he met their gaze evenly. His question was not stupid if his life might depend on the answer. Eventually the countess spoke, 'It is said that there were some of the Carstein bloodline who could transform themselves into creatures of the night.'

Max considered for a while. 'There is no reason why it should not be possible. Some wizards can manage the same trick using certain transformational spells. I have never seen it done, but I see no reason to doubt that it is possible. Many strange things are given the proper application of the correct forces.'

Things were looking worse and worse, Felix thought. It was possible that Krieger possessed all the powers that legend ascribed to the blood drinkers, and it was equally possible that none of the protections of which the tales spoke might work against him. He tried telling himself that he was looking at things in the worst of all possible lights but often in the past the worst had happened, so this was no comfort.

Where was Gotrek, Felix wondered? The power of that ancient axe would certainly be a reassuring thing to have around right now.

THE BUILDING STILL burned as they rode up to it. Thick oily clouds of smoke rose from the peat walls of the nearest huts. Felix had heard the living conditions of the peasants in Sylvania were even more squalid than those of such people elsewhere, and here was evidence of it before his very eyes. Farmers around Altdorf kept pigs in sties that looked more inhabitable than some of these huts must have been.

Felix had heard that things were hard in Sylvania, and that the lives of the peasants here were bywords for brutishness. Looking at this he could believe it. He had never seen dwellings so small and squalid. The peasants who had come filtering back when they realised the knights had arrived were smaller, thinner and more unhealthy looking than any human beings Felix had ever seen, and most of them bore pockmarks or possessed wall eyes or the look of congenital idiocy. Was there something in the soil here that twisted human life, he wondered?

He had not realised he had spoken out loud until he saw Max looking at him. 'The taint of dark magic is very strong in Sylvania,' said the wizard. 'And the soil was said to have been contaminated terribly by the warpstone starfall that preceded the Great Plague of 1111. Maybe that has affected the people, although this is probably neither the time nor the place to speak of it.'

Felix nodded his head. He had visited the Chaos Wastes and thought that there could be no worse place in the world, but now he was starting to have his doubts. The mark of darkness was much more obvious in the Wastes, but in some way the very familiarity of Sylvania made it seem worse. This was part of the Empire. These people were citizens of his native land and yet ruinous magic had tainted their lives in many ways and on many levels. He wondered what his own life would have been like if he had been born here.

Thinking of the somewhat eccentric appearance and manner of the nobles he had met, he wondered if they were at all different from their people. Perhaps they were changed on the inside the way these folks had been altered on the outside. Perhaps there was some truth in all those tales of madness set in this accursed province. He shook his head. He was making too many assumptions based on too few facts. He was letting the depressing atmosphere of this decaying place get to him.

He rode up to where some of the villagers were prodding a corpse. Or what at first looked like a corpse. He looked again, reined the horse in and dismounted then shouldered his way through the small knot of people around the body.

Maybe once it had been human, although it must have been a very lean and evil-looking man. He prodded it with his boot and the head rolled to one side. The face was shocking, as much for the ways in which it resembled a man as for the ways it did not. The skin was greyish and flaky with an oddly reptilian quality although Felix could not quite put his finger on what made it so.

The yellowish eyes were much larger than normal, and seemed to bulge out of their sockets so that the eyelids could not contain them. The face was very long, and very lean, and the jaw was very narrow. The mouth grinning in death's rictus was full of teeth that were discoloured and far too sharp. The nails on the hands were long and claw-like.

'What is it?' he asked quietly.

'It's a ghoul, manling,' said Gotrek, the crowd parting around him. 'An eater of manflesh.'

Felix was sickened. Like all the citizens of the Empire he had heard tales of these foul cannibals who gorged themselves on the meat of corpses but he had never really expected to encounter one.

'Goetz killed it yer honour, wiv 'is pitchfork,' said one of the peasants. 'Just afore two o' this thing's mates grabbed 'im an' made off. I guess we'll find his bones cracked for marrow one o' these days.'

Now, Felix really did feel nauseous. It was disturbing enough to see the bones of those who had been killed and eaten by beastmen, but if legends were correct this ghoul here had once been human till he developed a taste for forbidden meat.

'Look's a bit like Wilhelm, this one,' said another peasant with a sort of dull curiosity. 'I always did wonder what 'appened to 'im.'

'You're saying you knew this thing?' said Felix incredulously.

'Maybe. Wouldn't be the first around here to try a bit of sweet pork if you get my drift. Winter is long and sometimes food is scarce. Who can afford the butcher's bill?'

Felix did not know what horrified him more, the information the man had imparted or the casual way he had said it. Seeing Felix looking at him askance, the man flinched and added, 'Not that I've ever tried it myself, you understand.'

The thunder of hooves announced the arrival of Rudgar. 'These creatures are either very desperate or very confident to be attacking the town itself.'

The Countess Gabriella's voice was chill. 'I fear they are growing very confident.'

At that moment, the ghoul's eyes flickered open and it let out a chilling malevolent laugh. 'The Time of Blood is here,' it cackled and lunged upward at Felix. Before he even had time to step back, Gotrek's axe had parted the thing's head from its shoulders. There was surprisingly little blood.

The peasants had fallen back muttering with horror, making the sign of the hammer, and other wards that Felix did not recognise. 'The thing was dead, I knows it was,' said the peasant who had spoken of sweet pig.

'It is now,' said Gotrek and spat on the headless corpse.

'IT CERTAINLY LOOKED dead when I poked it with my boot,' said Felix, as they strode through the ruins at the edge of town. Here the walls were almost the height of four men and tipped with spikes in places. Of course, in other places there were huge gaps, where the stonework had tumbled and not been rebuilt. It was easy to see how the things had got in.

'Anyone can make a mistake, manling,' said Gotrek.

'It might have been dead,' said Max. 'Perhaps there was some residue of dark magic left within it, which allowed it to come back to a semblance of life one last time.'

'Maybe,' said the Slayer. 'Or maybe it was just wounded and faking.'

'You're most probably right,' said Max, but he still sounded a little dubious. Felix wondered if the atmosphere of this place was starting to get to the wizard as well. Normally Max Schreiber was quite sceptical.

'Vampires, ghouls, beastmen; what next?' muttered Felix.

'Some of these peasants look like they might want a good meal of sweet pork,' said the Slayer nastily.

'They just look like they could use a good meal,' said Felix.

'No need to concern yourself with these scum,' boomed Rodrik, striding up the muddy street. He had obviously overheard. 'They will get by. Their sort always does. Most likely have a whole sackful of turnips they should have used for taxes buried in their midden piles.'

'A whole sackful? Of turnips?' said Felix softly. His irony was obviously lost on the young knight who just nodded sagely.

'These villains are scum, pure and simple. Steal their liege lords blind, rob a passing stranger for his shoes and use them to make soup. If you don't treat them with the lash they'll go right back to their old ways. They were too long under the Vampire Counts.'

Too long under the likes of you more like, thought Felix, all the reasons why he disliked the aristocracy of his homeland coming flooding back to him. He gazed at the young knight with unconcealed distaste. If Rodrik noticed he gave no sign of it.

'There's nothing much more we can do here. Best get back to the schloss,' said Rodrik.

Felix nodded. They had better things to do than stick around and help this upper class brute oppress the peasants. Still, he had to admit, some of the peasants were looking at him rather hungrily.

MAX WAS HAPPY to be back on the road again, though less than pleased that Countess Gabriella had decided to accompany them, with Rodrik and his fellows as escort. It seemed that their routes ran together for many leagues. If what the countess claimed about Krieger having a claim on her husband's lands was true, then perhaps they might find themselves allies.

The conference of nobles had ended inconclusively. They had agreed to send aid to one another if attacked, but it seemed that the plan was mostly to remain within their castles till the end of winter and then summon their vassals and muster their armies to scour the land. In truth, there was very little else for them to do. Armies would not be able to march in the deep winter and keeping any large force supplied would be next to impossible. Only the desperate or the driven would be abroad now. Max smiled grimly. People like ourselves in other words. And those in the service of the dark powers, he added after a moment's consideration.

He wondered how much chance the Sylvanian nobles really had against any force Krieger might muster. Max doubted that it was good. This was a poor, infertile land, and could not support many people. The size of the nobles' forces was considerably smaller than any that might be mustered elsewhere in the Empire. He doubted that all of the rulers at the meeting at Waldenschlosse together could muster as many troops as the city guard of Praag. That was not an encouraging thought either.

There had been some talk of hiring mercenaries as well but Max doubted that anything would come of it. No mercenary in his right mind would want to come to Sylvania for the sums these impoverished nobles would offer, and even if they did most would, doubtless, soon be far more lucratively employed by the Emperor in the campaign against Chaos.

Max dismissed these thoughts and gave his attention to his surroundings. Snow crunched beneath the hooves of the ponies. The Kislevite warriors rode in a column, silently scanning their surroundings with wary eyes. Max did not blame them for their low spirits. He himself had never seen a more ominous-looking wood. The trees were sickly and, where not covered in snow, were blotched with some sort of parasitic mould that glowed in the shadows. The place was oppressive and deathly quiet save for the sounds made by the advancing party.

He shivered. This was the road to Drakenhof, a place with as bad a reputation as any in the world. At Drakenhof, the scourge of the Vampire Counts had first arisen. At Drakenhof, the first of the infamous von Carsteins had raised his banner and proclaimed himself ruler of Sylvania. The castle itself was said to have been built on a particularly ill-omened site, a nexus of terrible dark magical energies, a place so woven around by evil protective spells that any

mortal who spent time there went insane. It was said that
the siege engineers who had been set the task of destroying
the place by the Emperor Joachim had gone mad, and
devoured each other. All things considered, it was not a
place he was keen to visit. Unfortunately it seemed likely to
be the ultimate destination of Adolphus Krieger. It was a disturbing thought.

At least, whatever else they might have been, the folk back
at Waldenschlosse had been generous with their supplies.
They had replenished the stores of grain and hard tack on the
wagons out of their own meagre stocks. They had an ulterior
motive, Max supposed. If this expedition had even the faintest
chance of ridding them of Krieger then it was worth their
while supporting it. Judging by the looks they had received, as
they rode out, not too many rated their chances highly.

Max had other reasons to be grateful. While at the keep he
had taken advantage of the library and learned a great deal
of obscure knowledge concerning Sylvania and the Vampire
Counts. The family chronicles of noble houses here were for
the most part as dry and dull as those of aristocratic families
elsewhere but some surprising nuggets of information could
show up.

Mannfred von Carstein had had the whole approach to
Drakenhof lined with the crucified forms of his enemies.
One dark autumn evening he had them all set alight to illuminate his triumphal procession into the town. Many of the
victims had still been alive when the torch had been set to
their oil-soaked bodies. What sort of maniac would do that
sort of thing, Max wondered?

Unfortunately, the answer was all too obvious, when dealing with members of the Carstein bloodline. There seemed
to be something tainted in that brood, as if an ancient curse
of madness inevitably descended on its members. Not that
any of the undying ones were exactly sane. From his other
readings, Max knew that almost all of the bloodlines suffered this in some way. Max wondered if the vampires would
see it that way though.

How could he judge? Their lives were so long and their
perspectives so skewed by what they were that maybe to

them their behaviour was normal. If you had lived for centuries by treating people as cattle then maybe using them as
torches would seem natural. Somehow Max could not quite
convince himself of this. He thought it far more likely that
the creatures were so saturated by dark magic that their
minds and their souls, if they still had any, were warped by
it. It was a well documented process that occurred to dark
magicians and those who trafficked with the Ruinous Powers. There was no reason to assume that vampires were
immune; quite the opposite, in fact.

Max did not know where all of this speculation was leading him except perhaps to the fact that he knew several
spells of unbinding and dissipation against dark magic, and
that these might prove most useful against a creature which
owed its existence in part to those baneful energies. In some
ways too this was a tactical problem. If Krieger was one of
those who were affected by sunlight then Max knew several
spells for replicating the effect of the sun too. Those might
prove very handy as well. This was a problem that needed to
be considered from all angles. The stakes were too high to
allow for any errors of judgement. Not only his life but
Ulrika's and all of their party's might depend on such things.

'So, YOU HAVE written poetry?' asked the Countess Gabriella.
Felix nodded, wondering why she had asked him to join her.
Surely she had not asked him here simply to discuss poesy.
He glanced out into the gathering gloom before nodding.
Rodrik rode along beside the coach. He caught Felix's eye
upon him and glanced back with a look that could only be
described as jealous. Felix turned to look away. The last
thing he wanted was any trouble with the hotheaded young
noble.

He felt quite sleepy. The motion of the coach on its runners was lulling him into a daze. The countess's coach was
warm and the cushioned leather seats a lot more comfortable than the hard bench on the supply sledge. The countess
herself was far more pleasant company than the Slayer,
although that wasn't saying much since, on most days, so
was a dead badger. To be fair to the woman, she was a lot

better company than most people he knew – witty, erudite and charming.

'And where was it published?' He looked over at her. Behind her veil her eyes seemed to glitter in the dim light. The subtle, spicy smell of her perfume filled the coach's interior.

'In Altdorf, by the Altdorf Press. In their anthologies of new Imperial poetry for the most part.'

'So you wrote it in Imperial, not Classical.'

'It's the modern manner,' said Felix, a little defensively. Like most educated men he could read and write quite competently in the old tongue if he had to, but the idea of writing poetry in it had no great appeal. Too many of the great masters had used the language, and that invited unfavourable comparisons. 'Most publishers these days are aiming at the vernacular audience. It's larger.'

'Quite,' said the countess, a little sharply. 'But Classical is a much more elegant language, don't you think?' There was something a little challenging in her tone. Felix felt as if he were being quizzed by his professors back at the university.

'I don't know that I agree,' he said. 'I think it's the choice of words that makes a statement elegant, if that's what you wish, rather than the language it's written in. Certainly I can think of just as many bad poems written in Classical as Imperial. More, actually, since it was the language of scholars and poets for so much longer.'

'Interesting,' she said. 'You are a most unusual young man, Herr Jaeger, with an original turn of thought.'

Felix looked at her to see if she was being ironic. He had just told her what most intellectuals and professors would have told her. It had been something of an orthodoxy for the past twenty-five years. Yet there was no trace of mockery in her voice or manner. He supposed it was possible. Sylvania was after all a backwater place, far from the mainstream of intellectual life. Most of the books back in the Waldenschlosse library had been hand-written, copied by scribes rather than set in movable type. Considering the explosion in publishing since Johannes of Marienburg introduced his printing machine over a century ago that was unusual. Felix had heard someone say more books were now printed in any given year than had been scribed in all of Imperial history before the introduction of printing, and more new books were published in any year than had been written in any previous century. He did not know if that was true, but it certainly sounded correct to him.

He mentioned this to the countess just for something to say.

'Yes,' she said. 'Things used to be so different. Once you could keep up with all the new trends in literature and philosophy and natural philosophy. Now, sadly it's impossible. The world is racing forward at a much faster pace, and I fear it's rushing headlong toward no good final destination.'

She sounded very definite about that. 'I think the expansion of knowledge is a good thing,' said Felix. 'I think the more we can learn the better.'

She sighed. 'The confidence of youth.'

Felix was not sure he liked her tone. He did not feel very young these days. He worried that his experiences had aged him prematurely. The countess continued speaking as if she had not noticed his frosty look, although he was certain that she had. She was a very observant woman.

'Do you think it's good that knowledge of the dark cults is spreading? Or that soon the secrets of the darkest sorcery will be available to any lout who can read, where once they were the preserve of those who knew their dangers and their costs?'

'The wizards' guilds and the temples still hold their secrets close,' said Felix. 'So do the engineers and the alchemists.'

'How much longer do you think that will continue? How much longer do you think the world has?'

That was a fair question, Felix thought. He had seen the armies of Chaos on the march. It was all too likely that they were living in the final days. All the bright promise of natural philosophy and magical research might well never be fulfilled. Instead, the whole of the Old World might be ground under the iron-shod hooves of the Chaos hordes. Still, you could hardly blame the spread of printing for that. The countess watched him intently, as if deeply interested in his answer.

Felix felt as if he should say something reassuring, that the Emperor would triumph, and everything would turn out all right in the end, but he had seen too much to believe it. The forces of Chaos might have been halted at Praag but that was a temporary setback for them. They would soon recover and push ever deeper into the lands of men.

'I don't know,' he said eventually. 'These are dark times.'

'Darker than you think,' she said.

FELIX CLAMBERED DOWN from the coach, oddly disturbed by his conversations with the Countess Gabriella. She had a way of making him think about the things he did not want to, and she was a very erudite woman in her old-fashioned way. She seemed particularly interested in him as well, and he was not sure why. He would have said it was in the normal way a woman was interested in a man, and yet there was a reserve about her, a holding back, a quality of waiting and watching and judging so intense that it seemed abnormal. A most peculiar woman, he decided, trudging back through the snow to the supply sledge.

He drew his cloak tight against the wind. At least he felt a little better. His nose had stopped running, his cough no longer scourged his body and brought tears to his eyes, and he was not quite as feverish as he had been. Perhaps the stay at the castle had done him some good after all.

He clambered back up onto the sledge beside Gotrek and took the reins of the pony.

'Best be careful, manling. There's a fellow who looks like he might want to slip a dagger into your back.' The Slayer sounded amused in his own bleak fashion. Felix glanced around and saw Rodrik glaring at him, his handsome face contorted by what might almost have been hatred. It looked as if Rodrik were jealous of the time he had spent with the countess.

'Rodrik's too honourable to put a knife into my back,' Felix muttered.

'He might try a sword into your belly then.'

Felix laughed. 'I don't think now is the time to be fighting duels for the hand of the countess.'

'He might disagree with you.'

'I'll worry about it if it happens.' The Slayer chuckled maliciously. 'Might be too late by then.'

'It smells a bit fusty,' said Roche.

Adolphus Krieger looked around the entrance hall of Drakenhof. It looked good. His servants had undone some of the damage done by those vandals two centuries ago. The scorched walls had been rebuilt, the vegetation clogging the gateways had been removed and the huge tree growing through the roof had been chopped down. A fire burned in the hearth. He did not need the heat but he liked the look of it. Unlike many of his kind he did not take the fear of fire to great extremes. It was a good beginning, he decided.

'It smells wonderful,' said Adolphus, and meant it. 'It smells like home.'

He was surprised by how much that meant to him. He felt as if his decades of rootless wanderings were over. He sensed the flow of old magical energies course through the stones. This was a place of power where he could do what he needed to do. Here he would take the final steps on the road of his destiny.

Ulrika entered the chamber. She looked pale and she staggered a little. Her eyes had the glazed ecstatic look that so many mortals got after the dark kiss. She looked at him with a mixture of resentment, hatred and longing that had become familiar down the centuries.

'Show the girl to the guest chambers,' he said to the chambermaid. The faint flicker of jealousy that appeared in the woman's eyes amused him. She was one of his most faithful servants and bore herself with appropriate modesty although once she had been the proud daughter of one of the noblest houses of Kislev. She was beautiful but she had been too weak to interest him for long.

What was he going to do about Ulrika, he wondered? She was beautiful, intelligent and ambitious, and in his own cold way, he liked her. Her blood enchanted him, and there was a latent viciousness in her that he thought would make her truly one of the Arisen. Perhaps it was time for him to create a get. Perhaps he would grant her the gift of immortality. Not yet though. She was not quite ready. She still had to be won round to his point of view. If he granted her the final kiss, she might well go mad, or kill herself, or worse yet break free of him entirely and go her own way. He did not want that. It defeated the whole point of the exercise, which was to have someone at your side to go through eternity with. Thinking about himself and the countess, he did not know if he wanted to face that.

Of course it was inevitable she would leave. All gets eventually did. He had himself broken with his progenitor and made his own way out into the world. It was better if that did not happen too soon though. Still, if all went according to plan with the Eye of Khemri that was not something he needed to worry about. Using its power, he could well bind her and any others among the Arisen he wished to his will.

How the countess would regret ever sharing that knowledge with him! He chuckled. He would make his honoured progenitor sorry she had ever spoken of it all those long years ago. Of course at the time, it had been necessary to hide the desire that burned in his heart for the Eye. He had needed to acquire power and knowledge before making the break from the elder vampire and that had taken decades of quasi-servitude. It was not that he hated the countess for it. It was just that her cloying affection and concern for his wellbeing had reminded him too much of his own mother's overpowering interest in him. It had enfolded him and choked him and made him feel trapped and imprisoned. Just thinking about her brought those feelings back.

Soon now, he would not have to worry about her or any others of the Arisen. The ancient enchantments Nagash had woven around the Eye of Khemri would see to that.

EIGHT

ADOLPHUS FINISHED CHALKING the pentagram onto the floor. Around the edges he had made the symbols of all four of the great Powers of Chaos. He himself stood within a triangle in the centre of the pentagram. The scared young girl lay naked and bound before him. The Eye of Khemri glittered between her breasts. He could see the panic and bewilderment in her eyes. Only yesterday she had gone to sleep in her parents' hovel near the castle. Tonight she had awoken in its deepest dungeon, spirited away by his servants.

The witch-knife glittered sharply in his hands. She looked as if she wanted to scream.

Adolphus chanted the names of the Dark Gods, invoking their presence, as the ritual prescribed. The girl began to thrash, terror overcoming even the potent compulsion to obey he had laid upon her. Perhaps he should have bound her physically. Perhaps he had been too confident in his own abilities. He pushed the thoughts aside. Any loss of concentration now might prove fatal.

Dark magical energy rose all around him. To his mage-sight it appeared reddish, blood-like, droplets of it dripping from the stones of the cellar walls and flowing around the boundaries of the pentagram. To the girl's mortal eyes, nothing would have changed, but she seemed to sense what was going on and whimpered.

Adolphus breathed deeply. Dark magic had a scent uniquely its own, like blood but more so. It made his skin tingle and his brain buzz. He felt the beast start to stir inside him. What was happening? He had not felt like this since Praag. Why was the fury within him emerging now?

With an enormous effort of will, he fought the bloodlust down. He could not afford any loss of control for now. The girl started to rise. If she broke the edges of the pentagram, the dark magic would surge in uncontrollably. Worse, some of the daemonic entities that it attracted might enter too. Adolphus was not sure even his strength might prevail against such things, at least not until he had the Eye attuned.

He strode over to the girl, still chanting, and grabbed her by the throat. He lifted her easily with one hand despite the feeble beating of her fists and feet against his body. He raised her until her eyes were level with his and his gaze struck her with the impact of a hammer. Her pupils dilated, her mouth fell open slackly and soft whimpers emerged from her mouth as her whole body went limp in his grasp. Easily, he lowered her to the desecrated altar once more.

Ripples appeared in the tide of dark magic, taking on the shapes of evil entities. The ritual was starting to attract daemonic presences: huge hounds with great fleshy crests on their necks fought with clawed androgens; monstrously obese, pustule-covered things writhed on the floor in combat with strange disks whose edges were covered in eyes. They battled over a small proportion of the energy he drew up from the dark depths beneath the keep. It was enough to give them shape and form. Now even the girl's mortal eyes might be able to perceive them as shimmering shapes in the darkness. The beast howled within his breast, desperate for the combat that would ensue, even though that combat would most likely end in his destruction.

He needed to progress faster. If he did not use the power he had gathered before the creatures fully manifested, terrible things might happen. The dark magical energy rushed in through the gaps in the point he had left at the northern edge of the pentagram, the arm of the star that pointed towards the Chaos Wastes. Ancient Nehekharan poured from his lips as he continued to chant the words of the ritual. His thoughts were inexorably drawn into the necessary configuration for the spell to be complete. The torrent of words continued even as the evil presences surged around the pentagram's edges, attracted now to the souls they sensed within.

Adolphus fought down panic. He was not the best of sorcerers. There were mages who could have accomplished what he intended without the rituals and the extra power he needed to draw from the ancient evil beneath the keep. Perhaps he had made a mistake; perhaps he had attempted something beyond his ability. Perhaps this was the end.

No! He would not let that happen. He steeled his will and continued the chant he had memorised so long ago. He moved the knife through the elaborate ritual gestures, thrusting it in the direction of each point of the star in turn before finally raising it high above the girl and then plunging it into her heart.

She gave one long despairing wail as her soul was drawn from her body, and her blood splattered the altar. At that exact moment Adolphus felt the dark thirst within him. The beast wanted to lap up that blood. He fought with the urge and let the blood flow, until the trickle overflowed the altar and reached the floor. It touched the streams of dark magic and began to sizzle and dance, droplets jerking upward from the paving stones. A fine red mist filled the air inside the pentagram. From outside the spell walls Adolphus thought he heard the thin wailing and howling of the daemons. He continued to chant and gesture, guiding the twisting writhing mist until it touched both his flesh and the Eye of Khemri.

At that moment, a link was formed between him and the amulet. He sensed the power within it, and the ancient spells. He felt almost as if he was being sucked into it and he fought against it as a swimmer fights against the current of a raging river.

Then suddenly it was done. The amulet was his. He began the ritual of dismissal and the energies he had summoned began to drain away. The daemonic entities fought against it but there was nothing they could do to stop the process. As the flows of dark magic departed they were left high and dry like fish flopping on the bed of a sun-dried lake. One by one they disappeared, returning to whatever extra-dimensional hell from which they had come, leaving Adolphus alone with his prize. It pulsed in his hand as he attuned it to his own mystical energies.

As he did so he noticed lines of force shimmering through the night, so faint as to be almost invisible, leaving the pentagram through its open edge and flowing away towards the distance. These did not have the feel of the power within the amulet. They felt more recent, and bore the signature of a different wizard. Well, no matter. Adolphus reached out with the witch-knife and cut them. In a heartbeat they unravelled.

The amulet was his now, and he was about to use its power to serve his ultimate purpose. The dead girl looked up at him with empty sightless eyes. He reached down, dipped his fingertips in her blood and raised them to his lips. The blood tasted very sweet.

FELIX SAW MAX crumple forward and almost fall off the supply sledge. He jumped down from his own seat, leaving Gotrek clutching for the reins, and raced forward.

'What is wrong?' he asked. The wizard looked pale and drained. Sweat crossed his brow and he gave every impression of being a man in extreme pain.

'The spell I placed on the Eye of Khemri was just broken,' he groaned. 'It was not a pleasant feeling.'

'Can you still find it?' Max shook his head despairingly.

'No. I can't sense it any more.'

'Do you have any idea where the Eye might be?' Slowly and painfully the wizard nodded.

'I know the direction we must go. I can give a bearing from here, judging by the position of the sun.'

'That won't be much help. This trail winds its way through the forest. We can easily lose the way.' Max gritted his teeth and nodded once more.

'It gets worse,' he said.

'Oh good,' said Felix. 'Tell me all the cheering details.'

'Just before my spell was cut I had a strange sense that something was happening to the amulet. I could sense a surge of power, and a soul screaming in terror. I suspect that Krieger has used the darkest of all magic to bind the amulet to him. I think he sacrificed someone.'

From Max's expression, Felix could tell they were both thinking the same thing. 'Ulrika?'

'I don't know,' said Max. 'Maybe.'

'Damn!' said Felix, crashing his fist into the side of the sled. The pain of hitting the wood helped bring him back to his senses, and get control of his mounting panic and anger. He looked at Max again. The magician did not look too healthy.

'Are you all right?' he asked.

'I will be. Whatever Krieger has done, I intend to punish him.'

'I will help you,' said Felix, wishing he felt nearly as confident as he sounded.

'First we will have to find him,' said Max.

'Something tells me that it won't be too difficult. He came all the way to Sylvania for a reason, and I think we can both guess what it is.'

'To claim the whole bloody province, and that's just for a start.'

Even as he spoke, Felix knew Max was right. The wars of the Vampire Counts were about to start all over again.

MAX HUNCHED FORWARD in his seat, barely able to handle the reins. Fortunately the weary ponies could almost be trusted to follow the path themselves. The cold wind bit into his face, bringing tears to his eyes. He could not find the energy to recast a spell of warming. It was all he could do to keep himself upright and concentrate on breathing.

At first there was a niggling sense of loss. The link to the Eye, which he had held onto for so long, was gone completely.

Even when he had not been concentrating on the thing, he had always been aware that it was there. Now, he could not feel its presence. After a while he realised that he also felt better. It was as if he had just had a tooth pulled, one that had been giving him niggling pain for weeks.

In a way he was relieved. His contact with the ancient evil within the Eye of Khemri, no matter how far removed, had been oppressive, and had cast a pall over his spirits. Now, despite the circumstances he felt almost cheerful. It was difficult to keep a smile off his face, despite his worries over Ulrika and what the vampire might be doing. He knew this was not right, but he could not help himself. It was as if he had just started to recover from a long illness. The whole world looked somehow brighter.

ULRIKA LOOKED AT the talisman glittering on Adolphus Krieger's chest. Somehow, it made the vampire look taller, more commanding and more confident even than he usually did. He smiled at her in a way that was almost friendly. She shook her head and looked away, wondering why everything in the room seemed sharper and clearer to her sight than it normally did, despite the darkness. What was happening to her? She was not sure she wanted to know.

She glanced around the strange throne room he had brought her to. It was buried deep within this haunted castle with its strange corridors in which time and distance seemed to become all twisted. There was a stillness about the place such as you found only in the oldest of temples, and a sense of brooding evil power that left her in no doubt that she was at the heart of the wickedness that enshrouded this place. Ancient suits of armour filled the niches, clutching old but still serviceable weapons.

Overhead, amid the enormous beams of a gigantic vaulted ceiling, she thought she saw something move. Vast shadows seemed to shift above the huge chandelier, independent of the light being cast. There was a terrible sense of presence about the place that she very badly wanted to ignore.

'It begins now,' said Krieger, mounting the massive dais and lounging back on an enormous throne of carved and polished wood. The back of the throne was sculpted to resemble the wings of a massive bat or dragon. Over Krieger's head loomed the skull of an enormous bat. Glowing rubies gazed from its eye sockets.

Krieger's voice was deeper somehow, more resonant and thrilling. It was difficult not to believe someone who sounded like that. She fought the compulsion, reminding herself that he was an evil, soulless bloodsucker. Somehow she could not manage the vehemence she once had. It was hard to think of anything save the pleasure of his last embrace. She wondered how that could have happened, then dismissed the thought as irrelevant.

It had happened and she needed to fight against it. That was all she needed to know.

'The talisman is mine now, Ulrika. Soon I will be the Prince of Night.'

'I do not know what you mean.'

'The talisman was created by the Great Necromancer himself in the ancient days. One of its many attributes is to increase its wearer's... influence over the Arisen.'

'Why?'

'Nagash feared the growth of their power, and saw them as potential rivals. He made the talisman and with it bent many of the Arisen to his will: they became his hounds, creatures that are feared to this very day. The amulet was lost when Alcadizaar overcame him. It has drifted down the ages born by fools who were too blind to see what it was. All that is ended. Tonight, I have claimed it for my own, just as I have claimed von Carstein's throne for my own.'

'How do you know it will still work after all this time?'

'Not for nothing was he known as the Great Necromancer. The things he made do not lose their potency. He was the greatest sorcerer of his age, the greatest necromancer of any age. No one ever understood the magic of Undeath like he did. I know the Eye works. I can feel it. You are already responding to its influence.' The tone of his voice shocked her. She had never heard anyone sound quite so triumphant.

'What do you mean? Why should I feel its influence?' She suspected she already knew the answer.

'Because every night for the past three nights you have taken a step closer to joining me. It seems only fair that I should have someone by my side to enjoy my triumph. You will be the possessor of eternal life.'

Her mouth felt suddenly dry. She wanted to scream. She wanted to run shrieking from the hall. She wanted to drive her knife into the chest of this undead ghoul. And a surprisingly large part of her was almost pathetically grateful for the offer.

'No,' she forced herself to say.

'Yes,' he said, springing on her, his fangs emerging, his eyes glowing with a hellish light. She tried to dodge but she was dazed and slow. He caught her easily. His fingers burned on her neck. She grabbed his wrists and tried to pry his hands away but he was far too strong. Slowly, he bent over her, as if he was about to deliver the gentlest of kisses. His eyes blazed redly. His canine teeth gleamed like ivory. She could see they were long and sharp as needles.

A surge of ecstasy passed through her body as his teeth bit into her neck. Strength drained from her along with all will to resist. Slowly her vision darkened, and her hearing dimmed until all she could hear was the sound of her own heartbeat. She felt a bloody finger being forced into her mouth and she sucked at it as greedily as an infant at a mother's breast.

Even as she did so, the darkness continued to gather. Her heartbeat echoed in her ears like thunder and then stopped.

'At least this village has an inn,' said Ivan Petrovich Straghov gloomily, staring up at the sign of the Green Man. 'It certainly beats camping out in the snow for another night.'

Felix was not sure he agreed. The Green Man was an enormous fortified structure overlooking another nameless and partially ruined Sylvanian hamlet. His limited experience of this land's towns and villages had not left him filled with any great desire to spend time in them, although he had to admit the howling of the distant wolves made even this squalid place seem an attractive option.

He sniffed and looked at Gotrek.

'They will have beer,' said the Slayer, as if this was reason enough to spend a night in a flea-infested hovel.

'Snorri likes beer,' Snorri added, by way of clarification.

'I'm glad you told me that. I would never have guessed.'

'There's no need to be sarcastic, young Felix.' Felix reflected miserably that one of the worst things about his lengthening association with Snorri was that the dwarf's capacity to detect sarcasm had improved greatly with practice. 'A pint or two is just the thing to drive off the night chill.'

A pint or ten more likely, thought Felix, but did not voice the thought out loud. He realised he was just arguing for the sake of being contrary, to give vent to his anger and anxiety over Ulrika and their quest, and his own misery in his illness. He was not being constructive, or helpful, and anyway, it appeared that his opinion mattered not at all, since everyone else in their party appeared to be in favour.

All the tales of dark, haunted Sylvanian inns he had read as a youngster returned to him. They were often the haunt of murderers or monstrous vampires who preyed on innocent travellers. He felt like making dire pronouncements about how they would all regret this, but he resisted. There was no point other than to increase the pall of gloom that had already gathered over their journey.

Inside, the inn was not as bad as Felix had expected. The building was made of stone, perhaps an indicator of more prosperous days in the region, although Felix could not ever recall hearing of any time when Sylvania was prosperous.

The thin crowd of folk within fell silent at the entrance of the party of knights, Slayers and over a score of Kislevite horsemen. The landlord, a fat barrel of a man with cold calculating eyes in a jolly face, came round the bar to greet them. He rubbed his hand nervously on a soiled apron, obviously unsure whether they were customers or a bandit band.

Rodrik informed him of their purpose, and requested rooms for his companions and a separate chamber for the countess. Felix and Max took separate chambers. The Slayers and the Kislevites elected to remain in the common room. Actually, several of the horse archers elected to remain in the stables with their mounts. A number of obscene jokes concerning the love of the Kislevite cavalryman for his horse sprang to Felix's mind but he tactfully restrained himself from telling them.

Felix studied the patrons. This was a relatively prosperous inn for this part of the world, he realised. Few in the common room appeared to be locals. Most looked like merchants and their bodyguards, although it seemed to be a bit early in the year for them to be on the road.

A few looked like noblemen down on their luck, the sort of shabby genteel men who you always found in the remoter parts of the Empire, cheating the locals at cards and making outrageous demands based on their supposed superior status. More than a few looked like mercenaries, hard-faced dangerous men in worn armour. Most of them had a hungry, hopeful look. They reminded Felix of a pack of starving wolves scenting a wounded deer.

In one corner, sat a priest of Morr, in his black robes, a cowl obscuring his face. His presence was such a cliché in melodramas that Felix almost laughed. Instead he strode up to the bar, and ordered ale for himself and the dwarfs. Ivan Petrovich was already seeing to the comfort of his men, and Max and the nobles had disappeared upstairs to inspect the rooms along with the countess.

As he leaned on the bar, one of the dingy-looking men at the corner table sidled over to him. He was dressed in a tattered fur cloak and hat, and the soiled finery of those who belonged to the nobility. His eyes were quick and fear-filled, his face was gaunt and narrow, and his Adam's apple was very prominent.

'Just got in?' he asked. He had the look of a man gauging whether Felix would offer to buy him a drink or not. His accent marked him as a noble, or someone who had learned how to pretend to be one. He licked his lips. 'Where have you come from, sir?'

Felix noticed the man's fingers toyed nervously with the pommel of his longsword. The hilt was absurdly over-decorated. It went all too well with the man's pretentious tunic and codpiece. 'Waldenhof,' said Felix, more to be polite than because he was interested in anything the man had to say. The man quirked an eyebrow as if to say both he and Felix knew that Felix was kidding. Felix refused to take the bait.

'And yourself?' he asked.

'Here and there,' said the man. It was Felix's turn to smile ironically at him. Felix turned to watch the barman pour the drinks, hoping to indicate by this the conversation was over. 'Just came up the road from Leicheberg.'

'You're travelling at a bad time of the year,' said Felix.

'I could say the same about you,' muttered the stranger.

'I have urgent business in these parts,' said Felix.

'Must be. I can't help but wonder what urgent business might bring twenty Kislevite horse-soldiers, a pair of Slayers, a wizard, some Sylvanian knights and the Countess of Nachthafen to the Green Man on a winter night like tonight. And an educated man like yourself as well.'

Felix looked at the man with a bit more interest. He was not as drunk as he seemed, and his eyes and mind were quick. His count of the Kislevites was accurate. Felix kept his expression bland.

'Urgent business,' he said.

'Must be,' said the man.

'What brings you here?'

'This and that. Itchy feet, a desire to see what was beyond the next hilltop, some family problems.'

'Family problems?'

'A dispute with my brothers over an inheritance. I needed to put some distance between myself and the ancestral manor.' The man spoke confidingly, and flashed a quick, calculating look at Felix.

He seemed to think that by sharing a confidence, he would get Felix to do the same. Felix had encountered men with such a manner before, in the underworlds of Altdorf and Nuln. Most of them had been professional informers. 'You know how it is?'

'Not really,' said Felix. 'I always got on well with my brothers.'

'It's a bad thing when kin fall out over an inheritance,' said the man. He gave a long practiced sigh, but he did not look at all bothered.

'I imagine so,' said Felix. 'I mean it must be bad to bring a man like yourself to this out of the way place at this time of the year.'

The man's nervous gaze flickered around the room. He looked down at the counter-top and started drawing circles with his fingertip. 'I count myself lucky that I got here,' he said in an ominous tone.

'Why?'

'Buy me a drink and I'll tell you,' he said. 'If you're going south you will want to hear it.'

'Give me a hint.'

'The undying are on the move,' whispered the stranger, in a portentous manner.

'Really?' said Felix ironically. 'Tell me something everyone doesn't already know.'

The stranger smirked. 'Ghouls are gathering in the forests. The old castle at Drakenhof has been reoccupied. I saw strange lights flickering in the windows as I passed. We saw the lights in the woods and thought we might be granted shelter for the night. In this cold, any place is better than a tent. But when I saw those lights I thought differently.'

'We?'

'The lads over there at the table were with me. We were all travelling together. Safety in numbers is a good maxim but never more so than in Sylvania at a time like this.'

Felix looked over at the group the stranger had indicated. They were a rough looking crowd, down at heel mercenaries by the looks of them. He hadn't seen such a fine collection of cauliflower ears, broken noses and missing teeth since he left Karak Kadrin, the city of Slayers.

'They don't look to be the sort of men to be scared off by a few lights,' said Felix. Quite the contrary, he thought, they looked exactly the type to be drawn to them to see if they could rob anybody in the vicinity.

'You would have been scared if you saw them, and maybe even your Slayer friends too. Those lights were the work of evil magic, I have no doubt whatsoever.'

'You're an expert on evil magic then,' said Felix.

'There's no need to mock, friend. Anybody could have told these lights were the work of something wicked. They glowed green and sputtered, went out and then started to glow all over again. They seemed to float through the woods.'

Felix thought this sounded fairly convincing when compared to his own experience but he kept a disbelieving look on his face. 'When was this then?'

'Three nights ago.'

Felix nodded. That would be the night Max said the spell linking him to the Eye of Khemri was broken. There was a pattern here, even if the stranger knew nothing about it. Maybe he should make the man recount his tale to the wizard. He decided to tell Max himself and wait and see what the wizard said.

'So you're saying avoid Drakenhof keep,' said Felix.

'Like the plague. How about that beer then?'

Felix saw the barman looking at him. He nodded.

'This is going to be good,' said the stranger.

'WHAT DID THE tailor's dummy want?' asked Gotrek, a little too loudly, as Felix set down the beers. Felix recounted the man's tale in a low voice.

'I think we'll be visiting this keep,' said the Slayer. Snorri Nosebiter nodded enthusiastic approval.

'I knew you were going to say that,' said Felix.

'IT FITS,' SAID Max. He had listened intently as Felix finished the barfly's tale. Felix got up and walked over to the window. It was shuttered against the chill. He listened for a moment anyway then glanced around the room. It was surprisingly well furnished for such an out of the way place, although all the furniture looked ancient. The bed was a four poster carved with disturbing-looking dragons. The wardrobe was big and heavy and reminded him too much of a coffin.

Max sat on a claw-footed chair and regarded him with a clear-eyed gaze.

'I imagine Krieger would want to cast any spells in what had once been a place of power filled with dark magic, and Drakenhof is said to be that. And that was the very night when my spell was broken. A suitably potent and far-ranging spell might manifest itself with a display of lights such as he described.'

'It all fits a bit too well, don't you think?'

'What do you mean?' asked Max.

'I mean, what are the chances that this fellow downstairs just happened to be passing the keep with his mates on the very night this occurred, and then just happened to be here tonight to tell us about it?'

'Such coincidences do happen,' said Max. 'But I see what you mean.'

'Coincidences, Max? Come on. It's the dead of winter. Why would someone of his sort even be on the road? If he really were what he claimed then he'd have found a nice tavern somewhere in Middenheim to hole up for the winter, and you'd need a big spade to dig him out. I tell you, I didn't like his look at all. He was a weasel, and I've seen his sort before.'

Max had the tact not to ask where. Instead he stroked his beard for a moment and then drummed his fingers on the armrest of the chair.

'You think maybe Krieger sent him? That he's laying a false scent to get us off his trail?'

'I don't know. Maybe he's figured out how to make the talisman work for him and he wants us to walk into a trap.'

'This is all just speculation, Felix.'

Felix smiled grimly. 'This is a land that lends itself all too well to speculation.'

Max nodded his head in agreement.

THE LANTERN FLAME flickered and went out. Felix cursed the gust of chill air and the shoddiness of the device. It looked as if it had been lighting the way for guests since the time of Great Plague. He moved through the darkened corridors, one hand out touching the wall so that he could find his way in the gloom, walking his fingers along the stonework to feel when they encountered a doorway. The cool plaster beneath his fingers reminded him of the simple silly games of his childhood, and he smiled a little.

He knew his room was the third door on the right from the top of the stairs. He had to hunch low because of the sloping roof of the inn. It reminded him of the cramped conditions on the airship *Spirit of Grungni* which in turn reminded him of Ulrika. The thought sent a little surge of pain through his heart. Suddenly he sensed a presence ahead of him in the gloom, and his hand slipped to the hilt of his sword.

'Be calm, Herr Jaeger. It is only me,' said Countess Gabriella. By all the gods, Felix thought, the woman must have eyes like a cat's to be able to tell who he was in this gloom. 'I would like a word with you in private, if that is possible.'

'Certainly,' said Felix wondering what exactly she meant by that. He had some experience of ladies requiring a private word at this time of the evening. You could never tell. Cool, dry fingers closed on his, tugging his hand away from the sword hilt, and she guided him with surprising strength through the corridors. He heard a key click in a lock, and saw her silhouetted in the doorway of her room. She was very slender, he noted drunkenly, but her figure was surprisingly good. She stepped inside and gestured for him to follow.

The chamber was the best in the inn, finely furnished in an antique fashion. A faint smell of cinnamon fought the mustiness in the air. Felix doubted this room was used all that often. The countess closed the door behind him, and he heard the key turn in the lock once more. He had a sudden panicky feeling of being trapped. She gestured for him to take one of the overstuffed armchairs and relaxed into one herself.

Felix remained standing, his sense of unease growing, as he listened to the wind whistle past the windows. He started as a particularly strong gust rattled the wooden shutters.

'Do sit down, Herr Jaeger! I assure you I mean you no harm.' The countess sounded faintly amused. Felix suspected this small, slight woman could do him a great deal of harm if she chose to, but he slumped down into the chair, and let his long legs stretch out towards the fire.

'What is it you want to talk about?'

'You appear to be a sensible man, Herr Jaeger, and you seem to have encountered more than your share of… unusual situations.'

Felix smiled wryly. He doubted that he would be following Gotrek Gurnisson around if he was the former but the latter was certainly true. There were times when he was surprised his hair had not turned white with the horrors he had seen. 'Perhaps.'

'And I think you are a discreet one.'

'Is this a situation that requires discretion?'

'Please, Herr Jaeger, this is not what you think. I am about to entrust you with a secret that might cost both our lives.'

Felix felt his smile widen. There was something about Sylvania that inspired the melodramatic as well as the terrible.

'I assure you there is no cause for amusement.'

Felix could not help himself. He laughed. For a second the countess looked like she was going to rise and slap him but he waved her away. Felix spluttered. 'No. Please I am sorry. It's just here I am in a Sylvanian inn. Outside the wind scratches at the windows, the candles gutter and a beautiful woman is about to let me in on a terrible secret. I feel like I am in a Detlef Sierck play. If only a wolf would howl, things would be perfect.'

'You have a very strange sense of humour, Herr Jaeger.'

'It comes from reading too many tall tales when I was a youth. I am sorry. Please what is it you wished to tell me.'

'First, can I ask you for your word that you will pass on nothing of what I tell you here unless I ask you to?'

Felix considered this. 'As long as it would not cause harm to myself or my comrades.'

'You are a cautious man. That is good.'

'It should also tell you I mean to keep my word as long as my conditions are met. Why make them otherwise?'

'Quite,' she said dryly. 'Although it's also the sort of thing a good liar would say.'

'You are the one who asked me here. You are the one who wants to tell me secrets. You must already have some ideas concerning my trustworthiness.'

'You are quite correct,' she said. 'I pride myself in being a good judge of men. In my life I have made very few mistakes on that score.'

'You seem to be a woman possessed of formidable powers of judgement.'

Felix was quite serious. There was something about her that inspired respect. He steepled his fingers and leaned forward in the chair, resting his elbows on his knees. He looked at her closely, trying to study her features through the veil. 'What exactly is it that you wanted to tell me.'

'Tell me, do you believe all you have heard about the undying ones?'

'In this place, at this time, I don't have much else to go on,' he said honestly.

'Do you believe they are all what you would call evil?'

'What I would call evil?'

'Herr Jaeger, this is not one of your Altdorf university debates. We are not here to split hairs or discuss how many daemons can dance on the head of a pin. Time is getting short and many lives are at stake.'

Suddenly Felix had an inkling of where this was going, and he fought the urge to reach immediately for his sword. He doubted that it would do him any good if what he suspected was true.

'You have very good control over yourself, Herr Jaeger, for a mortal. But rest assured if I meant you harm I would have done it before now.'

Felix looked at her in horror, as if a gigantic spider were seated in the chair opposite him, not a small and attractive seeming woman. He felt like he was very close to death. He was very suddenly sober.

'A pity,' she breathed softly. 'Still to business. Not all of the undying are the monsters you believe them to be.'

'I find that hard to believe,' said Felix.

'Why – because they drink the blood of humans to continue their existence? That does not mean they are all murderers. Believe it or not, there are many humans who give their blood willingly. You would be surprised by the number in your own Empire who have done so.'

'I doubt that there is any wickedness done in the Empire that could surprise me.'

'Don't be so parochial, Herr Jaeger! What two consenting people do together in privacy is between them, providing they harm no one else.'

'That depends on how consenting one of them is.'

'I do not have time to debate the ethics of this with you. I need your help. A monster is loose and he must be stopped. You and your friends can do it with my help.'

'Why should I trust you?'

'You don't have much choice. You need my help if you are going to find Adolphus Krieger and stop him before he becomes too powerful for anything short of the Lords of Chaos to stop. You need my help if you are going to free your woman from his influence. Which, to be frank, by now I judge is impossible.'

Felix felt his heart skip a beat. His mouth felt dry. 'Why do you say that?'

'Because by now she is either a bloodless corpse, hopelessly enthralled by him, or she is his consort, and I judge the latter option most unlikely unless she is a most unusual and striking woman.'

'She is.'

The countess shrugged. It was a human gesture but Felix felt as if he had just watched a spider shrug. He watched her with a kind of horrid fascination. He supposed a worm might watch a bird like that, or a rabbit a fox.

'You are a vampire,' said Felix. He felt proud of himself. He had wanted to say the words for minutes but forcing them out had seemed somehow dangerous. The countess clapped her hands together ironically.

'Very good, Herr Jaeger, no one could accuse you of being slow on the uptake.' Felix felt his fingers tighten on the pommel of his sword.

'I should warn you this is an enchanted weapon. I do not know if it can affect your kind but I am willing to try if you provoke me.'

'I know it is a magical weapon and a formidable one, albeit not nearly so formidable as that rather terrifying axe your friend carries. They are among the reasons I think you have a chance of stopping Krieger if you are quick.'

'Why are you prepared to help us against one of your own kind?'

'Believe it or not, Herr Jaeger, we are as different and as fractious as humans. We are just a lot fewer. Most of us would prefer to live in some sort of harmony with your kind. You are far more numerous and in the past centuries have gained too much power for us to want anything else. Most of us wish to be left alone with our flocks.'

'Flocks?'

'Admirers, willing victims, whatever you wish to call them, Herr Jaeger. See – I am being frank with you.'

'Fine. Most of you, you say.'

'There are some who dream of a return to the elder days, who would have us rule the night as they believe we once did. Mostly they are young and don't realise that we never ruled the night in the way they think. Things were never that simple.'

Felix's mind reeled with all this new information. He had never considered that vampires might be as filled with fear of humans as humans were of them. What she was saying did make sense. Humans did have the numbers, and the ability to operate in daylight when the undying were weakest, and they did have powerful magic too.

The countess studied him for a moment, as if gauging the impact of her revelations, and then she continued to speak. 'As I have said, there are those who believe that we should claim our ancient glories, no matter how often they are told that such things never were. Adolphus Krieger is one of them.'

'I believe you.'

'Good. We are making some progress.'

'Tell me – does the count, and those other nobles at Waldenschlosse, know what you are?'

'Yes. There is a pact between those Arisen who would avoid a return to the ancient wars, and the current rulers of Sylvania. We have no wish to see a pogrom initiated against us.'

'What about Rodrik?'

'He and his followers are part of my flock.' Felix paused to digest all of this information. It was almost too much for him to take in. He found it difficult to believe that he was sitting here calmly discussing such a thing with the countess, and not either attacking her or trying to flee the chamber. A thought struck him. 'So the count and his friends were concealing something from us.'

'Why should he let you in on all of his secrets? You are strangers, after all. He has no reason to trust you.'

'And you have?'

'I have no choice. I know what Krieger is doing.'

'And what exactly is that?'

'He intends to unite all of the Arisen behind him and fulfil an ancient prophesy of our kind. A prophecy made by a madman and destined never to be fulfilled, but that will not stop Adolphus from trying.'

'Given what you have already told me, it does not seem likely that he can do it.'

'Herr Jaeger, he possesses the means to do it. You have seen it, touched it.'

'The Eye of Khemri?'

'If that is what you wish to call it. It would be better to call it the Eye of Nagash.'

'Is it really so powerful?'

'I believe it to be so.'

'Why?'

'It was created by Nagash to bind my people to him. It can call them over a great distance and compel obedience if the wearer is strong enough.'

'If?'

'You have doubtless heard tales of how the Arisen can impose their will on mortals.'

Felix nodded.

'It takes a great disparity in willpower for the binding to take place and even then it is only temporary in most cases.

To be frank, this is why I have not tried to bind you or your companions. I doubt it could be done without your consent, not without creating a blood bond. It is a less well-known fact that the Arisen can do the same to each other. Among its many gifts the Eye magnifies this ability in one attuned to it. It works far more effectively for one of us than it ever did for the Great Necromancer. Perhaps due to the affinities we have for each other. We are all, at base, of one blood after all. Whatever the reason, by using it Krieger really could summon us all and bind us to his will. In fact, I think he has already started the process. I feel a… tugging at the corners of my mind even as we speak. I do not doubt it will grow stronger over the next few nights as he grows more powerful.'

'How do you know all this?'

'Does it matter?'

'Yes. I want to know what we face here.'

'Herr Jaeger, I have lived a very long time. I have studied much strange and obscure lore and I have had many many centuries to assimilate it. Believe me, along with most of my kind I have an obsession with the Great Necromancer and his works. I have read all of the supposedly forbidden books – van Hal's translations of the *Nine Books of Nagash*, the *Book of the Dead*, the Forbidden *Grimoires of Tal Akhad*. I have travelled to the ancient places to collect knowledge of him. I have walked the sands of the Land of the Dead and visited the pyramids of Khemri. It would take me more time than we have to explain how I sifted through all the lies and myths and distortions and eventually put together the pieces of the puzzle. You will just have to trust me when I say what I am telling you is true.'

'It seems I have little choice. Perhaps I should ask Max to join us.'

'Perhaps later. At the moment, I would prefer this to remain between us and give you a chance to prepare your companions. It would be better for us all if they did nothing rash.'

Thinking of what Gotrek would do if he found out there was a vampire in their midst, that seemed the wisest course for the present to Felix. If the countess was a potential ally it would be best if her head remained attached to her shoulders. Or, he reminded himself, if she was very powerful, perhaps it would be best if the Slayer did not achieve his long-awaited doom until after Ulrika was free or avenged. He could see from the way the countess nodded that she already took his agreement for granted. Was she really so good at reading him, he wondered? He supposed that after living for centuries she might have gained such a gift for understanding mortals. He gestured for her to go on.

'The Eye was created by Nagash in ancient times specifically as a weapon to be used against my kind, when he feared we might challenge him for domination of the ancient world. He even used it to bind some of the Arisen to his service. That is when we learned of the power concealed in it. Fearing what might happen, the rest of the Arisen fled as far and as fast as they could and hid themselves with whatever spells they could muster.'

Felix listened enthralled as she told tales of ancient intrigues, of the war between Nagash and the skaven and the eventual dispersal of the Great Necromancer's treasures. She spoke of the disappearance of the Eye until its return in the possession of Mannfred von Carstein and how he used it to forge the undead force that fought the War of the Vampire Counts. She claimed it was the loss of the Eye at Hel Fenn that had ended those wars as much as the slaughter of the counts.

'Of course, after the fact,' she continued, 'It is easy to see what happened. Most of the Arisen believed the Eye destroyed or lost forever after Hel Fenn and were glad. The Eye must have been found by one of the mortals after the battle, and he took it as part of the spoils of war, a memento of that terrible conflict. Not being a magus and having no idea of what it was he held, it became merely a family heirloom. Eventually some of the heirs, needing money, sold the collection and it came onto the open market. It then passed from hand to hand till it ended up in Andriev's collection.'

'How did you and Krieger come to know about it?'

'Alas, not all the Arisen believed the Eye lost. Some coveted its power. Adolphus Krieger was one such.'

Felix looked at her. And what about you, he thought? Did you want this thing for yourself? Again she seemed to read his mind.

'There are some of us who feared the return of the Eye, Herr Jaeger. We feared the rise of another von Carstein. It would be the end for many of us and we are already too few. We cannot afford another War of the Vampire Counts.'

'You are saying you have no interest in the Eye of Khemri yourself?' Felix did not quite understand why he was taunting this woman who most likely had the power to kill him where he sat but he felt the need to do so. 'If it fell into your hands you would not use it?'

'I would do my best to destroy it, or at very least, take it to a place where it would not be found for a long time, if ever.'

'Really?'

'I don't expect you to believe this, but I have sound reasons for not wanting to use the thing.'

'And what would they be?'

'The Eye was created by Nagash. It contains part of his power, his spirit, if you will. Over time it corrupts anyone who uses it and leads them to disaster. Nagash was jealous of his creations. They will not truly serve any but him.'

'Surely Krieger knows this.'

'Perhaps not and even if he does, perhaps he does not believe it. Or perhaps he believes he can master it. Or perhaps he is already subtly under the thing's domination. He was close to von Carstein and was exposed to its influence centuries ago.'

'Perhaps we should simply sit back and wait for this dire fate to overtake Krieger then.'

Felix wondered what he was going to do. There seemed little choice but to go along with her suggestions. Until she proved false she represented a potential ally and one who understood their enemy far better than they could hope to. Still, he realised he was reluctant to trust this undying predator. He felt rather like a deer trying to negotiate with a wolf. Perhaps that was why he felt the need to keep chipping away at her position.

'I would have thought your kind would gladly do anything to aid the victory of the Dark Lords of Chaos. Are you
not their spawn?'

'We are not the creations of the daemon gods any more
than you are, and they love us no more than they do you.
They require only souls and slaves. Some of the Arisen have
served them in the past, but then so have many of your kind.
We have learned from the mistakes of those who thought
they could somehow get the Lords of Darkness to serve their
ends better than your sort.'

And there was some truth in that too, Felix guessed, at
least the part about many humans having given their souls
up to the evil ones. The countess leaned forward and gazed
at him intently. So swift was her movement that Felix backed
away, startled.

'Look, Herr Jaeger, it is really very simple. Either you believe
me or you don't. Either you trust me or you don't. I am the
one who has taken all of the risks here. There are those of my
own kind who would see my existence ended if they learned
what I have told you here. You could tell your friends what I
am and they would doubtless help you destroy me. I suspect
they have the power. Herr Schreiber is a most powerful wizard and in all my long existence I don't think I have ever seen
a weapon more powerful than Gotrek Gurnisson's axe.'

'I could, if you let me leave here alive.'

'You can go now if you wish. I will not stop you.'

Felix almost rose but he was reluctant to put her words to
the test. After all, they were exactly what she would say if she
wished to take him off guard. He would be at his most vulnerable trying to open the door, with his back partially
turned to her. Maybe he could call for help now but her
apartments were a long way from the others, and the walls
were very thick. With the wind gusting loudly outside perhaps no one would ever hear him.

He spoke again, as much to buy himself some time to
think as because he was interested in the answer.

'When I listen to you I sense something personal in your
animosity towards Krieger. What is the real reason you want
us to go against him?'

To his surprise she laughed. 'I had not thought I was so transparent. I have grown so accustomed to reading mortals that I have ceased to believe that they might be able to see through me.'

Somehow, Felix doubted this. He was beginning to believe that this ancient immortal never did anything without a reason, that all of her acts were the result of long deliberation, and that if she had given something away it was because she wanted him to see it. He decided that it would be better to keep such thoughts to himself. Instead he said, 'You have not answered my question.'

The silence was long and at first Felix thought he had misjudged the situation and that she was not going to answer.

'Krieger is my creation. My child if you like. I made him what he is today, to my lasting sorrow. In a way, he is my responsibility. He would have been dead centuries ago had I not intervened in his life, and we would not have to worry about any of the things he is doing now.'

'What do you want from me?'

'I want you to help me with your companions. I do not want to have to fight with them while I struggle with Krieger.'

Felix rose from the chair and headed for the door. She made no move to stop him. He saw the key was still in the lock. 'I will think on what you have said,' he said as he opened the door.

'Do not think too long, Herr Jaeger. The hour is getting very late.'

As FELIX MADE his way back to his room, he was troubled as well as frightened. He felt as if he had had a narrow escape. And what was he to do with the information she had given him, and about the request she had made?

Surely she must see she had placed him in an impossible position. Max Schreiber might accept what she was and ally with her, but he did not think Gotrek and Snorri Nosebiter would. He could imagine the Slayers' response to the fact there was a bloodsucker in their midst. They would attack first and think later. Ivan Petrovich Straghov and his men

were no more likely to accept the vampire than the dwarfs.
They were from the marches of Kislev, which did not breed
men who would compromise with the darkness.

Whatever she was, the countess was intelligent. She must
already know all this. What did she hope to gain? Turning
things over in his mind, he could not uncover anything. Just
because he could not see any advantage for her, did not
mean there was not one there.

It was only after all these thoughts passed through his mind
that Felix realised that he had in part accepted her case. He
was not going to go rushing to the Slayers and inform them
about her, at least not until after he had considered all the
implications. Still, he realised he needed to talk to somebody.

'THE COUNTESS IS what?' exclaimed Max Schreiber.

'Keep it down,' said Felix. 'I don't want the whole tavern to
know.'

An aura of fire played around the wizard's hand and Felix
saw that Max was seriously considering storming off to the
countess's room. Under the circumstances, it was the last
thing Felix wanted. A confrontation between a powerful sorcerer and a vampire might leave the whole inn in ruins. He
was starting to regret telling the wizard all that the countess
had shared with him.

'I can't believe you are just standing there, Felix. There is
one of those monsters in this house, and you do nothing.'

'I'm talking to you, aren't I?'

'I would have thought gathering a mob and storming her
room would be more appropriate.'

'You are the last person I would expect to hear talking that
way, Max. A wizard should have some sympathy. After all it
was not that long ago when people felt the same way about
your kind.'

'I think I resent that, Felix. I don't see any connection
between mortal sorcerers and undead mass murderers.'

Felix shrugged. It had been an undiplomatic thing to say
but he was still shocked by Max's response. The wizard normally showed more self-control. Perhaps the strain of the
past few weeks was telling more than he let show. Felix

wanted to respond hotly to Max's words himself but some-one here needed to keep calm, and it looked like he was the one chosen by circumstances. 'I am sorry I said it then, Max, but think about it. What if she is telling the truth? She might be our best ally against Krieger.'

Suddenly Felix felt a chill run through him. Max stared hard at him and he looked as if he was contemplating vio-lence. It was all Felix could do to keep from drawing his sword. 'Has she enchanted you?' the wizard murmured. 'Are you bound to her will?'

Felix flinched as Max gestured with his hand. A trail of glowing fire followed the wizard's fingers as he sketched an intricate symbol in the air. It hung there glowing. Felix shut his eyes but the after-image of the rune seemed burned onto his retina. He was tempted to lash out at the magician but he wanted an answer to the wizard's question too. He did not feel as if he had been put under a spell, but how would he know? Perhaps the binding prevented those who had been bound from noticing it.

After a few seconds he heard Max exhale softly. He opened his eyes. The wizard looked calmer. There was a thoughtful look in his eye. 'There are no persistent enchantments on you that I can detect.'

'You would know about such things better than I,' said Felix. Max walked over to his bed and slumped down on it. His roomer was smaller and meaner than the countess's. Felix sat down in the only chair.

'What are we going to do about her?'

'If you are really seriously considering accepting her aid, I don't think telling Gotrek about this is such a good idea,' said Max.

'That thought has already crossed my mind,' said Felix. 'I don't feel good about it but right now I think our first con-cern should be rescuing Ulrika. And preventing whatever Krieger is up to.'

More of the tension drained out of Max. 'I agree. The ques-tion is, can we trust the countess? What if she simply desires the Eye for herself? She could be just as bad as she claims Krieger will be if she has it.'

'I know. I think it would be best if we ensure she does not get it. I think it would be advisable to trust her no further than necessary, and if one of us keeps a wary eye on her at all times.'

'You seemed to be doing a bit more than that already.'

'She's a fascinating… woman.'

'It might be best if you stopped thinking of her as that.'

'Believe me I already have. Just being in the same room as her made my flesh crawl.'

'I have heard that some men enjoy the company of the undying. There are rumours about Detlef Sierck for instance.'

'Some men might, but I am not one of them. I don't like the idea of anyone looking at me like I might be their next meal.'

'Glad to hear it. What about the knights? Our impetuous friend Rodrik and his companions?'

'We should assume they are completely under her spell.'

'It seems she was very forthright with you.'

'It seems that way but she has travelled with us for a few days. Do you think it's possible that a few of our companions might have been ensnared?'

'It's possible. I will check on the morrow.'

'Discreetly.'

'Yes.'

Talking in hushed voices they spent several hours discussing their plans. In both their minds the possibility of treachery was foremost.

BOOK THREE
The Vampire's Lair

'And so, almost inevitably, our path led us to Drakenhof Castle, a place steeped in legends of horror. Unfortunately I am in a position to confirm that the old tales were in no way exaggerated. If anything, they do not go far enough. It is not my intention to disturb the dreams of my readers, or to engender nightmares, but honesty, and the need to set down a true chronicle of the events of the Slayer's career, forces me to set such things to paper. Readers of a sensitive disposition may wish to stop at this point. Those who continue cannot say they have not been warned.'

— From *My Travels With Gotrek* Vol IV,
by Herr Felix Jaeger (Altdorf Press, 2505)

NINE

'You SEEM VERY thoughtful today, manling,' growled Gotrek.

Felix flicked the reins and goaded the ponies into movement, then turned and looked at the Slayer. The Kislevites as always rode ahead of them. The Countess Gabriella and her escort followed behind in their coach. He could hear Rodrik talking loudly about how this part of the wood looked like a good place to hunt for beastmen when spring came. To Felix, it looked like a good place for beastmen to hunt them right now.

'I have a lot on my mind,' he said. He wondered whether in spite of everything he should tell the Slayer about the countess's revelations of the previous evening. After all, if she did prove to be treacherous, Gotrek deserved some warning. Felix felt he deserved at least this. He and the dwarf had been companions on many a desperate adventure and the dwarf had saved his life more times than he cared to count. Keeping this a secret from him felt wrong. For all he knew, the countess could just be a very persuasive liar, leading them all into a trap.

226

'I do not trust those Sylvanians,' Felix said eventually.

'You seem to be getting on well enough with the Countess Gabriella,' said the Slayer. He sounded amused.

'She is part of the problem.'

The Slayer looked at him quizzically. He seemed to be in unusually good spirits today, despite having consumed a great deal of ale the previous evening. Perhaps the prospect of facing Krieger and achieving his long awaited doom was cheering him. With dwarfs it was difficult to tell. 'Go on?'

'I am not sure I can.' The Slayer's grin widened.

'Why not?'

'It is a matter of trust. I have given my word on it.' The dwarf looked more serious now. His people took oaths very seriously. 'I will not pry then,' he said.

Felix was disappointed. He had been half-hoping the dwarf would ask some questions. He glanced at the path, studying their way forward through the snow-covered land. The path wound through a wood that was becoming progressively darker and gloomier with every pace they took forward. He did not like the look of the place at all.

'If it makes you feel any better, manling, I too have my suspicions about our chance-met companions.'

Felix felt a thrill of fear pass through him. Had the Slayer discovered the countess's secret all on his own? Felix knew that despite his brutish appearance Gotrek was far from stupid. 'What do you mean?' he asked.

'I do not think they are quite what they seem.' Felix wondered exactly what the Slayer was getting at. He could not know the whole truth already, otherwise he would have already charged the countess's coach, axe held high. Felix thought he had better take some action.

'Do you trust my judgement?' he asked suddenly.

The Slayer regarded him for a long moment. Looking into his single mad eye, Felix was reminded of just how alien Gotrek's race was. They looked human enough but they were not. They were a product of a different culture, and a different upbringing, children of different gods.

'Yes,' said the Slayer eventually.

'I know a secret concerning the countess which is very dangerous, and which may give you cause to distrust her. Will you promise me not to attack her or harm her in any way until after we have freed Ulrika or slain Krieger?'

Felix could see he had piqued the dwarf's curiosity now. The Slayer remained silent for a long time considering. Felix wondered if he had misjudged the situation and Gotrek was going to go and try and beat Gabriella's secret from her right now. Perhaps he was simply looking at things from all angles. He knew dwarfs took oaths and promises very seriously, and did not give them lightly.

'You've picked an interesting deadline, manling,' said Gotrek eventually. Felix realised he had. It appeared that, no matter how persuasive the countess's arguments had been, he was not prepared to trust her in the long term.

'Will you take it?'

'Providing she does not attempt to harm any of us, yes,' Gotrek said eventually. The words came out reluctantly, as if against his better judgement. Felix felt quite proud of the fact that the Slayer was prepared to trust him so much. It made telling him the whole story a lot easier.

As he spoke, he thought Gotrek was going to explode. It was plain from his manner that the Slayer was very unhappy with the thought of having one of the undying within striking distance and not being able to do anything about. Swiftly Felix went on to explain the reasons why they should accept her aid at least until Ulrika was free. Gotrek glared at him as if he had been tricked. At any moment, Felix half expected the Slayer to throw himself from the supply sledge and rush over to the coach, but he did not. He merely favoured it with a sullen glower. Felix could see his knuckles were tight around the shaft of his axe.

'I like this not, manling,' he said.

'But you will leave her alone. For the moment.'

'An oath is an oath.'

The Slayer's words sent a short spasm of guilt through Felix. He did not feel good about giving the countess's secret to the Slayer. He told himself that he was being ridiculous. He owed the vampire nothing. She was a monster who fed on the blood of innocent men and women. Despite his guilt, he felt as if a weight had been lifted from his shoulders. At least the Slayer was aware of what was going on, and would be on guard.

If the countess planned treachery, she would find herself on the receiving end of the axe she feared so very much. It was not much of a reassurance but at the moment it was the only one he had.

'Who else knows about this?' growled Gotrek.

'Only Max.'

'It would probably be best to avoid mentioning this to Snorri Nosebiter.' The Slayer sounded almost embarrassed.

Felix could not help but agree.

THE FOREST BECAME quieter and emptier as they progressed, the trees more twisted and stunted. Max glanced behind him constantly, seeking to keep his eye on the coach of the countess. He certainly did not trust her, even as much as Felix. He had held the Eye of Khemri and felt its power. He knew that it would be as useful to one vampire as another, and no matter what she claimed, he could not bring himself to believe her motives were entirely altruistic.

He sensed a change in the nature of the forest. The place was tainted in a very subtle way. He felt vaguely nauseous, as he sometimes did in the presence of Chaos. He was beginning to think that the tales of this land being corrupted by the warpstone starfall of 1111 were not far from the truth.

More than that though, he sensed the winds of dark magic in this place were strangely altered, almost like the way they had been channelled when the Chaos horde attacked Praag, although not so strong. Not yet anyway. He wondered if all these events were somehow connected. It seemed that the flow of dark magic at the present moment was rather too malleable to the will of evil mages. Perhaps the Lords of Chaos were putting forth their power to aid their supporters. Max shivered and not with the cold.

He opened his magesight and saw nothing surrounding the coach. At least the countess was not working any magic that he could detect, and that meant she was most likely casting no spells. Max was a sufficiently competent sorcerer to spot it if she was. Not even a master mage could conceal his spellcraft from Max now.

He reviewed the plan he and Felix had come up with the previous evening. Even if the vampire countess was what she claimed, it was best to ensure the Eye of Khemri did not fall into her hands. If possible, Felix was to take it. Max was reluctant to do so. Felix was not a mage and the thing was unlikely to be able to affect him as much as it would Max. Even if it did, his lack of magical ability would ensure he could work no harm.

Max tried to recall everything he could about the Eye from his brief contact with its secret heart. It certainly seemed possible that wondrously complex cluster of spells at its core could do what the countess claimed. There definitely had been spells of amplification and compulsion in there, of a most unusual kind. They had not seemed to be aimed at binding anything human either.

Max knew they were fumbling in the dark with little or no light to guide them. They had fitted together hints and vague memories and suspicions to make a theory concerning their foe and what he wanted, but it was by no means certain that what they thought was correct. All they could do was move on and hope that when the time came they would be ready for the vampire's onslaught.

OVERHEAD THE CHAOS moon burned so bright that Mannsleib seemed dim. Adolphus Krieger strode through the forest surrounding his new keep. So far his minions had not had time to clear the land and make a killing ground, but that would all change soon. He smiled, revealing his fangs.

He felt strong. The Eye of Khemri was his. His spell of summoning had gone out across the land. Already ghouls and other creatures of the darkness had begun to gather at his call. He knew that in their submerged dreams all of the children within a hundred leagues were beginning to feel the tug of his will. Soon the aristocracy of the night would gather at his home and plan the reconquest of all that had been theirs.

Tonight he had another purpose. His strides had taken him to the massive graveyard, hidden deep within the woods not far from the tumbled down ruins of Drakenhof town. It was a huge area, originally consecrated to Morr, the Lord of Death. It was a place where once men had thought to lie in peace through all eternity, a sanctuary, a place of rest.

Adolphus intended to change all of that. Tonight, the cemetery would be turned into a recruiting office for the mightiest army in all of history. Tonight, he would raise the first of many regiments to be drawn from the ranks of the dead.

He touched the talisman and felt its power. As he did so, he seemed to hear a voice whispering to him, telling him potent secrets of necromancy. Somehow, since he had attuned the Eye, his understanding of sorcery had deepened.

Ancient incantations that had once seemed meaningless to him were now pregnant with hidden significance. He could visualise and control the flows of dark magic with an ease that surprised him. He had always been an indifferent student of the magical arts, but now he felt given enough time he would prove to be one of their greatest masters. It appeared that there was no end to the gifts Nagash's ancient creation granted. Who knows, given time, he might match that ancient liche for knowledge and create such potent artefacts himself.

He pushed the thought aside. Such sweet dreams were for the future. Right now, he had more important work to do. Right now, he must take his next steps along the path of empire. There were prophecies to be fulfilled. It was his duty to herald the Age of Blood.

Lithely he leapt atop the defaced remains of an ancient mausoleum. From here, he had a fine view of the entire graveyard. He could see the masses of tumbled gravestones, broken-limbed statues, effigies of the now-forgotten dead who would soon return to be his soldiers.

He cast back his head, opened his mouth and began to enunciate the words of the ancient ritual.

'In the name of Nagash, Lord of Undeath, I call you…'

The Eye blazed at his throat, a beacon sending a cold clear light out to illuminate his surroundings. The winds of magic swirled around him, caressing him lightly as they flowed into the talisman.

'In the name of Nagash, Lord of Unlife, you must come…'

Burning snakes of fire twisted and turned in his belly. For once, there was no struggle to control them. All of this energy was his to command. Dark magical power flowed through him and down into the tainted soil of Sylvania.

The tendrils of power spread like an elaborate root system. He could sense through them, an odd mixture of sight and touch and other unnamed perceptions. He became aware of the many hundreds of corpses planted in the earth, preserved for centuries by the faint taint of warpstone in the soil. He saw the bloated white worms burrowing, and other twisted creatures that even he found dreadful to contemplate.

As the web of power touched the corpses there came a faint echo of the life that had once burned so strongly within them. Here was a proud nobleman who had ground his peasants to dirt. There was a knight who in life had been a proud defender of his faith. He touched a woman who had died painfully in childbirth and a man who had died of hunger during one of the many periodic famines that wracked Sylvania.

Krieger did not care how they had died. He did not care what they once had been in life. He only cared that they would serve him in death. His spell opened up a path to somewhere else, another world parallel to his own, a seething sea of wild chaotic energies in which evil presences lurked. Some of the weakest drifted towards the spirits and entered the rotting bodies, merging with them, lending them animation.

In his mind's eye, he saw green witchfires spring to life in empty eye sockets. He saw white bony limbs move, skeletal fingers flex. Worm-eaten skeletons shifted, swimmers plunging through a sea of dirt. It did not matter that they had been buried face down to confuse them in the event of just such a dark resurrection. They sensed the direction of the power that drew them, and they came.

Wriggling, writhing, twisting and turning, they clawed their way to the surface. His voice was a high-pitched wail as he recited the ancient forbidden words. The earth below him vibrated as hundreds of dead woke from their long slumber. Somewhere off in the distance a wolf howled in terror. The eerie hunting calls of ghouls ripped the night as they responded subconsciously to the energies they sensed being unleashed.

A grin of triumph twisted his lips. He opened his eyes. Lines of power shimmered in the air. As if in response to his thaumaturgy, a shower of glowing stars fell from the heavens, blazing across the leering face of the Chaos moon. Eerie green contrails raked the night, as if the talons of some huge predatory beast had shredded the parchment-thin surface of the sky.

A faint white speck appeared on the ground. It might have been the head of one of those albino worms he had seen in the depths, but it was not. It was a fingertip. Four near identical slivers of ivory then a whole skeletal arm followed, emerging from the earth, flailing in the empty air like that of a swimmer drowning in deep water.

The palm of the arm pushed flat against the ground, gaining leverage, and the rest of the skeleton appeared. First came the skull, with its glowing eyes and leering evil smile, then came the ribcage and the other arm, followed by the spine, the hips and the strangely elongated-looking legs. The first of Adolphus's newly recruited army emerged into the night, and stretched exultantly, lifting its arms skywards in triumph. As it moved, it clicked. Its grinning jaws opened and then shut in a deranged parody of a man sucking in huge breaths.

The stink of corruption and fresh-turned earth filled the air, as more and more animated corpses pulled themselves upwards in the moon's pale light. Gravestones tumbled; old markers fell as the skeletons emerged. Some of them looked around, heads scanning their surroundings, necks creaking faintly as they moved. Others danced wildly amid the tombstones, as if testing their mobility after centuries of being interred. A few nodded gravely as if they understood what was happening and approved.

Then one by one, clicking as they moved, they drew closer to Krieger and abased themselves like worshippers of some dreadful ancient god before a bloodstained altar.

Tonight, he thought, a new age begins. Tonight, I have taken my first step towards an empire that will last throughout eternity. Tonight will be remembered a thousand years hence. I too will remember it.

He spoke more words, drew more power and extended the spell outwards, sending dark magical energies tumbling in an ever-expanding sphere for leagues upon leagues. Everywhere the spell touched, the dead began to move in their graves.

At his throat the talisman of Nagash glowed like the eye of an evil god. The Time of Blood had arrived.

MAX LOOKED UP from the fire around which they sat huddled. He could tell that they all sensed it, the stirrings of that vast power somewhere in the forest. One did not have to be a wizard to notice. The pulse was so strong that even the most ungifted yokel would feel it and know dread. By the way even the most hardened Kislevite shuddered and glanced out into the surrounding gloom, he could tell that they felt it too.

If such a thing was noticeable to someone lacking the talent, it was like a thunderclap to Max. His entire being echoed to the power he sensed being unleashed. He knew that somewhere out there in the night, a spell of extreme potency was being woven. He could sense the direction as clearly as he could see a beacon burning in the night. He could feel the pressure of power moving across the land as surely as the pilot of a merchantman feels the wind. What was that undying madman up to, he wondered?

As if some celestial being were giving a sign of the evil to come, a clutch of meteors blazed through the night. From the colour of their fiery contrails, Max knew that they were made from warpstone, the concentrated essence of pure evil. What was it about this land that attracted the stuff so, Max wondered? Why did it seem to receive an inordinate concentration of this dreadful starfalls? An accident of geography? Like calling to like? The curse of the gods? Or was this starfall's appearance something to do with the spell he had just sensed being cast. Would he ever know?

Even as the thought flickered through his mind, he sensed a further rending of the fabric of reality. It was strong enough so he could tell the exact direction and distance, and yet distant enough so that he merely felt uncomfortable. He suspected that had he been closer he would be enduring far more than a faint sense of nausea and dizziness.

He rose reluctantly from the fire and walked towards the small pavilion where the Countess Gabriella was resting. A gesture and a word called a ball of light into being. It floated at his shoulder illumining his way. Another gesture and an incantation and a web of energy sprang into being around him, invisible to any eyes but that of a mage. Anyone or anything, any spell or malign influence, would trip a number of powerful defensive spells. Max was taking no chances.

Outside the tent, Rodrik's companions met him with bared blades but Rodrik himself was nowhere to be seen.

'What do you want, wizard?' asked the youngest of them. His voice was high-pitched and faintly effeminate. In the glow of the witchlight Max could clearly see his fresh face with a small caterpillar of a moustache crawling over his upper lip. The boy sounded at once a little scared and desperate to prove his bravery.

'I want to speak to the Countess Gabriella.'

'It's all right, Quentin. Let him pass.' The voice of the countess sounded from within the tent. The young warriors stepped aside reluctantly. Max gave them a pleasant smile, although his flesh crawled knowing what they were. Despite his defensive web, he half expected a sword in the back as he pulled aside the tent flap and let himself in.

Inside the air smelled of musk and cinnamon, a strong perfume meant to cover the smell of something else. Undead flesh, perhaps. An Arabian rug covered the floor. Two heavy chests were set to one side. Aside from his own glowing globe there was no source of light within the tent. He supposed its occupants did not need it.

Rodrik lay sprawled on the floor. He looked exhausted and ecstatic. His face was flushed. His lips were bruised and swollen. His eyes were unfocused, staring at nothing. His breathing came in ragged gasps, like a man who had just run a long race. The countess lay beside him. Her arms were wrapped round his shoulders. Her head was thrown back. Her veil was still in place. Judging from the scene, Max had no doubt he had just missed watching her take her evening meal from her follower's veins.

Coldly and deliberately, Max reviewed all the swiftest and most destructive spells he knew. With a gesture the glowglobe could be turned into an engine of destruction. A word and a more complex weave would send hundreds of streamers of razor-edged light slashing through the gloom. Another word would encase him in a cocoon of protective energies. He breathed deeply, and smiled in a relaxed manner, all the while ready to deal death in a heartbeat.

'There is no need for violence between us, Herr Schreiber,' said the countess. It was almost as if she had read his thoughts. She sounded amused.

'Let us hope so,' said Max, not letting his guard down for an instant.

'Do not dare to threaten milady,' said Rodrik weakly, struggling to rise to his feet. His voice sounded slurred, like a man who had drunk too much or overindulged in witchweed.

'It is unwise to threaten me,' said Max, in return letting his eyes move from the knight to the woman so there was no doubt as to his meaning. 'Leave us, Rodrik. I would have words with your mistress.' Despite himself Max could not help but stress the last word to play on its ambiguity.

Rodrik looked up blearily at the countess. She stroked his cheek almost affectionately and nodded her permission. The young knight gathered his wits and reeled to his feet, before staggering to the exit.

'If you need me, milady, I will be within call.'

'His devotion is truly touching,' said Max ironically, after Rodrik had executed a clumsy bow and left.

'His devotion is quite sincere and unforced I assure you, Herr Schreiber. And I am sure you did not come here simply to sneer at my admirers.'

'A nice way to put it,' said Max.

'I take it Herr Jaeger has told you all about me then. I thought as much from your manner on the ride.'

'Let us make one thing clear,' said Max. 'I do not like you or what you are. At the moment we happen to be allies because we have need of each other. Under different circumstances, we would be enemies.'

'You are forthright, Herr Schreiber. Very well, we need each other, as you say, so I will forgive your boorish manners and the way you have entered cloaked in power, and I will discuss things like a reasonable person. I suggest you do the same.'

Max smiled at her coldly. The rebuke had been delivered well, in the tone of a parent admonishing a surly child. Many men would have been cowed by that alone. Max was not one of them.

'Your protégé, Krieger, has begun his work. You must have sensed that as clearly as I.'

'Why do you think I took the risk of asking Rodrik to join me in my tent? I will soon need all the strength I can muster, so will you. I fear that my get has become very strong indeed.'

'I had understood that he was an indifferent sorcerer. The spell cast this evening was not the work of a clumsy journeyman.'

'Then we can assume that either he has learned a great deal over the past few years, or that the Eye of Khemri is augmenting his capabilities in that area.'

'If that is so we face a truly terrifying foe.'

'And one who is summoning an army to him unless I miss my guess, Herr Schreiber. What we both sensed was necromancy of the darkest and most potent sort. Believe me, I have enough experience of this to know.'

'And what does your experience tell you we should do?'

'Hurry to Krieger's fortress and destroy him, if we can. Already I can feel the power of the Eye growing in my mind.

He is summoning the Arisen, and it's a tug that few within a hundred leagues will be able to resist.'

'You are saying that perhaps he can turn you against us?'

'Yes, Herr Schreiber, that is exactly what I am saying. You see, I am giving you fair warning of all hazards.'

Max looked at her, measuring her words. In a way, he would welcome the chance to destroy this creature, but part of him also hoped it would not come to that, for then it would be a truly desperate situation indeed. She nodded her head, as if reading his mind once more.

'I believe I can fight Krieger's influence for a long time. I am much older, and more skilled in these arts than he.'

'I think the Eye of Khemri might change that.'

'You should know. You have had more contact with it than I.'

'Tell me all you know about it.'

Max settled down to listen to the vampire's tale, looking for any contradictions between what she told him and what she had told Felix. He already suspected he would find none. As he gave his attention to her clear, soothing voice, he found his thoughts turning to Ulrika. He truly dreaded what might have happened to her.

ULRIKA WOKE IN darkness. She felt weak and strange. There was something wrong with her eyes. She could see her surroundings quite clearly but they had been drained of all colour. Everything was in varying shades of black and white.

She pushed herself upright. The motion made her dizzy. Her whole body ached. Her head was sore. Her stomach churned. Pains stabbed through her mouth. She looked around. She lay on cold stone, in a crypt. It looked as if she were entombed in a burial chamber of some sort. A wave of panic passed through her. Was she imprisoned within some tomb, mistakenly believed to be dead, when all the while she had been alive?

It could have been worse, she supposed. She could have been interred within a coffin. At least she would be up and about when they came to bury her. If they came to bury her. What had happened? She suspected that Krieger had drunk so deep of her blood that she had fallen into a death-like trance. It would be a mistake that was easy to make.

The thought of the vampire and that final embrace sent a wave of conflicting emotions through her: hatred, resentment– and secret guilty pleasure. She stretched and rose to prowl around the room. It was small, with carvings of skeletons, skulls and other symbols of death engraved into the walls. She sniffed the air. Her senses seemed keener than once they had been. She could smell the dust, and the faint scent of a cinnamon perfume Krieger used. Underneath lay the faintest hint of decay. She could smell mould in the air, and off in the distance she caught the warm smell of living things. She listened and thought she caught the sound of footsteps far away.

The burning hunger grew stronger. Responding to some primal instinct, she moved towards the exit. She reached a stairwell and found it barred. A gate of rusty yet ornate metalwork blocked the way out. Typical of Sylvanians, she thought, to turn even their mausoleums into prison cells, as if somehow the dead might escape from their internment. She shook her head. What had happened to her showed that they might have some justification. That sent her thoughts racing in a direction she did not yet want to follow. Instead she tested the bars, feeling the cold of the metal beneath her fingers.

They seemed old and weak. Rusty, indeed, she thought thankfully, exerting her strength against them. Even weak as she was, she managed to bend the bars enough to make a gap for her to slip through, and she raced up the stairs. What was she going to do now? Where was Adolphus Krieger? Did it matter?

She was on her own at last, with a chance to escape. This was still her best chance to get away before he or his repulsive human followers came to check the vault. She considered her options. The burning hunger increased. She had no winter clothing and no weapons. In the snow, in this haunted land, she would not get far. No matter how risky it was she needed to find supplies and weapons and warm gear. That meant searching this house and praying to all the gods she did not encounter the vampire or his henchmen. Part of her rebelled against the very concept of flight, part of her wanted to experience the vampire's embrace again and again, no matter what the cost. Ruthlessly she squashed these thoughts. They would not help.

Quietly as she could she paced on. She was in part of the manor house she had never seen before, which was hardly surprising for mostly she had been confined to her rooms, except when summoned to Krieger's throne room. A whiff of cooking food reached her nostrils, all animal fat and charred flesh. In spite of her hunger it left her repulsed. Nonetheless she forced herself to move in that direction.

She passed door after door. She knew she should pause and check them out, looking for what she needed, but she found she could not. Some compulsion, only half-understood by her rebellious mind, drove her in the direction she knew she would find people.

Ahead of her she caught a flicker of movement. Her first thoughts were to throw herself through a doorway and hide, instead she found her stride lengthening, sending her racing towards the fat merchant, Osrik. He stood there, a look of astonishment and fear on his face, a drumstick of chicken in his hands, and a stream of grease dribbling from his blubbery mouth. He raised his hands as if to ward her off. All of his actions seemed terribly slow to Ulrika, as if she were caught up in some strange nightmare. She could smell the warmth of him, the sweetness of the blood coursing through his body. She could see the pulse beating in his neck. It hypnotised her, drew all of her attention. The hunger in her was irresistible. She felt like a passenger in a runaway coach, or a rider mounted on a wild stallion. She had no conscious control over her body now, and she did not want to have.

The pain in her mouth grew intense. She felt something ripping through the flesh of her gums. A taste of old, stale black blood filled her mouth. She leapt forward on the screaming servant, arms grasping his neck and drawing him closer into her embrace. Weak as she felt herself to be, his frantic struggles availed him nothing. He seemed about as strong as a small child.

All conscious thought was seared away as she leaned forward and felt her fangs puncture the flesh of his throat. Like a wild beast she ripped at the artery, widening the gap, causing the blood to spray everywhere. It rose in a red mist, obscuring her sight, clinging to her flesh. It did not matter. There was plenty of the warm red stuff to drink down.

As it slid down her throat, a wonderful warmth filled her, a glow of wellbeing stronger than any pleasure she had ever felt before. The embrace of the vampire had been but a dim echo. The pleasure blotted out all other sensations: all horror, all guilt and all restraint. She gulped the blood down greedily, never wanting this moment to end, not wanting to stop. She heard the shouts and screams of the other servants but she ignored them. Osrik spasmed in her grasp, but the convulsions of his muscles were nothing to her. She held him in place easily though he was much heavier than she.

Her whole universe contracted till there was only her mouth and the hot wonderful flow of life-giving liquid. She was aware dimly of Osrik's heartbeat slowing and then stopping, and the flow dying away until it became only a few drops. Still, the warmth of blood passed through her system. It passed from her stomach to her veins, with a sweetness so intense it was almost unbearable, then surged through some barrier where the pleasure became pain, and horror and fear came flooding back into her mind along with conscious thought.

Now she felt sick, nauseous, bloated beyond belief. She felt as if she might explode, like an overfull wineskin stuffed with stolen blood. Worse was the realisation of what she had done, of what she had become.

The sickness became so intense that she could barely stand up. She sensed the approach of other servants and could do nothing. She knew she should flee but could she could not. She knew that they would kill her and that she would welcome death. Instinctively, though, her body betrayed her. She reeled away down the corridor, nausea sweeping through her swift as fire. She hit a wall with her head, crumbled to her knees then crawled blindly down the corridor, retching up blood, bile and decaying bits of food as she went.

Swiftly the weakness overcame her and she slowed to a halt face down in a pool of filthy vomit, overcome with loathing for herself, and the thing she had become, and the one who had made her so. Darkness filled her vision again, and as it blotted out her consciousness she welcomed it.

'INTERESTING CHAT?' Felix asked, as Max settled down beside him. The wizard looked weary and more than a little grim. Hardly surprising under the circumstances, thought Felix. Dealing with one of the undying would put a strain on anyone. He was suddenly glad he had shared his knowledge of the countess with Gotrek and the wizard. In this case, it really was true that a burden shared was a burden lightened.

Across the fire, Gotrek looked up. His one good eye reflected the flames, giving the Slayer an eerie supernatural look.

'Very,' said Max carefully. 'The countess is a very learned... woman.'

He sounded like he was having some trouble saying the last word. Felix thought he knew how Max felt. There was a crawling between his own shoulder blades whenever he thought of her out there in the darkness behind him. It had increased ever since he felt that strange surge of unease earlier in the evening, the prickling of the hairs on the back of his neck that he sometimes got when magic was being used in the vicinity.

'Did you learn anything from her?' Felix coughed. He could feel phlegm moving in his lungs but he was feeling a little better, he thought. Not quite so weak.

'I learned we should beware of treachery.' Max glanced around the fire. Aside from Gotrek and Snorri Nosebiter they were alone. The Kislevites preferred the company of their companions around the other fire. Ivan Petrovich was lost in gloom and stood apart, staring into the night. Snorri snored loudly. Gotrek glared at them. Felix did not doubt that the Slayer's keen ears could hear everything Max said. 'She thinks the Eye of Khemri might be used to control her, to turn her against us.'

'Wonderful,' muttered Felix. This news amplified his unease. 'She also thinks we need to strike soon before others of their kind are drawn to the place. Who knows, they may already be on the way.'

'This gets better and better. Remind me again why I came here.'

'The same reason as I did, to free Ulrika.'

'What if we can't? What if she is dead?' Felix pressed.

'Then we avenge her.'

'And what if she has… gone over to the other side.'

'Then we kill her.'

Felix looked at Max and wondered if either of them were really capable of it. He caught the glitter in Gotrek's eye. If they could not bring themselves to kill the woman, the dwarf could. Felix prayed to Sigmar that things would not come to that.

UNDER THE MOON'S eerie light, the corpses pulled themselves from their graves. Cerements still clung to their flesh. Their hands were claws. They hungered for the flesh of the living but another more powerful urge overcame their lust for meat. Somewhere out in the night, something called them, with a strength they could not resist. Stumbling, shuffling, moving like sick blind men, they began to march towards their goal. All over the cursed land of Sylvania peasants hid themselves within their houses and prayed to Sigmar to save them. The undead were on the move.

'SO NOW YOU know,' said Adolphus. Ulrika was surprised. There was no triumph in his manner, only concern. He looked at her like a lover might, or a father, or a king contemplating a favoured vassal or some combination of all three. She glanced around at her surroundings. She lay on the great four-poster bed, in his chamber. Someone had taken the trouble to clean the vomit and the blood and to change her clothing.

'Let me die,' she said. She felt miserable, physically and mentally. Her body was wracked by sickness, her mind by self-hatred and guilt.

'You will not die now unless you kill yourself or someone kills you. You feel terrible now because you drank too much blood. It is a common mistake among the newly risen. In some ways it is like what happens when a starving man sits down to a banquet. His stomach simply cannot deal with all the food he eats. In other ways it's like what happens after a human indulges in too much wine. There is what you might call a hangover.'

'I do not want to live. I killed a man for no reason.'

'You killed a man to extend your life. People do it every day. We have discussed this. Oh, now you feel guilty because it goes against many of the hypocrisies you have been taught since you were a child, but believe me, this too shall pass.'

'I do not want to change the way I feel.'

'But you will. Trust me. You will.'

'I don't think so.'

'We all say that, at first.'

'You are so sure of yourself, aren't you?' Ulrika sneered. Adolphus Krieger shrugged.

'I have every reason to be. I have gone through what you have gone through. And I know that one day you will thank me for doing you the greatest favour anyone has ever done for you.'

'Turning me into a monster?'

'Turning you into an immortal.' Ulrika rose up on her elbow to stare at him.

She felt like lashing out. She wanted to take her nails and slash his face to the bone, to bury her fangs in his throat. He took a step back.

'It would be extremely foolish of you to turn on me now,' he said. 'I know things that you need to know. Without that knowledge you will be prey to any passing vampire who decides to take advantage of you.'

'It seems to me that you have already done that.'

'True, but I am your progenitor. You are my get. I have certain responsibilities to you just as you have certain responsibilities to me. In a very real sense, you are my child.'

'I already have a father.'

'You *had* a father. What do you think he will do to you, if he finds out what you are now?'

Ulrika paused for a second. She knew what her father would do. The people of Kislev did not suffer monsters to live in their midst. That thought sent a flash of pain through her chest; no matter how much her father had once loved her, he would do his duty. It would pain him unto death but he would do what he had to.

'Look at it another way,' Krieger continued mercilessly. 'What do you think you might do to him if you were near him when the thirst overtook you?'

An image of doing what she had done to the fat merchant to her own father flashed through her mind. It was at once horrifying and strangely attractive. She shuddered and tried to force the picture from her mind, but it would not go.

'I see you do understand. It is best if you break all mortal ties now. You are still a neophyte. You would not be able to control yourself when the killing lust came upon you.'

'Would I be able to one day?'

'Good – you are beginning to adjust to your new state, to accept it.'

Ulrika realised that she was. She had taken to her new condition far too easily. Part of it was sheer Kislevite pragmatism. She was what she was and nothing could change that now, but part of it was something else.

'You are doing something to my mind,' she said. He nodded like a teacher pleased with a particularly apt pupil.

'It is because I am your progenitor. There is a link between us that is very strong. Also it is this,' he said indicating the talisman at his throat.

Her eyes were drawn to it. She sensed its power. It was like watching a huge spider clinging to his neck. Did he not sense the wickedness and the power of the thing? 'It is as well that you understand your position from the start. There is much I have to teach you and we do not have a huge amount of time. Soon we will both be very busy.'

'Doing what?'

'Carving out a new kingdom here in Sylvania, ruling the night, and setting our servants to rule the day.'

'Do you really think you can do that?'

'I have already started. Now, listen! There is much you have to learn.'

Such was the compulsion implicit in his words that she fell silent, and simply stared at him, waiting for him to share his infernal wisdom.

'You will find that many things have changed. You no longer need to eat or drink as mortals do. Blood will provide you with all the sustenance you need. It is everything to you now. It is the be all and end all of your unlife. It will nourish you, heal you, and provide you with power the like of which you could only dream about when you were mortal. With it, you can maintain your existence forever. Without it…'

He paused for a moment and glanced out the window as if considering something.

'You will not die, not as others understand it. Something worse will happen.'

'Worse?'

'You will simply wither away, losing strength and youth and beauty. Your muscles will shrivel. Your mind will deteriorate. You will not be able to move or speak or think. Your body will become a withered desiccated husk, and yet part of you will live on imprisoned in it, aware in a very dim way of what has happened to you and of what you once were. It will be a long eternity of torment and hunger, tortured by the thirst but unable to slake it. It is something like hell.'

'You speak as if you have experienced it.' She said softly.

'The beginnings of it, once, long ago. I was saved when another brought me blood. It gave me enough strength to hunt for myself once more. But enough of these ancient memories – I was telling you what you need to know.'

'Then go on,' she said, a little sulkily.

He reached out and touched her cheek. A thrill passed through her body. The feel of his cold skin on hers aroused a strange sensation in her. He smiled as if he knew what she was feeling.

'I told you there was a link between us. Some of my blood is in you, just as one day some of your blood will be in your get. We are bound now by blood and by darkness.'

Ulrika considered this. On some deep instinctive level she knew it was true. There was a bond between her and Krieger such as she had never felt with any other human being. With any human being, she corrected herself bitterly, knowing she was no longer one herself.

'Tonight I will tell you the essentials of what you need to know. The rules are simple. Do not go out by day if you can possibly help it. Find yourself a safe place and keep out of the light.'

'Why? You sometimes do it.'

'I have a tolerance for light. Some do not. Sunlight burns some of our kind as surely as flaming oil. Some are merely made torpid unless they have taken a great deal of blood, and even then their minds are not sharp. The only way to find out which type you are is to risk it and see, and that is not something you should do unless you are in the greatest of danger and swathed in the thickest cloak you can find, exposing as little flesh as possible.'

'Could I not simply expose some skin, say, on the back of my hand, for a short space of time.'

'You could, if you are willing to see it melt away into a stump if you are one of those who are vulnerable. And sometimes, for some of the Arisen there is an increased risk. Sunlight does not burn them immediately. It scorches their skin after prolonged exposure, blistering it and cracking it and causing the most extreme agony. It's like a case of sunburn to a mortal, only a thousand times worse.'

'Why is this?'

'I am not a natural philosopher. I do not know. I can only tell you the stories I have heard. Some say the sun god of the long dead kingdom of Nehekhara cursed our kind. Others say it is because we are saturated with a dark magic that is disrupted by sunlight. The only thing I know for certain is that all our kind are almost blind by day compared to how well we see at night. Something in our eye changes, adapting it to darkness and making it too sensitive to the sun's light. It is best to sleep through the day. It is when we become naturally torpid anyway.'

'Can I fly? Turn myself into a bat?' She realised it was a childish question, but being able to fly like a bird was a childhood dream, and perhaps she could find something good in what had happened to her.

'Transformation can be learned but the mastery is a long and difficult process. I will teach you what I know of it when I have the time. For the present you should be content with what you have. Mortal diseases no longer affect you. You are now many times stronger and hardier and faster than any mortal man, and you are invulnerable to many of their weapons.'

'Why?'

'Most of your internal organs are useless to you now. Over time they will atrophy. A blade to the belly will do you no real harm. Most wounds will heal very quickly when you take enough blood.'

'What about a stake through the heart?'

'Ah, that old chestnut. Yes. That will harm you. Any blow there will. Your heart still beats, albeit so slowly as to be undetectable except after you have drunk. It still pumps blood through your body though. If it is shattered then it will take a long time to repair itself. You will still live, but all the things I told you about lack of blood will apply. It will be a period of torture, and at the end of it you may be too weak to feed.

'You should also protect your head. It is the seat of your soul, or at least your mind. If your brain is damaged you will go mad, or lose memories or become an unthinking soulless brute. Having your head parted from your body, having the brain scooped out and burned, is the surest way of finding a real death. You would do well to avoid it.'

'What about magical powers? I have always heard that vampires gain many sorcerous powers through pacts with the Dark Ones.'

'Our powers do not come from the Lords of Chaos but they are very real. There are many ways to compel mortals to your will, to fascinate them, bedazzle them and ultimately to command them. Again, these things take a long time to master and I will teach you how to use them as and when I can.'

'It seems you intend to keep me very dependent on you.'

'Why not? These are traditional roles in our society. I am the master. You are the apprentice. I will teach and in return you will obey.'

'And if I do not want to? What will you do then?'

He smiled, showing all his teeth, and gestured to the talisman at his throat. 'Believe me, you have no choice. I command you to obey me in all things, to serve and protect me, until I release you from this binding.'

Even as he spoke Ulrika felt the compulsion settle on her mind like burning fetters hot from the forge being hammered onto the limbs of a condemned prisoner. She wanted to scream and to resist but there was nothing she could do. The power of the Eye of Khemri and of the will behind it was too great. She knew she was overwhelmed now, as surely as she had been by the red thirst earlier. Part of her actually wanted to obey. The spell was very strong.

'This is a very great honour, Ulrika. You will be the first of many bound to my service. Together we will forge a new empire and bring a new age of darkness to the world.'

TEN

'WE ARE VERY close now,' said Max. His voice sounded gloomy and bitter, half crazed with fear and frustration, but Felix did not doubt that he was right. The cloying evil in the air was almost tangible. He felt as if eyes watched him out of every shadow. He wanted to turn and run before whatever it was that waited out there came to get him. It was an effort of will to keep from constantly glancing over his shoulder.

It was these ruins. They were depressing him more than even the normal buildings of Sylvania. He told himself to be glad they had found some shelter. Even this old abandoned manor with its tumbled down walls and collapsed roof was better than nothing with a storm coming. At least the walls provided some shelter from the wind. He just wished it did not remind him so much of those tales he had read as a youth.

The forest was deep and dark. The sense of corruption was more intense. The snow here was a thin crust over the tainted earth. A miasma of evil rose from it. There were times when Felix found it difficult to breathe. It was late afternoon, and the shadows were lengthening. The ponies whickered nervously. Felix drew his cloak tighter about him, and then made sure his sword was loose in its scabbard.

From up ahead he could hear the sound of horses forcing their way forward. It had started to snow again, big flakes falling fast, so many of them that they obscured vision more than a few feet away. Their coldness brushing his cheek felt like the touch of dead men's fingers. He cursed and wondered whether they would all die in the blizzard. It would be ironic after they had come all this way.

Felix wiped his running nose on the edge of his cloak and looked at Gotrek. At that moment, he heard soft sounds of approaching movement from up ahead. His hand flew to the hilt of his sword.

The Slayer held his axe negligently in his hands. He looked as relaxed as he ever did. 'Tis just the scouts returning, manling.'

A moment later Felix saw that he was right. Two of the Kislevites had returned, Marek and another man. Their faces looked at once excited and afraid. They rode up to Ivan Petrovich and Marek spoke swiftly in a loud voice so that all could hear.

'Drakenhof Castle ahead of us about two hours' fast ride. A terrible sinister place it is, half in ruins, but at least partially occupied. We saw many men marching through the snow towards it. At least they looked like men – but they moved slowly, as if under some evil spell.'

Ivan Petrovich cocked his head. 'How many?'

'Many. Coming from all directions and converging on the castle. And we saw other things. Their tracks, anyway, before the snow started to fall.'

A thrill of fear passed through Felix.

'What do you mean?' asked Ivan Petrovich.

'We saw footprints in the snow around the mansion. Lots of them. They appeared to be human…'

'Appeared to be?'

'They were bare-footed, no shoes or boots.'

'And there were small indentations at the toes that looked like… well, like the marks of claws.'

Felix thought back to what they had seen on the outskirts of Waldenhof. It sounded like the tracks of ghouls. He caught enough of the rest of the scout's speech to guess that they thought the same.

'We could camp here tonight,' said Marek. 'There is no sense in going on through this storm.'

Ivan Petrovich listened to the rest of the scout's reports and then wheeled his horse round and rode towards them. Max had already stridden over to stand beside their sled. Rodrik was with him.

'It seems we have found what we were looking for,' said Max. 'I think we have tracked the monster to his lair.'

'Aye, but there is no way we can reach there tonight. Not in this weather.'

'What are we going to do?'

'We should camp here,' said Ivan Petrovich. 'The men will be tired and hungry. I say we wait till tomorrow morning and push on then.'

Max nodded his agreement, as did Rodrik. Gotrek looked around as if he was going to disagree but to Felix's surprise he glanced over at the countess's coach and then kept his mouth shut. Felix thought he could read his mind. The Slayer did not trust the countess and did not want to abandon these men to their mercies. Besides, if she attacked them, his oath would end and he could fight her. Felix did not doubt that one vampire was very much as good as another for Gotrek's purposes.

'We will post a very careful watch tonight,' said Max.

'I will double the sentries and make sure they guard in pairs tonight to keep each other awake,' said Ivan Petrovich.

'I will keep a careful eye open myself,' said Gotrek. He rubbed his eye patch so ostentatiously that Felix wondered if he was making a joke.

'THEY ARE OUT there,' said Adolphus Krieger, leaning forward on the Throne of Blood.

The ghoul who had brought the word lay sprawled on the cracked mosaic of the floor, its arms stretched out before it in a gesture of abject fealty. Adolphus paid it no more attention than he would any other piece of furniture. He glanced around at Ulrika, Roche and the rest of his followers. They looked around uneasily. Overhead, in the shadows, something vast flapped leathery wings.

'Who are they?' Ulrika asked. Obviously she had difficulty following the ghoul's slurred words. Krieger smiled fondly at her. She seemed to be adapting well to her new role. She was docile and obedient. If he detected a look of trapped horror far back in her eyes, he chose to ignore it.

'Our enemies. Warriors of some sort, strangers mostly. Outlanders it seems, sheltering in the ruins of the old Rattenberg house. The ghoul does not know enough to tell us any more.'

'What do you intend to do?' She walked over and stood in front of the dais, staring up at him boldly. He wondered how she felt. This was all new to her. He could remember his own horror and wonder at the strangeness of his condition when he was freshly risen. He felt a surge of affection such as he had felt for no other being in a very long time. Was this what humans felt for their children, he wondered? Was this what the countess had felt for him? Had he really not been able to return that feeling with a fraction of the intensity? Did Ulrika feel the same way about him as he had once felt about the countess? He dismissed the thoughts as being of no account, even as he came to a decision.

'I will go and take a look at them. Perhaps I will teach them the folly of trespassing in my domain.'

'Perhaps I should go, master,' suggested Roche.

'Tonight is not the night for a mortal to be abroad, old friend,' said Krieger. Fear passed over the faces of the other coven members. They did not want to be left alone here, in this haunted place, with the newly risen Ulrika and the army of the undead gathering. They all knew what had happened to Osrik. Krieger let his malicious amusement show.

'Do not worry. I will return.'

THE BLIZZARD HAD stopped, leaving the forest cloaked in a mantle of deep fresh snow. Adolphus Krieger stalked through it, lithe as a leopard, confident as a king. He knew no mortal eyes could pick him out unless he wanted them to. The night was his home. It would cloak and shield him until he chose otherwise.

What fools were these, he wondered as he saw the distant campfires flickering through the trees, to be abroad in Sylvania in the depths of winter, and to have strayed so far from the beaten track? Surely they must know how close they were to the haunted keep at Drakenhof? Were they fortune hunters keen to prove their bravery and despoil the ancient castle of its mythical treasures? If so, they were in for an unpleasant surprise.

Perhaps he would be merciful. Perhaps he would kill a few sentries silently and unseen and leave them as a warning that would terrify the others. Or perhaps he would summon the ghouls and the skeletons he had raised and massacre them all, leaving only one to carry word of the killing back to the lands of men. That might be better. It would spread fear and terror in advance of his armies, and those had always been the greatest allies of the Arisen when they went to war.

He moved forward swiftly, from pool of shadow to pool of shadow. Tempting as that course of action was, perhaps it was not the wisest. He was not yet ready to begin his campaign yet. True, several hundred animated corpses and skeletons had joined him but there were other hidden burial grounds to be visited. More ghouls were drawn to him every night. Soon the first of the Arisen themselves would arrive. Only once that had happened could he be certain of his power. It would be folly to strike too early and forewarn his foes. Perhaps the first method would be best after all. Or maybe he should summon the wolves and have them deal with the intruders.

The Eye tingled on his throat. He sensed something was wrong in the night. Surrounding the old ruins was a flow of power that should not be there. He opened his magesight to its fullest and studied his surroundings. Nearer to the fire, he could perceive a subtle webwork of force, a spell of some sort, a ward or an alarm, no doubt. It was fine work, near invisible. He suspected that had he not been wearing the Eye he might not even have noticed it. There was a wizard present in that camp. He needed to be careful indeed.

Moving with exaggerated caution he proceeded through the snow, easing his weight down to minimise the sound of the white stuff crunching underfoot. Within the tumbled down walls was a large camp, with a coach, several sledges and many horses pegged within what was left of the stables. Some of them neighed nervously as if catching his scent. There were a lot of warriors, probably too many for the wolves to deal with unless his other servants supported them. If the wizard was powerful, perhaps even that would not be enough.

Who were these people, he wondered: some noble and his retinue, perhaps? Only the nobility were rich enough to hire wizards to travel with them. Or perhaps the coach belonged to the wizard himself, and these were his bodyguards. It had been known for sorcerers engaged in all manner of dubious practices to seek refuge in the wilds of Sylvania in order to continue their nefarious researches untroubled by the authorities and by witch-hunters. Perhaps he had stumbled on one of these. Or perhaps the man had come to investigate his own spellcasting. His use of the Great Ritual must have been noticeable for a dozen leagues to one sensitive enough.

Someone called out. Krieger froze. Had he been spotted? He listened. No. It was merely one nervous man making sure another was there. Perhaps the unease of the animals had transmitted itself to the sentries. He would have to be careful. Under normal circumstances he would have used his powers to cloud their minds, but the wizard down there would be able to sense it.

Krieger told himself not to be foolish. He was a power now. He possessed the Eye of Khemri. There was nothing those mortals down there could do to harm him. Still, he had not survived as long as he had by throwing caution to the winds. He needed to be careful now, more than ever with his destiny so close to being fulfilled.

There was something naggingly familiar about the voices. They were speaking with the accents of Kislev! These men had strayed far from home. Perhaps they were merely wandering mercenaries or perhaps the whole party were refugees fleeing the advance of the Chaos army. Or perhaps they were connected in some way to his recent stay in Praag. He knew that he had better find out.

As he moved closer, he saw that most of them wore the garb of Kislevite horse-soldiers. They were short, stocky men, bandy-legged from so much riding. One of them seemed very tall. He caught a flash of blond hair as the man strode off to relieve himself.

He sniffed the air, and found a whiff of some familiar scents. Dwarf, he thought. Near one of the fires he caught sight of a squat figure with a towering crest of hair and a massive axe in one hand. It seemed that Gotrek Gurnisson had taken his oath seriously and tracked him here! How had the dwarf managed to track him over hundreds of leagues of winter forest, Krieger wondered. Perhaps the wizard had done it.

Krieger moved around the camp, staying out of the light. He could see that there were some Sylvanians present. Their horses were larger than the rangy steeds of the Kislevites; chargers intended to carry men in full plate. The sign of Waldenhof covered the raiment. These were all ranged around a pavilion and a large coach on runners.

This was a strange mix indeed. What were dwarfs, Kislevite archers, a local lordling and a wizard doing so near to his home all at once? He paused to consider this for a second. Obviously the Slayers had come to fulfil their vow. Perhaps they had hired the wizard, or perhaps it was this Max Schreiber that Ulrika talked of. The more he thought about it, the more likely it seemed. The tall blond man he had spotted would be Felix Jaeger. Maybe the Kislevites were mercenaries or had been sent by the Praag authorities to bring him to justice. The locals could have come along as guides. Doubtless they would aid anyone who set themselves up against him. He could not be completely certain, of course, but all of this seemed to be the likeliest explanation.

The question was – what was he to do against them? Here, on his own, he doubted he could prevail against so many.

Particularly not a wizard and warriors so formidably armed as Gotrek Gurnisson and Felix Jaeger. He could kill many but doubtless they would drag him down. He did not want to risk his life against that axe.

He could summon the wolves and the ghouls and the skeletons and attack their camp. But it would take most of the night to assemble such a force, and perhaps the wizard would sense the summoning. If the fighting was not done by morning, he would be far from shelter and surrounded by enemies when the sun rose, and that was a fate he wished to avoid at all costs.

If they were coming against him, it would be best to fight them on his home ground in a place that he knew, on a field of his choice. At Drakenhof, if the worst came to the worst he could drain some of his human servants of blood and fight in the light. It would be better though to send the wolves to harass and slow them, to use the ghouls to set ambushes and traps so that they would arrive at his home as late as possible. Better yet would be to lure them into the ruins and pick them off one by one.

And back at the mansion he had a potent ally. Ulrika would be doubly useful. She was strong and deadly, and more importantly, because of her relationship with Felix Jaeger, the mortals would be unlikely to attack her until they were absolutely certain she was his ally. Perhaps he could even use her to lure them into a trap.

Yes, he thought, that would be the best plan. He could refine it on his way back. When his pursuers set out tomorrow, they would find several unpleasant surprises in store for them.

'SOMETHING WAS HERE during the night,' said Marek the tracker, a frown creasing his leathery brow. 'You can see here if you look closely. These are boot prints that the snow has not yet had time to fill.'

'They are very close to the camp,' said Felix. 'Were the sentries asleep?'

'None of my men slept last night, Felix Jaeger,' said Ivan Petrovich Straghov wearily. Felix thought he looked dreadfully old. 'I have ridden with these men from the Marches of Chaos, and I swear to that. They are veterans and they are honourable men.'

'Nothing disturbed my wards,' said Max. 'I would have woken if anything did. Nothing and no one came into or left our camp last night.'

The way Max stressed the possibility of someone leaving the camp, Felix knew they thinking along the same lines. It seemed no one in the camp had set out to warn Krieger.

'Snorri thinks it does not matter if one man came to spy,' said Snorri.

'It matters a lot if it was Krieger,' said Felix. 'He is more than a man.'

'Or less than one,' said Max.

'The tracks lead away in the direction we are going,' said the tracker.

'I suggest we prepare ourselves for an ambush then,' said Felix. 'If it's Krieger he may have friends in the area.'

'Perhaps the countess and her men should be sent on their way,' said Ivan Petrovich Straghov. He was chivalrous in his way, and would not want to see the woman in danger. 'She might wish to take a different road.'

'I will suggest that to her,' said Felix striding off in the direction of the coach.

'Don't take too long about your suggestions, manling. We leave immediately,' said Gotrek.

'YOU THINK IT was him then,' said Felix. As the coach swayed on its runners, he braced himself, not wanting to be thrown any closer to the countess than he already was. He had already put as much distance between the two of them as was possible in the enclosed space.

The vampire adjusted her veil and covered her mouth while she yawned. Felix was not sure whether she was trying to tell him he was boring her or whether she was feeling the effects of the daylight. He told himself that he didn't care. 'Who else could it be? Who could have got so close to the camp without being spotted by sentries or setting off your friend the wizard's defences?'

'You think he could have penetrated them?'

'No. I inspected them myself and I doubt the Great Necromancer himself could have pierced that weave without setting it off. Max Schreiber is a very competent mage.'

'I am sure he will appreciate that ringing vote of confidence.'

'Tell him what you will. Just be sure he is alert. Drakenhof is a place of power, sacred to the Arisen. Strong wards protect it. The very stones are steeped in bloody magic, and there are potent weaves of illusion and masking on the place that will affect all save the Arisen or those bound by blood to them. Krieger is not going to allow us to walk right up and decapitate him. I think right now he is preparing a very cold reception for us indeed.'

'That is not reassuring.'

'This is not a pleasure jaunt, Herr Jaeger. We are heading towards the lair of a very dangerous beast.'

'I'll bear that in mind.'

Suddenly from outside came the whinnying of panicked horses and the shouts of warriors, intermingled with blood-curdling howls.

Felix let the door of the coach swing open and jumped out into the snow, wrenching his sword from his scabbard as he landed. Up ahead a melee swirled. From out of the shadows beneath the trees long loping forms emerged to strike at the horses. Enormous red-eyed wolves sprang from cover to hamstring mounts and rip the throats of the riders who fell from the saddle.

Felix raced forward. In front of him a wolf worried at a Kislevite horse-soldier. The man had got his arm between the creature's jaws but the white-furred beast was massive and strong. It kept the man off-balance and unable to draw his knife while its kin circled closer. Felix kicked the wolf's head, sending the beast tumbling backwards. It bounded back up immediately and returned to the attack, madness in its eyes. Vile sorcery was at work here, Felix thought, whipping the beasts into a rabid frenzy.

Felix took the hilt of his sword in both hands and swung it in a great arc, slashing across the chest of the pouncing wolf. The impact of the massive body almost knocked Felix over. He recovered his balance and lashed out again, half-severing the wolf's head. He glanced around to see what had become of the other wolf and saw the soldier wrestling with it, rolling over and over in the snow. He had one hand at its throat while he stabbed it with the dagger held in the other.

Off in the distance, an explosion sounded, swiftly followed by the smell of burning flesh. Max was using his magic, Felix guessed. Ignoring the distraction, Felix took careful aim at the second wolf and stabbed. His blade passed through the animal's ribs. Blood gouted from its mouth. It gurgled as it died. The warrior pulled himself to his feet and wiped himself down. Felix saw that it was Marek.

'A handy stroke,' he said. 'And thanks for it.'

Felix nodded his acknowledgement and took in the scene of the battle. Dozens of wolves bounded through the snow. Here and there a few lay pierced by arrows. Still more had their skulls crushed by the hooves of horses. Many lupine corpses lay in puddles of red blood, testimony to the deadly skill with which the men of Kislev wielded their sabres. In the distance, smoke billowed and golden light flared. Max Schreiber was still alive and invoking his terrible powers.

Gotrek and Snorri stood atop the supply sled, bellowing war cries and daring the wolves to attack them. Both of their ponies were dead. A small hill of white furred bodies showed that the two Slayers had not been idle. Rodrik and his companions had formed up around Gabriella's coach, determined to protect her from harm but taking no part in the battle. No wolves had come near them. Felix wondered why.

At least a dozen men and horses were down. And judging by the screams more were going to be. He strode across to the two Slayers, the Kislevite at his heels.

'This is not natural. Wolves do not attack large bands of armed men unless provoked!' Felix shouted.

'Your powers of observation amaze me, manling,' sneered Gotrek leaping down from the sled. 'I think we can take it for granted that this is the handiwork of our bloodsucking friend up ahead.'

Snorri plunged into the snow behind Gotrek. 'Snorri thinks it's not right, sending these poor wolves to fight for him. He should have come himself.'

'Be sure to tell him that when we run into him,' Felix suggested mildly. 'Right now we'd best go help Ivan Petrovich and his lads.'

Gotrek glanced significantly at the four knights surrounding the coach and making no move to aid the Kislevites. 'It would seem that some folk here would disagree with you.'

'We'll deal with them later. First things first. Let's kill some wolves.'

'Fair enough, manling.'

'Snorri still doesn't like it. Poor beasts.'

'You've picked a bad time to start having scruples about killing things, Snorri,' said Felix.

'Snorri didn't say he wouldn't kill them. Snorri just said he doesn't like it,' said Snorri Nosebiter racing off towards the fray.

'HOW MANY MEN have we lost?' Felix asked.

Ivan Petrovich looked at him wearily. His breath rasped heavily from his chest. He wiped blood and sweat from his balding forehead with the sleeve of his tunic. 'It's not as bad as it looks. It's a good job Max was here to do some healing. We've three men dead, and five more wounded. Two of those can still fight once their wounds are bandaged. The other three won't be good for anything for a while.'

'What are you going to do?' Felix knew what he wanted to suggest, but Ivan was the leader of the horsemen, and this was his decision. Ivan sucked in his cheeks and considered for a moment. 'Under normal circumstances I would leave the two who can still fight to guard the ones who can't, along with the sledges we don't have ponies for, but right now I am loath to do it. The wolves might come back, or other things might come for them, and I would not wish that on my worst enemy, let alone these lads.'

It was as Felix had feared. The whole purpose of the attack had been to slow them down, and the wounded were going to do that. It was suspicious how the wolves had fled once about half of them had been cut down. They had attacked as if they were starving but had left without taking any food. It was not natural. Felix looked over at Max. The magician was sweating a little and his chest still rose and fell like a bellows.

'How are you feeling, Max?'

'I've felt worse.'

'Can you still cast a spell?'

'Yes.'

'I suspect this attack was meant to wear us down.'

'I wish I could disagree, Felix, but I can't.'

'We should expect more attacks before we get to Drakenhof.'

'That will slow us down too. We'll need to move cautiously.'

'Let's hope we can still get there before dark,' said Felix. Somehow he doubted they would.

THE SHADOWS LENGTHENED; the wind grew colder. Felix drew his cloak tighter around him and trudged on through the snow. His nose still ran. He felt a little feverish. Behind him, he could hear the grunts of Snorri Nosebiter and Gotrek as they dragged the sled along. He was still amazed by this display of strength. The two dwarfs had drawn the heavy sledge along for most of the day without showing any signs of weariness. Except for the odd grumble and curse they even seemed to be enjoying themselves. Felix thought: I will never understand dwarfs; the worse things look, the happier they seem.

'If I had known you two were so good at this, I would have had you pull the sledge sooner. The ponies could have ridden with me.'

'Snorri thinks we could have eaten them,' grumbled Snorri.

'In the mines dwarfs carry their own burdens and pull their own ore trucks,' said Gotrek. He sounded almost nostalgic.

'Snorri once pulled a truck up and down the Black Pit shaft for three days without stopping. Fought off a tribe of gobbos at the end too. Bastards tried to steal Snorri's truck.'

'And you couldn't have that, could you?' said Felix ironically. He glanced over his shoulder. A small lantern glowed on the countess's coach and Felix could see Quentin and two of his companions riding alongside it. Doubtless Rodrik was inside, providing the vampire with some nourishment. Well, tonight they would most likely have need of her strength – unless she betrayed them.

The young Sylvanians looked pretty sullen, as well they might after the haranguing Gotrek and Snorri had given them earlier about not joining the fight. It had been all the countess had been able to do to restrain them from attacking the two dwarfs. Of course, Gotrek had let them have a few well-chosen words about being brave now that the big bad wolves had gone. That hadn't helped things either. Still, he could understand the dwarfs' anger and the smouldering resentment the Kislevites held towards the knights. It was not good to have companions who did not pull their weight in a fight. Even though Felix knew the reason why this had happened, he resented it himself.

Now, of course, the knights were desperate to prove their manhood and work off this slur against their honour. They glared belligerently at anyone looking at them. Felix saw Quentin notice his own glance and he was rewarded with an angry glare. Felix shook his head. Idiot, he thought. At least Ivan Petrovich had stopped trying to send the countess on her way. He could not do that when there were wolves about and maybe worse things waiting in ambush.

Ahead, the wounded lay on the second sledge where Max could tend them. Ivan Petrovich rode alongside sharing a comforting word or two with his injured soldiers. All things considered the old march boyar was holding up pretty well, Felix thought, considering his age and all his worries. Felix felt bad about not letting him in on the countess's secret. On the other hand, given the fact that his daughter was in the hands of the countess's own 'son', who knew how Ivan would respond? Felix had decided it was better not to take the risk.

He wondered what would happen when they found Ulrika. He supposed it depended on how she was. If she

were a prisoner, they would free her, but if she had been
changed into one of the undying, what then?

Felix still wasn't sure of how he felt about the woman.
Once he had thought they had been in love, but after the initial infatuation had passed, it had been a troubled and
difficult relationship. She had not been the easiest person in
the world to get on with, although, he supposed, neither
had he. Still, there was something there, some emotional
bond between them, at least on his side. He did not know if
he could bring himself to try and kill her. No, that was not
true. He was certain he could not, nor could he stand by and
let Gotrek do so either. He felt pretty sure that Max felt the
same way.

But would she feel the same way about them? That was
the real question. He had talked with the countess about
this, and she had done her best to allay what she called his
superstitious fears. He had grown up believing that vampires
were possessed by monstrous, malefic spirits that would
turn them against their own flesh and blood in an effort to
slake their terrible thirst.

The countess had told him this was not so. Vampires were
driven to drink blood but they maintained all of their old
memories and loyalties and affections. The problem was
that for a newly risen vampire the thirst was near uncon-
trollable and they would attack whoever they could find
when in its grip. All too often that proved to be their kin,
unless another older, wiser vampire was there to guide
them. Felix was not at all sure that the countess's explanation reassured him. In its way, this sounded as bad as the
daemonic possession theory.

More to the point, she had told him that if she were one
of the Arisen now, Ulrika would almost certainly be under
Krieger's sway. The countess claimed that no newly risen
vampire could hold out against the power of the Eye of
Khemri. She had urged him to do his level best to restrain or
slay Ulrika. A strange note had entered the countess's voice
when she talked about her. She sounded almost jealous. Did
she see Ulrika as a potential rival for Krieger's affections? If
so, what did that say about her true motives?

In the gathering gloom, surrounded by this sinister forest, it was all too easy to believe that this was all some complex scheme to lure them into a trap. Would the countess really side with mortals against her own kind? It did not seem likely. Felix could not imagine ever siding with the Arisen against his own folk.

He shook his head, and gave a bitter laugh. What a hypocrite you are, Felix Jaeger, he thought. Only a few minutes ago you were considering that very thing, when you were trying to decide whether you would let Gotrek slay Ulrika. It seemed that these situations could indeed be complex. If you could judge the motives of a vampire by the motives of a human.

Somewhere off in the night, a wolf howled.

'Furry bastards,' muttered Gotrek.

WHEN THEY BREASTED the last hill and Drakenhof came into sight Felix was surprised. It seemed impossible that they had not noticed so massive a structure before now. Even though logic told him that the trees and the roll of the hills had concealed it until that moment, there was something sorcerous about its sudden appearance. Felix had been expecting something small, like one of the fortified manors of the Kislevite nobility. What he saw now was built on an entirely different scale. It appeared as if a huge hill had been carved into a castle. The building had once surely been as large as the citadel of Praag, and its architecture was just as twisted, albeit in a different way.

The stonework was not as intricate. Even in the fading light of the blood red sun, he could see that. The dominant motif was one of skulls and bones. The casements of the windows had been carved to resemble skulls. The monstrous main gateway was encased in the gaping maw of another gigantic fleshless head. Gargoyles clutched the side of the building, bat-winged, skeletal. Felix half expected them to come to life and flap down to attack. Snow had settled like a crust on the stonework, adding to the haunted look of the place.

It was obvious that the castle had lain in ruins for centuries, and that it had fallen to siege. There were huge holes

in the walls where war engines had battered through them.
Many of the statues had been defaced and someone had
obviously taken a hammer to the stonework in an effort to
deface the symbols. If anything this added to the atmosphere of faded grandeur surrounding the place, and
contributed to the sense of sinister evil hovering over it.

Coming on such a massive structure so deep in the forest
was something of a shock. He had become used to thinking
of Sylvania as an impoverished land, a place where everything was smaller and meaner than in the rest of his
homeland. He had not expected this. He pointed this out to
Max.

'It just shows what can be done with undead labour,' said
the wizard.

'What do you mean?'

'Doubtless this place was raised using necromancy, by
what laymen call zombies and animated skeletons. They
require no food, no sleep and no wages. All the builder
needed do was provide the raw materials and they would
work until it was done. If we searched around here we would
find quarries from where the stone came from. Probably the
wood was local too but in two centuries it would all have
grown back.'

Felix gaped at the wizard. 'What about those carvings? I
doubt mindless automatons could have made them.'

'The Vampire Counts enslaved the whole population of
Sylvania, Felix. They bound them with fear, superstition and
sorcery. Doubtless they had craftsmen in their service who
would do this work in return for their lives and the lives of
their families.'

'You are correct, Max Schreiber,' said the countess. Felix
was startled. In the gathering gloom the undead noblewoman had approached so quietly he had not noticed. Max
did not seem surprised though. Either the wizard had some
means of detecting her approach or he was better at concealing his feelings than Felix was. Probably both.

'I can remember this place when it was the capital of all
Sylvania, when the aristocracy of the night sipped blood
from crystal goblets, by the light of glittering chandeliers.

When the most beautiful youths and maidens garbed all in white waited to be tapped, and all the while hoped to be selected to join us.'

'There's no need to sound so nostalgic,' said Max.

'It was a beautiful and terrible time,' said Gabriella, and her voice had a sad haunted quality. 'Not since the fall of Lahmia had the Arisen ruled mortals so openly or indulged themselves so unstintingly. It is well remembered in the chronicles of the undying. Few who were there would ever forget it. Some have never stopped wanting to recreate it.'

'Of course, you are not one of them.'

'I am ambivalent, Max Schreiber. I would have thought that you of all people would have some sympathy. Wizards too have been outcasts, shunned by those who feared them and resented their power. Can you not imagine what it means, not having to hide what you are, but being able to glory in it?'

'Wizards have never tried to set up their own kingdom, and never tried to oppress those who did not possess their powers.'

Gabriella's laughter was tinkling, silver and utterly flaying. 'You are being wilfully naïve, Herr Schreiber. History is littered with examples of wizards who have sought to carve themselves dominions. What was Nagash if not a wizard, and he conquered the greatest empire of antiquity. My people have cause to remember it. Many other mages have succeeded in carving out their own lands, if only temporarily. Believe me, I am old enough to remember some of them.'

'Perhaps, but as a race or a class or a breed we have never sought to set ourselves up over others.'

'Not yet, perhaps, but I think it's only a matter of time before someone thinks to try it. Mortals experiment restlessly with their forms of government. Sooner or later someone is bound to think: why not a land where those who wield magic rule? Are they not usually wiser, and more learned than their fellow man as well as more powerful?'

'I would oppose such wizards,' said Max. Felix could feel the tension in the air. The wizard and the vampire resented each other, perhaps because in some ways they were so alike.

'Perhaps we could save this discussion until tomorrow,' he said. 'There will be time enough then for such a debate. Right now we are wasting time, and the lair of our common enemy lies before us.'

Both of them looked at him for a moment, and seemed on the verge of a snappish rejoinder. He met their gazes as calmly as he could, and slowly the tension dissipated.

'Your words make sense, Herr Jaeger,' said the countess.

Max nodded agreement. Felix saw that the rest of their party was already disappearing among the trees down slope.

'Then let us join the others before they get too far ahead of us, and we have to work our way through this accursed forest on our own.'

As THEY CAME closer to the mighty keep, Felix felt more and more as if he were walking in the shadow of some terrible giant which might at any moment spring to life and crush him.

The sheer scale of the ruin was oppressive. It made even the ancient trees around them seem no more than weeds. Its sense of antiquity made him feel like a mayfly. What sort of person would choose to dwell here, he wondered? Or was it simply the power of the warding spells the countess had warned about that he was feeling?

Wearily the warriors trudged towards the building's gaping entrance. Their earlier courage seemed to have evaporated. No one spoke. The only sounds to break the silence were the occasional groans of the wounded as the sled hit a rut in the earth.

The cold wind tugged at Felix's cloak. Flakes of snow struck his face. Under other circumstances he might have looked forward to getting inside out of the wind and the chill. Now he found his feet dragging, as if reluctant to carry him any closer to their destination.

As the darkness deepened, he heard a shout from up ahead. He glanced up and saw what the commotion was about. An eerie green witch light had appeared in one of the highest towers. It flickered for a moment and then receded. It seemed that the place was occupied although what sort of

creature used one of those devilish lights did not bear thinking about.

'Looks like we're expected,' Felix said. Gotrek glanced at
him.

'There's a surprise, manling.'

'What do you think of this place?'

'The stonework is crude even by human standards.'

'That's not what I meant.'

'I think we shall see what we shall see once we are inside.
There's no sense in speculating until then.'

Felix shook his head, astonished by how calm the dwarf
could remain in the face of horror and danger. No, that was
not true. He knew the Slayer well enough to recognise the
underlying note of anticipation in his voice. A frenzied light
had appeared in the dwarf's one good eye. His expression
might be as bleak and uncaring as usual, but Felix knew
Gotrek was as tense as himself.

As well he might be, Felix thought.

'THIS PLACE IS wrapped round with spells,' said Max. He
stood for a moment, leaning on his staff and appeared to
reconsider his words. 'No. That is not quite correct. The
walls hold all the usual defensive wards you would expect in
a castle of this size, but they seemed twisted somehow.'

'What do you mean?' asked Felix.

'I am not sure I can explain it to one who is not a magician.'

'Try!' said Gotrek.

The magician started walking again, easily keeping pace
with the two of them. Felix thought he detected a small flow
of heat from around him. Was he using magic to keep himself warm, Felix wondered? That would certainly explain a
lot of things.

'There is something else at work here. The whole keep is
saturated with dark magic. Tainted in some way, as if some
of the stonework contained warpstone or somewhere deep
below is a mother lode of the stuff. Whatever it is I think its
influence has modified the defensive spells, mutated them,
if you will.'

'And?' Felix probed.

'And I don't know what the overall effect will be. I suspect it might be nasty, and I also suspect that it will interfere with the casting of spells within the keep.'

'Wonderful,' said Felix sardonically. 'You are saying that your magic will be useless.'

'Not necessarily. Just that their effects might be dampened or unpredictable.'

'You think it's the effect of the talisman?'

'No. The very stones here are steeped in evil magic. It would take centuries for that to happen. I think this place is a locus of dark power. I have no idea why.'

'Any more vague warnings you would like to give us?' sneered Gotrek. 'Maybe I should consult Snorri Nosebiter and see what he thinks. It would probably be clearer.'

'We are all a little tense here, Gotrek,' said Max with what Felix considered to be a masterful use of understatement. 'There's no need to be sarcastic.'

Gotrek grunted and then spat on the ground. Ahead of them the entrance to the keep loomed massively. Felix could see that once there had been a portcullis but the blades had rusted into position. The metal struts that had once reinforced the door lay in pieces on the ground. It looked deserted, but appearances could prove deceptive. Ahead of them, the Kislevites paused to light torches and pour oil into their few lanterns. The horses whickered nervously. Max gestured and a ball of golden light came into being just above his outstretched fingers. Another gesture sent it orbiting outwards.

Felix wished he knew the trick for doing that. He could imagine that once he was within the keep the ability to conjure light would prove very useful.

'THIS IS THE great hall,' said the Countess Gabriella. She had the trick of speaking in a quiet-sounding, calm voice that somehow managed to carry to the furthest of the group.

'You don't say,' said Gotrek.

'Snorri would never have guessed that,' said Snorri and then chortled at his words.

It was huge. The vaulted ceiling was almost lost to sight above them. Massive galleries ran round the chamber. The posts of the banisters were carved to resemble naked skeletal humans. The floor underfoot was covered in a vandalised mosaic that Felix guessed had once shown the heraldic symbol of the keep's owner.

The air smelled of rot and chill. A massive staircase at the far end of the hall rose up to the galleries. Max's gesture sent his sphere of light arcing towards the ceiling. It stopped at the remains of a massive crystal chandelier, and its beams were reflected eerily about the chamber.

Gotrek wandered around the edges of the vast room. Felix followed him. He had long ago learned that his best chance of survival lay in sticking close to the dwarf and his massive axe. There were many doorways leading off into smaller passages and chambers. Here and there were vandalised pictures. Huge patches of black mould covered parts of the walls. Massive cockroaches scuttled away from the light.

'This is an evil place,' said Felix.

To his surprise, the dwarf laughed. It was a sound as cold as ice floes cracking together.

'It seems our wizard is not the only one with a gift for stating the obvious.'

They strode back towards the assembled troops. All the warriors and their mounts were present, and the sledges had been dragged through the huge gate of the keep. The countess and her knightly companions seemed to be debating something with Max and Ivan Petrovich. As they closed Felix could hear what was being said.

'I say we set up camp here for the evening, set the fires burning brightly and ready ourselves for an attack,' said Ivan Petrovich. 'I do not doubt one will come.'

'This is not a very defensible position if an enemy comes at us in any numbers,' said Max. 'It's too open, with too many entrances. We should find a smaller chamber.'

'And be trapped in it like rabbits in a burrow when a weasel comes?' asked Ivan Petrovich. The use of such an analogy told Felix how nervous the Kislevite was beneath his bluff exterior.

'You forget who and what had this place built,' said the countess. 'The whole mansion is riddled with secret passages. At least if we camp here we will see our opponents coming at us.'

'And we will have a clear field on which to fight,' said Rodrik. 'I will not cower from the foe.'

'Not like when we fought the wolves, eh?' bellowed Gotrek. If looks could kill, the knight's glance would have struck him down on the spot. He glanced contemptuously at the countess. 'Secret passages, eh? I am a dwarf and the secret passage has not been built that a dwarf could not find.'

'Are you suggesting we should hide like frightened children?' said Quentin. His high-pitched voice sounded even closer to breaking than usual.

Gotrek looked at him nastily. 'That is certainly what you remind me of.'

Ever the diplomat, thought Felix. A room full of armed people, scared and ready to come to blows, and what do you do? Try to set a spark to that dry tinder. 'No one is suggesting that we hide,' said Felix quickly before the situation could deteriorate further. 'We are discussing the best plan to proceed and destroy the monster that dwells here. That is all.'

Much to his surprise the others nodded as if he had just said something sensible; even Gotrek managed to hold his tongue. He decided to press his advantage. 'We need a place to keep the wounded safe, and our supplies guarded. We will need them when we leave, unless any of you have discovered a way to eat snow.'

He glanced around. 'This darkness is probably not the best time to go searching through the adjoining chambers looking for a refuge. Who knows what we will find, and we don't want to split our forces.'

He saw they were getting restive once more. They did not want a balanced assessment of their situation. Most of them were scared and wanted decisive leadership. Just this once he would give them it. 'We build fires here, split into watches and wait for the night to pass. On the morrow, when there is more light, we will seek our foe.'

They nodded agreement. Men had already begun to move off to build fires in the centre of the chamber. Some of them tethered the horses to the runners of the coach and the sledges. Men nocked their bows and put lanterns up where they could provide the most light. Max set more balls of light spiralling towards the ceiling. They wavered and flickered eerily but at least they continued to provide some illumination.

From somewhere in the distance came the high-pitched shrieking gibber of a ghoul. With all the echoes it was impossible to tell from where the call had come. From the opposite direction came a response.

Felix was suddenly glad that they were not going to check the adjoining rooms. He could tell the others were too.

FROM THE BALCONY above the grand hall Adolphus Krieger looked down on the assembled mortals. His magesight saw the glittering web of magical wards the wizard wove. They flickered as the keep's own wards interfered with them but somehow maintained their integrity.

The vast setting made them look like ants but appearances were deceptive. He was not going to underestimate his foes. That was the cardinal mistake so many of his kind had made when dealing with mortals. He considered using overwhelming force, assembling all the walking corpses and animated skeletons and throwing them against the intruders in one mighty hammer blow, and dismissed the idea. There would be time enough for that later. This was his home ground. The ghouls and his mortal followers knew their way around it better than those men down below and the old wards would not interfere with their movements. First of all, he would pick off a few of the interlopers, one at a time, and then when the force was weakened and morale low, he would destroy them.

He watched them, feeling quite pleased with himself until he caught sight of a familiar figure moving through the assembled mortals. The countess! What was she doing here? He had not expected to see her so soon. It was strange how she still affected him after all these years. He still felt like a schoolboy about to be confronted by a domineering mother. He told himself not to be ridiculous, he had the Eye of Nagash, and there was nothing she could do to him now. It was all very well telling himself this but it did not lessen the shock or the strange echo of old emotions washing through his brain.

Doubtless she was scheming with his enemies, but why? How would accompanying these foolish mortals advance her schemes? He shrugged. It was fairly easy to understand. She obviously hoped that they would kill him, and allow her to take the Eye of Khemri. As ever, she preferred to use others as her cat's-paws. The wonder of it was that she had come all this way and exposed her precious self to danger. He smiled revealing his teeth as anger flowed through him.

He stalked along the balcony fingering the precious talisman. Then again, she had never been a coward, and he supposed she was desperate. It was unlikely those particular mortals down there could simply be tricked into taking the Eye back to her. And now that the summoning had begun others of the Arisen would soon be here. She could hardly take the risk of them getting it. It seemed her motives were simple and comprehensible after all.

He wondered if her mortal dupes knew what they were letting themselves in for. They were caught between him and the countess and there was no way they could survive the experience. In a way, he would be doing them a favour by killing her before she could work her will on them.

Of course, they would serve him too, in their own way, as soldiers in his resurrected legions.

'I FEEL AS if there is something watching us,' said Felix. He glanced upwards, his flesh crawling, knowing somehow that there was something on the balcony above, looking at them with the same glance a hawk gives a field mouse.

'That would be a fair bet, manling,' said Gotrek. 'Perhaps we should go up and take a look.'

Are you mad? Felix wanted to ask, but didn't. He already knew the answer. The Slayer was not sane as most men measured sanity. So instead, he said, 'I don't think that is a good idea.'

However, the Slayer was already stomping off towards the huge staircase. Felix considered letting him go alone for an instant but then followed. In part because he had sworn an oath to follow the Slayer and record his doom, and in part because he suspected that in this place it was safest to stay close to the Slayer and his axe. Then, realising he had no light, he rushed back into the mass of men and grabbed a lantern.

'Oi! Where are you going?' Snorri Nosebiter shouted. Felix could see the others around the fire were looking at them.

'Just going to scout about for a bit,' Felix responded.

'Not without Snorri you're not. If there's fighting to be done, Snorri wants to be part of it.'

'Suit yourself,' said Felix, as the second Slayer rushed over to join them. Seeing the uneasy looks of the men around the fire, Felix was not surprised when there were no other volunteers.

KRIEGER LOOKED DOWN in disbelief. The two dwarfs and the human were actually coming looking for him. Either they were mad, or they were supremely overconfident. In either case, he did not really care. This was a hell-sent opportunity. His foes had split their forces and thus reduced their effectiveness. He intended to take full advantage of it. For the moment, all he had to do was wait.

'THIS PLACE COULD use a little cleaning,' said Felix, as they stalked upstairs. Cobwebs hung between the spokes of the banister. Very big spiders scuttled away from the light. The stairs creaked eerily beneath his boots. Not for the first time he wished he could see in the dark like the dwarfs. This lantern made him an easy mark for anything in the dark. None of the creatures they had encountered so far seemed to have any difficulty functioning without light.

'Complain to the servants, manling,' said Gotrek, pausing at the top of the stairs to inspect their surroundings for a moment.

'I suppose good help is hard to find these days,' said Felix, glancing over the dwarf's shoulder. 'My father always used to say that.'

The stairs ended in a gallery running left and right around the edges of the great hall. There were more doors leading off into more chambers. Here and there large paintings covered the walls. About halfway down the hall on either side, more stairs led off upwards. It was very quiet. Felix could hear the voices of the men below, and the soft, scared whinnying of the horses. Felix ran his fingers over the edge of the banister. They came away caked with a thick layer of dust. There was no sign of any enemy but still Felix's flesh crawled. He looked up at the ceiling, half expecting to see a massive spider about to drop on his head. Instead he saw nothing except the painted and blotched plasterwork of the ceiling, which was also the floor of the gallery above.

Felix stepped forward onto the gallery. The floor flexed beneath his foot. He wondered how safe this place was. After all, it had not been maintained in two centuries. He proceeded forward cautiously, half expecting the floor beneath him to give way at any moment.

He moved over to the nearest painting, holding his lantern up close so that he could inspect it. Within an elaborate gilded frame was a portrait of a tall, pale woman, classically beautiful, black hair piled high in an ornate coiffure. She stood by a window. A huge crescent moon dominated the night sky behind her. In one hand she held a crystal glass of what Felix hoped was red wine. The other rested on the head of a kneeling man. There was something disturbingly bestial in the features of the man.

The painter had contrived to convey the impression that the woman was stroking him, as a noble lady of the Empire might a pet leopard. A broken silver chain dangling from the man's neck added to the impression.

'Snorri thinks she was a bad one,' said Snorri Nosebiter, from just behind Felix. He had to agree. There was something about the woman's features that suggested great power and a refined cruelty. Perhaps it was the faint flaring of the nostrils and the slight twist to those pouting red lips.

'One of the vampire countesses, no doubt,' said Felix. 'They all gathered here once or so I am told.'

They stalked on across the crumbling gallery to the next portrait. This time it was of a tall, pale-skinned man, bearded and aristocratic looking. His clothes were rich and dark. He too held a goblet of red wine in one hand. A massive golden hunting horn dangled from his neck. His booted foot rested on the chest of a dead man like a hunter standing triumphant over a stag. Once again it was night. This man smiled confidently, revealing two long prominent fangs. He radiated power and confidence, certain of his authority and right to dominate others. Like the first, this painting was executed with a skill amounting to genius. It almost seemed like the subject was about to step out of the painting. Felix shivered. That was a concept that did not bear thinking about.

They passed more pictures, alternating male and female, and all as beautifully executed and as disturbing as the first two. All were nightscapes. One showed a woman modelled as a goddess with a crown of laurel leaves on her head and a bow in the other. There was a powerfully built man stripped to the waist who looked strong as a bull. His head was shaved and he possessed an enormous walrus moustache. He toasted the viewer with a glass of red liquid while an adoring child clutched at his leg. The child's eyes glowed a sinister red.

Felix paused in front of the fifth picture, for he thought he recognised the features of the countess. Certainly the proportions were correct, and the face looked like the one hinted at through her veil. It was not possible to be certain, of course, but he knew that it was possible that she had posed for the artist all those long centuries ago.

He hurried past this painting. Neither Gotrek nor Snorri Nosebiter had spent as much time in the company of the countess as he had, so he doubted that either of them would recognise her. He did not want to take the chance of Snorri doing so now. He might just go charging back into the camp and give the game away although that might not be such a bad thing. He glanced over his shoulder. Gotrek and Snorri were checking doors, inspecting the rooms beyond. He decided to take a look at the next painting and then wait for them.

He recognised the man in it immediately. It was beyond a shadow of a doubt Adolphus Krieger, dressed in heavy black robes, a book tucked under his left arm, a glass of the red liquor held in his right. Two adoring women crouched beside him, naked save for diaphanous robes, looks that could only be described as worshipful engraved on their faces.

Felix paused to consider the picture. Krieger looked every inch the aristocrat: arrogant, swaggering, unafraid. A secretive smile played on his lips.

'It's a very good likeness, isn't it?' said a voice from nearby. Felix whirled, tearing his blade from the scabbard. He looked in the direction the words had come from. It was almost as if his earlier fantasy about the pictures coming to life had happened. Krieger stood there looking unchanged from the picture.

'Belardo was a genius in his way. He was one of the greatest of the Tilean painters, I always thought. Of course, the common folk never forgave him for taking our commissions. I heard that after Hel Fenn he was burned atop a pile of his works in the public square in Talabheim. Someone betrayed him as he tried to pass through the city in secret.'

Without taking his eyes from the vampire, Felix set the lamp on the floor.

Krieger looked as relaxed as he had in the picture, but instinct warned Felix that charging him would be most unwise. Instead he began to inch forward, blade held ready, nerves keyed. He doubted he had ever been more wound up in his entire life. Without taking his eyes off the vampire, he shouted, 'Gotrek! Snorri! Look what crawled out of the woodwork.'

'Now, now, Herr Jaeger, that's not very polite. I come here to make pleasant conversation with you, and you start tossing insults.'

'I'd rather toss you over the balcony. What have you done with Ulrika?' The vampire smiled, showing all his fangs. The sound of pounding feet told him that the Slayers were rushing to join him.

'I have not done her any harm, I promise you. I am sure she will be delighted to see you.'

Felix edged ever closer. He was all too aware of the long drop into the great hall below. He did not doubt that the vampire was swift enough and strong enough to toss him over the balcony without difficulty given the slightest opportunity. He did not intend to let that happen if he could help it.

'Where is she?'

'If you want her, you'll have to find her yourself. She's somewhere in the castle.'

Felix was almost within striking distance now. He tested the floor beneath him pressing gently with his foot before putting all his weight on it, fearing a trap. He did not like the vampire's look of confidence. He had not even drawn his weapon yet. The Eye of Khemri glittered hypnotically at his throat.

'Now you die, bloodsucker!' bellowed Gotrek.

Krieger's smile widened. He raised his arms wide. Mist bubbled around his feet and enshrouded his form. As it did so, he began to fade, almost as if his body was dissolving into the swirling fog. A faint hint of decay hit Felix's nostrils. He leapt forward and slashed with his sword at where he thought he saw the vampire's outline.

His blade encountered no resistance. Instead there was a sickening lurch as his foot passed through the rotting floorboards. The whole world wheeled around him. He dropped his blade, desperately trying to catch hold of something to prevent himself falling all the way to the hard floor of the great hall so far below.

'Gotrek! Snorri! Stop! It's a trap!' he shouted. Evil, distant laughter rang in his ears. The floor gave way beneath him and he began to fall. Felix grabbed the edge of the hole with his hands. Splintered wood bit into his palm. Pain surged along his nerve endings. He fought the urge to let go, knowing that if he did so, he would most certainly fall to his doom. The old rotten boards began to come apart. Frantically he flailed about with his right hand, trying to get a better grip. The shift of weight swung his body around, and he felt his fingers losing their grip. A long way below his boots, death beckoned.

Groaning he tried to find something to grip on and failed. His last tenuous handhold gave way. His stomach lurched as gravity gripped him and pulled down towards certain death.

ELEVEN

STRONG FINGERS GRIPPED Felix's wrist. It felt like his arm was being pulled out of its socket by the wrenching shock. Looking up, he saw the Slayer's tattooed arm. Gotrek was taking all of his weight one-handed. Snorri stood wide-legged, his hand gripping the Slayer's belt, anchoring Gotrek in case the rotted boards beneath him gave way. A moment later he was pulled back out of the hole.

Felix's breath came in gasps. He wiped sweat from his brow and tried to calm his racing heart. Neither of the dwarfs showed any sign of strain. Snorri walked calmly over to where Felix's sword lay, picked it up and returned it to him. 'Snorri thinks now is not a good time to be throwing your weapons away, young Felix,' he said.

'I am inclined to agree with you,' said Felix, limping over to where the lantern stood. As his fingers closed on its handle, he winced. Splinters of wood from the broken floor were driven deeply into his flesh. He inspected his hand for a moment, and used his dagger point to pick them out.

'What was that all about, manling?' rumbled Gotrek.

Felix looked up at the dwarf. 'He has Ulrika. She is here somewhere. Or so he says.'

'Perhaps he just wants us to go running off looking for her.'

Felix nodded. It seemed very likely, considering what had just happened. This was the vampire's home territory, after all. He knew it well. He could lead them around by the nose until they fell into more traps. Still, he did not see what other options they had.

Even as he thought this, he saw that Krieger had reappeared much further down the balcony. He waved mockingly as if challenging them to come and get him. Snorri Nosebiter raced forward, with Gotrek in hot pursuit.

'Wait,' shouted Felix. 'What if he's leading us into a trap?'

'We wouldn't want to disappoint him then, manling. Would we?'

'I suppose not,' muttered Felix, following swiftly on the heels of the dwarfs.

MAX SCHREIBER GLANCED up at the ceiling. For a moment, he had seen Felix's feet dangling through a gap in the floor, and then the man had vanished back through the hole.

'What's going on up there?' Ivan Petrovich asked.

'Exactly what I was wondering, my friend,' Max replied.

'We should go up there and help them.'

'I did not hear any cries for aid,' said Max. 'And I can't think of three people better able to look after themselves.'

'I suppose you are right.'

'Don't worry. They'll be back soon.'

One of the archers came over. 'I thought I saw another man up there in the gallery with them.'

Max knew the man had been standing at a better angle than he had been to see. 'Describe him.'

'I could not see all that well in the gloom. But he was tall with black hair and pale skin. Sounds like the one we are after.'

The horse-soldier sounded scared, and Max did not blame him.

'Maybe we should go up there,' said Ivan. Max shook his head. Instead he concentrated his mind and began an incantation. A wave of dizziness swept over him as he fought to overcome the strange resistance in the place, then he looked out from the sphere of light hovering over his shoulder. There was a moment of disorientation until his brain adjusted to the fact that the man beneath him was in fact himself. He willed the sphere to rise and watched the camp dwindle beneath him, then sent it arcing up to the hole in the gallery floor. There was a faint queasy feeling in his stomach. He had never liked using this spell. When he moved his point of view up to great heights it made him nauseous with vertigo.

He looked through the hole and saw nothing. Swiftly he sent the light darting around the gallery, knowing he would have to act quickly. Turning the sphere into an eye entailed setting up a complex weave of forces that was difficult to maintain here. It would swiftly unravel even with the utmost concentration. Under his breath he cursed the dark magical wards on this place.

His eye swept through the gallery of portraits. He saw no one, no signs of a struggle, no bodies, no blood. His comrades had simply disappeared. The most logical explanation was they had left the gallery through one of the many doorways. But where and why? There were too many exits for him to explore before his spell faltered. All he was doing was wasting power. He opened his own eyes and let the spell unwind. Overhead the golden eye disintegrated in a shower of sparks.

'They are gone,' he said to Ivan Petrovich.

'Dead?' The old boyar sounded dismayed.

Max shook his head. 'Just vanished beyond the range of my mage sight. There's no need to assume the worst.'

'In this place?'

Max shrugged. 'They can look after themselves.'

He wished he felt as confident as he sounded, and cursed the Slayers for going wandering off on such a wild goose chase.

'I will take some of the men and go look for them.'

'That would not be wise, Ivan Petrovich. Our forces are already far more dispersed than seems sensible. Why chance losing more?'

He suspected that in this place, at this time, it was going to take all of their combined resources to survive. He noticed that the countess and her henchmen were looking at him appraisingly. Max sincerely hoped that they had not brought an enemy within. Judging by those looks he would not have bet gold on it.

THERE WAS ONE good thing about dwarfs, Felix reflected, as he jogged down the corridor. They were easy to keep up with. Because of their short strides any chase involving them was naturally a very slow one. The vampire could have left them behind any time he wanted to, which meant that he had his own reasons for luring them deeper and deeper into this ancient stronghold.

He had completely lost track of time and distance since they had left the great hall. He had no idea where they were or how they were going to get back. This whole place was a maze. The pursuit swept them through an endless succession of rooms of decaying grandeur, rotting fittings, and crumbling beauty. He remembered fleeting glimpses of peeling wallpaper and walls blotched black with mould, of painted ceilings where god-like vampires depicted in fading paints glared down from scenes of hellish cruelty. The stink of mould, decomposing leather and stagnant water filled his nostrils.

Ten more minutes of running through the decaying chambers convinced him of something else. One of the bad things about dwarfs was that by human standards they were near tireless. Felix's long bout of illness had not left him in the best physical condition. Sweat ran down his brow, and his breathing was laboured. He felt winded and he had a stitch in his side. Far off in the distance, the mocking figure of Krieger loomed. Felix decided that for the moment he could go no further.

'Wait!' he gasped, bending double, bracing his hands on his thighs. 'Wait! This is getting us nowhere except lost.'

The Slayers reluctantly halted and turned to look at him. 'Dwarfs don't get lost,' said Gotrek.

'That's not exactly correct,' said Felix. 'I can remember a few occasions. When we were coming back from the land of the Border Princes for example–'

'Let me rephrase that, manling. Dwarfs don't get lost underground, in mines or deep delvings.'

'I may be being a little obtuse here but we're not in a mine.'

'We're in a building. The principle is the same. I can remember all the twists and turns of every passage we took. So can Snorri.'

'That's right,' said Snorri. 'Snorri could find his way back to the entrance with his eyes closed.'

'I don't think that will be necessary,' said Felix. He glanced along the corridor. Krieger was nowhere in sight. 'It seems that our bloodsucking friend is sulking now that we're not playing his little game.'

'Maybe not, manling.'

'What do you mean?'

'I think he's brought along some playmates.'

Felix looked at the Slayer. He had no idea what Gotrek meant.

'Listen!' said the Slayer. 'Can't you hear them?'

Felix shook his head. All he could hear was the sound of his own rasping breath, and his heartbeat drumming in his chest. Gotrek and Snorri grinned at each other in anticipation. This was a bad sign. Felix's heart sank.

A few moments later he heard what they were talking about: a distant stealthy padding of many feet, strange high-pitched chittering voices that yet had something horribly human about them.

'Ghouls,' he said mournfully, and whipped his sword through the air in practice passes to loosen his muscles for the struggle.

'Lots of them,' said Snorri happily.

'Coming from behind us as well,' added Gotrek almost gleefully.

'A trap,' said Felix.

'We'll see who for,' said Gotrek, smiling nastily. He dragged his thumb along the edge of his blade. A bright drop of blood appeared. Feeling hopeless, Felix glanced left and right. In both directions he saw faint pinpoints of reddish light, the reflections of his lantern in the eyes of monsters.

KRIEGER SMILED HAPPILY. Things were going very well. The foolish dwarfs had been lured away from their compatriots with remarkable ease. Now his army of ghouls would overwhelm them. This might actually be a good time to change his initial plans and take the Kislevites in the great hall. He sped along the corridor, fingers stroking the Eye of Khemri lovingly, sending his silent call speeding through the darkness. Everywhere in the massive building his undead minions responded.

MAX OPENED HIS eyes when he felt the vampire touch the web of warding spells woven around him. He came awake instantly, glad to leave the nightmares behind, and looked at the countess.

'I would not come any closer if I were you,' he said cautiously. The thought of this creature approaching while he slept was a disturbing one. 'You will trigger some particularly nasty wards.'

The countess adjusted her veil. 'I noticed. That is why I have made no attempt to touch you.'

So she could see his spell webs well enough to know what would trigger them. That was worth knowing. Max filed the information away for future reference. The countess shivered. 'I came to tell you that Krieger is doing something, sending out a summons to anything dark within this place that can respond. There will be many such things here.'

'I believe you,' said Max. He was more than a little disturbed. His own wards should have woken him at the first trace of any such thing happening. It seemed the dark magic saturating this place was doing more to suppress his powers than he had realised. Once more he cursed whoever had cast them, then pushed the thought aside as childish. Curses wouldn't help him or Ulrika now.

'I think we should be prepared for an attack,' said Gabriella. 'I have already sent Rodrik to waken the others.'

All around him the Kislevites wiped sleep from their eyes and reached for their weapons. The horses shifted restlessly, as if they knew something dreadful was going to happen. Damn, he thought, why couldn't Gotrek and Felix have stayed here? Their blades would have made a big difference in any battle. No sense in wishing for the impossible. What is done is done. Work with what you have.

'You can sense other presences in this place?' he asked, realising the implications of what she had just said.

'Only if they are very close. A spark of dark magic animates most undead constructs. You should be able to see it as well as I. I am merely deducing that if Krieger sends a summons then he expects it to be answered.'

'That would seem logical.'

Gabriella nodded. 'Herr Schreiber, we will soon be fighting for our very existences, and the penalty for losing may be something worse than death. I would have some things understood clearly before the fighting begins.'

'Such as?'

'Such as that we are both on the same side here. I wish no accidents to happen to myself or to my men in the heat of battle. Things will be difficult enough fighting one enemy without having to worry about another at our backs.'

'I was thinking the same thing myself.'

'Then we have a truce?'

'We have had that since the Green Man. I will not be the first to break it.'

'Nor will I.'

'I truly hope so.' The vampire turned to walk away.

'Countess!' She looked back at him over her shoulder.

'If you do break our truce, your existence will end. Be assured of it.'

For a moment the fires of hell flared in her eyes. Anger, naked and unmasked, burned there. She bared her fangs threateningly. 'I do not like threats, Herr Schreiber.'

Max shrugged. 'That was not a threat. It was a promise.'

* * *

ROCHE GLANCED OUT from the cover of the doorway, laced his fingers and fought down the urge to crack his knuckles. It defied belief that such a small number would dare enter this keep and think to challenge his master. Why, there were almost enough of the so-called coven members here to match them. When you added the number of magical constructs the master had reanimated, they would be swept away like a child's sandcastle by the tide.

Of course, they did not know what was here, he told himself. If they did, they would not have come. They would have remained hiding in their pitiful keeps until the master came and winkled them out. Roche drew his short stabbing blade and glanced around.

Far back down the corridor, skeletons moved, their bones softly clicking as they took up their positions in answer to their master's silent command. Roche smiled as he saw the coven members flinch at the sight of them. They might be wealthy and powerful people back in their own lands, but they were finding that this was a place apart. Roche wondered what they would do when they realised that the master had no idea of granting them immortality. Probably whine and backbite and do nothing, he decided. Those that did show some spirit would swiftly learn the folly of opposing the master's will. And then they would end up serving him as animated corpses just like those fool Kislevites. The master's skill at necromancy had grown impressively over the past few days. It was another testimony to the fact his great plan was working.

The master's new consort would be the only mortal raised to near divinity in this place. Roche admitted to himself that he was a little jealous. Deep in the back of his mind, there had always rested the faint hope that he might be granted that ultimate boon. It could still happen, he thought.

Roche saw that the Kislevites were rousing themselves. Did this mean they realised that their doom was close? Roche did not really care. He rather liked the thought of them being awake and realising what was happening to them. He always liked it when the victims struggled a little.

* * *

FELIX CHOPPED DOWN another ghoul. His blade crunched through its skull. The hideous creature went down with the top of its head sheared off. Felix hacked at another, and then another. Clotted blackish blood covered his whole body along with the strange green slime that oozed from the ghouls' innards when he gutted them. He felt sick with the stench and the killing.

The monsters were strong and terribly swift and their claws were as sharp as knives. He bled from a dozen small cuts and bites. Sweat almost blinded him. His muscles ached. At least he had more than held his own against the ghouls. His method had been simple. He stood between Gotrek and Snorri Nosebiter and let the Slayers do the bulk of the killing. In the narrow corridor, only a few of the monsters could attack at a time, and the dwarfs had wreaked terrible havoc. The ghouls were fearsome but the Slayers were engines of destruction. Felix knew that few things in the world could stand against Gotrek when the killing rage was upon him, and Snorri was far more than a match for a ghoul.

To begin with Felix had only to stand there, and stab any of the monsters that got past the dwarfs. As the battle had raged longer and the dwarfs waded into the throng, more and more had somehow got by them and attacked Felix who must have seemed far easier prey. At one time, Gotrek fought at one end of the corridor, Snorri at the other, and Felix had been on his own against a trio of ghouls. Things had been desperate until the Slayers had fought their way back into a closer formation.

Felix hacked another ghoul, then suddenly, to his surprise, it was over. Everything went quiet. The only other things moving were the two dwarfs. Dozens of dead and decapitated ghoul corpses filled the corridor. Gotrek spat on the nearest.

'I hope the bloody vampire puts up a better fight,' Gotrek complained, wiping ghoul blood from his forehead with his tattooed arm.

'Snorri thinks Felix could have taken them on his own,' said Snorri Nosebiter.

Felix tried to grin. Snorri Nosebiter was probably idiotic enough to believe such a thing, but he didn't. He had no illusions whatsoever about what his chances of survival would have been without the Slayers.

'Next time, we'll leave them to you, manling. Snorri Nosebiter can just stand there and give you some pointers on your fighting style.'

'Thanks,' said Felix. 'I look forward to it. But what now? Krieger is nowhere in sight. Shouldn't we head back to the others? They'll be wondering what happened to us.'

Gotrek looked around and nodded. 'Might as well. Who knows – they might need our help.'

ULRIKA HEARD THE sounds of fighting off in the distance, and wondered what was going on. Adolphus had told her to wait in her chamber, and keep as far away from the intruders as possible. She was only to leave if her existence was threatened or if he came for her. He seemed to be worried that in her newly arisen condition she might prove vulnerable to attack, but she sensed there was something more to it than that. She wondered if he were hiding something from her.

She wished that the compulsion to obey was not quite so strong. The thirst gnawed away at her mind, and no matter how much it horrified her, she was filled with a deep need to slake it.

She sat down on the bed, and considered her predicament. The power of the Eye was such that she could not disobey a direct command. Or could she? She made for the door. She did not even reach it before her feet carried her back to where she had come from. She growled like an animal at bay.

There was one thing. If she could hear the sounds of fighting that had just faded, perhaps the warriors could hear her. It was worth a try. She opened her mouth and let out a long, hideous scream.

MAX SCHREIBER CONCENTRATED on remaining calm. It was not easy. The panicked horses raced around the huge hall, desperate to find an escape from their predicament. If something was not done soon they were going to trample someone to death. Ivan had obviously reached the same conclusion.

The old boyar nodded to two of his men. 'Open the main door! Let the beasts out!'

The two Kislevites were not happy. Max could tell they were thinking about what might happen if they were stranded here without mounts. 'Do it!' bellowed Ivan. 'Now!'

The soldiers hastened to obey, casting a nervous eye in the direction of the great staircase. Like everyone else, they had figured that whatever was making their steeds nervous was over there somewhere. Max knew a way to find out.

Once again he created the floating eye. A touch of his will sent it in the right direction, covering the ground faster than a running man. From its point of view, Max caught sight of things moving beneath one of the arches. He sent the eye to investigate.

Suddenly, he saw what waited and horror filled him. All along the corridor skeletons marched, with rusting, notched weapons clutched in bony fingers. Animated corpses, rotting skin peeling back from gangrenous flesh, clad in the ragged remains of grave clothes, shambled slowly along, a hellish glow burning in their decomposing eyes. Here and there, armed and armoured men waited. Most of them looked as sick as Max felt. Their leader was a gigantic man with a shaven head and the gaunt ascetic face of a fanatic.

All of the mortals looked up, seeing the glowing sphere. One of the men rushed at it and slashed with a sword. Max broke the link before impact.

'Get ready to fight,' he told the Kislevites. 'The dead walk here. Ready yourselves!'

Pale, nervous faces turned to look at him. He could see that some of the younger ones wanted to run, but would not shame themselves.

These were men brought up on the marches of Kislev; they had seen more than their share of horrors. Just as well really. Their chances of survival were higher here with their fellows than fleeing through the winter darkness outside.

Rodrik and his companions clustered around the countess, preparing to defend her with all the ardour of Bretonnian knights fighting for the honour of their lady love. The sight at once astonished and sickened Max. He took a deep breath and began the mental exercises designed to calm his mind. He forced himself to relax and be receptive to the flow of the winds of magic.

The currents of power were turbulent here, roiling like the waters of a fast flowing stream passing through rocks. The strange corrupted wards in the walls and the evil power buried deep within the keep caused weird swirls and eddies. It was going to take all of his skill and concentration to work powerful magic.

He pushed his palms together, interlocked his fingers and flexed them, feeling some of the tension in his shoulders unknot. The waiting was over. Conflict beckoned. His destiny was in his own hands. By his skill and power he would survive.

Or at least, send as many of his foes back to hell as he could before he fell himself.

ADOLPHUS KRIEGER LOOKED down from the gallery once more, watching the Kislevites and their wizard preparing to meet his forces. Give them some credit, he thought, they are brave. Few men could stand their ground against the forces of undeath at night within the walls of this keep. Of course they did not yet know what they truly faced. And it was always possible that the countess had enthralled them. It took no courage to stand and fight when your will was bound to it.

He was tempted to probe the defences the wizard had set around the camp, but resisted. He was not yet confident enough in his sorcerous skills to risk a direct confrontation with a powerful mage. It would be best to wait for an opportune moment, then strike. He composed himself to watch the battle until that time arrived.

'WHAT WAS THAT?' asked Snorri, as the echoes of the scream faded.

'It sounded like Ulrika,' said Felix, wondering if this were yet another trap. Even if it was, they had to investigate it. They had come so far in search of her that they could not afford to ignore any possible trail.

'It came from this direction,' said Gotrek, stomping off down the corridor towards the source of the noise. Decision made, thought Felix. A thrill of fear and anticipation at what they would find passed through him.

BONES CLICKING HORRIBLY, the skeletons marched into the great hall and deployed themselves in an evil parody of a human regiment. No human force had ever marched with such precision, thought Max. The whole mass moved in unison in response to a single will.

Another force of skeletons entered the chamber, and then another. Walking corpses followed them, and then finally came the humans he had seen earlier, garbed in their black surcoats and britches bearing the sign of a skull flanked by two mirrored half moons. Max tried to count the numbers of the enemy. He guessed that they were outnumbered by at least ten to one. It was a second before he realised that he had spoken aloud.

'Not bad odds,' he heard Ivan Petrovich mutter. The old boyar chuckled. His men looked at him admiringly. So did Max. Straghov obviously knew how to reassure his troops under difficult conditions.

'Maybe half of the lads should stand aside to give these ghoul lovers a sporting chance,' said Max. It was a weak joke but most of the men laughed as if he had said something uproariously funny. 'Perhaps you should all stand aside and I'll deal with them myself.'

He could tell by the awestruck looks that some of them thought he was serious. The clicking of bones grew louder as the enemy surged towards them. Their lack of war cries and boasts was as unnerving as the sight of them. No human army would advance without a mighty roar.

'Allow me to demonstrate,' said Max, spreading his arms wide and opening his mind to draw the winds of magic to him. A nimbus of light appeared around his head and each of his hands. He spoke words of power, focused his mind in the patterns he had been taught. The flows resisted him. As he forced one part of the pattern into place, another oozed out. It required utter concentration, far above the norm, to bind the winds of magic to his will.

In the air above his head, between his outstretched arms, an intricate web of light sprang into being. Shimmering strands of power flowed into one another weaving among themselves like a basketful of snakes. Max strained to keep the magical structure in place while he drew all the power he could to himself. The strain was enormous. His head felt as if it would explode from the pressure. Pain stabbed through his mind. His forehead felt as if it was caught in a huge vice. His arms shuddered as if he tried to hold the weight of the world above his head.

Power attracted power. Like was drawn to like. More and more magical energy swirled inwards now, drawn into the vortex he had created. Tendrils of it touched the real world; phantom fingers made his robes ripple as if in a breeze. His skin tingled. The tips of his fingertips felt like they were touching red-hot iron.

Where at first he had struggled to draw power into the weave, now he was having difficulty releasing it. Power buffeted him from every direction, all of it being pulled inward. He took a deep breath, howled the final syllables of the incantation and focused every iota of willpower, every ounce of magical sinew, to cast the sphere of destruction he had created towards his foes.

He felt something give way but was not sure whether it was in himself or the binding. An enormous weight lifted from him, and a blaze of light flashed across his sight.

ADOLPHUS KRIEGER WATCHED in awe as the wizard struggled to cast his spell. He would not have thought it possible for any mortal to draw such power to himself in the face of the wards on this keep, but not only was the mage doing it, he was controlling a mightier flow of energy than Krieger had ever seen bound before.

Snakes of light flickered from every corner of the room, searing the air as they were pulled into the sphere above the sorcerer. They were so bright that Krieger's sensitive eyes almost could not bear the sight of them, and he had to force himself to watch.

A wind sprang up from nowhere and passed through the room. Krieger wondered how it was possible for any man to contain so much power. It seemed impossible that any human form could do so for more than a few moments. Every inch of the wizard's skin glowed. His eyeballs were molten spheres of gold.

Then the wizard unleashed his spell. Dozens of serpents of golden light flickered through the air towards the undead horde. They covered the distance in a heartbeat. As each one impacted, a skeleton disintegrated into a clattering pile of bones. The lights in the skulls faded and died. As each shimmering snake touched a zombie, the walking corpse shrivelled and collapsed into a desiccated husk and came apart in a shower of dust. Where the lights touched men, they screamed and burned. Krieger was suddenly very glad he had chosen not to lead the attack.

THE KISLEVITES CHEERED as about half of their foes went down to Max's spell. The rest sent a wave of arrows hurtling towards their attackers. Some buried themselves into the flesh of walking corpses and quivered there, seemingly having done no harm. Others clattered through the empty ribcages of the animated skeletons. A few took down some of the men. The effect was not what Max would have hoped for, but was hardly surprising. The walking dead were fell foes.

Max felt the tug of magical energy being drawn to someone else. His magesight saw a wave of dark magic being drawn to the countess. A web of darkness came into being around her then tendrils leapt from it towards the undead. When it touched them they simply stopped in their tracks.

It was a good casting under difficult circumstances, Max judged, but it was neither as strong nor as destructive as his own had been. Barely half a dozen of their foes went down.

The rest covered the distance between the two sides in a few more strides. Max snatched up his staff and prepared to defend himself.

All around him the blades of man and undead monster rang against each other. He had done all that he could. He only hoped that it was enough.

'I WISH SHE would stop screaming like that,' said Felix. He was angry but he suspected that his anger merely concealed a deeper-seated worry. There was something profoundly disturbing about the voice, a faintly inhuman note that suggested a mind either just on or just over the brink of being unhinged.

'Be sure to tell her that when we see her,' said Gotrek. He moved warily, the monstrous axe held in his right hand. With the ghoul blood covering him he looked as terrifying as anything they were likely to encounter here.

They crossed a massive hall, its floor chequered in tiles of bone white and blood red. Old fusty tapestries depicting mounted men and women hunting naked people in the woods covered the walls.

'Whoever furnished this place was not sane,' Felix muttered. He expected no reply and got none. They passed a long crumbling flight of marble stairs and halted in front of the door from behind which the screaming was coming. As they reached it, the screams halted. Before Felix could reach for the handle Gotrek's axe smashed into the wood, splintering it. The runes on the blade glowed. With swift chops the Slayer made an entry into the room.

Ulrika waited within. She looked very pale and had lost a lot of weight but seemed otherwise unharmed. The room was richly furnished and cleaner than most in this foul place, although there were still massive cobwebs in the corners of the ceiling, and a faint smell of rot in the air.

Felix wanted to rush over to her and take her in his arms and reassure her but some instinct stopped him. She looked up at him and smiled – and as she did so long fangs extruded themselves from her gums. A red glow entered her eyes. Seeing these changes come over that well remembered face, turning it into something at once evil and eerily familiar, Felix felt his own sanity teeter on the brink.

'Sorry, manling,' said Gotrek, striding into the room, axe held ready to strike.

'Snorri's sorry too, Felix,' said Snorri Nosebiter as he followed.

Felix stood by the doorway, unable to decide what to do. Looking at them, a hideous hissing sound emerged from Ulrika's mouth.

ROCHE AIMED A blow at the Kislevite in front of him. His mighty arm drove his blade right through the man's leather armour and buried it deep in his guts. The man screamed as he died. Another servant for the master, thought Roche happily as he pulled his sword out. Warm ropy entrails spilled over his hand. He glanced around to see how the battle was going.

Somewhat differently than he had hoped. Well over three quarters of the master's forces were down. The wizard stood with his back to the coach, two zombies coming for him. As Roche watched, the mage struck one in the head with his staff, stepped away from the second and spoke a word. Something emerged from his mouth and hovered shimmering in the air for a moment, a blazing pattern of light that brought tears to the eye and hurt the brain. In another heartbeat the zombie's head exploded, spurting brains and fragments of bone into the air and covering everyone nearby in a rain of jelly and splinters. Roche licked his lips. The taste was interesting. Briefly he considered charging the wizard and trying to overwhelm him with a hail of blows. It might work, he thought. The wizard gestured and a bolt of golden light ripped through the spine of a nearby skeleton. It fell on the floor in two halves, the glow of animation fading from its eyes. Then again, it might not.

Off to his left the battle had taken another surprising turn. A small, frail-looking woman leapt amid the coven members. With one sweep of her arm, she tore off Gaius's head. Roche knew he was strong. He could break a man's neck with his bare hands if he needed to, but there was no way he could rip a head from its shoulders even using both hands. What sort of woman could? Instantly the answer swept into his mind: one like the master. This was not good. Why had the master not warned him? Roche dismissed the thought. Doubtless the master had his reasons.

The intruders were not having it all their own way. Many of the Kislevites were down now, and most of the Sylvanian knights were dead. By Roche's count that left only the wizard, the fat old man, the countess, and one of the knights. A quick glance told Roche that more than a dozen of the zombies were still on the go, and a couple of the coven. It would be enough, he told himself. It would have to be.

He raced towards the old man hoping to take him unawares and then get on to the wizard. As he moved he suddenly came to a halt, anchored to the spot by a slender arm. He caught sight of long fingernails dripping red blood. He noticed a ruby glittering on one of the fingers. Automatically, he appraised its worth, even as a low, surprisingly gentle woman's voice whispered in his ear.

'Now, lackey, you go to the grave.'

There was a flash of pain, a terrible strain on his neck, and then the pain and the strain were gone. He watched the roof wheel and found himself looking up at a massive headless corpse tottering above him. With a shock, he realised that the body belonged to him. It seemed that a brain was capable of living for a few moments after being separated from its body. His lips formed a prayer for help to his master but there were no lungs to push air into his mouth.

MAX SUMMONED POWER and gestured. A bolt of golden light sheared through the chest of an animated corpse, chopping it in half like an enormous cleaver. The body flopped to the ground and remained horribly animated for a few moments. Its top half still tried to crawl towards him, while its bottom half drummed its feet on the flagstones. Max took no chances. Another gesture and another blast of power incinerated the creature.

Here and there a few knots of fighters were still locked in combat. Ivan Petrovich hacked down a pair of animated skeletons with one stroke of his sabre. The old man was covered in cuts and bled profusely from a massive wound in his arm. Rodrik fought beside the countess, guarding her back. Not that she needed much guarding. The vampire moved with phenomenal speed, rending and tearing anything that got in her way. To his horror he realised that they were the only members of their party remaining on their feet. All of the other Kislevites were down. Many cried in pain. As Max watched, a skeleton bit out the throat of one of the wounded.

Still fighting against the strange warping power of his surroundings, Max wearily drew on his magic once more. A blast of energy ignited the brittle bones of the animated thing. Molten bone splattered the corpses surrounding it.

Suddenly, all was silent, save for the cold whisper of the breeze carrying snowflakes through the open doorway. Max glanced around and realised that it was over. Only he, Ivan, the countess and Rodrik remained standing in the hall. After the terrifying din of battle, the quiet was almost as unnerving.

Max looked at his companions, and smiled without warmth or any sense of triumph. It was the weary smile of a man who had remained alive while most of his companions had fallen, and the other two men mirrored it. The countess did not smile at all. Instead she stood with her head cocked in the attitude of one listening, although what it was she listened for, Max could not begin to guess.

Max saw that Ivan Petrovich was staring at the countess, as if contemplating driving his blade into her back. The old boyar must have seen the carnage she had wrought and doubtless he now wondered exactly what had travelled with him to this place. Perhaps like Max he was searching his memory, trying to remember if any of the Kislevite casualties had been her work.

Max could not recall any, but in the heat of battle he might have missed some. He regretted his bravado and his threats from earlier. Manipulating the powers of magic had cost him dearly. Overcoming the resistance of this place had taken almost as much of his strength as working the magic itself. He felt as tired as if he had walked for days without sleep. He took a deep breath and calmed his mind. He was not about to let any of this show.

Instead he strode across to Ivan Petrovich. 'Let me see your arm,' he said gently.

Absent-mindedly the boyar stretched out his arm, but his gaze never left the Countess Gabriella. 'Did you see what she did?' he asked.

Max nodded. The Kislevite nobleman's expression mingled awe and horror in equal parts. 'What evil have you brought here?' he asked.

Max ran his fingers over the wound and concentrated. A gentle golden glow passed from his fingertips to the boyar's arm. The flow of blood stopped. The flesh knitted beneath his touch. The boyar winced at the pain of the procedure but made no sound. The countess turned to look at them. Max saw her gaze at the blood on the closed wound as if hypnotised. She licked her lips. The gesture reminded the wizard of the flicker of a serpent's tongue.

'He is close,' she said after a moment of silence. 'And so is the talisman. I can feel its presence gnawing at my mind.'

'Where?' Max asked.

'Somewhere above us.'

Max was about to summon his golden eye for the third time that day when she winced. 'He is moving away from us.'

'He has seen what we have done here and flees in fear,' said Rodrik stoutly.

'Then we will follow him,' said Ivan Petrovich.

'First we will burn these bodies,' said Max. 'I would not have him draw them back to life. I do not want to have to face the corpses of those who fought so bravely alongside us.'

'How will we burn so many?' Rodrik asked.

'Cover them with lantern oil,' said Max. 'I will do the rest.'

FROM BEHIND THEM came the sickly sweet smell of burning flesh mingled with aromatic lantern oil. Max walked beside Ivan Petrovich. Ahead of them walked the countess and then

Rodrik. He was sure this was a deliberate gesture of bravado on her part, turning her back to them, letting him see that she trusted them enough to leave herself vulnerable, even if they did not trust her. Or perhaps, thought Max, she was simply contemptuous of them. Weak as he currently felt that contempt might well prove justified. Max prayed that the wounded would be all right until they returned. He would have healed more, but he knew he needed to conserve his remaining power.

'Be very careful,' the countess said, in that deceptively gentle voice. 'There could still be ghouls and worse in this place, and not a few of his coven fled the battle before it was over. Adolphus Krieger is not the only foe we might have to face, although he is doubtless the worst.'

Max glanced around. This had never been the most reassuring place and now, without the troops, with only Ivan Petrovich and the vampire and her minion for company, it was even less so. Every shadow seemed to conceal some hidden threat. Every open doorway was a gaping maw that he expected to spew forth a horde of undead monsters.

What now? Were they going to have to search this whole horrid place to find Krieger or would he come to them? What other nasty surprises did this place hold?

'No!' SHOUTED FELIX. 'Don't!'

For a moment everyone in the chamber froze. Ulrika stood legs flexed, ready to strike. The two Slayers had covered half the distance between them and her.

'Surely we can settle this sensibly.' Felix was not sure how, but they had reached an accommodation with the countess – surely they could do so with Ulrika, surely she had not changed that much.

He moved between the dwarfs and the woman and turned arms open wide to beseech Gotrek and Snorri Nosebiter not to attack. 'Nobody here need die.'

'That is not true, Felix,' he heard Ulrika's voice whisper in his ear, as a very strong arm looped around his neck. He struggled but he was like a mouse caught in the jaws of a cat. Gods, she had become very strong. His feet were off the

ground. He found himself being held as a shield between
her and the dwarfs.

'So you're going to kill me then,' he said, relaxing completely. He felt resigned to his fate. If he was going to die
here, so be it. It was ironic that it would be at the hand of
the woman he had come so far to rescue.

Snorri and Gotrek had moved apart, one on either side,
flanking Ulrika. One or the other of them was going to get a
strike at her, or him, if she chose to interpose his body
between herself and the blow.

Suddenly, the world tipped and he was hurtling through
the air towards Gotrek. From the corner of his eye, he saw a
blurred figure leaping between the two Slayers towards the
door. Gotrek leapt to one side to avoid him. Felix hit the
flagstones rolling. Pain slammed through his body with the
impact. He kept rolling hoping to absorb the impact and
slammed into the wall. Stars danced before his eyes.

He pulled himself erect and glanced around to see the two
Slayers gazing mournfully out of the door. 'She was too
quick for us,' said Gotrek. 'She has got away – for the
moment.'

A bewildered expression flickered across his brutal face.
He shook his head annoyed and spat on the ground. Felix
looked at the Slayer. For a moment there he had been certain that Gotrek was not saddened by Ulrika's escape and
that fact shamed him. Now did not seem a good time to
check his observation.

'What now?' he asked instead. Snorri shrugged. Gotrek
glared at him.

'The next time we meet her, don't talk, manling, strike!'
Felix remembered how he had felt in Ulrika's grasp. He was
certain that he had come very close to death. He knew that
the Slayer was right. Next time, there would be no attempts
to negotiate and no mercy.

ULRIKA FLED THROUGH the vast maze of the keep. She shook
from reaction. The thirst was on her now. She was not sure
how she had found the willpower to avoid burying her fangs
into Felix's neck and draining him dry.

She stretched her legs and bounded up a flight of stairs, boots soundless on the moth-eaten red carpet. Perhaps it was some residue of the feeling she had once felt for Felix that had saved him. She would have liked to think so but she was not certain. It seemed equally possible that it was a deep buried instinct for survival. If she had allowed herself to be overcome by the thirst just then, she would have given the Slayers a clear shot at her. Many mortals might flinch and flee from the sight of one of the Arisen in full feeding frenzy but she knew that neither Gotrek nor Snorri Nosebiter could be counted among that number. She was certain that allowing the Slayer one clean stroke with that axe of his would have been the end of her, and horrified as she was by her new condition she was not yet ready for the final death. For one thing, she intended to repay Adolphus Krieger for what he had done to her, if it took all eternity.

She might be bound to him now by her need for knowledge and the power of the talisman, but she would find a way to slay him. She knew it had to be possible. After all, if she were cautious, she had all the time in the world, and over the centuries surely anything would eventually become possible.

The question was, what was she to do right now? She needed to avoid her pursuers and find Krieger. Failing that, she ought to get away from here, and then see what happened next. It was not the best of plans, but she could think of no other. For many conflicting reasons, she was not about to stay and fight with Felix and the Slayers.

Why had Krieger not told her they were here? Why did he keep it a secret from her, and what other secrets was he keeping? These were other scores to be settled with him when the time came.

Some instinct told her to head to the right, taking a long corridor into a massive dining room. Why? Could it be the talisman still called to her? Would the call lead her eventually to Krieger? It was possible. She decided to trust the feeling, and follow her instincts. What else was there to do? She raced along the path leading to the throne room.

* * *

'HE WENT THIS way,' said the countess. She paused at the junction of two corridors and indicated the one to the left.

'How can you be so certain?' Max asked. The walk had left him feeling a little worse. The castle was covered in spells of mazing and warding intended to confuse anyone but the undead and their servants. Using his magesight to overcome them had left him feeling queasy.

'He is using the talisman to summon all of our kind here. Perhaps he has not thought to cease the summoning. Perhaps it is something he has overlooked.'

Or perhaps, thought Max, he is luring us into yet another trap.

THINGS COULD HAVE gone better, thought Krieger. The vanguard of his invincible undead army was gone, defeated by the enemies who still roamed free in his castle. All of his careful preparation had gone for naught.

On the other hand, things could be worse. Ulrika was still free, as he could sense through their bond. And the countess was here. Foolish of her, really, to put herself in his power like this. It meant that potentially he still had two very powerful pawns within the building.

All it would take now would be to arrange matters as he wished, and choose a spot where he would dispatch his enemies. Where better than his throne room? He would gather what were left of his forces in the building and draw matters to their inevitable conclusion there.

'AH, ULRIKA, I am so glad you could join me,' said Adolphus Krieger.

Ulrika entered the throne room. It was a hideous place, dominated by a massive ebony throne inlaid with skull motifs. Each of the skulls had rubies for eyes. The walls were covered in tapestries depicting the great triumphs of the wars of the Vampire Counts. The floor was tiled in black and white, save for a mouldering carpet that lay around the base of the regal dais. Adolphus Krieger lounged in the throne. As she had suspected, she had been drawn to him by the power of that evil talisman blazing at his throat.

'I did not have much choice,' she said bitterly.

'True, but that in no way lessens my joy at seeing you.'

'Why did you not tell me Felix was coming here?'

'Would it have made any difference? You would still have had to do as I wished.'

'I wish you had told me anyway.'

'Why? You sound regretful. Did you kill him?'

'No.'

'A pity.'

'He and Gotrek almost killed me though.'

'I would have been sorry about that. The Slayer and his cohorts are still alive, then?'

'When I last saw them they were, very much so.'

'I suppose they will have to be dealt with too then.'

'Too?'

'Your wizard friend also came here with some Kislevites, and a former associate of mine. I think they seek what I now have.'

'Kislevites?'

'Your countrymen, my dear. Led by a fat old man.'

A spasm of fear and guilt passed through Ulrika's mind. It could only be her father. Of course, if Max and Felix could find her here, he would have come with them. He would ride into the gates of hell themselves to save her. In a way, he had.

'Are they dead?'

'Who?'

'The wizard and the Kislevite leader.'

'Regrettably both were still alive when I last saw them, but don't worry, that will soon change. Did you know the old man?'

Ulrika considered for a moment. She could see nothing to be gained by denying the truth. And perhaps if worst came to worst she could see her father's life spared. 'He is my father.'

'Ah… That would explain why he came all this way to find you then. I should have suspected as much.'

'You are not going to kill him, are you?'

'That certainly was my intention, my dear. Why? Do you have something else in mind?'

'Spare him!'

'Such sentimentality, Ulrika. He is no longer your father. I am. I doubt that he would spare you if he finds you.'

Ulrika had to admit there was truth in that. Ivan Petrovich's upbringing on the marches of Kislev left him little room for compromise with the powers of darkness, to which she now undoubtedly belonged. He would have come all this way to make sure his only daughter was truly dead, as much as to rescue her. It was the only honourable thing to do, and Ivan Petrovich Straghov was a man of honour. Even so, even if he would kill her, she did not want that to happen to him.

'Nonetheless, I ask you to spare him.'

Adolphus Krieger leant forward on his throne and stroked his chin with the fingers of his left hand. 'He came here to try and slay me. I am not inclined to show mercy.'

Overhead, in the shadows of the vault, massive things moved.

MAX BLASTED THE last of the animated corpses. It flew apart as if sited atop a keg of exploding gunpowder. The stench of charred flesh filled the air. Max was too used to it by now to feel nauseated. He glanced around and saw that there had been no casualties among his comrades.

'There are fewer of them,' said Ivan Petrovich with a weak grin. 'And they do not seem so well organised.'

'I think these were just remnants of the main force left wandering aimlessly around the keep,' said the countess. 'I do not think they were sent to attack us specifically.'

Max agreed. There had been too few of these zombies to pose a threat. The countess could have torn them apart herself. In fact, Max resolved, the next time this situation arose, he would stand aside and let her do just that. 'How much further?' he asked.

'Not far now,' said the countess. There was a strange gleam in her eyes.

'SHE WENT THIS way,' said Gotrek.

'Are you sure?' Felix asked. He tugged at his cloak nervously. The sense of oppressive evil had deepened. He really did not want to be in this place. In answer to his question, the Slayer shook his head doubtfully.

'I am not the tracker Marek is, but these are her prints in this mould.'

'Perhaps those lights up ahead are a clue as well,' said Snorri Nosebiter. Both Felix and Gotrek glanced in the direction he indicated. Felix thought he caught sight of Ulrika slipping through a low archway. He felt sure that neither the archway nor the lights had been visible moments ago. He felt certain that either he or Gotrek would have noticed them.

'That's very convenient,' said Gotrek.

'Isn't it?' said Felix. Without further discussion they moved towards the light.

'Herr Jaeger! Herr Gurnisson! It gives me great pleasure to renew our acquaintance.'

The throne room was vast, quiet and appeared to be in good repair. On a massive ebony throne lolled Adolphus Krieger; Ulrika crouched down by his side. His left hand played with her ash blonde hair the way a man might idly stroke the head of a favourite hound. His right hand toyed with the familiar talisman at his neck.

'Snorri Nosebiter is here too, you cheeky bastard,' said Snorri.

'My apologies. I was not sure whether to call you Herr Nosebiter or not,' said the vampire with an amused smile. His face was clearly visible in the light of the enormous chandelier.

How had it been lit, Felix wondered? And why? Around the walls stood countless suits of antique armour, filling every niche. Each held a sword, a pike or some other weapon of antique design but obvious utility. He thought he detected movement overhead. A quick glance revealed only deeper shadows moving in the blackness above the lights.

'It doesn't matter,' said Gotrek, advancing towards the throne. 'You are dead.'

The vampire raised his hands. 'Wait a moment,' said Krieger. 'My other guests are about to arrive.'

* * *

MAX ENTERED THE enormous throne room just behind the countess. His gaze swept past the massive throne and was drawn as if by a magnet to Ulrika. She looked so pale. Fangs were visible in her mouth. His heart sank when he realised that she had become a vampire.

Max asked himself what he was going to do. He had come all this way to rescue her, and it looked like she was beyond salvation. Could he really kill her? Could he really stand by and watch as Gotrek attempted to do so?

He was almost glad when a sudden massive surge of magical power drew his gaze to the throne.

FELIX SAW MAX Schreiber, Ivan Petrovich, the countess and her lapdog Rodrik enter from the other side of the chamber. They looked just as surprised to see him as he was to see them. He saw the look of horror and despair sweep over Max's face. He understood it all too well.

What was Krieger planning now? Why had he brought them here? Surely he must have some sort of ace up his sleeve or he would not look so confident. Not unless he was completely mad. Or utterly secure in his power.

'Countess Gabriella. It's been a very long time. I am so pleased that you are the first to answer my summons. Rest assured you won't be the last,' Krieger smiled.

'I should have put you down when I whelped you,' said the countess, her voice chilly with hate. Any doubts about the animosity between the two Felix might have had vanished. The countess sincerely wished Krieger dead. Well, that makes two of us, Felix thought. Gotrek watched the confrontation between the two with interest and began to move towards the throne, holding his axe ready.

'Alas, countess, the time for such regrets is long past. I am the master now. You will serve me as surely as young Ulrika here.'

Was there something fluttering among the rafters of the hall? Felix was sure he had heard something. As he looked up again he felt certain he could see massive scraps of black shadow fluttering about. Things were not as they seemed here at all, he told himself. He needed to be very careful. He placed his lantern on the ground and held his sword warily.

'We shall see,' said the countess. Felix was certain he heard a hint of doubt in her voice.

'Indeed we shall. I have mastered the Eye now. Allow me to demonstrate.'

The talisman at Krieger's throat flared dazzlingly. Just the sight of it made Felix dizzy. Gotrek halted for a moment, covering his eye with his arm. The countess gave a shriek and fell to her knees. Rodrik ran to her side, solicitously. Max watched everything very carefully, as if following the invisible flow of power with his mage sight. Snorri Nosebiter looked just as bemused as Felix felt.

Ulrika stared miserably at her father. He stared back disbelievingly. Felix wished he did not have to look at their faces; they were such studies of horror and misery. Quickly he looked back at Krieger. If anything, the vampire appeared to be enjoying himself even more.

The countess raised her head. An odd glow entered her eyes. Her whole expression changed. She stood up, moving jerkily and mechanically, as if her mind fought with something else for control of her body. Fear, hatred and impotent rage flashed across her face. Rodrik moved to her side, reaching out for her with all the tender concern of a worried lover.

Gotrek prepared to charge. Felix made ready to follow him.

MAX WATCHED THE incredibly complex flows of energy emerging from the vampire on the throne. Doing so distracted him for a moment from his horror at what had happened to Ulrika. The mesh was of incredible complexity, speed and subtlety. It reminded him of the defences he had encountered when he had probed the Eye of Khemri himself.

It was difficult to follow such a swift, complex casting but Max did his best. There were elements of compulsion there, reinforced with strong threads of dark magic. The power of the thing was incredible. Max doubted that such a spell could be used on a mortal; it was too finely attuned to the dark magic-saturated physiognomy of a vampire.

Thin tendrils of dark magical energy, emanating from the throne, coiled down to the stones of the castle. Great roots of magical energy delved down through the floor into the stonework. Krieger had attuned himself to the castle, which was why he was not struggling to overcome the wards the way Max had to.

Closer inspection revealed the tendrils were connected through the throne to the Eye of Khemri itself. At this moment Krieger was drawing power from the keep for some purpose Max could not yet guess, although he could see the dark magical energy beginning to shimmer around the vampire's form. The power was so great he was surprised that no one else in the room could see it.

The countess had claimed that Krieger was an indifferent mage. Something had certainly changed. He was maintaining two very potent spells with superlative skill. Max doubted he could have managed quite so well himself.

Max would have been willing to bet that Krieger had not always cast spells like this. He was attuned to the talisman now, and it was affecting his magical signature, changing it to resemble its creator. It was likely not all that had been changed either. Doubtless the vampire's mind was being subtly altered too. He shivered briefly at the closeness of his own escape. Who knew where such a process might end up?

The countess moved towards him. Max prepared to defend himself.

ULRIKA KNEW AS SOON as she saw the woman called the countess that here was a fellow vampire. Perhaps it was like calling to like, she did not know. Ulrika could tell at once that this new woman was immeasurably stronger and older than she herself was. She watched in despair as the countess tried to resist Krieger's binding spell and failed. She saw her put up an enormous struggle. It seemed that she could feel the echoes of that struggle in her own mind, and even as she did so, she felt the bonds holding her weaken a little.

Was it possible that while Adolphus used his strength to subdue the countess, his grasp on her was somehow weakened? If so, would his grip return once her struggles ceased?

Ulrika knew she could not take the chance. Frantically she tried to break the mental shackles holding her, to force her way to Krieger's side and attack him.

FELIX SAW ULRIKA begin to move, and Gotrek react as if to a threat. The Slayer raised his axe and prepared to strike, although at least twenty paces separated them from the dais. Noticing this, Krieger gave a laugh and gestured with his right hand.

Something massive and dark flashed downwards from the ceiling. Enormous wings spread to break its fall, massive jaws, full of razor sharp fangs and glistening saliva opened to rend and tear. It was a huge bat, its body larger than any man's. The hooks on its wing tips were razor sharp. It slashed at Gotrek, and the Slayer whirled and ducked, striking at thin air as the creature swept past.

The displacement of air behind him was the only warning Felix had. He threw himself flat even as a winged shadow loomed on the floor in front of him. Pain seared his shoulder like vitriol as flesh parted. An upward glance revealed another of the huge bats hurtling away from him, up towards the cavernous ceiling of the hall. Eerie high-pitched chittering filled Felix's ears.

The clang of metal announced a new threat. One of the massive suits of armour stepped down from its pedestal and began striding towards him. More clattering told him that others were springing into a similar horrid semblance of life.

'Look out!' he cried as several of the armoured forms lumbered towards the Slayer.

ADOLPHUS KRIEGER FELT his two captives struggle against the chains he had placed around their minds. He knew it was futile. There was no way they could resist him. He had the power of the Eye of Khemri; even two women as strong-willed as they could not resist him. The Servants of the Throne would take care of the other interlopers.

A crash of metal on metal drew his attention. He looked down and saw the accursed Slayer piling through the armoured figures of his guardians. His mighty axe smashed through their metal breastplates, cleaving metal to reveal the bones of the animated skeletal constructs within. Even as Krieger watched, a skull rolled from its helmet and the red light of its eyes faded and died.

The monstrous Servants swooped from above. Felix Jaeger ducked the sweep of one's massive membranous wing, and slashed it with his sword, ripping flesh and sinew. The gashed wing interfered with its flight and the Servant tumbled to the stone flagstones. Another Servant grabbed Snorri Nosebiter in its claws and raised him into the air. The Slayer struggled like a mouse in the talons of an owl as he was borne high into the vaulted ceiling. The Slayer's furious struggles allowed him to slip from the creature's bloody talons. Snorri dropped like a stone, tumbling through the air, arms and legs flailing. Krieger grinned. There was no way anything could survive that.

FELIX WATCHED SNORRI tumbling to his death. A growing sense of helplessness filled him. There was nothing he could do to save the dwarf. Then Snorri lashed out with his axe, hooking the massive chandelier. He hung there, as the monstrous bat closed in for the kill and the chandelier swung like a pendulum. Two more massive bat-winged creatures dropped towards Felix. It was going to take all of his attention to stay alive. There would be time enough later to worry about Snorri Nosebiter. He ducked the slash of one razor-sharp talon, rolled under two talons that tried to grab him and stabbed upwards into the belly of the wounded one. Black bile spurted, obscuring his vision.

MAX WATCHED THE countess turn her eyes towards him. Their gazes met with an impact that was almost physical. He had heard much of the vampire's hypnotic glance before, but experiencing it was something completely different. He felt as if all the will were draining out of him: all he could do was stand there like a small bird fascinated by a serpent.

His head spun from trying to maintain his concentration amid the wards of the castle. At that moment, all he wanted to do was give in. Normally, he would have been able to resist her easily, but these were not normal circumstances. He was drained of strength from the long battle, and his mind reeled under the influence of the castle's warding spells. It was all he could do not to simply surrender to her power immediately.

As he stood there paralysed, Rodrik, the countess's faithful lapdog, advanced towards him, blade bared.

IVAN PETROVICH LOOKED up at his beloved daughter, knowing that she was no more. Her soul had been devoured. A daemon had taken possession of her body. There was nothing he could do now but slay her, and lay her body to rest. Hopefully doing so would free her soul to go to eternal rest. So all the old tales claimed.

Yet he found himself reluctant to advance and do his duty. He could remember what she had looked like as a small helpless infant, smiling and glad on the day he had received her first pony, torn by grief at the death of her mother.

How could he forget holding her in his arms as a child or all of the memories of their shared lives? How could he kill her now?

She is gone, he told himself. There is nothing left of her, only a daemon wearing her form. You must do your duty now, even though it's the hardest thing you will ever do. Anything else would be a betrayal of all those fine soldiers you left dead on the way here, and of Ulrika herself. You can mourn afterwards. You must do this thing even though it kills you.

He kept his eyes fixed firmly on her as he charged towards the dais, blade in hand. It was only at the last moment he heard the swish of wings in the air, and felt razor-sharp claws bite into his neck.

ADOLPHUS KRIEGER LOOKED down from his throne and saw that things were going well. The fat old man was dead. The stupidest of the two Slayers was about to die. The countess and her lackey would take care of the wizard. Felix Jaeger was on his knees blinded by blood as two of the Servants flapped overhead, circling like hawks about to swoop for the kill. All that was left was Gotrek Gurnisson and his axe. He would take care of it himself.

The Slayer crashed through the last of the armoured guardians and stood at the foot of the dais, brandishing his mighty weapon. His beard bristled and his one mad eye glittered with insane fury. He looked like some unleashed god of battle. For a moment, Krieger felt almost afraid, but only for a moment.

It was time to put an end to this farce he decided, throwing wide his arms, and drawing on the full power of the Eye. His bones rippled and elongated, and his skin stretched. His features flowed into a new configuration. Long talons ripped the flesh of his fingers. Enormous strength flowed into him, and he knew there was nothing he could not do.

FRANTICALLY, FEARING AT any moment to hear the hissing of air and the slash of talons, Felix wiped the black stuff from his eyes with his arm and scrabbled for his blade. As he did so, from the corner of his eye he caught sight of Adolphus Krieger's transformation.

The vampire's skin cracked open. Reddish flesh erupted through the pallid, broken skin, flowing like melted candle wax into a new shape. His face became longer, his ears became larger and his hair seemed to withdraw into his head. White bones emerged from the mass, lengthening and thinning; translucent folds of flesh wove themselves around them, becoming monstrous bat-like wings that ended in weirdly human hands. Huge scythe-like talons sprang forth from his fingertips. His eyes became larger and darker, his head more triangular. Massive ears emerged from his head, and his nose flattened.

Krieger's whole body lengthened and grew taller, forcing him to hunch forward in a bestial manner. Within seconds an awful hybrid of bat and man loomed over the Slayer, casting a terrible shadow. Even as it did so more of the armoured guardians sprang forward to assail Gotrek. The monstrous bats assaulting Felix withdrew to join the attack. Gotrek swept his axe around in a huge arc, striving to hold them at bay with its fury.

As he did so, the Krieger thing sprang forward with awful speed, so fast that Gotrek had no time to strike. In an instant those razor-sharp talons were digging into his throat. Droplets of red beaded the dwarf's skin. For a terrified heart-beat, Felix wondered whether this was where the Slayer's saga ended. If it did, he knew his own tale would end shortly thereafter.

ULRIKA SAW HER father fall, and horror and despair swept over her in a tidal wave. For a moment, she had been worried that the old man was going to kill her, and she had undergone a brief surge of guilt at the relief she felt when she saw him fall. She knew that he was the one person in the world she would not have defended herself against. This guilt amplified her anger and her despair. Her rage sought an outlet and found it in the monstrously mutated form of Adolphus Krieger. He was responsible for all of this. He had brought her here. He had changed her. It was because of him that Ivan Petrovich had come here looking for her, and found his own death instead.

She threw all the force of her will against the bonds that held her. Strong as they were she felt them shiver. And distantly, she sensed she was not alone in the struggle. Another will joined hers in resisting Krieger's evil spell, the will of a being much older, stronger and more disciplined by dark sorcery than her own. Together they began to throw off the chains that bound them.

MAX WATCHED RODRIK's blade descend. It was all he could do to force himself to duck to one side. The blade caught his arm and drew blood. He saw the vampire lick her lips hungrily. She leapt forward to pinion him, pushing aside her lackey. Ivory fangs flashed nearer to his neck. Her eyes had expanded to vast pits that filled his consciousness and threatened to swallow all awareness.

Suddenly, she stopped, and the hellish light in her eyes flickered. Max felt the will bearing down on his weaken, as if it were distracted. Perhaps it was. He could sense the bonds of Krieger's spell begin to weaken. Those incredibly strong hands loosened themselves from his throat. He fell to the floor and caught sight of the monstrous bat-creature that had been Krieger dash Gotrek to the ground. He loomed over the Slayer like the shadow of doom.

TRIUMPH FILLED ADOLPHUS Krieger. The dwarf had proven no match for his altered form. Look at his pathetic struggles as even now he tries to rise to his feet, he thought.

Krieger bared his fangs. It was time to end this. Even as he did so, he felt Ulrika and the countess threaten to break free from his influence. The backlash from their efforts almost paralysed him. He threw all of his willpower into the struggle and drew deeply on the power of the Eye. Their despair was like nectar to him. They knew he was invincible. Just at that moment, he heard something moving above him. He looked up, and in a shocked second saw the enormous crystal chandelier descending towards him, the metal spike on the bottom glittering like a sword-blade.

A BELLOWED WARCRY from overhead drew Max's attention. He saw Snorri Nosebiter had somehow clambered up onto the chandelier and chopped through its chain. It crashed downwards, hurtling down onto the massive hybrid thing that was Krieger. At the last second the monster sensed its peril and looked up, a peculiarly human look of despair flashing through its eyes, as the spiked tip at the base of the huge structure smashed through its chest, driven by all the weight of Snorri Nosebiter and the momentum of its long fall.

Krieger surged to his feet, desperately casting off the remains of the chandelier. His unnatural shape was already changing back to human. The marks of mortality were etched on his face. Max summoned the last of his remaining power and sent a bolt of dazzling light flickering towards the transformed vampire's eyes. Krieger let out a screech of unnatural rage and pain. It emerged from his warped throat and the pitch heightened until it seemed to reach a realm inaudible to human ears.

Gotrek pulled himself to his feet and sent his axe thundering at the vampire's neck. His blade impacted on the Eye of Khemri and drove right through it, burying itself deep in Krieger's chest. As the enchanted axe smashed through the ancient talisman, all of the armoured guardians lost their animation and collapsed. The huge bats, no longer guided by a single will, fluttered upwards, away from the battle. For a moment, everything seemed frozen in place. An aura of unnatural energy crackled around Krieger's form as the talisman discharged the last of its power, then a vast explosion of unleashed magical energy ripped outwards, tearing the vampire apart.

The force of the blast smashed into the weakened Max, knocking him from his feet and down into darkness.

Without taking his eyes off the countess, Felix bent down and retrieved his sword. He ached all over but he still offered up his thanks to Sigmar for sparing him. His clothing was scorched, his hair was burned and his face felt toasted. All in all though, things could have been worse. Looking at the countess however, his gratitude vanished. She glared at him hungrily.

'Come and die,' growled Gotrek from somewhere behind Felix's back. Felix braced himself for the inevitable attack. It did not come. Instead the countess merely looked at him and then at the Slayer, and shook her head like someone awakening from a bad dream.

'There is no need for us to fight,' she said. 'We have done what we came here to do.'

'Are you sure?' Felix asked.

'The threat of the Eye is ended forever.'

Felix glanced down at where the corpse of Krieger should have been. All that remained were some putrefying chunks of flesh, and a few fragments of the broken Eye. As Felix watched the shards turned to dust.

The countess looked at Ulrika. She extended one of her hands. 'Come with me child. Your progenitor is gone, and there is much you must learn.'

Ulrika strode over to where her father lay. She looked as if she wanted to cry but could not quite remember how. 'I must bury him first.'

The countess nodded. Ulrika bent and picked up the old man's corpse as if it were weightless. Felix looked at Gotrek.

He wondered if the Slayer were going to attack her. At the moment the dwarf did not look as if he was up to overcoming a puppy let alone a vampire. The explosion had covered him in filth. His eyebrows and crest were singed and smouldering. He bled from a dozen cuts. He appeared barely capable of standing let alone fighting. Snorri Nosebiter sprawled amid the remains of the chandelier. No help there either, Felix thought.

'What she did was done under the influence of something she could not resist,' said the countess. 'She bears you no malice.'

For the first time Ulrika seemed to see them. 'That is true,' she said. There was nothing apologetic in her tone though. Her voice was cold and distant and alien. Felix wondered if any trace of the woman he had once known remained.

'She was as much Krieger's victim as anyone here. She does not deserve to be punished for something that was not her choice. I will take her and teach her and see that she does no one any harm,' said the countess. The Slayer started as if he was considering an attack. Felix was surprised at his restraint. Gotrek looked at Ulrika and an odd mixture of emotions flickered across his brutal features.

'See that you do,' he said eventually. 'Or I will come looking for you both.'

The countess knelt down beside Max and touched his forehead gently. 'He will live,' she said eventually. 'When he recovers he will heal you.'

Together the countess and Ulrika left the chamber. Rodrik followed like a lapdog. Gotrek surveyed the shambles of the throne room bleakly and then stared towards the door, as if trying to decide whether he should follow the departing vampires. Eventually he shook his head and slumped wearily to the floor. Felix suddenly realised just how much effort it had cost the Slayer to remain upright.

'I am spending too much time with humans,' Gotrek said quietly. 'I am getting soft.'

'I don't think so,' Felix said. 'What now?'

'The forces of Chaos are abroad. There is a war still to be fought, manling, and monsters to be slain. I am sure we will find something to do.'

Groaning, Snorri Nosebiter rose from the wreckage of the chandelier. 'Good thing something broke Snorri's fall,' he said. 'Now where's that bloody vampire?'

'You killed him,' said Felix.

Snorri Nosebiter looked pleased.

ABOUT THE AUTHOR

William King was born in Stranraer, Scotland, in 1959. His short stories have appeared in *The Year's Best SF, Zenith, White Dwarf* and *Interzone*. He is also the author of seven Gotrek & Felix novels: *Trollslayer, Skavenslayer, Daemonslayer, Dragonslayer, Beastslayer, Vampireslayer* and *Giantslayer*, four volumes chronicling the adventures of the Space Marine warrior, Ragnar: *Space Wolf, Ragnar's Claw, Grey Hunter* and *Warblade*, as well as the Warhammer 40,000 novel *Farseer*. He has travelled extensively throughout Europe and Asia, and currently lives in Prague.